THE STONE OF AUTHORITY
THE STONE CYCLE BOOK 3

THE STONE OF AUTHORITY

THE STONE CYCLE BOOK 3

ALLAN N. PACKER

LUMINANT PUBLICATIONS

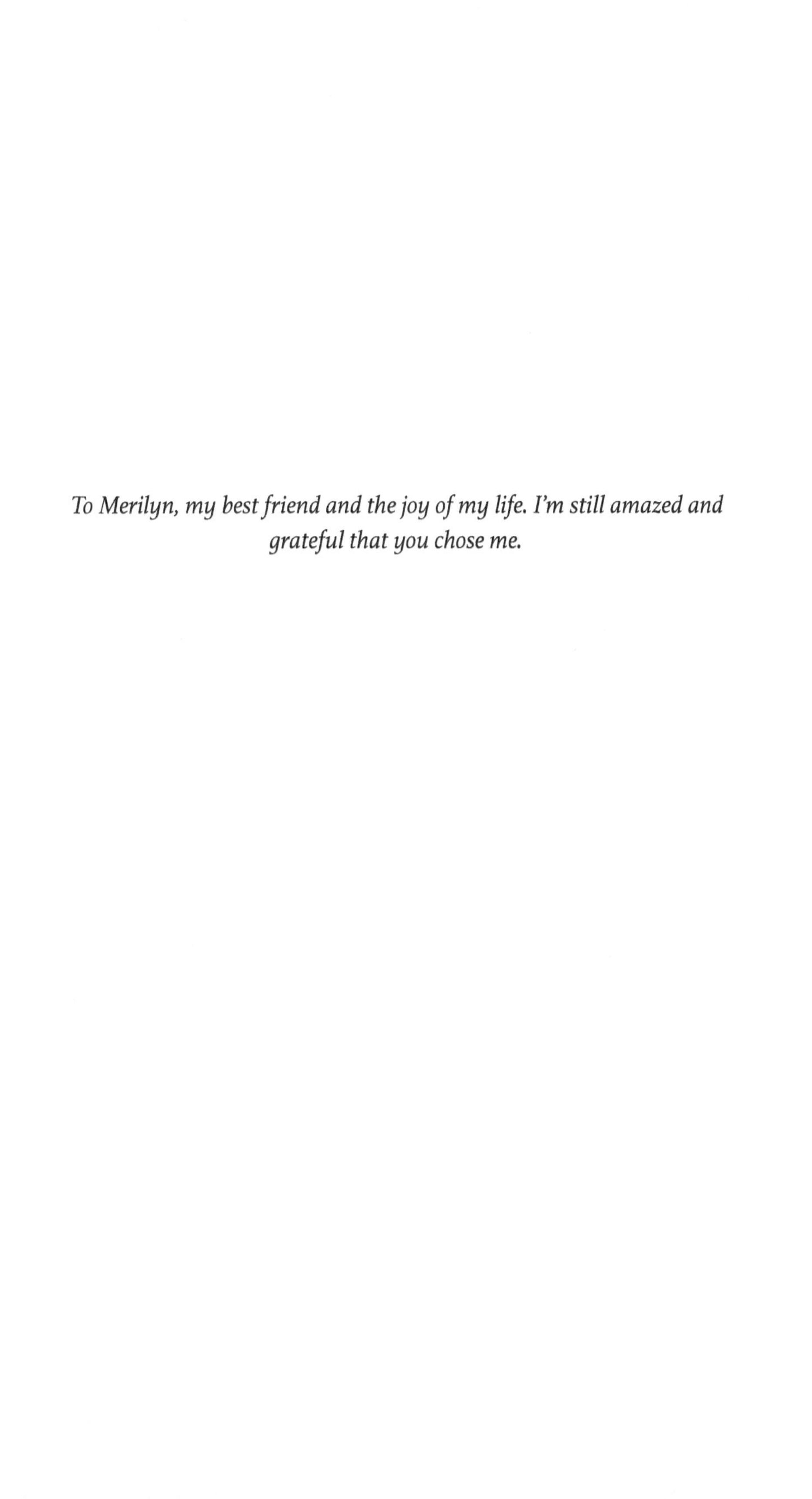

To Merilyn, my best friend and the joy of my life. I'm still amazed and grateful that you chose me.

Castel
Castel Citadel
Deadman's Pass
Steffan's Citadel
Arven
Maranelle
Duchy
of
Erestor
N
W
E
S
Arvenon
& surrounding Kingdoms

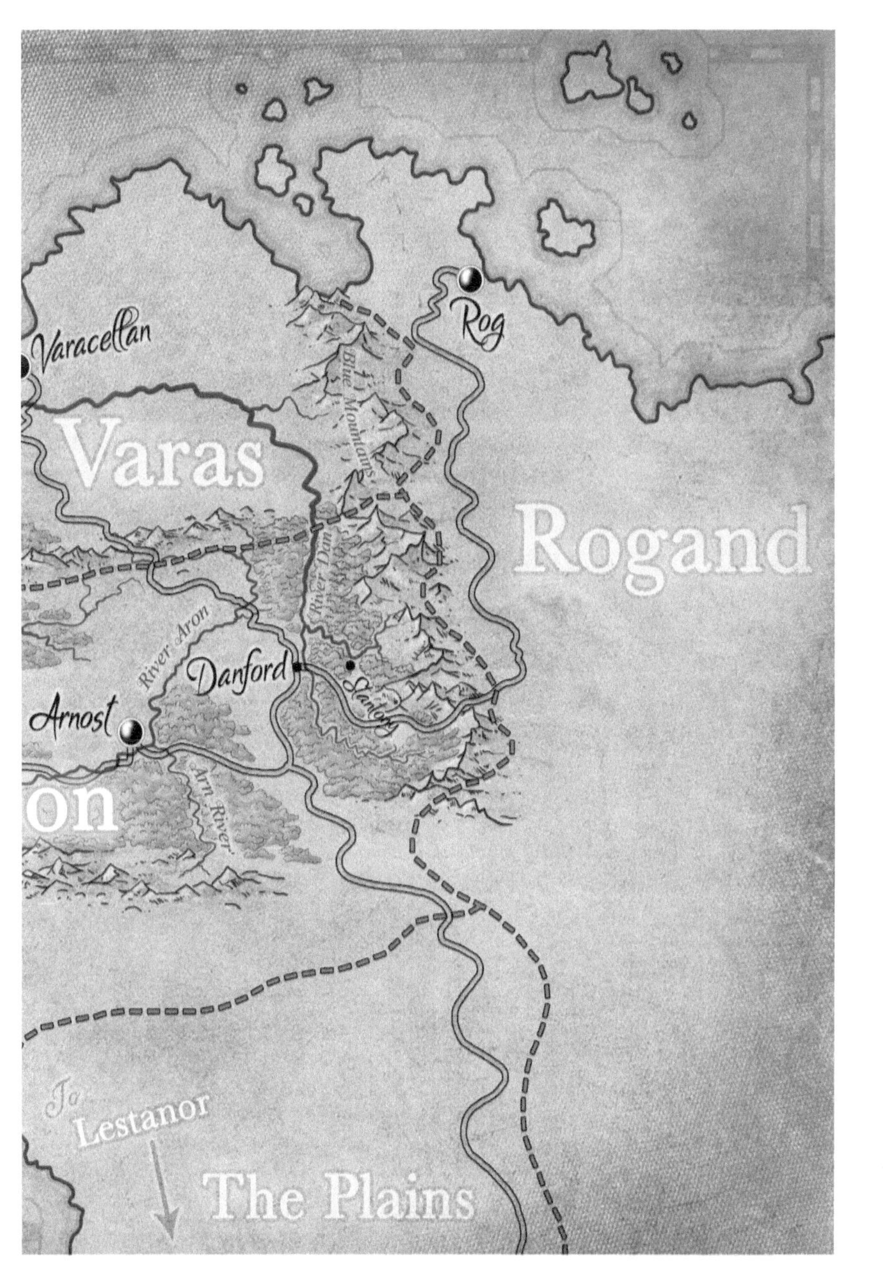

Varacellan
Varas
Rog
Rogand
Blue Mountains
River Aron
River Dan
Danford
Station
Arnost
on
Arn River
To Lestanor
The Plains

VOLUME 1—STORM CLOUDS GATHER

PROLOGUE

Almost 30 years before Thomas Stablehand finds the Stone of Knowing,
The future King Steffan has just been born in Arvenon;
Rogand is ruled by King Ugar;
The Seer has begun to make a name for herself in Lestanor

The eagle soared high on the midday thermals, attentive to the tiniest movement in the desert terrain below. It ignored the little figures and the beasts of burden beside the colorful tents around the oasis. Humans held no interest for it. The monarch of the skies cared nothing for their hopes and fears or the rise and fall of their kingdoms.

The majestic predator glided effortlessly over the series of low hills above the oasis. Sometimes reptiles or rodents were foolish enough to risk exposure in the open. They provided a tasty snack.

A solitary figure briefly caught its eye as a young tent dweller picked his way slowly down the slope of a small hill. The eagle watched dispassionately as the ground suddenly opened up, swallowing the figure in a puff of dust.

Serenely indifferent to the fate of the hapless creature below, the hunter wheeled south, searching for less unsettled hunting grounds.

A RICHLY DRESSED youth sat beneath the eagle as it glided off into the distance. The crown prince fidgeted uncomfortably, struggling to keep every inch of his body sheltered within the shade of a large rock. His idleness was shattered momentarily as something repulsive slithered past, almost startling him out of his wits. It was only a lizard, but he frowned in irritation anyway as he anxiously scanned the dirt nearby.

The tents of the royal caravan lay clustered before him, workers scurrying around them like ants. Prince Agon knew he could be sitting in luxury down there, away from the dust and the heat and creeping things. He would be waited on by bustling servants whose sole purpose in life was to satisfy his every desire. But it would be insufferably boring. And it would also bring him within reach of his father's foul temper.

Thankfully he had managed to slip away, right under the noses of the royal guards. His father would punish them cruelly for their negligence, but he didn't care. It served them right.

Only moments before, a faint cry—quickly cut off—had interrupted his musing. It sounded like a cry for help. Most likely it came from Vilkami, his boyhood companion.

The pointless meanderings of the youth must have finally landed him in some kind of trouble. Agon's first instinct had been to wonder whether he himself might also be in danger. He quickly concluded that he had little cause for concern. The most deadly predators in this region were humans like himself, and they shunned the outdoors in the heat of the day. Apart from serpents, the only other truly dangerous creatures here were nocturnal.

Perhaps Vilkami had disturbed a snake. The prince yawned. The young idiot could bleat all he liked—losing him would hardly be a great loss.

There was a time when Agon might have called the overeager

sixteen-year-old his friend. That was back before he knew better. He had long since realized that a prince didn't have friends. He only had servants.

Just one month earlier Prince Agon had celebrated his eighteenth birthday, attended by the greatest noblemen from across the land, each of them bowing low as they presented him their gifts. He was the most important person in the kingdom, and therefore in the world. The one exception was his father, as the old fool never tired of reminding him.

He spat into the dust. King Ugar's day would come, no matter how often his noblemen greeted him with "Great king, may you live forever!"

Another cry came to him faintly. "Agon! Over here!"

He sat up straight this time, frowning in anger. No one, not even his most faithful boyhood companion, had the right to address him by name. Perhaps he had overlooked such behavior when he was a child, but no more. The young cur needed to learn there was a price to pay for daring to be familiar with the crown prince of Rogand.

Agon got up and set off haughtily in the direction of the voice. Wrathful as he was, he wasn't going to hurry. He had no need to scamper about like a servant.

The moment he left the shade he began to feel uncomfortably hot. The desert might be cold at night, but it was sweltering during the day. He had journeyed with his father and a bevy of royal attendants into the far south of Rogand, and the colder climate of the capital, Rog, seemed a world away. Their reason for being here was a mystery to him. It undoubtedly had something to do with Lestanor, though, since Rogand's border with Lestanor was not far from their current location.

He squinted up at the sun as he walked. The glowing orb in the sky appeared to be making common cause with the boy in failing to show due respect for his royal station. It irked him greatly, not least because he knew he could do nothing whatever about it.

Ahead of him a series of low hills rose out of the desert. The eager summons had come from that direction. The voice had since gone silent—perhaps something had happened to Vilkami. His lip curled in a smirk of satisfaction at the thought. He always enjoyed it when other people suffered.

Then a horrible notion occurred to him—what if the boy had discovered something? Agon quickened his step. He had incontestable rights to whatever it was, and he needed to be on hand promptly to assert those rights.

Cresting the hill he spotted a section of hillside—halfway down the slope—where the earth had caved in. Dust drifted up into the air from around it. There was no sign of his companion.

"Vilkami! Where are you?" he called.

"Down here," a faint voice replied.

Agon knelt beside the hole and tried to peer in. It was too dark to see much of anything in there. "What are you doing?"

"I was investigating a small opening in the hillside," a muffled voice replied. "Then the ground collapsed, and I fell in."

"What's down there?"

"It's a tomb of some kind. A very old one."

Agon shuddered. The idea of falling through the dark into an unknown tomb unnerved him. Vilkami, however, had a peculiar taste for the macabre. He was probably enjoying it.

"Have you found anything interesting?" asked the prince.

"Maybe. I'm not sure."

"Can you get out?"

"I think so."

Agon heard a scrabbling sound, and further sections of the hillside disappeared into the hole. He moved hastily back from the edge.

A head appeared, and Vilkami struggled slowly out of the ground. Trees must once have stood on this hillside, because a tangled mass of ancient roots was providing him with a precarious ladder.

The youth came out covered in dirt from head to toe.

"What's that in your belt?" Agon asked him.

Vilkami brushed himself off. Then he reached down carefully and withdrew a sheathed sword from his belt. "I found it in there. I couldn't really see what it was like." He began to dust it off, and a scabbard richly encrusted with jewels slowly emerged from beneath the clinging detritus of the ages. He slid the sword from the scabbard to reveal a shiny blade without hint of rust or tarnish. The edge was still sharp and true—he tried it on his tunic, and the blade sliced cleanly through the fabric.

A glint came into Agon's eye. The sword was finely crafted—the workmanship was clearly superior. It was exquisite, quite unlike anything he had ever seen. And it fully aroused his insatiable lust.

"What else is down there?" he asked.

Vilkami peered uncertainly into the hole. The idea of going back clearly didn't appeal to him.

"Are you scared to risk your precious life?" Agon asked, a sneer on his lips.

His companion stiffened. "I'm not scared!"

"Climb down, then. I'll hold the sword for you," said Agon.

Vilkami looked very uncertain. After a few moments he reluctantly handed over the sword and climbed back into the hole. He was gone for some time before emerging once again.

"What did you find?"

"It was hard to see in the dark. There wasn't much else down there. Mostly a lot of old bones. And this." In his hand he held a small stone.

Exposed to the sun once more after uncounted years, the tiny object dazzled Agon's eyes, splashes of bright red shining brilliantly out of a gray surface. The stone was thin and flat and almost perfectly round. It was shaped like a miniature version of the low circular loaves that bakers pulled from their ovens every day.

It appeared to be little more than a colorful rock, but there was something mesmerizing about it. The prince wanted it, and he intended to get it.

Vilkami held out his hand for the sword.

"The sword is mine," Agon told him. "You gave it to me."

"Only to hold!" Vilkami retorted indignantly. "While I went back into the hole for you!" Outrage twisted his face.

The prince shrugged. "You didn't say that. You gave it to me, and that's the end of it."

The youth's features contorted as he struggled to master his fury.

Agon watched on thoughtfully. "I'll offer you an exchange," the prince finally said. "The sword for that stone."

Vilkami's face flushed, and he frowned angrily.

Agon smiled to himself. No doubt the young fool thought that since he had found the objects, they belonged to him. He would soon discover otherwise.

After a long pause Vilkami finally nodded. "I agree to the exchange. You can have the stone."

In spite of his words, he seemed reluctant to give it up. He stared hesitantly at the brightly colored object in his hand.

"Well?" demanded the prince impatiently.

Vilkami looked down at the stone once more, then he slowly held out his hand, the stone resting in his open palm. At the same time he stretched out his other hand for the sword.

Agon reached out greedily, his fist closing over the stone. A smug smile twisted his face.

He made no move to honor his end of the bargain.

Vilkami continued to hold out his hand. "Give me the sword," he said fiercely. "You gave your word."

"I changed my mind," Agon said in a bored tone.

"I'll tell my father!"

"'I'll tell my father,'" Agon echoed in a high pitched whine. "I'm so terrified! Ha! As if that old dotard could do anything about it." He snorted scornfully. "The sword is mine anyway. And the stone. Whatever's found here rightly belongs to ME."

He leaned forward, sneering. "Look and learn, little boy. It's time you grew up. Your father will be gone before long, and his title will be yours. You won't have a daddy to run to then.

"I've just done you a princely favor—I've demonstrated a lesson I learned from my father. He taught me that nothing worthwhile in life ever comes as a gift. People always expect something in return. If you want it, then you pay for it, or you take it. The strongest get to take whatever they want. The weak don't matter."

Then his voice hardened. "Don't think this advice is free. It's payment—in full—for anything you've ever done to benefit me. And don't threaten me again, Vilkami. I won't overlook it a second time.

"Oh, and one other thing. As far as you're concerned, I don't have a name. To you I am 'Your Highness'. Don't ever forget it."

With that he spun on his heel and headed in the direction of the royal caravan.

VILKAMI WATCHED HIM GO, blinking back tears of helpless rage. For years he had borne the brunt of Agon's petty cruelty. He had loathed the prince for as long as he could remember, and that seed had slowly been ripening into a passionate hatred.

The future king enjoyed every advantage that came with royal blood—power, prestige, and the divine right to do pretty much anything he pleased. Why had the gods bestowed all this on a person with no more honor than a snake?

He hated everything about Agon. It was surely a punishment from the dark gods to be stranded in this barren desert with him. Every day he asked himself why he was here.

He knew the answer, of course, and he could only grind his teeth in frustration. The king went wherever he pleased, and Vilkami's father—powerful nobleman though he was—followed him like a faithful hound.

And, if he was honest with himself, he was no better. He had always tagged along behind the prince like an obedient puppy.

Vilkami had been born to the nobility, but Agon showed no more consideration to him than he would to a servant. It was time he began learning from his persecutor.

From now on everything would change. "His Highness" might eventually find himself trembling at some of the changes.

The prince had taught him that nothing mattered except power. So Vilkami would learn the ways of power. And he would play by the prince's rules. He would use power ruthlessly, and use it for his own gain.

He would do whatever the prince demanded, but first he would search tirelessly for the way of doing it that would benefit him most.

Vanity was not one of his weaknesses. He had never cared about appearances—he was willing to abase himself and refer to the prince as "Your Highness" if that was what it took. And when Agon eventually became king he was prepared to abase himself even more. When Vilkami came into his own inheritance, he would become Agon's most dependable nobleman.

But he would never forget what had happened here today. Sooner or later an opportunity would arrive for the tables to be turned, and he would pay Agon back in full—for every insult and every humiliation he had endured over the years. His lips twisted in satisfaction as he indulged in vengeful daydreams.

Before long the heat dragged him back to the present.

He pictured again the peculiar stone from the tomb. The prince had defrauded him of it. Royalty or not, the sheer arrogance of Agon's deception infuriated him. He would take it back, and the mysterious sword with it. He had found them, and they belonged to him.

His thoughts were drawn irresistibly back to the stone. Someone important had been laid to rest in that tomb—no ordinary person could ever have owned such a sword. And the other object buried with him had been the stone. He sensed that its unusual appearance was not its only notable characteristic. The stone was significant—he was sure of it. It possessed a strangely alluring quality, and handing it over had been surprisingly difficult.

He wondered if old histories might refer to such an object. He derived endless fascination from poking around in decaying scrolls. The priests of the dark gods loved to hoard ancient documents, and his father had already used his connections to arrange access for him to their main library. He would begin a search there as soon as he returned to Rog.

He couldn't lose himself in the future, though. As he reluctantly dragged his thoughts back to the present, the pain of his humiliation flooded his awareness.

Standing in the heat and the dust, he reached a momentous decision. Taking back what rightly belonged to him would just be the beginning. He vowed to himself that he wouldn't stop until he had found a way to eliminate Agon, however long it took.

Vilkami had no particular desire to become king of Rogand. The title of Lord Drettroth—along with all the wealth, power, and prestige that came with it—had apparently satisfied his forebears well enough, and he fully expected it to satisfy him too.

He wanted revenge.

He would be subtle, and he would be stealthy, but from that day forward he would never rest until he saw the crown pried from Agon's unworthy head.

1

Two weeks after the Battle of Torbury Scarp

King Agon of Rogand paced impatiently, fuming as he waited for his senior agents to arrive. Although the sun had yet to clear the horizon, the first hints of daylight were already visible in the small audience room that adjoined the grand reception hall of his palace in the capital, Rog.

Lorik and Jorvan were the best agents he had. That simply meant that the king placed high expectations on them. It didn't mean that he should be required to wait on their pleasure.

Their appearance did little to improve Agon's mood, even though they came at first light as instructed. He didn't offer them a seat.

"What have you learned about the death of Drettroth?" he demanded. "I expect answers!"

The two men bowed low before daring to speak. "Great king, may you live forever!" began Lorik, the older man.

"Get on with it!" snapped the king.

"Lord Drettroth was poisoned, Your Majesty," Lorik told him.

"Poisoned."

Agon was careful not to show it, but he was shocked at the news. Such a death was surely ironic given that Drettroth had made a particular study of poisons and used them to silence many of his own opponents.

"Who poisoned him?"

"A dispatch rider discovered his lordship's body, Your Majesty," Jorvan replied. "A youth, most likely Lord Drettroth's food taster, was lying dead nearby, also poisoned. His lordship had been run through, apparently with his own sword, although he appeared to have been poisoned first, which would explain why he couldn't defend himself. The dispatch rider found a monk in the same room, in the act of unchaining a prisoner, so he assumed that the monk had killed both Lord Drettroth and his food taster."

"Where is the monk?"

"The dispatch rider killed him, Your Majesty," Jorvan replied.

"Who was the prisoner?"

"An Arvenian youth," said Jorvan. "The monk succeeded in freeing him, and he escaped in the confusion."

Agon scowled in annoyance.

"How did Drettroth allow himself to be poisoned by a monk?" growled the king.

"We believe it was actually the food taster who poisoned Lord Drettroth," said Lorik. "He would have needed to consume the poison himself, which is why he also died. But he managed to free the monk first. And the monk in turn freed the youth before he was killed by the dispatch rider."

"Why did Drettroth imprison the youth?" Agon asked.

"Apparently he had something Lord Drettroth wanted, Your Majesty," said Lorik. "An item his lordship wanted very badly. His lordship expended a prodigious amount of effort to capture the youth and the monk. He sent agents throughout Arvenon searching for them, and also deployed several regiments for the purpose."

Agon's eyebrows furrowed. He knew nothing of this. What had Drettroth been playing at?

"What item did the youth have that Drettroth wanted?"

"The object of his attention seems to have been a small stone, Your Majesty," Lorik replied.

"A stone?" Agon glared at them, shaking his head in contempt. "Do you think I am stupid?"

"Of course not, Your Majesty!" Jorvan replied. He reached for a pile of scrolls with a trembling hand, selected one, and passed it to the king. "We also dismissed it as nothing more than hearsay at first," he said. "Until we read this scroll. We found it among Lord Drettroth's papers."

The scroll was old and appeared brittle. Agon unrolled it carefully and peered down at it. Almost at once his head snapped up again, and he fixed them in a glare. "Do you expect me to read this?"

The agent looked at him blankly.

"It's written in Arvenian!" snapped Agon.

Jorvan stared at him in confusion. "Would Your Majesty care for us to prepare a translation?" he stammered uncertainly.

"I have no need of a translation, you fool!" Agon's eyes narrowed as he stared at them. "You have the audacity to confront me with the language of my bitter enemies, and then you pretend surprise at my reaction?"

Both men stared at him, open mouthed in fear.

He shook his head in disgust. "You'd better pray it's worth my while," he snarled.

Ignoring the men he turned to the scroll and silently began to read. "*Three talismans of great potency are abroad in the world, uncelebrated, unrecognized, and hidden from any certain knowledge. Perhaps I alone know their true history, long forgotten with the passing of many scores of years...*"

At first he scanned the handwriting dismissively. But as he progressed further through the scroll his eyes widened, and his heart began to race. He sped to the end, then started again from the beginning, this time reading slowly and carefully.

Finally he looked up. "Where did Drettroth find this?" he asked.

"We think he might have discovered the scroll here in Rog, Your Majesty," suggested Jorvan, "in the temple library."

"It seems that Lord Drettroth spent many hours there," Lorik added. "The library holds a large number of documents, some of them very ancient. They also have a substantial collection of scrolls written in Arvenian and other languages."

"Who has seen these scrolls?" the king demanded.

"Apart from Your Majesty, no one except us," Lorik replied.

Agon's eyes narrowed. "For your own sakes you'd better keep it that way!" he said. "That applies to this entire investigation."

The men both bowed low.

"You are dismissed," the king told them. "But do not leave the palace. I want you on hand the minute I call!"

The men scurried away.

Agon's memory had begun to stir as he read the scroll. The moment he fully grasped the implications of its words, his excitement had intensified until he was struggling to conceal his agitation from his agents.

The Stone of Authority described in the scroll sounded remarkably like the stone Vilkami had handed over so many years ago. Could that object, long forgotten, truly deliver the powers claimed by the scroll? He felt certain that Drettroth had thought so. From the moment he asked himself that question, nothing mattered to him except finding the missing stone.

The problem was that years had passed since Agon had last seen it. He had been aware from the beginning that Vilkami desperately wanted both the stone and the sword he had found with it. The little brat would have snatched them back the moment an opportunity presented itself. So Agon kept them well hidden. After he returned to Rog, he placed both objects in a secret and very secure hiding place for safe keeping. Then he had forgotten about them. The sword had obvious value, but he had little real interest in either artifact beyond making sure that Vilkami couldn't have them.

It occurred to him now to wonder if Vilkami had somehow contrived to ferret them out in the years since he came into his inheritance as Lord Drettroth. But it couldn't be so. The scroll had described three stones and the powers associated with each of them. It would have been obvious to Agon if Drettroth possessed any such powers.

No, the stone must have remained wherever he had hidden it. The problem was that having disregarded it for so long, he no longer had any clear memory about the location of the hiding place.

AGON STRUGGLED to master his agitation as he waited for Lorik and Jorvan to return to his audience room. He couldn't sit—he was pacing restlessly back and forth like a caged lion.

For days he had searched in vain for the stone. He had upended both his current and his previous apartments without finding a trace of it, and his jangled nerves had long since frayed to tatters. Already today he'd demanded the heads of three of his servants. That must surely have brought the total to fifteen this week.

He could not afford to have these two decapitated though. Not yet. They still had information he needed.

He began breathing slowly and deeply in an attempt to calm himself.

When the men finally entered the room he saw that they were visibly trembling. Agon felt his rage welling up inside him as he witnessed their obvious terror. Hadn't he appointed these men because of their reputation for remaining calm in a crisis? He was surrounded by incompetent fools.

Even as he opened his mouth to spew out his fury, his reason somehow asserted itself. He remembered that he still needed these agents.

With a mighty effort he restrained himself. Gritting his teeth, he snapped his mouth shut without saying a word.

They stood there paralyzed, staring at him wide-eyed in mortal dread. Staring back, he realized he needed to greet them—normally if at all possible.

"Welcome," he sputtered. "You are...welcome." He peeled back his lips to reveal his teeth. It probably didn't look much like a smile, but it was the best he could manage.

He waved them to a pair of seats, and they sank into them. The agents still trembled with fear, although they seemed visibly relieved at his unexpected restraint. Agon didn't find it hard to imagine what was being said about him around the palace.

He thrust such trifles from his mind. There were important matters to address.

He began with a question that had been plaguing him over the last few days.

"You told me that Drettroth went to great effort to capture an Arvenian youth, because he believed the youth had one of the stones mentioned in the scroll," said Agon, managing to speak evenly again. "Which stone?"

He knew that Drettroth could not have been on the trail of the Stone of Authority. The nobleman would have been well aware that the stone was already accounted for.

The men continued to stare at him, wide-eyed. Neither of them said a word.

"Well?" he snapped. His irritability was bubbling away just below the surface, and it took a conscious effort to keep it down.

Lorik finally found his voice. "Great king, may you live forever!" he began. "We believe that Lord Drettroth was looking for the stone that the scroll refers to as the Stone of Knowing."

The king's heart beat faster. From the moment he had read the scroll, the Stone of Knowing was the one he lusted after the most. Could it truly have been almost within Drettroth's grasp?

"What makes you think it was that particular stone?" he asked. He kept his tone mild, but danger lurked below the surface. Lorik had dared to raise the king's expectations, and the man would suffer if he'd done so without good reason.

Lorik bowed respectfully before replying. "Our investigations have revealed that almost twenty years ago Lord Drettroth sent a number of his men to capture a woman renowned as a seer. If she had this stone, its powers could have made her appear to be a seer.

We believe that Lord Drettroth might have drawn a similar conclusion."

"And what happened?" the king demanded.

"The men were unsuccessful, Your Majesty," he replied. "The woman eluded them. The trail went cold in Arvenon. It seems that Lord Drettroth's special interest in Arvenon began at that time."

Agon's eyes narrowed. How had the ambitious army commander managed to conceal all this from his king? *What other games were you playing, Drettroth?*

"How did you learn of this seer?" the king asked.

"Lord Drettroth immediately executed all of the men involved. But a few of them deserted rather than return home. We were able to track one of them down. We pried the whole story from him before he died."

Agon grunted in satisfaction. These men were good.

"So this youth somehow acquired the stone. What do we know of him?" he asked.

"One of Lord Drettroth's agents tracked down the youth and the monk in Arvenon, after the invasion. We have interviewed the agent. He discovered the fugitives hiding in a monastery. Lord Drettroth personally went there with two regiments of soldiers. His men demolished the monastery, but the youth and the monk escaped. They were eventually captured some weeks later."

"So this youth—you have his name and description?"

"Yes, Your Majesty. We believe that his name is 'Tomas'. And we have a reasonably complete description of what he looks like."

Agon scowled as he considered these revelations about his army commander. Drettroth had persuaded him that the annexation of Arvenon would multiply the power and the glory of Rogand, and in particular that it would elevate King Agon. The nobleman had brazenly traded on the king's lust for power. Agon was furious to discover that he had been manipulated.

All along Drettroth had been pursuing an agenda of his own—he must have been laughing at Agon behind his hand the entire time.

The king licked his lips, imagining what he would have done to the commander if he had still been alive.

"What efforts have you made to find the youth and retrieve the stone?" Agon asked.

"We have attempted nothing, Your Majesty," Lorik replied innocently. "We've been awaiting your instructions."

The man was almost certainly lying. His face projected calm, but Agon could see the veins in his neck standing out. And those veins were throbbing. It was hardly surprising. How could any normal man resist the lure of such a prize?

"No further response is required on your part," the king replied haughtily. "I will give the matter more thought before deciding on a course of action."

He would select an entirely different set of agents to renew the search for the youth. He would tell them no more than they absolutely needed to know. It wouldn't serve his purposes if they fully understood what they were searching for.

"I want a report, and I want it in writing," the king ordered. "Every detail of your investigations and everything you have learned. I expect it to be completed in two days."

The men bowed, and he dismissed them.

The agents would not include everything in their report, of course. They were far too clever for that. But it made no difference. Agon would personally squeeze every last detail from them.

He would have no further use for Lorik and Jorvan after that. They knew too much. From the time of their first meeting a few days earlier, Agon had arranged for them to come under constant observation. They had been monitored every minute, day and night. He immediately issued instructions for the watch on them to be doubled.

King Agon sat on the floor laughing maniacally. The Stone of Authority was his. He had found it at last.

There had been moments when he feared the stone would

remain lost forever—he had never been more ecstatic about being proven wrong.

The problem had arisen because he acquired the stone when he was crown prince. The crown prince occupied a lesser wing of the sprawling castle that was now the royal palace. The moment Agon became king he had relocated to the king's much more luxurious private apartments. His old accommodations were soon forgotten. He hadn't spared a thought for them in years.

That day—and not for the first time—Agon had focused his search on the suite he once occupied as crown prince. The rooms lay silent and empty, neglected by all except the servants who periodically cleaned and dusted against a day when the suite might be needed again.

He had been leaning on the wall of the little balcony, staring out across a small garden. In a corner of the garden stood an ancient tree, one that he had climbed many times in his youth.

A memory came to him of a young Vilkami falling from that tree and breaking his arm. The injured youth had been too scared to tell anyone that his fall was not an accident. Who would have listened if he revealed that his future king had deliberately pushed him out of the tree? Agon chortled out loud as he recalled it. The broken arm had been just one of the indignities Agon visited upon his supposed friend.

Neither Vilkami—nor Lord Drettroth as he later became—ever found an effective way to pay Agon back. But Agon could not deny that the nobleman had come dangerously close to changing that situation. If Drettroth had taken control of the Stone of Knowing, the balance of power would have massively tilted in his favor.

As Agon gazed at the tree, another memory sprang suddenly to mind. A low stone wall stood behind its spreading limbs, and among the stones he had once discovered a hollow cavity. He remembered occasionally hiding small treasures in there.

Agon immediately dismissed every servant from that wing of the palace. Racing outside he hurried to the stone wall and worked feverishly to locate and expose the cavity. When he at last discovered it, he saw to his excitement that a long metal box lay inside it. The memories came rushing back. He had concealed the box within the wall after placing the sword and the small stone inside it.

Impatiently he wrested the rusted container from the cavity.

He was shaking with excitement when he carried the box inside. After taking a deep breath, he forced open the lid.

Within the box lay the ancient sword, just as he had left it. Beneath it, folded into an old piece of cloth, he found the Stone of Authority.

Grasping it in his hand, he threw back his head and began to howl with laughter. His body shook, and the tears ran down his cheeks. He hadn't been so deliriously happy for years. Not since pushing Vilkami out of the tree. The thought set him off again.

Eventually his body became calm, and his laughter turned to gloating. Everything was about to change in Rogand.

From the moment he ascended the throne, he had found himself surrounded by ambitious schemers. The Rogandan nobility was little more than a pit of vipers, awash with poisonous intrigue. Now, after years of wrestling with the nobles and the priests, he dared to hope that he could bypass completely the power plays and the political maneuvering. He bared his teeth with anticipation at the thought.

The scroll had made it very clear what he should expect from the stone. It was time to stop gloating and to try it out.

2

Five months after the Battle of Torbury Scarp

The crowds bumped and jostled together, forced shoulder to shoulder as they attempted to pass through the narrow entrance at the gates of Arnost. The guards stationed on either side of the entryway gazed on with bored indifference as the human tide ebbed and flowed. It was just another market day at the capital of Arvenon.

A weary traveler approached the gates, leading a donkey. His weathered brown cloak was topped by a broad rimmed hat that covered his face, and he plodded forward with head down, looking neither to the left nor to the right.

His animal bore an unusual burden—an old crone, perched in the saddle uncomfortably with bent back and misshapen shoulders. Her face was concealed by the expansive hood that crowned her black cloak.

Having arrived at the gates the wayfarer halted. His hat swung slowly from side to side as he quietly scanned the faces around him, alert to any possibility of danger. Annoyed at the obstruction, the other travelers called out impatiently, pushing and shoving as they attempted to force their way past him and his donkey. He ignored them.

Apparently finding nothing to interest him, and seeing that the guards were about to intervene, the traveler lowered his head once more and shuffled forward, disappearing through the gates with the donkey and its unsightly passenger in tow.

The main thoroughfare was no less crowded inside, but the wayfarer soon abandoned the main road in favor of a broad alley that wound its way steadily into the heart of the city. He soon turned aside to a narrow road that led upward until he stood directly beneath the walls of the castle.

To one side lay a pair of wooden gates. He pushed them open and entered the courtyard that lay beyond, closing the gates behind the donkey. A small stone cottage lay before him, with smoke drifting lazily upward from its chimney.

He came and positioned himself beside the donkey, glancing pensively up at its rider. Then he stood silently, as if deep in thought, making no move to approach the door of the cottage. He had remained there unmoving for some time when the door opened abruptly.

A man emerged, coming to a sudden halt when confronted with the spectacle before him. The newcomer frowned, seemingly more in revulsion than in puzzlement.

"Who are you, and what is your business here?" he asked brusquely.

"Hello, Father," the traveler replied quietly. "It's your son, Thomas."

Axel Stablehand stood in stunned silence, contemplating the extraordinary prospect before him. Then his face hardened, and he frowned. "You've chosen a strange way to return home, Thomas," he said.

Thomas stiffened, and his misshapen companion reached down

quickly and placed a gentle hand on his arm. He glanced up at her, then stood silent for a moment as he composed himself.

"Is my mother at home?" he asked.

"Yes, of course she is."

"Then may we come in?"

His father cast a sharp glance at the dark figure on the donkey before addressing Thomas. "Why should you need permission?" he asked roughly. "It's your home."

Thomas might have responded in kind, but the gentle pressure on his arm persuaded him otherwise.

The older man turned and opened the door again. He stared at them over his shoulder for a moment before disappearing inside, leaving the door ajar behind him.

Thomas watched him go. He shook his head once. His father was mistaken—this wasn't his home. Not anymore.

After removing his hat, Thomas helped his companion down from the donkey and led her into the cottage.

The first thing he saw upon entering the main room was the startled face of his mother. She took one look at him, then she burst into tears. Rushing to him, she enfolded him in her embrace, sobbing loudly. After a few moments she composed herself and stepped away, holding him at arm's length and studying his face. Finally she smiled in contentment.

Apparently allowing herself to register at last that he wasn't alone, she turned uncertainly toward his companion.

"Mother and Father, this is Elena, the girl I am going to marry."

His father's expression plainly showed his shock and distaste. His mother swallowed, then smiled resolutely. "You are very welcome, my dear!" she said brightly.

Turning to her husband, she saw the look on his face. She frowned. "Could you please fetch us some fresh water from the well, Axel?" she asked firmly.

Thomas suppressed a smile as his father obediently headed outside. His mother's question might have sounded like a request, but both he and his father knew better.

He turned to Elena. "It's safe here," he assured her.

She nodded, then quickly proceeded to shed her cloak and the bundles hidden beneath it.

Finally she stepped away from the pile at her feet. She looked anxiously toward Thomas. Then she faced his mother, her beautiful face flushed and uncertain. "Thank you very much for your welcome," she said softly. "I am very privileged to be able to meet Thomas's parents at last."

The incredible transformation in her appearance must have been no less shocking to Thomas's mother than it had been to him when he first witnessed it. But his mother put him to shame, recovering herself almost immediately.

"Well, now! What a blessed sight you are for these old eyes of mine!" she said, shaking her head in astonishment. "I don't doubt there's quite a tale to be told here."

She reached out and took Elena's hands. "I'm Marya," she said, beaming across at her, "and you truly are very welcome in our home, Elena. You must be tired after your journey. And hungry, too, I don't doubt."

She released Elena's hands and began bustling about, setting up stools at the table, gathering bowls, and stoking the fire.

Thomas turned to Elena and grinned. "She likes you," he whispered.

Elena returned a nervous smile.

The door opened, and Axel reappeared. When he spotted Elena he almost dropped the pail of water. His glance flitted around the room, as if he was trying to locate the old crone. Finally, seeing the robe lying on the floor, he turned to Elena with face flushed.

Thomas decided not to prolong the agony. "Father, this is Elena. Without her disguise."

The stable master reddened with embarrassment, and Thomas realized with a start that he couldn't remember ever witnessing such a reaction from his father.

Thomas addressed his companion. "Elena, this is my father, Axel. He is stable master to the king."

She looked up at Thomas's father, her face pale but determined. "It is a great honor to meet you," she said earnestly.

Axel flushed briefly again. He had not earned the courtesy she was showing him, and it was obvious to Thomas that he was well aware of it.

"I...I am...pleased to meet you, too," he finally blurted.

Thomas suppressed a snort when he saw the look on his mother's face. His father would undoubtedly gain the benefit of a few of her insights when they were next alone.

"Please! Sit down, all of you!" Marya said cheerily, clearly unwilling to tolerate her husband's blundering for another moment.

"Tell us where you've been Thomas, and what you've been doing! Will visited us some weeks ago, and he told us that you were safe and that we should be very proud of you. He wouldn't say any more than that. I've missed you so much, and every day I've been waiting to hear from you!"

"I'm sorry I couldn't come sooner," said Thomas. He had long anticipated this interaction, but had never been able to settle on exactly what to say to account for his prolonged absence.

He hadn't reckoned on Elena.

"Please don't be angry with Thomas," she exclaimed. "It's me who's to blame!" She spoke with such disarming sincerity that his mother's face immediately lit up with an understanding smile. Even his father's frown softened slightly.

"Thomas only delayed coming to Arnost so that I could come with him, too. We waited until spring arrived so it would be easier to travel. I've been so much looking forward to meeting Thomas's parents! My father and I have a great deal to thank you for. Thomas has been such a help to us!"

His mother flushed with pleasure.

"We've come to rely on him very much," she continued. "He saved my father's life when he was dangerously ill with fever. Did you know he had skills as a healer?"

His mother shook her head in surprise.

"And when the Rogandans came, he led them away to protect us. He was so brave!"

"Well, just look at you now!" said Marya with a smile. "What young man wouldn't want to protect you?"

"Oh no, you don't understand!" she exclaimed. "He thought I was an ugly hunchback. Like when you first saw me."

Marya raised her eyebrows in astonishment.

"Thomas led them away, and he was injured and captured as a result! He was taken to their leader's fortress. They would have killed him if he hadn't managed to escape."

Thomas watched her, wide-eyed. Who could resist her? Certainly not his mother—she was hanging on Elena's every word.

"And he persuaded you to marry him?" Axel's question probably sounded more abrupt than he intended.

A delicate blush came to her lovely cheeks. "I don't think he needed to do a good deal of persuading," she said, lowering her eyelids bashfully.

She was incredible. Thomas marveled anew at the fact that she had promised herself to him.

"So we're going to have a wedding," said Marya enthusiastically. "That's just wonderful! I understand that you have connections now, Thomas. Perhaps you'll be allowed to hold the ceremony in the cathedral!"

"The cathedral?" he replied in alarm. "Please, Mother! I'm a commoner. You know as well as I do that commoners don't marry in the cathedral. Our wedding will be small and very quiet. If a church isn't available, we can marry here at home. All we need is a priest to bless the marriage."

"Nonsense," said Marya. "We'll find a church for you, don't you worry."

Axel faced Elena. "You mentioned your father," he said evenly, apparently managing at last to regain some composure. "Did he travel with you to Arnost?"

"Yes," Elena replied. "We parted just before we entered the city.

He didn't want to intrude on Thomas's homecoming. He is hoping to meet you, though."

"We would very much like to meet him, too," Marya assured her. "And what about your mother?"

"She died when I was quite young. My father raised me on his own."

"I'm so sorry to hear that, dear," said Thomas's mother. She reached out and took Elena's hand. "I've never had a daughter, and you don't have a mother. Perhaps we can be friends."

"I would like that very much."

Marya positively glowed. There was no need at all to guess about her opinion of Elena.

Thomas glanced across at his father, and saw that a distant look had come to his eye.

"You might be wondering where Simon is, Thomas," he said. "I don't know myself. He just vanished during the siege. I've heard nothing of him since. I don't suppose you've learned anything of him in your travels?"

Thomas had been anticipating this conversation too, and once again he hadn't decided what to say. This time Elena couldn't help him out.

Thomas knew he had to tell his father something—Axel Stablehand might have been the person who cared most about the youth. And Thomas was determined to acknowledge Simon's courage.

"I actually met Simon—when I was imprisoned at the fortress of the Rogandan leader. I escaped largely thanks to him. Simon behaved very heroically during his time there. I'm sorry to have to tell you, though, that he did not survive."

Axel frowned in disbelief. "He's dead? How did he come to be at the Rogandan fortress?"

Thomas paused, determined to ignore his father's tone. What would his father say if he told him that Simon had left Arnost solely to betray Thomas to the Rogandan leader? How could he explain that Simon had been pressed into that leader's service as his food taster, and that he had lost his own life when he fatally poisoned his master? It would raise too many questions—awkward questions that Thomas was either unwilling or unable to answer.

"The Rogandans captured him outside the city walls. As to how and why he came to be there, those are questions that only he could properly answer."

His father stared at him. "You said he was a hero."

"He was. It was through his efforts that the Rogandan leader was killed. Unfortunately Simon also died as a result."

"Who else knows this?"

"Will Prentis knows. I don't know if he has told the king."

Axel looked at Thomas with narrowed eyes. But he said no more and asked no further questions.

Thomas could not help wondering what he was thinking. But he had never used the Stone of Knowing to spy on his father's thoughts, and he didn't plan to start now.

A NEW DAWN broke over Arnost, sending the sun's rays peeping into the house containing Axel and Marya and their two guests. Marya had set up blankets for her son in the main living area to allow Elena to sleep in his old room.

Thomas had slept badly.

His parents' house was pleasant and familiar, but it held too many mixed memories for him. He missed the rough comforts of the cabin in the woods.

When the four of them were sitting around the little table breaking their fast with newly baked bread and fresh milk, Thomas turned to his father. "Could you please let Will know that we are here?"

"I'll get one of the stable boys to pass on a message," Axel returned gruffly.

Thomas responded with immediate alarm. "Please don't do that! I don't want anyone else to know we're here."

"Why not?" Axel demanded.

Thomas groaned inwardly. He had left Arnost out of fear that his secret would be exposed. The last thing he wanted now was to advertise his return. He couldn't say that, though.

If he refused to answer his father's question it would lead him onto a familiar path, one that wouldn't go anywhere good.

"I'm sure Thomas is thinking of me," Elena interjected, blushing faintly. "He knows I'm dreadfully shy."

His father subsided. "Don't worry," he said. "I'll tell Will myself."

"Thank you so much!" she replied with evident relief.

Thomas had a far greater need for concealment than Elena did, but once again she'd come to his rescue.

The look on her face had clearly softened Axel. Her shyness was charming rather than awkward—it only made her more endearing.

The contrast between Axel's reaction to Elena and his reaction to his own son could not have been more striking. His father plainly saw no particular reason for secrecy when Thomas requested it. Nevertheless, he'd readily agreed to it for Elena's sake.

Thomas had come here to introduce Elena to his parents, and as expected she'd made a good impression on both of them. But he'd also hoped to make a new beginning with his father. That wasn't proving at all straightforward.

Axel sought out Will and delivered the message. Will responded immediately with the proposal that Thomas and Elena meet him later that afternoon in the castle. He suggested the familiar small tower room that Will, Rufe, and Thomas had used as a hideaway in the days before the Rogandan invasion.

At the appointed time Thomas set off with Elena to find the upper room in the tower. They entered the castle through a small postern door and stayed away from heavily trafficked passageways. Both of them wore cloaks and kept their faces concealed.

Will and Rufe were waiting for them when they arrived.

"Thomas! Elena! It's good to see you both again," said Will, a broad smile creasing his scarred face. Rufe, too, greeted them with a warmth and a gentleness that belied his intimidating stature.

Thomas was more delighted than he could express to see his friends again.

"We've heard rumors about you, Will," he said with a smile. "I hear you're an important person now. Well, even more important than you were before, if that's possible."

Will dismissed the comment with a wave of his hand. "To my old friends I'll always just be Will," he said, "whatever happens."

"I hear the two of you are planning a wedding," Rufe said to Thomas and Elena with a grin. "Will you hold it here in Arnost? We'd love to attend if we're invited."

"We would be honored to have you!" Thomas assured him.

Elena said least of all in the energetic conversation that followed, but Thomas noticed her looking on with a contented smile.

After a while Will interrupted them. "There's someone who would like to meet you both," he said.

"Who?" asked Thomas curiously.

"You'll find out very soon. We're expecting her at any moment," Will replied with a grin.

"Her?" asked Thomas, raising an eyebrow. "Is there a lady in your life now, Will?"

The question drew a loud guffaw from both Will and Rufe. "No!" they replied.

As if on cue, a youthful face appeared in the doorway. Seeing Will and Rufe, a smile covered her face as the owner stepped into the room.

"Your Majesty," said Will and Rufe in unison, bowing deeply.

"Your Majesty," echoed Elena, performing a more than serviceable curtsy.

Thomas realized he was standing upright, staring at her with his jaws wide. He snapped his mouth shut and bent low.

"Your Majesty, I would like to present Elena and Thomas," said Will smoothly. "Elena and Thomas, you have the honor of finding yourselves in the presence of Queen Essanda."

Thomas had seen the queen before, but this was his first opportunity to observe her up close. She was indeed a girl. But the merry eyes twinkling out at them seemed somehow older, as if she had witnessed things that aged her prematurely. Knowing a little of her role in the Battle of Torbury Scarp, Thomas was not surprised.

The queen turned to Thomas. "I'm told you were present when Lord Drettroth was brought down," she said admiringly.

"Yes, Your Majesty. I can't take any credit for it, though."

She smiled. "I've heard you were very brave."

Thomas didn't know what to say.

Seeing his discomfort, she turned to Elena. The youthful queen gazed at her silently for a long moment. "I know many elegant young ladies," she said. "But you seem somehow different."

Elena blushed deeply.

A shy smile covered the queen's face. "Would you be willing to spend some time in my company?"

She seemed surprisingly vulnerable as she asked the question, and Thomas had to remind himself that she was scarcely older than a child. Observing the way she conducted herself, even putting to one side her remarkable reputation, it was easy to forget her real age and think of her as a mature young woman.

Elena must have sensed her hesitation, too, because her own shyness quickly gave way to her instinctive kindness. "It would be a great privilege, Your Majesty," she said, extending a warm smile of her own in return.

The queen took her arm, and they disappeared down the tower steps together, the queen already beginning to whisper conspiratorially as if Elena was an old friend.

QUEEN ESSANDA LED Elena to a small room in her private apartments that featured two windows overlooking a distant forest. The room was illuminated cheerfully by the afternoon sun, and they sat down together in two well worn but comfortable chairs. The young queen chattered away cheerfully, and Elena soon found herself relaxing in her presence. She immediately saw that her hostess wanted to be treated as a normal person, not as a lofty monarch needing to maintain an appropriate distance.

While walking to the queen's private apartments, Elena had once again concealed her face beneath the hood of her cloak. She removed the cloak only when they were out of sight indoors.

"Why do you hide your face in public, Elena?" the queen asked her curiously. "I'm surrounded by young women who love to parade themselves, and none of them are half as beautiful as you."

It was a frank question, but Elena could see that the queen had no desire to make her uncomfortable. She simply seemed puzzled.

"I'm very shy, Your Majesty. My father and I have lived alone in the woods for many years, and I'm not accustomed to being out among people. Most of my life has been very sheltered."

The queen sighed. "I will never look like you," she said wistfully. "I know my husband cares about me very much, but I sometimes wonder if he'll find me attractive when I'm fully grown."

"I don't think you need to worry, Your Majesty," Elena said with a ready smile. "You have lovely features! Besides, attraction isn't just about appearance. Thomas fell in love with me when he thought I was ugly."

"How could he possibly think you were ugly?"

"I wore a disguise, and he'd never seen me without it. My face was always covered, and I looked like I was deformed."

The queen didn't try to hide her astonishment. "But why?"

"When I was growing up, people thought I was a witch."

"Because you had a beautiful face?"

Elena could only shrug.

The queen sighed. "Some people have said nasty things about me because I went to the battle at Torbury Scarp."

"But Your Majesty!" said Elena, completely astonished. "Thomas told me the battle would have been lost without you!"

It was the queen's turn to shrug. "People don't seem to like it if you're different. If it made you worse than others, I could understand it. But they seem just as unhappy if you're different in a good way."

Elena shook her head. "I'm not sure I understand people very well," she said. "Apart from my father anyway. And I think I'm starting to get to know Thomas." She felt herself blushing faintly.

Queen Essanda smiled. "Learning comes from living. Or so my father has always said." Then her face took on an earnest look. "I've been told you probably won't stay in Arnost for long."

Elena nodded a confirmation.

"I would like to see more of you while you're here," said the queen. She hesitated for a moment, then she seemed to come to a decision. "I have some questions I'd like to ask you. There are things I need to talk about with...with a woman. Someone who isn't one of my maids." She spread her arms helplessly. "I don't have a mother to talk to."

"I'm not sure I'll be able to answer your questions," Elena replied awkwardly. "I've grown up without a mother myself." Then she brightened. "Thomas's mother would understand—she's already given me some helpful advice. I could ask her." Seeing the hesitation on the young queen's face, she hastily added, "Without mentioning you, of course!"

The queen nodded. After a pause she said, "You don't have to meet with me of course. Only if you'd like to."

"It would be an honor to spend time with you, Your Majesty," Elena replied. Then she added self-consciously, "And I would enjoy it, too."

Queen Essanda released a breath and smiled. "It's settled, then," she said. "I often have official duties to perform, but I will send you a message."

The queen provided directions to the tower room, and Elena hurried back with her face hidden. She felt considerable relief when she found herself once more in the presence of Thomas and Will and Rufe.

Thomas smiled at her and raised his eyebrows questioningly. She smiled back and gave him a look that said, "All is well. I'll tell you everything that happened later."

THE DAYS PASSED QUICKLY. The queen was true to her word and sent often for Elena. As they became more relaxed in each other's presence they spoke of personal things as well as everyday matters, and the two of them became firm friends.

If Elena could have known, her friendship provided a refreshing change for the queen. At her young age Queen Essanda had already found herself overwhelmed with the subtle and less than subtle maneuvering for power and position that was a constant feature of court life. Elena expected nothing from the queen, and so was able to satisfy that most basic of human needs—the need for a soul mate, a trustworthy friend who saw her as a person, not as a potential rung on the ladder of power and influence.

THE DAY after Thomas and Elena arrived in Arnost, they brought Rubin to meet Thomas's parents. Thomas felt anxious about the meeting, but the outcome exceeded his expectations. Rubin was as even-tempered by nature as Axel was abrupt, but both men were skillful and practical in their own way and they found plenty of common ground.

Rubin was soon spending most days with Axel in the stables. His confidence around horses increased in leaps and bounds. And Axel became noticeably less terse than usual.

3

———

After several months living in the forest with Rubin, Elena, and Thomas, Haldek had no interest in remaining there alone when his companions set out to visit Thomas's parents. He was devoted to Elena, and the idea of her leaving the safety of her isolated refuge alarmed him considerably. Reluctant though he was to travel openly in Arvenon so soon after the end of the war with Rogand, he immediately decided to join the little party. There was also talk of a wedding, and he wasn't willing to miss that under any circumstances.

As far as Haldek was concerned, he was going as Elena's protector. He liked to describe himself as her uncle, but he could scarcely have cared about her more if she were his own daughter.

When he learned that their destination was Arnost, he was dismayed. He had no expectation that any Rogandan would receive a welcome there. He had last seen the city as a soldier in the army besieging it. None of the residents of Arnost could possibly know that, of course. But he knew it.

When they eventually arrived in Arnost, Haldek was pleased to be there for one reason only—he hoped to see Will again. When the two men had last met, Haldek had been facing a future that seemed bleak indeed. Now he could never remember feeling so contented.

Will had been entirely responsible for the change. Haldek was plodding back to Rogand on foot with a band of other demoralized Rogandan soldiers when he encountered the Arvenian army commander. After the decisive defeat of the Rogandan army at the Battle of Torbury Scarp, Haldek was anxious to leave Arvenon as quietly and unobtrusively as possible. He had been tired, miserable, and hungry when Will's men flushed him out.

Will had been riding in search of Elena and Rubin, accompanied by a group of his soldiers and Thomas. He singled Haldek out and separated him from his companions, attaching him instead to his own party. Haldek had no idea why. But he was forever grateful.

THE FORMER ROGANDAN soldier didn't know it, but Will was acting purely out of gratitude.

He did not recognize the commander as someone he had ever met before, and Will did nothing to enlighten him. But he recognized Haldek immediately. The Rogandan had twice assisted him at crucial moments—once at Lord Drettroth's wooden fortress in the wilderness, and once when Will appeared in the Rogandan army camp outside Arnost in the guise of a priest.

Will later encouraged Rubin, Elena, and Thomas to allow Haldek to join them in their forest refuge near the town of Tallesford. They had done so willingly and quickly came to appreciate him as a genial and capable companion.

RUBIN AND HALDEK had entered Arnost the same day as Thomas and Elena, and Rubin quickly found a cheap room in a small inn to share with Haldek. The following day Thomas took Rubin to meet his parents. Haldek did not join them.

Haldek was grateful for the opportunity to hide himself away. In the secluded cabin in the forest there was no reason for his Rogandan heritage to cause a problem. Openly wandering around in the capital of Arvenon was another matter entirely. His Arvenian language skills had been improving steadily, but he spoke with a thick accent that he knew would betray him as a foreigner. Arvenian merchants traveled widely in Rogand before the recent war, and there would undoubtedly be more than a few who would recognize his accent. His features were distinctively Rogandan, too.

Haldek was determined to limit his forays beyond the four walls of the inn where he was staying with Rubin. But he still needed somewhere to eat and to enjoy an ale. The inn's public serving room proved ideal. The food was barely passable, and the ale was watered down, but the lighting was dim and neither the staff nor other customers appeared to be overly curious.

A couple of days after they arrived, Haldek rose early and headed downstairs alone to break his fast. Few other customers were in the public room at that time of the day, but his eyes were drawn to a couple of men dressed as merchants sitting in a shadowy corner of the room, well away from the bar and the entrance to the inn. There was a furtiveness about them that roused his interest—their demeanor suggested they had something to hide. He chose a table that was near them without being too close. Having ordered some food, he pulled his hooded cloak about him and leaned back in his chair.

Snatches of conversation from the men made him instantly alert. They were speaking Rogandan. Unable to hear them clearly, he strained his ears to catch anything he possibly could of their conversation. He heard the words "Castel", "Varas", and "Agon", and he thought he also heard "murder".

He leaned a little closer, and in doing so accidentally knocked against another chair, causing it to scrape loudly on the flagstone floor. The men looked up abruptly and peered at Haldek for a moment. After exchanging a sharp glance, they rose to their feet and quickly left the inn.

Haldek restrained his immediate urge to get up and follow them. For all he knew they would be waiting outside the inn watching to see if anyone followed them. Hasty action might put him in danger, and drawing attention to himself in a strange city was the last thing he wanted to do.

Haldek hastened back upstairs to his room, where he found Rubin still resting.

"I am hearing something," he said, the words tumbling out roughly as he struggled to speak quickly in his accented Arvenian. "We must see Will at once. It cannot wait!"

Rubin stared at him in surprise for a moment, then nodded his head and got up. They were downstairs and outside in a couple of minutes, but it wasn't quick enough for Haldek. As they headed for the castle, he glanced around him for any sign of the men. But he acknowledged to himself that he probably wouldn't recognize them in the light of day. Their faces had barely been visible in the inn, and their clothing was little different from that of any merchant.

When they arrived at the castle, Rubin approached one of the guards and asked to see Will Prentis. The guard looked them up and down disdainfully. His gaze lingered suspiciously on Haldek, then he turned to Rubin with a frown.

"Who wants to see him?" he asked skeptically.

"Tell him that Rubin and Haldek need to meet with him."

"The commander is a busy man. Come back tomorrow."

"He will want to see us," Rubin replied firmly. "And he will not be pleased if you delay our meeting." He studied the face of the guard carefully through narrowed eyes as if committing his features to memory.

The guard frowned again, but after a moment's hesitation he turned aside and spoke quietly to one of the other guards before disappearing into the castle.

After a short delay, another soldier appeared with the guard and greeted Rubin and Haldek courteously.

"Please follow me. The commander is busy at the moment, but he will see you as soon as he is available."

Before many minutes had passed, Will did indeed appear, with Rufe beside him. Both of them greeted the two men warmly.

"Rubin! It's good to see you again," said Will. "Are you and Elena both well?"

"We are! I know you must be busy—thank you for seeing us so quickly."

Will gave a friendly nod in response, then he turned to Haldek.

"Uncle!" he said loudly. "It's been far too long since I saw you last!"

"Welcome to Arnost, Haldek!" said Rufe enthusiastically.

Haldek was bemused by the greeting. But he quickly guessed the purpose behind Will's little charade. A number of soldiers were standing within hearing range. They would undoubtedly spread the word that Will's "uncle" was in town.

Haldek had once asked Will how he came to be so fluent in Rogandan. Will had explained that he had been adopted by his uncle as a small child, and raised by him and his Rogandan wife. Will's aunt was responsible for his fluency in Rogandan. Haldek had the impression that the aunt had little else to commend her, but she had certainly done a thorough job as a language teacher. Perhaps she might have made a poor sister for Haldek, but he nevertheless clearly understood the value of being seen as Will's long lost uncle.

Haldek knew that after defeating the Rogandan invaders, Will was held in the highest esteem by all Arvenians, from the king down. The commander was trading on that credibility to transform Haldek's obvious Rogandan heritage from a liability into an asset.

A wave of gratitude flooded over the Rogandan. He didn't understand the reason why Will was being so considerate to him, but it made him more appreciative than ever of the Arvenian commander.

"We have something we need to tell you," Rubin said quietly.

Will nodded to Rufe, and the giant guardsman led them all to a small room that boasted several comfortable chairs. Rufe ushered them in and pointed to a seat. Then he shut the door.

Will looked at them curiously. "What is it I need to hear?" he asked. "It sounded important."

Rubin leaned forward. "Haldek overheard some merchants. They were speaking Rogandan." He indicated to Haldek that he should continue.

"I am only hearing a bit," Haldek said. "But they talk about Castel, Varas, Agon, and murder."

Will raised his eyebrows. He turned to Rufe. "Could you please bring Thomas?" he asked. "You may find him at the stables. I'd like him to hear this conversation as well."

Rufe set off without delay.

Will turned back to Rubin and Haldek. "While Rufe is gone," he said with a smile, "you can catch me up on all your news."

RUFE DID INDEED FIND Thomas in the stables.

Thomas was spending a large part of each day working with his father and Rubin, while Elena helped his mother. The two women were getting along famously. That was no surprise. What was more surprising was that his father had become less abrupt when speaking to Thomas. Perhaps Axel's exposure to Rubin was having an effect.

When Rufe arrived he greeted Axel before turning to Thomas. "Can I tear you away from your work here, Thomas? Will would like you to join him as soon as possible."

Thomas raised an inquiring eyebrow toward his father.

"You go, Thomas," his father said. "I can continue on here."

"What's happening?" Thomas asked Rufe as they hurried back to Will.

"Haldek heard some men talking in Rogandan. Will wants you to be there when Haldek tells us what happened."

Thomas thought he understood. Will probably wanted him to use the stone to ensure that no details were lost. While they were walking he unobtrusively retrieved the stone from his pouch.

When they arrived Will greeted them with a smile.

"What is he good for?" Haldek asked, jerking a thumb at Thomas. "He speaks terrible Rogandan." He winked at Thomas as he said it.

Will laughed. "Just ignore him if you like. Tell us what happened."

Haldek switched to Rogandan and began describing the men and their conversation as best he could. While he talked, Thomas studied him closely, working hard to limit his focus to the recent incident.

"We will send some men to try to find these merchants," Will said, switching back to Arvenian. "I am grateful to you, Haldek. Your alertness might prove significant."

"I'm heading over to work with Axel in the stables," said Rubin. "Would you like to come with me, Haldek?"

"No, I head back to the inn," Haldek replied.

"On your own?" asked Thomas.

"I am just fine," Haldek insisted.

As Rubin and Haldek left, Will had a few quiet words with Rufe. The guardsman left the room as well, leaving only Thomas and Will.

"Did you learn anything useful?" Will asked.

"Yes. I was able to see their faces, and in more detail than from Haldek's description. I think I would recognize them if I saw them."

"Did you understand any more of what they were saying?"

"No," Thomas replied regretfully. "Haldek wasn't close enough to hear much of their conversation."

"Was he being too cautious? Or are the men worth investigating?"

"I think he was right to be concerned. I don't know what they are doing here, but I suspect these men are much more than simple merchants."

"Thank you, Thomas. Once again you have proved your unique value to the kingdom."

WHILE WILL and Thomas were questioning Haldek, three men sat huddled together in a dark corner of a quiet tavern in Arnost. They were sipping ale from large mugs. One of them was a thickset man with a scar across his chin. He sat opposite the other two men, one with a thin angular face and another with a crooked nose. To any casual observer they would have appeared to be a group of friends enjoying a well earned break after a hard day's work. Anyone sitting close enough to overhear their conversation, though, would not have understood a word unless they happened to be conversant in Rogandan.

The thin faced man was talking. "The Rogandan went to the castle with another man," he said. "I followed them. When they arrived they asked to see Will Prentis." He spat on the rough stone floor as he voiced the name.

The thickset man frowned. "Who is this Rogandan? What have you been able to find out about him?"

Bent Nose shrugged. "We know nothing about him. I overheard some of the guards talking, and supposedly Will Prentis has a Rogandan uncle visiting him." He snorted dismissively. "I don't believe the story for a minute. He's clearly a traitor."

"Interrogate him. No need to be gentle. Find out what he's doing here and what he's up to."

Thin Face smiled—an ugly smile with no trace of humor in it.

Gulping down the last of their ale, the three men pushed themselves to their feet and left the tavern. Once on the street they pulled their hoods down low over their faces and slipped away in different directions.

***

HALDEK LEFT the castle and headed back into the city. He kept his head down, careful to mind his own business. He didn't want trouble.

Sensing the underlying tension in his body as he walked, he consciously worked at calming himself. His edginess wasn't just because he was a foreigner in a strange city. He had never found it easy to relax around crowds and noise. In recent months he had come to realize that the peacefulness and seclusion of the forest was the only setting he could truly call home.

He had never lost his sense of wonder at the sights and the sounds of a city, though. Urchins dashed in and out of alleyways, street sellers loudly hawked their wares, and ordinary people called greetings to each other as they went about their business. Occasionally a lord or a lady passed by in a carriage, dressed in their finery. The garments of the nobility splashed reds, blues, and yellows onto a scene dominated by the brown wood and whitewashed walls of the buildings and the dull fabrics and hardwearing leather of the commoners' clothing. Arnost might be a foreign city, but it had much in common with any large city in his native land.

As he approached the inn, the road narrowed, and the houses on either side drew closer together. With the prospect of hot food and a mug of ale occupying his attention, he paid no mind to his surroundings.

Suddenly he was grabbed from behind and pulled into an alley. He registered a brief glimpse of two men before a blow to the head sent him staggering.

"What do we have here?" said a harsh voice. "A traitor, up at the castle making common cause with these vermin. Likely a deserter, too. We know how to deal with scum like you!"

Another blow to the head almost caused him to black out. Then pain dragged him back to awareness as punches began to rain on his body.

Haldek reacted instinctively, aiming a vicious kick at the shins of one of his attackers. The man cried out in annoyance and drew back.

Haldek used the respite to land blows of his own on the other attacker. Gathering all his strength, he aimed a knockout punch at the second man's head. His target swung away at the last moment, and his blow went wide. With Haldek's arm fully extended, the attacker leaned in swiftly and punched him hard in the midriff. Completely winded, Haldek doubled over, gasping for air. Something heavy hit him on the head, and everything went dark.

HALDEK WOKE to find himself in unfamiliar surroundings. Colorful paintings of cherubs gazed down at him from an ornate ceiling.

"Where am I?" he asked the cherubs. His head was pounding, and he ached all over.

Rufe's face appeared above him. "It's good to see you awake again, Haldek. You've been beaten up pretty badly."

Haldek tried to sit up and almost passed out with the pain. He lay back down again.

"Rest!" ordered a voice that seemed to belong to Will. The commander's face appeared over him as well.

"Do you know who the men were?" Rufe asked.

Haldek shook his head, wincing as the pounding in his skull increased in intensity.

"How you find me?" he asked weakly.

"I asked Rufe to keep an eye on you," said Will.

"And a good thing he did," Rufe added. "They probably would have killed you if I hadn't disturbed them."

"You catch them?" asked Haldek, unable to stifle the groan that escaped with his question.

"Unfortunately not," Rufe replied. "They took off fairly quickly. Do you know who they were? Were they the men you overheard in the inn? Or were they local robbers who didn't like the look of you?"

Haldek closed his eyes and drew in a slow breath. Then he opened his eyes again. "They are Rogandan."

"Are you sure?" asked Will.

"Yes. No doubts about it. They speak to me."

Haldek slowly repeated what they had said.

"Were they the men from the inn?"

"Maybe. I have no chance to see faces."

"From now on you're staying at the castle," said Will. "And you won't be walking around in the city on your own again."

THE THREE STRANGERS had once more retreated to a quiet corner of the tavern.

"We cornered our Rogandan friend. We were interrupted before we got anything out of him," said Thin Face.

"We've been asking plenty of questions, though," said Bent Nose. "He's been seen with a youth. And with a girl who is always cloaked. The youth—and the girl—are staying beside the royal stables."

"There are vague rumors about the youth," Thin Face added. "Someone who sounds a bit like him attended a meeting of the Council of Lords during the siege. The meeting supposedly ended in uproar."

"Something strange is going on," said the thickset man with a scowl. "Have all of them watched closely. Especially the Rogandan and the youth. I want to know everything they do and everywhere they go. Stay well away from them, though. That includes the Rogandan! Pay the local street rats to do the snooping for you. Make sure you stay out of sight!"

Both of them nodded.

"We're going to need more money," said Thin Face. "To pay our informants."

The dull clink of coins could be heard as two bulging bags were pushed up onto the table. Thin Face and Bent Nose each took a bag and hid them away in their cloaks.

A moment later, all three men were gone.

***

WILL STOOD with King Steffan in an inner chamber in the castle. The room was the king's location of choice for private audiences, and Will had become very familiar with it. He had just finished delivering a full report to the king of everything that Haldek had discovered.

King Steffan frowned. "Do you believe the story of this Rogandan friend of yours? Haldek, isn't it?"

"Yes, Sire. I have no doubt whatsoever about it."

The king raised his eyebrows. "No doubt at all? Well, you usually seem to know what you're talking about, Will, so I'll take your word for it."

A thoughtful look came over his face. "Are these men here for a reason? Or are they just merchants with a bad attitude?"

Will shrugged helplessly. "Without proof I can't be certain," he acknowledged. "But I don't want to assume the best and miss something important. I'd rather assume the worst and be proven wrong."

The king nodded. "Find some of our soldiers who speak Rogandan, and send them into the marketplace. Make sure they do it quietly. It's possible they might discover something."

"Yes, Your Majesty."

Will bowed and withdrew.

Before two hours had passed, Will had chosen twenty reliable soldiers and sent them off with clear instructions. The men set off in twos and threes and spread out around the city. They paused to browse among the wares in the marketplace, they sat quietly on wooden stools in busy inns and quiet taverns and watched and listened as they sipped their ale. All day and into the night they kept a vigilant eye out for anything unusual. The following day they did the same.

They witnessed noisy merrymaking and drunken brawls, and apprehended several pickpockets.

They discovered no sign at all of the Rogandan merchants.

4

Elena had no mother of her own to help prepare her for her wedding, but Thomas's mother stepped into the gap with eager delight. Having delivered only a son, Marya never expected to share such an experience with a daughter. Now finding herself in precisely that situation, she could barely contain her excitement. She leaped in with unbounded enthusiasm and every ounce of her restless energy.

A small church and a priest were quickly secured for the event, and Marya began planning a special meal at her home to follow. The guest list was small. Thomas and Elena could not invite extended family members—none of their relatives lived anywhere near Arnost. The wedding would be celebrated by the immediate families, a few close neighbors, and some of Thomas's friends from the army. Of those who had traveled with Thomas during the Rogandan invasion, only Will, Rufe, and Nestor were in Arnost. All three of them readily accepted the invitation to attend.

Marya began the food preparation several days in advance, helped by Elena. They chattered away merrily as they worked, and both of them seemed equally excited to be sharing the effort with the other.

Whenever Thomas had the opportunity, he stole a few minutes to watch them at work. It pleased him immensely that Elena and his mother were getting along so well.

Just two days before the big event, he found them sitting together at the kitchen table, taking a welcome break from their preparations. He slipped onto a stool beside them.

"Axel has given me some coins for the wedding feast," Marya was telling Elena excitedly. "Tomorrow we will buy a few treats at the market."

Elena's eyes widened.

"My only regret," his mother continued, "is that we're not able to provide you with a suitably magnificent gown." She shook her head sadly.

"Oh, I don't mind at all," Elena replied contentedly. "I'm very happy with the dress I have." She beamed a smile at Thomas, who smiled back encouragingly. However humble her garments might be, he never doubted he would truthfully be able to proclaim her the most beautiful bride in the world.

His musing was interrupted by a voice at the door of the cottage. "Is the mistress at home?"

"Come in!" called Marya.

An old woman appeared in the doorway. "Beggin' your pardon," she said, "but I have a package for the lady of the house from Her Majesty."

The visitor handed it to the astonished Marya, then left immediately.

Marya laid the package on the table. "I have no idea what this could be," she said, bemused.

Whatever it held, its contents had been wrapped in fine paper. Unable to bring herself to wantonly destroy such delicate and expensive material, Marya carefully began to unwrap it. Then she caught a glimpse of what lay inside, and her hands froze in shock. She looked up at Thomas and Elena, her eyes wide.

Then abruptly she recovered herself. Frowning down at Thomas on his stool, she waved him away impatiently. "Off you go, then! Now! This is women's business!"

When he didn't immediately move, she put her hands on her hips and glared fiercely at him. "Out! Be off with you!" she cried, pointing to the door.

He finally got the message, and she wasted no time in bustling him out of the cottage.

Thomas stood outside shaking his head in bewilderment. Then he shrugged. Turning on his heel he headed for the stables, chased all the way by the sound of excited squeals from the kitchen.

ON THE DAY of the wedding, Marya ejected her son from the cottage almost from the moment he woke. Thomas hadn't been entirely abandoned though. Rubin, Haldek, and his father had established themselves in one of the stable buildings, and he joined them there. The men had brought with them everything they needed to dress themselves for the wedding, and Marya had sent ample food supplies with Axel. Before long Will, Rufe, and Nestor arrived as well, bringing with them a small cask of ale.

Every necessary ingredient was on hand for a merry party. The three soldiers were soon entertaining the men with tales from their travels. To Thomas's dismay, most of the stories were at his expense.

"I remember the time when Brother Vangellis was ill," said Will. "Thomas was sent off to find feverwort."

"Yes, and he came back with a poisonous plant," said Rufe, grinning hugely.

"Our female companion was not at all impressed," chortled Nestor. "She let him know exactly what she thought about it."

All three soldiers laughed uproariously.

Will leaned in close to Thomas, a huge grin on his face. Then he whispered in his ear, "Shall I tell them what she said that day when she was riding in front of you?"

Seeing the horrified look on Thomas's face, he laughed and slapped him on the back.

After a steady flow of embarrassing yarns, Rubin clearly decided that his future son-in-law had been punished enough. "You might not know it, but Thomas used feverwort to save my life," he said seriously.

"I'm not at all surprised," said Will. "The truth is that we could never have managed without Thomas."

Rufe and Nestor agreed wholeheartedly. It clearly took some effort for them to swallow their grins, but they nevertheless accepted the change in tone cheerfully.

"There never was a better horse master for the army," Rufe asserted soberly, every trace of irony extinguished from his tone. "He got Will back into the saddle after his injury at Danford. At the time I couldn't imagine Will ever being able to ride confidently again. Thomas proved me wrong."

The remainder of their time together passed very agreeably for Thomas. His companions succeeded admirably in making him feel valued.

Before long it was time to go. Rubin left them, and the others escorted Thomas to the church. He felt conspicuous and awkward in his new doublet and breeches, and his friends didn't help by grinning at his discomfort.

As the big moment approached Thomas's nerves began to surface, and he broke out in a sweat. Apparently deciding to take pity on him, Will threw an arm around Thomas's shoulder and proceeded in low tones to relate a juicy tale about Rufe. He reported that a determined young woman had singled out the giant guardsman as the man of her dreams, untroubled by his lack of interest in her bountiful charms.

Will provided a hilarious account of Rufe's frantic and often futile attempts to avoid her, succeeding so completely in distracting Thomas that at first the groom failed to notice that wedding guests were filing into the church. Thomas tried hard to put on an appropriately solemn demeanor as he redirected his attention to the guests. All of them were known to him, and when they caught his eye they beamed him smiles of encouragement.

A slight girl that he didn't recognize also slipped into the church, choosing to sit at the back. She glanced briefly in his direction, but her face was covered by a hood, and he wasn't able to make eye contact. She was clearly at pains not to be known.

His brows drew together briefly in puzzlement. He knew very few girls, and none of them were close enough friends to be invited to his wedding. Then with a shock he realized who it must be. A brief glimpse of soldiers outside the church confirmed it. The uninvited guest was no lesser personage than Queen Essanda.

This new discovery might have melted his courage away entirely, but at that moment his bride appeared. A hooded cloak had apparently concealed her wedding finery on her way to the church, but as she entered the porch her father helped her out of it. Then she stepped through the door, her delicate hand resting on her father's arm.

Thomas stood with Will at his side, and he heard a gasp escape from his friend. He understood Will's reaction entirely.

Elena took his breath away. He had expected her to be clad in a simple dress with bold colors, much like every other bride he had ever glimpsed. Instead she wore a delicate gown made from a pale fabric he did not recognize. She was beyond beautiful. This was her day, and she shone with a wondrous radiance.

His family and friends stood to honor the bride. But the groom ceased to be aware of them. As Elena and her father made their stately progress toward the altar, Thomas saw only the face of his bride, illuminated with a joyful smile—a smile intended for him alone.

Dazzled as he was by her beauty, he remembered again what had first attracted him to her. Believing her to be surpassingly ugly, he had been captured by the beauty of her spirit. She was gracious, she was guileless, and she was unfailingly kind.

The most amazing thing about this day was that she had entrusted her heart to his keeping. He could never deserve her, but he would always strive to be worthy of her.

The ceremony passed in a blur. He only knew that he could have drowned in his joy.

Vows were spoken, and the newlyweds received a blessing from the priest. Then the congratulations flowed freely as their friends and family shared in their delight.

Only as they were leaving the church did it occur to Thomas to look for the young queen. There was no sign of her. She had slipped away as unobtrusively as she had entered.

A SMALL CROWD had gathered when the wedding party arrived, cheering the bride heartily the moment they caught sight of her.

One observer in particular had looked on with eager interest. He noted that the Rogandan traitor had finally emerged from the safety of the castle, and that he was appearing in the company of both Will Prentis and Rufe Sarjant. His eyes narrowed when he saw the queen's guards escorting her to the church.

The youthful groom and the stunning young woman at his side would warrant further attention.

The moment the ceremony finished and the church had emptied, he had eased his way through the crowd and stole away. Neither his arrival nor his departure attracted attention. Just as he intended.

MARYA HAD LAID out a tempting feast for the wedding party under a shelter beside the stables. Freshly baked bread rolls, meat dishes featuring fish and fowl, tasty sweetmeats, and even dried fruit from Lestanor adorned the tables. Ale, too, was available in plenty. Everyone was soon eating and drinking heartily.

The well wishers might have been few in number, but they kept Thomas and Elena busy.

Elena was smiling and laughing with Thomas's father when his mother bustled up to him. She enveloped her son in a joyous embrace.

"What do you think of your bride's dress?" she asked him breathlessly.

"It's magnificent!" said Thomas, gazing in admiration at his beautiful wife.

"The dress was a gift," gushed his mother. "From no lesser person than Queen Essanda! I even met her at the wedding! Elena was expecting to wed in a much more simple garment. She's such a humble person, after all, in spite of her looks. But the queen said it was fitting for Elena to be seen in her full beauty on her wedding day. So she personally arranged for a silk gown to be made! Silk! Just look at it! Who could have imagined such a thing?"

Thomas gazed at it, feeling like he was seeing it properly for the first time. He saw a brocaded bodice above an expanse of shining lace, but the fabric and design meant little to him. He did notice the way the garment flowed around her, though, serving to accentuate the shapeliness of her figure.

Even he could see that the dress was elegant without being overstated. The overall effect was magnificent. It was a regal gift.

Thomas could not take his eyes off his bride. Everything about her captivated him, from her graceful movements to her shy laugh. The knowledge that she would be his partner for life filled him with amazement. How had he become the one to receive her love?

With his own joy overflowing, he remembered he needed to spare a thought for other people.

From time to time he had caught a glimpse of his new father-in-law glancing wistfully at Elena. He couldn't help wondering if the sight of Rubin's radiant daughter was bringing to mind visions of his own departed wife.

He headed over to speak with him.

"I was wondering if the wedding has brought back memories for you," he began tentatively, hoping he wasn't being insensitive.

Rubin smiled at him encouragingly. "It has. Happy memories. Elena's mother was beautiful, inside and out, just as her daughter is."

Rubin had become a second father to Thomas in the months he had spent with them. "I hope you know how grateful I am to you," Thomas said. "You've helped and encouraged me more than I can say."

Rubin responded with a smile, reaching out a gentle hand and clapping Thomas on the shoulder.

Elena soon joined them, and a tear came to Rubin's eye as he embraced his daughter. Thomas quietly left the two of them alone together.

Thomas found himself near Haldek, who called out to him with a beaming smile, "Congratulations!"

"Thank you," he replied with a grin.

He wondered if Haldek might be missing their quiet home in the forest.

"Does all this feel strange?" he asked, waving a hand vaguely across the celebrations.

The Rogandan gave him a knowing smile. "You are smarter than you look," he said with a wink. He shrugged. "I am not loving change," he acknowledged. "But it is good anyway. Sometimes. Very soon, you, Elena, Rubin, me—all of us are going to the forest again. Then I am happy."

Thomas attempted a response in Rogandan, and his friend was soon laughing at his stumbling attempts. After a while Will joined them, and Thomas left them to converse freely in Haldek's mother tongue.

Thomas noticed that his father was not currently engaged in conversation. He couldn't help wondering what the stable master was thinking and feeling at that moment. The stone, secure in the pouch at his waist, could have answered the question, but he refused to even consider using it to pry into the thoughts of anyone close to him.

The time had come to talk to his father. He felt awkward and apprehensive, but there were things he needed to say. He approached him with as much confidence as he could muster.

"I know I haven't always been as grateful and appreciative as a son ought to be, and I'm sorry for that," he said. Then sucking in a deep breath, he added, "I love you, Father."

He'd done it. He relaxed, slowly releasing the breath.

Axel was too astonished to reply. He stood there uncomfortably for a moment, then thumped Thomas on the back and turned away to get another ale.

Thomas noticed that Elena had witnessed the interaction. She shot him a knowing smile. He raised his eyebrows and shrugged. He'd tried.

He saw that his mother had also been watching, her hand to her mouth. Elena joined her mother-in-law and placed an arm around her. Marya responded by leaning her head on Elena's shoulder.

Then Rufe and Nestor approached Thomas, and his attention was drawn away.

He eventually began to think the celebrations would never end. But the time finally came for the revelers to send off the bride and the groom. Thomas's parents had offered the newlyweds their cottage for their first night, and Marya had set up a bed for Axel and herself in one of the stable buildings.

Everyone walked them to the door of the cottage. Final good wishes and warm embraces were accompanied by cheeky winks from Will and his friends. Then all of them departed and went their separate ways.

FINALLY ALONE INSIDE THE COTTAGE, Elena looked across at Thomas and began to giggle. Taken aback, he felt a deep blush rising to his face. What could possibly be prompting such a reaction?

The giggles died on her lips when she saw his confusion. Taking his hands, she gazed up at him earnestly. "Please pay no mind to me, Thomas," she said. "I think I must be nervous."

Thomas could certainly relate to that.

Rubin had offered Thomas some tips in the lead up to his wedding. He had also received a different kind of preparation for marriage during his time in the wilderness with Brother Vangellis.

Although the monk had been single all his life, he had seen the fruit —both sweet and bitter—of many marriages over the years, and in response to Thomas's curiosity he had freely shared many valuable insights with his young friend.

Thomas later discovered that his mother, never one to be troubled by shyness, had also held a number of frank conversations with her future daughter-in-law.

As a result, both of them had some inkling of what might await them on the journey of life stretching out before them. They were also prepared, at least in part, for the delicate dance that was their first night together.

In spite of all the words of preparation and encouragement, though, Thomas found himself standing red faced and awkward before his bride. Elena decided to help. With a self-conscious smile, she bent low over the candle and snuffed it out. Then she reached out and drew him to herself.

When finally they settled themselves side by side, wide-eyed and breathless, Thomas could only wonder if greater happiness was even possible.

At that moment Thomas might have been tempted to think that he was now a man in every way that mattered. But he knew that a lifetime of responsibilities came with the steps he had taken.

Young as he was, he had boldly reached for the mantle of manhood. Time alone would reveal if he proved worthy of it.

5

One month after the Battle of Torbury Scarp

King Agon gave his horse its head, reveling in the sensation of the sun on his face and the wind in his hair. The nobleman at his side was hard pressed to keep up.

Lord Krasmir, one of Rogand's most wealthy and powerful barons, had come to the palace in response to the king's summons. It was possible that the baron had no desire to spend the afternoon galloping across the extensive grounds surrounding the royal palace. The king neither knew nor cared. Over the preceding weeks Agon had watched on in growing excitement as the stone brought about complete turnarounds in the attitudes of a number of lesser men. The time had come to test it on an unusually difficult subject.

King Agon gradually slowed his horse to a walk and pulled in closer to his riding companion. The man was heavy set and roughly clad. Agon looked at him in disgust—the nobleman dressed himself little better than a hairy animal, for all his wealth. In poor light Krasmir could have been mistaken for a bear.

Never before had Agon chosen to spend an afternoon with Krasmir, not least because the man had a reputation as a callous beast. The king had no cause for apprehension, though—not with a squadron of soldiers following closely behind the two men. The captain of the royal guard left nothing to chance.

Agon had something very specific to say to Krasmir.

"I've decided to levy a new tax on the western barons, Lord Krasmir," said Agon casually. "I wanted you to be the first to know about it."

The nobleman glowered at him through bushy brows.

"You can thank the late Lord Drettroth for this initiative," Agon told him darkly. "He was the one who emptied the royal coffers. All that effort and expense to support his little adventure in Arvenon, and I have nothing whatever to show for it!" He raised an empty hand to the heavens.

"What is the nature of this tax?...Your Majesty," Krasmir asked. He managed to make his words sound more like a snarl than a question, and his addition of the royal title was belated enough to be pointed.

"Think of it as an 'Excess Assets' tax," the king replied evenly. "I'm glad to tell you that only those who possess enormous resources will be required to participate. Barons with lesser means will need to wait for another opportunity."

Krasmir's frown deepened. "What rate of tax are you proposing?"

Agon smiled genially. "Just twenty percent of income. In addition to existing taxes, of course."

Krasmir was too stunned to reply.

"And only for the next five years," the king added.

Agon watched with malevolent satisfaction as a storm began brewing on the baron's face. He knew what the baron would be thinking. Drettroth's armies had tramped through Krasmir's lands on their way to invade Arvenon. As they passed, the soldiers had heedlessly stripped the fields of cattle and sheep, and much else besides. After they were defeated, the surviving rabble had slunk back the same way, desperate and hungry. They'd taken whatever they could without giving it a moment's thought.

Krasmir had suffered more than most. And that was before taking his manpower losses into consideration. Many of his able-bodied men had been forcibly enlisted in the army; more than half of them had not returned. Slapping the new tax on Krasmir was entirely unreasonable—deliciously so.

The nobleman finally found his voice. "The Great Council will have something to say about this!" he snarled.

Agon smiled to himself. The baron's response was predictable. Rogand's council of lords could not actually override a royal decree, although only kings who were supremely powerful—or completely stupid—ignored the council entirely.

"The Great Council has already endorsed the tax wholeheartedly," Agon returned, affecting a bored tone. "Regrettably you were absent during the session. I am told you were unavoidably detained."

Krasmir preferred to pull political strings in private, so he rarely bothered to attend council meetings. That meant he had no one to blame but himself.

The nobleman pulled savagely on his reins, prompting his horse to rear with a high pitched scream. Agon's mount backed away in alarm.

Fearing a confrontation, members of the royal guard thundered up with swords drawn.

Agon waved a hand lazily to indicate all was well. "Lord Krasmir's horse seems to have been startled by a bee," he ventured.

He nodded to Krasmir with an indulgent smile. "I wish you a pleasant afternoon, My Lord."

With that, he turned his horse toward the palace and galloped away.

THE FOLLOWING morning Agon sat in council with his advisors. None of the king's advisors were bold enough or stupid enough to actually offer him advice, but Agon found their pearls of wisdom quite entertaining at times.

"Lord Krasmir is reportedly furious, Your Majesty," one of the advisors suggested. "He is even said to be threatening revolt."

Agon smiled condescendingly. In spite of Krasmir's unpredictability, the nobleman offered no real surprises to the king. Krasmir was a volatile brute—a man after his own heart.

"Would it be wise to approach him with caution?" the advisor concluded. "Even animals can be dangerous when cornered."

The advisor's attempt at wise counsel came across to Agon as comical. The king shook his head in disgust. There was a reason he rarely met with his so-called advisors. These toads could barely boast a working brain between them. They simply didn't get it.

The king was not at all shocked by Krasmir's reaction—it was exactly what he had anticipated. Agon had conceived the tax with the baron in mind. It was hardly surprising that the Great Council had so readily endorsed it. None of the other noblemen were affected by it.

"What will you do, Your Majesty?" another of the toads asked anxiously.

Agon looked at him pityingly. "What will I do? I will invite Krasmir to join me in the procession to the temple tomorrow."

ONCE EACH YEAR the king was expected to lead a procession to the gates of the main temple in Rog. Agon found all such rituals extremely tiresome. Nevertheless he went through the motions, as his predecessors had done before him.

This particular day was a holiday throughout Rogand in honor of the dark gods. The day began and ended with a feast, and no one was expected to work on that day, not even slaves.

It hardly needed to be said that someone must feed the animals, milk the cows, build the fires, fetch water, prepare food, serve at the feast, and tend to every whim of the masters. Apart from that, slaves were not expected to work.

As soon as the sun reached the halfway point in its journey from noon to sunset, the festivities began in earnest. Led by the king and an immaculately presented contingent of the royal guard, the procession started at the palace and descended to the huge central market square before climbing again to the gates of the temple. The streets had been adorned with flowers to honor the dark gods—white lilies for Nehrvina the Awful, and red and white carnations for Malzakh the Destroyer. In keeping with tradition, crudely constructed effigies of corpses painted white were carried on the shoulders of the crowd.

The people marched slowly through the streets in eerie silence, their numbers swelling each time the procession passed a new district of the city. All but the poorest had clad themselves symbolically in funeral attire—black from the waist down, and white above the waist.

The king soon found himself at the head of a massive column that stretched behind him all the way to the central market and beyond.

Finally the column approached the gates of the main temple. Inside the grounds lay an imposing and ominous looking structure shaped like a gigantic mausoleum. However the procession came to a halt before it passed the temple gates.

A large delegation of priests waited at the gates bearing flaming torches. The priests were clad in dark cloaks with black leather belts and shoes. Large cowls covered their heads, and the faces that protruded from beneath the cowls bore long streaks of deep blue paint.

As soon as the procession stopped, the crowd began passing forward the effigies. They flowed in a seemingly endless stream until a massive pile of dummy corpses had risen before the gates. As one man the priests stepped forward and threw their torches onto the pile. A moment later the king and members of his royal guard hurled pitchers of oil onto the blaze.

The flames roared upward into the sky, and the crowd erupted in a deafening cheer. Handheld drums and cymbals appeared among the people, and men and women were soon dancing with abandon from one end of the column to the other, shrieking out the names of their dark gods as they spun and twirled to the hypnotic beat of the drums.

As soon as the flames began to die down the king and his party turned away from the temple and set out for the feast awaiting them at the palace. The crowd gradually dispersed behind them as people headed for their homes and the prospect of abundant food, cheap wine, and bawdy songs.

Throughout the procession, Krasmir marched at the king's right hand. The baron was too angry to speak—he had reportedly been incandescent with fury since learning of the tax—but he nevertheless accompanied the king as commanded.

Agon was not at all concerned by Krasmir's silence. He had nothing to say to the baron himself. Apart from ensuring that the nobleman constantly hovered nearby, the king ignored him completely.

The two men parted the moment they reached the palace. The king did not offer the courtesy of a farewell.

THE FOLLOWING days proceeded in a similar fashion. Before long Agon was spending so much time with Krasmir that people began referring to the baron as the king's shadow.

After two weeks had elapsed, Agon decided that the right moment must surely have arrived. He had come to heartily loathe the baron's company, and he was impatient to sever the cord as soon as possible.

Since announcing the tax to Krasmir, Agon had never referred to it again. He did so now.

"It has been suggested to me that you had reservations about the new Excess Assets tax, My Lord. Was that report accurate?"

Krasmir turned to his sovereign. "I have no objection to the tax, Your Majesty," he replied.

For a fleeting moment as the baron was saying it, he looked confused. He appeared thoroughly convinced that the tax was worthwhile, yet some part of him seemed baffled by his own ready acceptance of it. The moment of confusion quickly passed, though, and his face cleared.

"I was hoping you would see it that way," said Agon mildly.

Krasmir returned a stern nod.

Agon said nothing more, keeping his face expressionless. Inwardly he was shouting with glee.

IN THE WEEKS before his first approach to Krasmir, Agon had witnessed with growing excitement the stone's influence on a few carefully selected subjects. Nothing remained but to present it with the greatest available challenge. Drettroth would have been the perfect candidate, except that he was dead and buried. Agon accordingly turned his attention to the most difficult of his barons—Lord Krasmir.

The man possessed a fierce and independent spirit. He bowed the knee to his king in public, but his will belonged to him alone. Inwardly he yielded to no one.

The king knew from the scroll that the Stone of Authority did not take effect instantly—prolonged exposure was needed. Consequently, having enraged and alienated the baron, the king found a myriad of excuses to make constant contact with the nobleman. A furious and bemused Krasmir had no way of knowing that Agon's real intent was to bring him under the influence of the stone.

The results had been nothing short of spectacular. The king had looked on in awe as Lord Krasmir's way of thinking was slowly transformed before his eyes. Nothing now prevented Agon from fully exploiting the power of the Stone of Authority.

The only remaining question was where to focus his attention next.

BEFORE HE HAD COME CLOSE to exhausting the possibilities of the Stone of Authority, Agon was already dreaming of bigger things. Giddy as the stone's power had made him, he quickly became hungry for more—much more.

With Lord Krasmir confirmed as his obedient puppy, the king devoted himself to recruiting a new set of agents to pursue the Stone of Knowing. He sent them to Arvenon with instructions for their leader, a man named Biel, to return regularly to deliver a report.

The moment he was informed that Biel had returned to Rog for the first time, the king summoned him to the audience room adjoining his grand reception hall.

"What progress have you made in tracking down this Tomas?" Agon demanded.

His agent bowed respectfully. "We have not yet identified any person matching his description in Arnost, Your Majesty. But we are vigorously pursuing our investigations. We have people watching the gates, and we are establishing a network of informants throughout the city. There is some suggestion he was involved at the royal stables at one time, so we will watch the stables as well."

"Bring me news," Agon warned him. "And do it soon if you want to keep your head."

The man began to sweat visibly. Agon dismissed him before disgust made him do something he might later regret.

He would give Biel and his men ample time to prove their worth. If they failed to deliver on the king's expectations, he would replace them without a second thought. His patience had a limit.

But if they should succeed...

With two such stones under his control, he would become almost invincible. It was hardly surprising that his lust for the Stone of Knowing was increasingly consuming his waking thoughts and troubling his sleep.

With the Stone of Authority secured and a search underway for the Stone Lof Knowing, a new issue began to loom large in Agon's mind. Opportunities beyond his wildest imaginings had already fallen within his grasp. But Agon was now in middle age. It was becoming clear that his own life span would eventually prove to be his undoing.

The Stone of Vitality could prolong his life—if he could somehow get his hands on it. This final stone would not grant him immortality though. It would merely delay the inevitable.

Given all this, his thoughts were increasingly drawn to another scroll buried in the midst of Lorik and Jorvan's pile. It appeared to have been authored by Drettroth. The text was rambling and even incoherent in places, and its content was bafflingly theological in nature. But Agon understood the general idea well enough.

The deceased nobleman had seen the Stone of Vitality merely as a stepping stone. Apparently he believed he had discovered a way to completely overcome the limitations of mortality. Endless delving into old scrolls had led him to a startling conclusion: for the right price, a limitless life span could be purchased from the dark gods.

Drettroth intended to invoke an arcane and sinister ritual that involved human sacrifice on a grand scale. Although he had not detailed the actual ritual in his scroll, he did make it clear that the outcome would be to extend his life in exchange for prematurely ending the lives of others. The price would not be cheap—a steady flow of victims would be needed. Drettroth expected the tally to run into the tens of thousands.

The king was beginning to grasp the reason why Drettroth was so eager to annex Arvenon and the surrounding kingdoms. Having stripped them bare, he would probably have turned south to Lestanor. Eventually he might even have turned east to Rogand itself.

The very notion of such a bargain was utterly absurd. But was it more absurd than the idea that a tiny stone could convey unimaginable power?

Agon would have given a great deal to be able to discuss the scroll with its author. But Drettroth was beyond such concerns. The king might have analyzed the scroll with Lorik and Jorvan if he hadn't already executed them. Only one other way to test Drettroth's conclusions had presented itself. He would need to consult with the High Priest at the temple in Rog.

The very thought left him cold. It still gave him shivers to recall his childhood responses to the priests. Their appearance, their behavior, their very existence—everything about them was profoundly disturbing.

Agon still vividly remembered his first visit to the temple as a child. His nostrils began to twitch uncomfortably as he recalled the sickly atmosphere inside the building. In his childish imagination the temple seemed more like a tomb than a place of worship. Within a few minutes of entering, he had emptied his stomach violently onto the dull stone floor. He had still been retching helplessly as he was carried outside. His father had been furious.

He had learned to master his reactions while among the priests, but his occasional encounters with the High Priest sent a chill up his spine, even as a grown man.

Still more disconcerting, His Eminence never left his temple. He made exceptions for no one, not even the king.

Much as it galled him to admit it, Agon could not force the High Priest to do anything. When he was crown prince his father had tried to impress upon him the principle that a kingdom was only as strong as its foundations. The Kingdom of Rogand rested on the foundation of three powerful institutions—the throne, the nobility, and the priesthood. Agon could no more afford to alienate the priests than he could wish away the nobles.

It might have been possible to bend the High Priest to Agon's will using the Stone of Authority. But the king was not willing to spend the number of days required in the High Priest's presence, and he was certain that the priest would never consent to it anyway.

The High Priest agreed to meet Agon at the temple, and when the day arrived the king set off accompanied by a large contingent of the royal guards. The soldiers were on hand to bolster his courage more than to protect him.

The streets bore no resemblance to their appearance the last time he had made his way through Rog. The procession was no more than a memory now, and filth and squalor had replaced the flowers and the revelers.

Beggars stepped forward eagerly as he approached. As soon as they became aware of the identity of the rider, they scurried away like rats from a flame. Agon stared fixedly ahead, steadfastly refusing to countenance any sight he didn't wish to see.

As soon as Agon arrived at the gates of the temple compound, he dismounted. His men did the same.

He was met by a thickset priest clad in black.

"I bid Your Majesty welcome to this sacred place," the priest said with a bow. "Please, follow me."

Agon proceeded through the gates, followed closely by his men.

"Not the soldiers," the priest said sharply. "They must wait outside."

The men drew back at once.

The king's first reaction was an angry scowl. Then he reminded himself he had come seeking information.

"Wait for me here," he instructed his captain before turning and following the priest.

Agon had visited the temple many times, but never alone. The entrance to the temple building felt no less dark and foreboding than on his previous visits, and Agon paused awkwardly at the threshold before trailing in behind the priest. The light inside was dim, the vast space illuminated only by small clusters of candles that guttered and flickered feebly. A heavy smell permeated the air—a cloying union of incense, smoke, and blood.

His guide led him past a group of priests who appeared to be in a trance. They aimed an empty stare in the king's direction, and he returned their gaze, noticing in the dim light that fresh blood mingled freely with the blue paint on their faces. He tore his gaze away in distaste.

The priest ushered him into a small room where the High Priest sat in an ornate wooden chair. His guide then left without a word.

By that time, Agon's mind was reeling. The otherness of this place overwhelmed him. He was the king. He understood the subtle ways of power and the complexities confronting anyone bold enough to rule a people. But he felt adrift in this temple, far beyond his depth. He had no comprehension of the dark gods, nor did he understand what motivated the men who devoted their lives to ministering to them.

He labored to push all such thoughts from his mind.

"Welcome, Sire," said the High Priest. "What has brought you before me?" He nodded Agon to a seat. He did not get up from his own chair.

A flush of annoyance rose in Agon. The High Priest might rule in this place, but he had no need to flaunt it.

He forced his displeasure down and seated himself. "Thank you, Your Eminence. I have come to you with a delicate question."

The High Priest did not immediately respond. Agon peered at him curiously. The man's skin had the appearance of leather, and the wrinkles on his face were deeply creased. He had already been old when Agon was a child, and he seemed little different today.

The king wondered briefly if the man opposite him possessed the Stone of Vitality. He soon rejected the idea. The High Priest might appear almost ageless, but nothing about him conveyed the vaguest hint of vitality.

"What is your question?" the High Priest finally asked.

"Do the dark gods offer any possibility of relief from the curse of mortality?"

Agon winced as he said it. Surely the question must seem foolish to the priest.

The High Priest did not treat his query with scorn. "You are not the first person to ask me such a question," he observed.

"Lord Drettroth?" the king responded immediately.

His Eminence did not reply. He simply gazed expressionlessly at Agon with his timeworn eyes.

As the seconds ticked away, the king began to fidget. He was accustomed to others feeling uneasy in his presence. Nothing about this place felt normal, though.

Still the High Priest remained silent. As time continued to pass, Agon's need to fill the emptiness became a compulsion.

"Is there a ritual that grants long life in exchange for a sacrifice?" he blurted out.

No answer was forthcoming. Agon shifted awkwardly in his chair, trying hard not to squirm.

After what felt like an eternity, the High Priest's mouth slowly opened. "Nehrvina the Awful grants life. And she reclaims it when she chooses," he droned.

What did that mean? It certainly didn't answer the question.

Agon squinted across at the High Priest, and a frown began to form on his brow. How had His Eminence managed to preserve his own life for so long? And if the High Priest himself was indeed benefiting from such a ritual, how likely would he be to confess his secret?

Was it possible that Drettroth had asked himself the same questions?

The king decided to try again. "Does Her Awful Majesty ever choose to extend the life of a favored person?"

A long pause followed. Agon began to feel lightheaded. Was it the incense in the air, or was it the disconcerting gaze of the High Priest? He shook his head in an attempt to clear it. It was becoming difficult to focus his thoughts.

Once again the High Priest's mouth opened. "Her ways are inscrutable," he slowly pronounced.

Another non-answer. It was increasingly obvious to Agon that he would learn nothing useful here.

When his vision began to swim he decided he'd had enough. He needed to get out of there before he collapsed.

Pushing himself to his feet, he stumbled to the door of the small room. The High Priest sat unmoving, watching his departure dispassionately. Neither man uttered a word of farewell.

Agon lurched unsteadily through the temple and staggered out of the entrance into the open air. Once clear of the building he bent low and placed his hands on his knees, sucking in great gulps of fresh air.

A small group of priests wandered past and glanced at him curiously. He ignored them.

When he had recovered sufficiently he stood upright again and made his way to the gate.

His men were waiting for him there. None of them commented on his appearance—they wouldn't be so foolish. All of them mounted their horses. Agon rode away without a backward glance.

The further he went from the temple grounds, the more normal Agon began to feel. Slowly his head started to clear.

He had left without answers. What had been going through Drettroth's mind when he emerged from his own interview with the High Priest?

Nothing had been said to confirm or deny Drettroth's idea of a bargain with the dark gods. Perhaps no confirmation was needed though. The High Priest's longevity might itself provide the answer. Surely his great age could not be natural. Agon felt sure he had stumbled upon something significant.

The specifics of the ritual were still a mystery, which left important questions unanswered. The king promised himself he would carefully revisit the pile of scrolls inherited from his former army commander.

His spirits rose higher as the temple slipped further away behind him. In spite of his unsettling experience with the High Priest and the unsatisfying outcome of the interview, Agon saw no reason at all to feel discouraged.

6

Six months after the Battle of Torbury Scarp

A brand new sunrise saw King Agon of Rogand standing silently on the balcony of his private apartments, gazing sourly across the extensive woodlands that surrounded his palace. From this vantage point he could see beyond the palace grounds to the capital city of Rog that lay below them. In the far distance he caught a glimpse of the walls that encircled the city.

Birdsong rose from the trees to compete with the muffled din of the city that penetrated the palace's borders. The palace might be a haven from the squalor of the capital below, but the city's proximity provided the king with a daily reminder of the reality that lay just beyond his privileged existence. Agon had no interest in any such reminder, and he had instructed his servants to find a way to block out the sights and sounds of the city. It annoyed him intensely that they had so far failed to satisfy his demands. Perhaps it was time to lop off a couple of heads. That might provide the necessary motivation and focus.

Turning away from the city, he reentered his rooms.

His personal slave hovered nearby, as always.

"I haven't seen you in a while, Ennawi," said the king. "Have you missed me?" He smiled ironically.

The slave did not respond.

"I've been busy," Agon continued. "Not something that could ever be said about you."

The king glanced at Ennawi scornfully. "I hear that my servants have been whispering. They regard you with universal contempt. They simply cannot understand why I retain a person incapable of performing any kind of useful service."

Ennawi offered no response. He could not have answered even if he wanted to of course—having no tongue, he was incapable of speech.

The king had never made any secret about his attitude toward Ennawi—anyone within earshot knew that the royal vitriol was directed at him more than at any other person. Yet whatever Agon said, and however loudly he shouted it, the slave simply ignored it.

Agon couldn't help admiring his composure—no other person who ignored the king had ever lived to see another sunrise. Ennawi was extremely bold or extremely stupid. Either way he was beyond fortunate. Many slaves had come and gone; Ennawi had outlasted them all.

Regardless of the whispers, Ennawi seemed determined to reinforce the widely held view of his usefulness. Silent and unmoving, he simply stood there.

Agon shrugged. How could such a slave be useful anyway? A person without hands was good for almost nothing.

Ennawi was certainly reliable though—he was always there without ever being in the way. Most curious of all, while he was unarguably the most attentive of Agon's servants, he gave no sign of understanding a single word the king said.

Agon did not tolerate idleness in those who attended him. Nevertheless, he tolerated Ennawi.

He came and stood before the slave, studying him silently. Then he shrugged. "Others can think what they like," he murmured. "I'm the king, and I do whatever I please."

The status of his slaves held no lasting interest for Agon, and he soon pushed the issue from his mind. Already his thoughts were taking him in a different direction—there were matters he needed to address. Important matters.

He hastened away from his private rooms without sparing a further thought for Ennawi.

AGON HAD BARELY VANISHED before another slave hurried into the apartments in his wake. The king did not notice her arrival. He never did—she made certain of that.

Spotting Ennawi near the balcony, she immediately bustled across to him.

The woman, Nistinaa, had been Ennawi's carer since before he came to the king. The two slaves were not related, but over the years she had come to care for him as a mother cherishes a son.

Agon had encountered Nistinaa only once, and the contact had been brief. She was well into middle age and no beauty, and the king had looked straight through her. She had no desire to meet him a second time.

She scanned Ennawi carefully. "So he hasn't struck you again," she said with a little grunt of satisfaction.

A bowl appeared in her hand, and she began to spoon food into his mouth. He chewed and swallowed instinctively, offering no hint that he even registered her presence. She was not perturbed by his apparent indifference.

Finally she held up a small vial filled with a dark blue liquid. The appearance of the liquid finally earned her a reaction. His eyes flickered briefly, betraying what she knew to be distaste. She tut-tutted once, raising an eyebrow. He responded by tilting back his head obediently and drinking.

She patted him lightly on the shoulder and smiled sadly up at his impassive face. Then, after whispering a few quiet words of encouragement, she slipped away as quietly as she had come.

DAYLIGHT WAS ALMOST SPENT by the time Agon laid aside his pressing business and returned to his private chambers. He found Ennawi exactly where he had left him. If the slave had moved during the time he was gone, it wasn't obvious.

"My new army commander is no better than the fool I executed last month," he snarled. "I'll give him another week to muster up some intelligence, then I'll have his head!"

He scowled in anger. "Where is Drettroth when I need him?"

Picking up a delicate marble statuette, he hurled it at the far wall. The object shattered into smaller pieces that scattered across the floor. The act of destruction calmed him for reasons he couldn't fathom.

"Drettroth might have loathed me, but he served me well. He only did it to boost his own power and influence of course." He smiled mirthlessly. "I respect that in a person."

He gazed at the slave thoughtfully. "Drettroth might be dead and buried, but he wasn't a complete failure. He did at least give me the Stone of Authority, back when we were youths. I don't pretend it was an ungrudging gift. But I wanted it, and when I want something badly enough I always get it."

Ennawi appeared unmoved by this information.

The king picked up a bunch of grapes from a bowl and began rhythmically popping the dark purple juice balls into his mouth. He chewed them carefully, then he spat out the pips in random locations. He made a mental note to punish his servants appropriately if they failed to locate and remove them all.

"It was Drettroth who learned the truth about the stone. And he hid it from me! But I've discovered his secrets, and I've mastered the stone. The world is about to change!"

He looked pityingly at the slave and shook his head. "Someone like you could never understand how difficult it is to be king, Ennawi. I'm tired of doing things the hard way. I deserve this stone."

The human statue didn't move.

"It's just the beginning. My stone isn't the only one—there's another even more useful one called the Stone of Knowing. I have agents searching throughout Arvenon. In Varas and Castel as well. I intend to find it!"

Agon rubbed his hands together. "With both stones under my control, I'll be unstoppable."

Was that a flicker in Ennawi's eyes?

Agon peered attentively at the slave for a few moments before shaking his head. He was imagining things.

His mind turned to another subject, and he stood brooding for a while.

Eventually he faced Ennawi again. "My nobles have been whispering behind my back. They're saying I need an heir. Perhaps they think that manipulating a prince will be easier than manipulating me."

He snorted. "A crown prince might make the nobles happy, but any intelligent king knows that princes are liabilities. They have a nasty habit of becoming impatient."

He shot a shrewd glance at Ennawi. "I should know. My father died of natural causes—every one of his physicians said so. I made very certain it looked that way," he added with a sly wink.

"There's plenty of time for me to father an heir. It can wait until I'm in my dotage. But I've got a better idea. I've decided to live forever."

He leaned in close to the slave. "Drettroth believed he could do a deal with the dark gods—rivers of blood in return for a life without end. I like the sound of Drettroth's deal," he whispered conspiratorially.

"Every day my nobles exclaim, 'May you live forever'. Given the number of times they say it, it must surely be their fondest wish. So I'm going to grant that wish."

He came and stood before Ennawi, his eyes searching the face of the slave. "I would like to live forever," he said. "I would like it a lot."

He peered intently into the other's eyes, vigilant to detect the faintest hint of a response. "Would you like me to live forever, Ennawi?" he asked softly.

The human statue did not move. Not one of his muscles betrayed a single twitch.

7

Eight months after the Battle of Torbury Scarp

The sun had begun its downward journey in the sky when Ander at last cleared the foothills. He found himself at the base of a steep path that wound its way steadily up the side of a small mountain. His horse was just as weary as he was, but he didn't hesitate to guide it onto the path.

It had been dark when he last traveled this path several months earlier. He remembered it well, and the memories were not comfortable.

Part way up the mountain the path emptied onto a broad plateau. It had been the place where Will Prentis ran Brother Vangellis to ground. Needing a guide, the army commander had forcibly dragged the fallen monk away from his sanctuary. Memories flooded over Ander, sweeping him back to the tumultuous events that followed. A great deal more than Brother Vangellis's life had changed when the monk began to reengage with the world.

Once he reached the top of the path, Ander peered around,

frowning. He had expected to find buildings here encircled by a wall with a large wooden gate—the monastery of St. Rodrig the Martyr. Nothing remained now except blackened timbers and broken fragments of stone.

Ander dismounted and picked around for a while in the ruins. It seemed abundantly clear what had happened. The Rogandans had come, and they'd left nothing standing when they departed.

The monastery had never been what he was seeking, though. He had come in search of the monks.

In particular he sought an old man with a long gray beard and bright eyes. After all that had happened in the months that had followed, he still recalled the penetrating gaze of Brother Elias. He had told himself at the time that the old monk was weak, but he was willing to consider a different interpretation now. He remembered a wiry frame and a gentle manner, but even then he had sensed a toughness and wisdom beneath that exterior.

Ander had pinned great hopes on finding Brother Elias here.

He was not dismayed, though. There were no recent graves anywhere in sight, nor scattered bones picked clean by the vultures and bleached by the sun. The monks must have received some kind of warning before the Rogandans arrived. It seemed apparent that they had fled in time.

Ander glanced up at the sun, now sitting low above the horizon. With dusk almost upon him, he began to prepare for a night among the ruins.

There would have been villages in the area, although the Rogandans had probably destroyed them as well. But farmers should have returned by now, and they would have information to share.

He would begin searching for the monks in the morning.

ANDER ROSE with the dawn and guided his horse back down the mountain path. Before long he came upon a small flock of goats tended by a young boy.

The little goatherd froze the moment he spotted the soldier. He stood rooted to the ground, staring wide-eyed at the horseman and trembling with nervous apprehension.

Ander pushed down his anger at this apparent reminder of the ongoing legacy of the Rogandan invasion. There was a time when the goatherd's reaction might have seemed odd. But after the months of war and turmoil that lay behind them, he had become accustomed to such fearfulness. He wondered what the boy might have witnessed.

"Hello," he said, trying to speak in a gentle tone. The boy probably saw him for what he was—a war hardened soldier—but he was determined to make an attempt at being unthreatening.

The boy offered no reply.

"Do you know where the monks have gone? The ones who lived up the mountain." He gestured toward the path.

The goatherd still didn't respond verbally, but he pointed away to the southwest, beyond some low hills.

Ander returned a civil nod.

Wanting to relieve the boy of his anxiety, he set off immediately, heading southwest.

Before long four armed riders came into view. As soon as they spotted him they diverted in his direction. Ander had been around for long enough to sense trouble when it headed his way. He began to wonder if the young goatherd's anxiety had more to do with bandits than with the Rogandans.

When the riders reached him they flowed smoothly around him until he was surrounded.

"Good morning," said Ander evenly. "I'm looking for some monks. Perhaps you can give me directions."

One of the men wore a calculating expression. He appeared to be their leader. "What do you want with the monks?" he demanded.

"I'm planning to join them."

His announcement earned him snorts of derision from all the men.

"He might be big, but he's soft," one of them pronounced with a sneer.

"You won't need that horse if you're joining the monks," said the leader. "They've already donated to us anything they had of value. Hand the horse over now, and we might let you go with nothing worse than a beating."

Ander shook his head.

"Why don't we fight him for it?" asked one of the men eagerly.

The leader responded with a mocking nod. "I suppose that would be more sporting," he sneered. "He doesn't have a sword. We can use staffs."

One of the men dismounted. Leaving his sword sheathed, he reached up and loosed a staff secured to his saddle.

With no other option available, Ander dismounted and faced him. "Where's my staff?" he asked.

His question drew a guffaw from the men. "You don't get a staff," the leader replied. He nodded to a second member of his band, and the man slid from the saddle grasping a staff of his own.

The two men circled Ander with broad grins on their faces. One of them poked his staff tauntingly in Ander's direction. Then the other man aimed a stinging blow at Ander's legs, intending to bring him down.

Leaning swiftly aside, Ander reached out to grab the staff as it swept past. Then he yanked the staff hard, pulling its owner off his feet. The second man came for him at once. As the new attacker raised his staff to strike, Ander pulled the downed man to his feet and swung him around to face his comrade. Ander's human shield took a glancing blow to the head and collapsed to the ground the moment the big soldier released him.

Before the two mounted men could react, Ander grasped the fallen man's staff and strode in to aim a crushing blow at his other opponent. The man brought his own staff up in time to defend himself but went down hard when Ander struck him a second time.

With both of his men out of the fight and the unarmed stranger untouched, the leader apparently decided he had seen enough sport. Anger twisted his face as he spurred his horse forward with sword raised high. Ander lifted his staff to block the blow, and the wood splintered as it absorbed the full force of the stroke. Before the leader could raise his blade a second time, Ander reached up and pulled him from the saddle. The man crashed to the ground and lay there stunned.

The final horseman looked on with wide eyes. Clearly neither he nor his companions had been at all prepared to deal with a man like Ander. Guessing what he might try to do next, Ander called to him, "If you run I'll come for you, and it won't end well."

The horseman hesitated.

"Tie them up," Ander ordered him. The man looked at the big soldier uncertainly for a moment, then he dismounted and approached his fallen comrades.

After ensuring that the men had been properly trussed, Ander tied the hands of his helper and hoisted him back into the saddle. Then he secured the other three men across the backs of their horses.

A well traveled road lay near at hand. "Is there a town along there?" he asked.

The other man nodded. "Blackmere," he said dispiritedly. "Don't go there—the headman is a fool."

Ander ignored him and led the party along the road toward Blackmere. Less than an hour passed before a large town came into view.

As Ander led in his unusual procession, people stopped in the streets to stare at them.

A man ran toward them. "Those are the men who robbed me!" he shouted.

Other townspeople gathered around as well, many of them calling out accusations.

Eventually the locals stepped aside as an official—presumably the headman—strode through the crowd importantly. "What is happening here?" he demanded.

Many voices called out at once, and he raised his hands for silence, a scowl on his face.

He turned to Ander. "Who are you?"

"I am a traveler, and I was set upon by these men. I overpowered them and brought them to you for justice."

The man sneered. "You're one of them more likely," he said. "I've seen before what happens when your kind fall out."

"He's not one of us!" spat the fourth member of the gang. "Everything was going good until he showed up!"

The headman stared at the gang member but offered no response. He turned back to Ander, clearly still suspicious. "You say you're a traveler. Where are you going?"

"I'm heading for the monks who used to have a monastery near here," he replied.

"Why?"

"I want to join them."

Ander ignored the snorts of incredulity that greeted his statement.

The headman did not seem entirely convinced by Ander's story, but he shrugged dismissively. "You'll find them in that direction." He pointed away into the distance. "I'll be watching for you," he promised.

The headman issued orders, and men came and took the robbers away.

Ander turned his back on the town and rode off, more than happy to see the last of Blackmere. He remembered his captive's description of the headman, "He's a fool." Ander heartily agreed with the assessment.

He had been traveling for no more than thirty minutes when he crested a low hill and spotted a monk in the distance. The robed figure was sitting beneath the spreading boughs of an ancient oak. At the sight of the monk, all of his mixed feelings about what he was doing rose up once again. He ignored the inner debate and guided his horse toward the man.

Seeing a rider drawing near, the monk rose to his feet, calmly awaiting his arrival.

Ander pulled his horse to a halt and dismounted. He was astonished to see that he had found his way to the very man he sought.

In spite of his long anticipation of this moment, he felt uncomfortable and tentative. He bowed awkwardly.

"Brother Elias," he said. "I have been looking for you."

A pair of intelligent eyes gazed calmly back at him. The monk did not immediately speak. Then he nodded. "I remember you," he said.

His tone was reflective rather than reproachful, but Ander felt himself redden.

The monk watched him silently, waiting for him to say more.

"My name is Ander. I have come here because I want to join your monastery."

Had one of Brother Elias's eyebrows twitched slightly? He couldn't be sure. The monk seemed rooted to the ground, like the oak tree above him. Ander found himself wondering what it would take to startle him.

"Why do you wish to join us?" the monk asked simply.

"I've always been a soldier. But that life no longer satisfies me. I want to be different."

"What brought about this change of heart?"

"Brother Vangellis."

This time the monk's eyebrows definitely lifted.

"Do you know what has become of him?" Brother Elias asked.

"He is dead." Ander hung his head. He was not normally given to displays of emotion, but Brother Vangellis's passing had hit him hard. The monk had saved his life, and Ander felt that he had never properly thanked him. He had foolishly assumed there would be many opportunities.

Brother Elias apparently misunderstood the gesture. "Did you have a hand in his death?"

Ander looked up again. "No. Although there was a time when I did not wish him well," he admitted. "I set out to harm him, and it almost brought about his death."

The monk gazed at him with his searching eyes. "Are you hoping to join a monastery to atone for your past?"

Ander shook his head. "I have no idea how to atone for my past."

"Sometimes people come to us to escape from the world. That is not the right reason to join a monastery. The only valid reason is out of a desire to follow God."

"All I know is that I need a different purpose for living. Arvenon will always need soldiers, but I want to be something more than that."

Was it possible to be free of that life? The war had ended months ago, but even today he'd resorted to violence.

He had to try. He swallowed and took a deep breath. "I want to learn to do what Brother Vangellis did," he said. "At least in a small way."

Brother Elias considered his visitor thoughtfully. Then he slowly sat down again, waving Ander an invitation to join him. The soldier settled himself under the oak across from the monk.

"So you want to be like him? That must mean that Brother Vangellis found a way to escape the snare into which he had fallen," the monk offered.

"Yes. It happened gradually, but he became a very different man from the one we took away from the monastery."

Brother Elias nodded to himself, but said nothing further.

"Thomas Stablehand—the young man who was traveling with us when we came here—spent many weeks with him and learned his whole history," Ander told him. "He was with him at the end. Brother Vangellis revealed to Thomas what had caused him to give up hope and become a drunk."

Ander looked at Brother Elias uncertainly. "Thomas told me the story. I hope he didn't do wrong."

Brother Elias shook his head. "I do not think that Brother Vangellis would have minded."

"Thomas said that Brother Vangellis was grateful to me." Ander shook his head. "Me! After what I did to him."

"Would you be willing to tell me what happened?"

"Gladly."

The sun rose slowly into the sky as Ander retraced their journeys. He related everything that had taken place, particularly the events involving Brother Vangellis.

It was a long tale, and Brother Elias was clearly moved by what he heard. Ander appreciated the monk's attentiveness.

"He saved my life," Ander said, "even though he knew I hated him. I didn't understand at all why he did it. I still don't understand." He shrugged.

"Since then I've led men into battle—the greatest battle of our time. I'd wanted to command soldiers ever since I was a boy, and I finally had my chance. I've been told that I led well. I got what I always wanted, but it didn't satisfy me. I wasn't expecting that.

"Brother Vangellis's life counted for something. I've found myself asking what I will leave behind when it's my time to die. Will I be remembered as nothing more than a soldier who was good at killing?"

Ander shrugged, then he shook his head.

The monk sat silent, patiently waiting for him to resume.

Ander stood up and began pacing around restlessly. "A lot of good men died in the fighting. I don't know why I've been spared, but it must be for a reason."

Brother Elias watched him for a while. He seemed to reach some kind of decision. "So you wish to become a postulant?" he asked.

"What's a postulant?"

"It's what you become when you want to enter a monastery."

Ander shrugged. "I know nothing about that."

"Postulants take vows—of poverty, chastity, and obedience. Then they learn what it means to live that way in practice. The whole process takes a few years. Eventually, if they wish to continue and they have shown that they intend to live by their vows, they become full members of the monastery. After that they remain monks for the rest of their lives."

He looked at Ander intently. "Is this what you want?"

Ander could only shrug again. "I know what I want to become, but I don't know how to get there. If this is the pathway, I'm willing to walk it."

"It won't be easy for you."

"Because I'm a soldier?"

"Perhaps. But I was thinking more about your age."

Ander frowned in puzzlement.

"Most postulants start much younger, as Brother Vangellis did. It's harder to change when you've established your own ways of doing things and responding to the world around you."

Ander's eyes narrowed as he stared at Brother Elias. The monk claimed he was too old, but surely the truth lay elsewhere. More likely he simply thought Ander wasn't good enough.

"Are you saying you won't accept me?" he asked, an old bitterness beginning to stir within him. He began wondering what had possessed him to imagine he could measure up in the eyes of these people.

Brother Elias shook his head firmly. "It isn't about accepting or rejecting you. If we had to be accepted on our own merits, none of us would meet the standard. I welcomed Brother Vangellis into our monastery, and you saw the state he was in."

The monk's reference to Brother Vangellis shook Ander loose from his simmering anger. It was true. Brother Vangellis had been a hopeless drunk. There was no way he could possibly have measured up to any kind of standard the monks might have set. Yet Ander himself had witnessed Brother Elias's attempt to prevent Will from dragging him away from the monastery.

Some religious people deserved contempt—Ander knew that from bitter experience. But his own experience had shown him that superficial impressions could be misleading. He had been wrong about Brother Vangellis. Eventually he had recognized that the monk was far from contemptible, in spite of initial appearances. He sensed that Brother Elias might deserve his respect too.

Ander forced himself to calm down.

Many times he had tried to imagine how it would play out when he tracked down the old monk. But he hadn't known what to actually expect. He'd sometimes wondered if Brother Elias might poke and prod to uncover his guilty secrets, leaving him exposed and vulnerable like a child caught with his finger in the baron's honey pot.

More than once he'd even wondered if a public shaming of some kind might be required of him, perhaps as a condition of joining the monastery. The truth was he had plenty to be ashamed about.

Brother Elias didn't seem particularly interested in a roll call of his past misdemeanors though. And Ander acknowledged that he didn't appear to have approached Brother Vangellis's wrongdoings that way either.

The old monk had been watching him closely as he wrestled with his reactions, and Ander had an uncomfortable feeling that he either knew or guessed much of what was going on in his head.

"I would never lightly dismiss anyone who felt called to a vocation as a monk," Brother Elias told him. "And you seem to have a clear sense of call, even if such language means little to you."

Brother Elias studied Ander quietly with his penetrating gaze. "You're an intriguing person, Ander," he said.

He took a deep breath and exhaled slowly. Then he spread his hands wide, his face softening into a smile that reached to his eyes. "Come and spend some time with us. There's no rush about deciding anything—we can discuss the future later.

"And please, don't be troubled about being accepted—no one is going to reject you. As for joining the monastery, I am sure that any final decision we reach will be reached together."

8

———————

Three and a half years after the Battle of Torbury Scarp

King Agon of Rogand sat enthroned in state in the grand reception hall of his palace in the capital, Rog. Before him lay a gleaming mosaic of marble tiles, depicting horsemen with leveled spears charging across a field of green. Beyond the mosaic, at the opposite end of the vast hall, a pair of gigantic doors stood wide open.

Agon's throne, magnificent and imposing, overshadowed it all.

Sunlight flooded into the hall through huge windows, bathing the throne in dazzling brilliance. During the hours of daylight, no visitors, be they commoners or monarchs, could long gaze upon the king on his gilded throne without being obliged to avert their eyes.

Marble columns rose majestically on either side of the throne, and identical pairs of columns marched the entire length of the hall. Flanking the columns, a long line of tall armor clad guards stood an arm's distance apart, stretching from the entryway to the throne at the distant end of the expanse. Every guard wore a shining silver helmet plumed in black and carried a golden shield bearing the royal standard of Rogand: a winged eagle above a writhing snake.

Many petitioners and ambassadors entered the reception hall hoping for an audience with the king. Every one of them was sent on the long trek from the threshold to the distant splendor of the throne, enduring as best they could the endless lines of watchful guards.

The experience was overwhelming and intimidating. It was intended to be.

On that particular day, the person journeying the length of the hall was a foreigner of noble birth. This supplicant had not come to Rog on his own initiative—he was there by invitation, a chosen guest of King Agon.

Agon calmly inspected his progress toward the throne. Since he inherited the crown the king had observed many such approaches. He looked on as a coiled serpent coolly watches a scurrying rodent wander within reach. Some petitioners hurried forward, tripping over themselves in their urgency to get the journey over with. Others shuffled restlessly, as if searching for any possible way to postpone the inevitable.

Years of careful scrutiny had shown Agon that a bold approach with a confident stride was rare indeed. It warranted special attention, just as a serpent offers wary respect to a mongoose. Agon never wasted time when dealing with potential threats. Bold petitioners quickly found themselves firmly under the thumb of the king. Either that or their lives soon came to an end.

Agon looked on impassively as the foreigner approached.

His latest guest showed every sign of tension. An entire regiment of Agon's soldiers had escorted the nobleman to Rog. The men had been under instruction to treat him with courtesy and satisfy his every need, while never permitting him to relax. A sizable ceremonial guard detachment had ushered him to the throne room and dumped him at the entranceway, leaving him to travel the length of the hall alone.

Agon smirked to himself in satisfaction. The necessary tone had been set.

Arriving at the throne, the nobleman hesitated, clearly uncertain about what was expected of him next. Like every petitioner who preceded him, he had received no briefing on appropriate formalities and conventions. Agon made sure of that. He liked his guests to be wrong footed from the beginning.

The foreigner stopped short of the throne and made a low bow. Agon allowed a slight frown to play across his face, as if his visitor had caused offense by breaking protocol. The nobleman registered the king's reaction before the radiance of the throne forced him to look away.

After allowing the visitor to stew for a while, King Agon decided not to prolong the farce any further.

He addressed his guest directly. "Welcome to my humble hall, My Lord." He then added pointedly, "You are undoubtedly unfamiliar with our ways, but you are nevertheless welcome here."

The nobleman winced momentarily, then clearly decided to put a brave face on it.

"You are most gracious, Your Majesty," he replied. "I am honored to be in your presence."

"I understand that you have been driven from your home," said Agon, coming straight to the point, "though you did nothing worse than make an honest attempt to serve your king and country."

The nobleman bowed once more. "Your Majesty is most understanding."

"Perhaps we can find a way to aid one another," said King Agon. "You will join me for dinner tonight, and we will discuss it further."

The man smiled—a self-congratulating simper that filled Agon with disgust, though he was careful to mask his reaction.

The nobleman bowed again, and Agon dismissed him.

The king sat brooding on his throne, watching the visitor retrace his lonely steps along the hall.

. . .

As USUAL, the food served at Agon's table was magnificent. The cuisine was sumptuous and varied, the dishes were beautifully presented, and every selection tasted delectable. The wine had no peer.

"Drink up!" Agon bellowed. "I insist! You're my guest!"

The former nobleman had already imbibed much more of the intoxicating liquid than he should have—the servers made sure of that. Every sip of wine led to his cup being refilled. Few people had the presence of mind to keep track of how much they were drinking under such circumstances. The fool would have a very sore head in the morning. In the meantime, he was becoming increasingly unguarded and far too relaxed.

Agon leaned closer to the foreigner.

"I am willing to extend generous resources to you," he said. "As much money as you could reasonably need as well as a constant flow of useful intelligence."

The foreigner could not hide the satisfaction in his eyes. Agon's agents had informed him that the disgraced lord had grown up accustomed to great wealth. He had not been doing well at adjusting to life without it.

"I warn you, though," Agon growled. "I will expect a bountiful return on my investment."

"Of course," the nobleman said eagerly. "I promise that you will be sa...satisfied—entirely so—with the outcome."

He was already beginning to slur his speech. And he was far too eager.

He would learn that Agon gave nothing away. The king was not understating the truth when he spoke of his expectation of a bountiful return. This man would be discarded if he could not deliver it. Agon would eventually discard him anyway, of course. But the fool would not find that out until it was much too late. In the meantime, with Agon's active assistance he should be able to do significant damage to the enemies of Rogand.

Agon departed from the banquet hall, leaving him to his feasting.

Based on current indications, the man would be carried away senseless to his quarters before the night was out.

It was already obvious that the foreigner was an insufferable bore. But Agon would be seeing much more of him in the coming days. At least two weeks of intensive contact would be needed before he had come thoroughly under Agon's spell. Or, rather, under the spell of Agon's unique and formidable talisman. Once that had happened, the transformation would be complete, and he would become a loyal servant of the king of Rogand, in his presence or away from it.

The process was extremely tiresome, though. He shook his head in annoyance. Unfortunately there was no way to avoid it—the investment of time was essential.

HAVING STEPPED outside the palace into the cold night air, Agon surveyed a sky dotted with countless sparkling lights. It struck him that the same stars had dispassionately looked down on every schemer in history, royal or otherwise, and they would continue to do so when he was gone. Such thoughts diminished the gravity of his grand strategies, and he quickly banished them from his mind.

He turned his attention back to the harsh realities of the present.

His current tactics had been made necessary by the failure of Lord Drettroth. Three years had passed since the ruinous debacle at Torbury Scarp. No one dared mention that name in the king's presence, but Agon would never permit its lessons to fade from his memory. He daily nurtured a bitter hatred toward his enemies.

Agon had always desired dominion over the kingdoms around him. He had never been content with what he had—he always wanted more. Now, dominion over the neighboring kingdoms would not be enough. After the shame his enemies had dared to visit on him, nothing less than their abject humiliation would satisfy him.

He paused long enough to master his fury. Then he demanded his horse. A brisk gallop would help clear his thoughts.

When the animal arrived he mounted it and set off, flicking his fingers imperiously to indicate to his guards that they should maintain a respectful distance.

The wind whipped at his hair as he rode, and the cold bit into his ears and cheeks. He paid no regard to it.

Astride a galloping horse, his body blending with its movement, he experienced a welcome release from the clinging demands of his daily round. King as he was, he was subject to frustrating limitations. Chief among them was the burden of being surrounded by fools and incompetents.

The only effective solution was frequent personal intervention to ensure that his purposes were appropriately advanced. Such interference was needed all too often.

But it wasn't always possible. The search for the Stone of Knowing provided a perfect example. Progress had been extremely disappointing, and entirely replacing his agents twice had so far achieved nothing useful.

Good agents were becoming harder and harder to find. Executing everyone who disappointed him was not proving to be a sustainable long term policy.

His thoughts were drawn once more to the late Lord Drettroth. The nobleman had been gone for three years now. As much as Agon had always despised the man, the painful truth was that he was proving difficult to replace.

It had now fallen to Agon to complete Drettroth's unfinished business, and to arrange for the destruction of the kingdoms that had dared to defy his armies. There would be little need for soldiers this time, though. The damage would be done much more subtly. With the right encouragement, the foreigners would simply destroy themselves.

The fool currently drinking himself under Agon's banqueting table had a part to play in the looming conflict. With proper planning and the right level of assistance, he would strike a heavy blow against Rogand's enemies. It would only be the first.

In the private wing of King Agon's castle, a human statue stood on the balcony of the king's apartments. It was Ennawi, entirely alone and staring fixedly into the outside world.

When the sun set Nistinaa appeared quietly at his side. She spooned food into his mouth with practiced fingers before administering his deep blue potion. Then she took a candle and led him to a small room tucked out of the way in a far corner of the suites. The room contained nothing apart from the low bed upon which Ennawi whiled away the hours of darkness.

Nistinaa set the candle down on the floor and guided him to the bed. Once he was reclining she gently pulled a blanket over him. Then she knelt beside the bed, mouthing silently. He gave no indication that he heard what she was saying, but her words were not directed at him anyway.

With her work done, she kissed him lightly on the head, blew out the single candle, and departed.

Ennawi lay unmoving where she had left him, staring up at the ceiling. Many hours passed before his eyes closed and the last traces of Agon's world slid away. Then he slept.

9

———————

Three and a half years after the Battle of Torbury Scarp

Brother Ander ambled beside Brother Gerome on a sheep path, heading for the town of Blackmere. Free medical treatment was available to all comers at the monastery every weekday morning, and the monks also offered treatment in the town twice each week. On this occasion the two men were walking into town to see if further help was needed.

The former soldier was now a part of the monastery, having completed his novitiate and taken his simple vows. He would not be invited to take his solemn vows for another couple of years, so he had not yet committed himself to the monastery for life.

The afternoon sun warmed him pleasantly as he walked, and it occurred to him that he was actually feeling happy. He closed his eyes momentarily and let out a deep sigh.

Hearing it, Brother Gerome looked up at him with a smile. "That almost sounds like contentment, Brother Ander. Did you somehow manage to find enough food to fill your stomach for once?"

"Don't get me thinking about food," the big man grumbled. "It's already difficult enough to keep my eyes off those sheep over there." He waved his hand toward some particularly well fed specimens grazing just off the path.

Brother Gerome laughed. "I suppose when you were a soldier you took sheep whenever you were hungry."

"It wasn't that simple," Brother Ander replied. "Sheep always belong to someone, and farmers don't take kindly to soldiers walking off with their property. But we did enjoy some very tasty venison when the need arose." He rubbed his stomach wistfully.

Brother Gerome raised his bushy eyebrows. "Venison," he said. "I think I might have tried it once." He never seemed concerned about food.

Brother Ander shook his head in wonderment. The two of them were different in so many ways.

Many of the monks had responded with wariness when Brother Elias brought the big soldier into their midst. Some had even been openly hostile. Yet Brother Gerome had welcomed Ander from the moment he arrived, and had done everything he could to ease his initial adjustment. The resulting friendship came as no surprise— Ander saw no reason to dislike a person who so obviously enjoyed his company.

"I imagine your life here must seem strange at times," Brother Gerome continued, "even though you've been with us for almost three years now."

"There's plenty that's strange about living in a monastery," the former soldier replied.

"Like what?"

He glanced down at the other monk. "Like you. I've never known anyone who asked me so many questions!"

His friend laughed again. He did it a lot—it was one of the characteristics Brother Ander liked about him.

"As to what's strange, it isn't the obvious things," Brother Ander said. "I don't find the vow of poverty too difficult. Except for food, as you seem to have noticed—I could do with plenty more of it. I seem to be forever hungry, and I wouldn't complain about some variety." He stole another rueful glance at the sheep before shaking his head.

"I think I can live with the vow of chastity. Nothing ever prevented me from finding a wife and starting a family before I came here, but I never made it a priority. It probably sounds crazy to you, but I spent all my energy working on becoming a better fighter."

He shrugged. "Even the vow of obedience is probably less of an ordeal for me than for some. A soldier is forever doing what he's told."

"It sounds like you've had an easier adjustment than most of us," said Brother Gerome.

Brother Ander shook his head emphatically. "Absolutely not! A number of the brothers are still a bit suspicious about me. And life in the monastery drives me crazy at times. It's the peace and quiet that I struggle with most. My life never lacked action before. It wasn't so bad when we were rebuilding the monastery. These days I feel like I'm watching my fingernails grow."

He gazed down at his friend. "I'm not patient like you. I haven't mastered the art of sitting silently and contemplating. Most of the time meditation feels like punishment. I'm slowly starting to make sense of why we do it, but that doesn't make it any less monotonous."

His friend gave him a grin that suggested this information came as no great surprise to him.

The big monk-in-training decided to ask a question that had been on his mind for a long time. He turned to Brother Gerome. "Why did you join the monastery?" he asked bluntly. "I know why I came, but what brought you here?"

Brother Gerome looked up at him calmly. "Are you wondering if I joined because there was nothing else I was capable of doing?"

Brother Ander shook his head immediately. "Not at all. I can't see you as a soldier, and you wouldn't make much of a blacksmith. But I can think of plenty of other things you'd be good at."

In some ways his friend fit the image of a monk perfectly. He was calm and compassionate and slight of build. Physical strength was certainly not one of his assets. His robes always seemed baggy over his thin frame, and he wasn't tall—Brother Ander towered a full head above him.

But there was a wiry strength about him. He was very intelligent, and he demonstrated more persistence and determination than many men who boasted far greater physical stature. His capabilities could easily have been applied to a range of callings in life.

"Thank you, Brother Ander. It's generous of you to say so."

He paused, then a serious look came over his face. "There is a reason why I became a monk. When I was young I witnessed terrible injustices. The Rogandans were not responsible—this was long before they invaded. Arvenians were callously oppressing other Arvenians, the strong robbing and defrauding the weak.

"The local baron didn't seem to care. It felt like there was nowhere to turn for justice. A young friend of mine decided to take it upon himself to right some of the wrongs. It wasn't long before we buried him.

"Only the monks were doing anything effective to help the needy. I came to the monastery because I wanted to do something about it, and I saw no better option. But when I arrived I got more than I expected. It was obvious to me that the strong do whatever they like, so I thought the Creator had abandoned us. But I came to see it differently. Somehow I always knew that I would be held accountable for my actions. Now I believe that everyone will eventually be called to account."

Brother Ander nodded. "Injustice is a problem everywhere," he said. "There was a time when I traveled with Will Prentis, the commander of the army. On one occasion we came upon a situation of great cruelty, and the commander decided to do something about it. It was in a remote Arvenian village. I know Brother Elias teaches us that the Creator will hold a future reckoning, but we didn't wait for that. We fought the nobleman and his men. We called him to account ourselves and ended the oppression then and there."

"The commander has the right to act in that way," said Brother

Gerome. "He represents the king, so it's his responsibility to do something about oppression."

"I was badly wounded in the fight and nearly died," Brother Ander continued. "I wouldn't be here today without Brother Vangellis and a girl called Elbruhe who'd run away from the Rogandans. They were there when I needed them. I think God might have had something to do with that.

"They went to great lengths to heal me, even though Brother Vangellis in particular had no reason to save me. We'd only met Elbruhe by accident, too—if you can believe such things are accidental."

"I believe less in luck with every passing year," said Brother Gerome. "I've come to the conclusion that it's actually God who's responsible for much of what we call luck."

They had almost arrived at their destination, and they fell silent.

Brother Ander could smell the town long before they entered it, and he wrinkled his nose in disgust. Brother Elias made sure the monks worked hard every day to keep the monastery clean and tidy. At first Ander saw little point to it; he was well accustomed to dirty hovels in foul smelling towns and villages. But he must have gradually adjusted, because now he was finding it hard to put up with the filth and stench that always greeted him in this place.

He had never seen a town like this one. Garbage and human excrement were simply thrown into the streets, and dead animals were left to rot wherever they happened to expire. The only agency that ever attempted to clean the streets was the weather. A heavy downpour usually removed at least some of the refuse, but even then the rain left behind deep puddles filled with fetid water.

Brother Elias believed the rotting waste was partly responsible for the unusually high incidence of sickness and disease in the town. He had raised the matter with the headman more than once, but his warnings had been ignored. Brother Ander had not forgotten the first time he met the headman. The obstinacy shown by the official on that occasion had proven to be entirely characteristic.

The two monks walked through the streets of the town, stepping carefully to avoid the rubbish strewn across their path and keeping an eye out to dodge anything thrown from upper story windows. As they turned a corner near the building used to treat the sick and injured, they came upon a tense confrontation.

The town headman was glaring angrily at Brother Elias.

"As you know," Brother Elias said calmly, "I am greatly concerned about the state of the streets. I believe disease is breeding freely here. The foul air is a warning sign."

"So you do nothing to heal my son," shouted the headman, jabbing his forefinger into the old monk's chest, "and then you blame me for his illness?" The man's face was red with fury. Spittle flew from his mouth as he yelled.

When Brother Elias failed to respond, the man leaned forward and yelled in his face, "Are you deaf?" Then he planted both hands on the monk's chest and shoved. Brother Elias fell backward to the ground.

Brother Ander didn't pause to think. He strode forward and positioned himself between the two men, thrusting out his chest belligerently toward the headman.

His action made the headman even angrier. He quickly reached down and pulled a knife from his belt. Before he could attempt to use it, the big monk grabbed his knife hand by the wrist and slowly squeezed. The man cried out in pain and dropped his weapon.

The intervention of Brother Ander snapped the headman out of his fury. He glanced around him, his eyes narrowing. Many bystanders had been watching the conflict open mouthed, but not one of them met his glance. Several backed away, their heads bent low.

Finding no source of support, the headman took a slow breath and stepped back himself. Then he aimed a poisonous look up at the big monk. "You will pay for that!" he said, targeting Brother Ander with a single stab of his finger. Then he spun on his heel and left.

The crowd quickly dispersed as well.

Brother Gerome helped a shaky Brother Elias to his feet, and ushered him into the building, followed by Brother Ander.

"What was that all about?" asked Brother Ander.

"The man's son is very sick with fever and diarrhea," replied Brother Elias. "Anything he drinks is vomited up immediately. We have been treating him without success. The boy is unlikely to recover, and the headman is worried and upset."

He pointed to a small bed inside the room. Two other monks stood beside it, and they looked up dejectedly as the three men appeared. A woman stood behind them, fear twisting her tear streaked face.

Brother Ander went to the bed and stared down at the pale figure lying there. The boy might have been ten years old. His breathing was shallow, and his face wore an ominous pallor.

"The headman will follow through on his threat," said Brother Elias. "He will feel shamed by what happened." He glanced across at the woman, who stared back at him for a moment, then nodded once.

Brother Ander frowned unrepentantly. "He can't be allowed to push you around like that just because he's the headman!"

"We are not soldiers," replied Brother Elias. "We do not respond to violence with violence."

"So I should have stood there and let him knife me?"

The old monk sighed. "I know you meant well, but he didn't intend to do me any real harm. There was no need to defend me."

Brother Ander shook his head in frustration.

The old monk turned sadly to the woman. "We have done everything for this poor lad that we know to do. I am truly sorry that our best efforts have failed. We will not leave you alone, of course, but I fear we can do little more now than pray for his soul."

She began to sob silently at his words.

Brother Ander looked down at the pale figure once again. It was obvious that the boy was close to death. As he gazed at the child something rose up within him. He, too, had once been written off as a hopeless case. He was alive only because a stubborn monk had refused to admit defeat.

He set his jaw. "I'm not ready to give up," he said. "I will stay with him."

"I will stay, too," said Brother Gerome.

Brother Elias looked at them quietly for a moment. Then he nodded. "You will find a supply of herbs over there," he said, pointing to a large jar near the head of the bed. "May God guide your hands."

He led the other monks from the building. As he was leaving he paused in the doorway and looked back toward his big disciple. "The headman will come to the monastery. He will expect to take you. I will try to reason with him," he said. Then he was gone.

The woman approached the big monk tentatively. "Thank you," she said, tears glistening in her eyes. "Thank you for trying."

Brother Ander nodded, then he turned his full attention to the patient. He felt the boy's forehead. He was burning up with fever.

The monk cast about in his memories in a desperate attempt to find anything that might be useful in treating the boy's fever. He had seen much sickness throughout the course of his life and observed many men suffering from fever during his years as a soldier. But had he ever witnessed a situation where a seemingly hopeless case had responded to treatment?

An incident came to mind where a number of soldiers had been laid low with fever. Unable to keep down treatments of any kind, their prospects had not been good. The only accessible water had been brackish. It had been too salty for Ander—he had spat it out when he tasted it. Nevertheless, with no alternative supply, the water had been given to the men. To the astonishment of everyone, they had slowly improved.

He called Brother Gerome to his side and told him the story.

His friend heard him out, then pondered silently for a few moments. "It's worth a try," he finally said with a shrug, although Brother Ander heard the doubt in his voice.

The big man turned to the boy's mother. "Do you have any salt?" he asked.

"Yes," she said. "I will get it." She immediately left the building.

"What can I do?" asked Brother Gerome. "I feel useless."

"You can pray," Brother Ander replied. "You're much better at that than I am."

"Yes, of course," said his friend, brightening. "Thank you!"

The mother returned with some salt, and Brother Ander mixed some of it with clean water. Then he began to spoon it into the boy's mouth. The lad took in very little of it, but the monk persisted.

"Can you prepare a broth with feverwort?" he asked Brother Gerome.

His friend nodded and set about the task. When he had finished, Brother Ander alternated between the water with salt and the feverwort broth.

True to his promise, Brother Gerome knelt and began to pray. Inspired by his example, Brother Ander himself began pleading silently for the boy's life.

The hours dragged slowly by. When the sun set, the boy's mother lit candles and brought them to the bed. Then she sat down. Before long she fell into an exhausted slumber.

As the night wore on, Brother Gerome began to visibly droop as well.

Brother Ander did not falter. His quest to save the boy's life had given him new purpose, and he pursued it with passionate intensity.

DARKNESS HAD YIELDED to daylight and the morning was well advanced when the headman again marched into the room. This time a squad of armed men filed in behind him. Noticing his arrival, his wife leaped at once to her feet and ran to him, a joyous smile covering her face. She reached up on tiptoes and whispered in his ear, pointing first to her son then to Brother Ander. He frowned at her, then glanced across at the bed.

Clearly nothing had prepared him for what he saw there. The boy lay unmoving on the bed as before, but his eyes were open, and his face had lost its deathly pallor. Brother Ander stood beside him, still mouthing silent prayers as he replaced the damp cloth on his brow.

Seeing his father, the boy managed a weak smile.

The leader of the squad pushed past the headman. "Is that him?" he asked, pointing to Brother Ander.

The headman turned to him in annoyance. "Stay out of the way," he snapped.

"But you wanted us to arrest him," the man protested.

"Are you blind?" the headman demanded, pointing to the boy on the bed. "Do you think I'm going to arrest the man who's just saved the life of my son?"

The squad leader frowned in confusion. When he did not move, the headman rounded on him. "Get out!" he snarled. "Now!"

The leader shook his head in bewilderment. Then he turned and left the building, his men trailing out behind him.

The headman came to the bedside and knelt down beside his son. His wife joined him there.

Judging that the boy could safely be left untended for a while, Brother Ander stepped quietly away to give the family some time alone. He went outside and basked in the sunshine, stretching his aching limbs. He was there when Brother Elias appeared around the corner.

"The headman hasn't come for you yet?" he asked.

"He's inside," Brother Ander replied.

Brother Elias raised his eyebrows in surprise. He disappeared into the building.

He did not reappear for many minutes. When he did, he was smiling. "The boy appears to be making a remarkable recovery!" he said. "You have done well, Brother Ander."

He studied the big monk for a moment. "I am pleased to say that the boy's father no longer feels a need to take action against you." He paused before adding, "Now would be a good moment to go to him and apologize."

Brother Ander was stunned. "Apologize? For what?"

"For using force against him."

"Has he apologized for pushing you to the ground?"

"No," Brother Elias replied. "Nor is he likely to."

"*Should* he apologize?" the big man demanded.

The old monk sighed. "Of course. But the choices he makes are not our responsibility."

"And you think I need to apologize to him?" The very idea left Brother Ander cold.

"We are not here in any official capacity," Brother Elias said. "We have no rights that we can insist upon."

Brother Ander shook his head. Then he shrugged. "Very well then." He took a deep breath and walked into the building, Brother Elias hurrying along behind him.

The big monk went straight to the headman. Seeing him coming, the man drew back defensively.

Brother Ander ignored it. "I wish to apologize for the way I behaved yesterday," he said roughly.

The man's face was unreadable. He said nothing for a long moment. Then he said, "I am willing to overlook it this time. Only because of your services to my son." Then his face hardened. "Don't expect me to be so forgiving another time."

Brother Ander opened his mouth to speak. Just as he was about to say something he would later have regretted, he caught sight of Brother Elias. The old monk's head was cocked and his eyebrow raised. Brother Ander closed his mouth abruptly. He gritted his teeth and contented himself with a nod.

The headman turned and left the building without another word.

Brother Elias came to Brother Ander with a smile. "Well done," he said softly.

Brother Ander shook his head again. Then he returned to the bedside of his patient.

"How are you feeling?" he asked the boy.

"A bit better, thank you," the child replied. He was visibly brighter, cheered by his father's visit.

Brother Gerome had taken over the role of tending to the boy's needs when Brother Ander stepped outside. He now looked up at the big monk. "Go and get some rest," he said. "I slept for a few hours last night, and I will stay with him."

Brother Elias nodded his approval. "I will send someone to relieve you as soon as I get back," he told Brother Gerome.

The old monk placed a hand on Brother Ander's shoulder. "Walk with me to the monastery," he said.

They left the building together and walked in silence for a time.

Finally Brother Elias turned to him. "I believe you might have found your calling," he said.

Brother Ander returned a questioning look.

"I'd lost hope for the child," Brother Elias said frankly. "You did not. Fierce as you appear to be on the outside, you have a gift for compassion, and you show considerable promise at leechcraft. I believe your calling is as a healer."

The big man's eyes went wide. Could his mentor be right? He had spent so many years gaining mastery at ending lives. Could he now become adept at giving life back?

He drew his eyebrows together. "I was only doing for him what Brother Vangellis did for me," he said.

Brother Elias offered no further comment, and the big monk fell silent, musing.

Before long the monastery appeared before them. Seeing it, Brother Elias abruptly came to a halt. Brother Ander stopped as well, and the old monk gazed up into his face. "You showed great restraint when you spoke with the headman," he said.

"I apologized. He should have done the same!" Brother Ander growled. "He had at least as much to apologize for."

His mentor was silent for a moment. "You asked for forgiveness," he finally replied. "Perhaps what you really wanted was justice."

Brother Ander frowned. "What's wrong with that? Isn't God interested in justice?"

"He is," Brother Elias confirmed, "although he doesn't always seem to be in a hurry to provide it."

"Am I supposed to be happy about that?" grumbled Brother Ander.

Brother Elias didn't answer, contenting himself instead with an inscrutable smile.

.   .   .

WHEN BROTHER GEROME returned to the monastery he brought news from the town. "The headman has not been idle since you left," he told Brother Elias. "He has gathered many men and set them to work cleaning up the streets."

10

Four years after the Battle of Torbury Scarp

King Steffan of Arvenon sat restlessly in his audience chamber. One final matter needed to be dealt with today, but it couldn't be completed until the Varasan ambassador arrived.

He glanced across at Queen Essanda, sitting patiently beside him. She must surely find these sessions supremely dull. Yet she had never complained. And she didn't fail to offer useful insights later when they debriefed together.

She was no longer the girl he had first met in Castel Citadel more than four years ago. Her features and her figure had filled out. More importantly, her character had further blossomed and matured. She had developed into a truly arresting young woman—in body, mind, and spirit.

Apparently sensing his gaze, she turned to him and flashed him a smile. Her face was always beautiful, but when she smiled it lit up the room. He returned a happy smile of his own, then turned away, unwilling to allow himself the luxury of distraction. They were here for a reason.

It was especially fitting that she attend this particular session, since she had contributed significantly to finding a solution to the issue that had first been presented to him three months earlier.

Eventually the arrival of the ambassador was announced, and Steffan called for the merchants to be brought in.

The king turned his attention to the spokesman for the Arvenian merchants. "Some time ago you asked for permission to bring a complaint against two merchants from Varas," he said. "Your request has not been forgotten, in spite of the delay in granting you an audience."

The merchant bowed. "We are grateful for your consideration, Your Majesty."

"Since that time," King Steffan continued, "I understand that the Varasan merchants have discussed with their ambassador bringing a complaint of their own against you."

"Some of our number may have been a little vigorous in expressing their displeasure, Your Majesty. But I believe they did so with good reason."

"Your complaint is that Varasan merchants are being allowed to operate stalls in the main market of Arnost. Is that correct?"

The man bowed again. "Yes, Your Majesty. The complaint may sound trivial. But Arvenian merchants are barred from setting up stalls in the markets of Varacellan. When trading in Varas we are forced to sell our wares from outside the capital walls. We simply wish to see the same rules applied to foreign merchants here in Arvenon."

Steffan entirely understood their frustration. Since any change in the policy of the Varasans seemed highly unlikely, his initial inclination had been to agree to the request of the local merchants, and to bar their Varasan counterparts from selling in the markets in Arnost. It seemed the simplest and most even-handed solution.

In the end the simple solution had been discarded, though. And that change had come about solely due to Essanda's persistence.

King Steffan addressed the merchant. "I believe that we have found a fair and equitable solution to the problem," he said. "The Varasan ambassador, Lord Haldenset, wishes to make an announcement."

He nodded to Lord Haldenset. The ambassador bowed to King Steffan, then stepped forward and unrolled a scroll. "The following proclamation is being read today in the Varasan capital of Varacellan," he said formally.

"His Royal Highness King Delmar of Varas, after consultation with his friend and ally, His Royal Highness King Steffan of Arvenon, is pleased to announce that Varas has concluded a trade agreement with Arvenon. From this day forth, merchants from Arvenon will enjoy the same access as local merchants to markets throughout Varas. In return, King Steffan has agreed to extend the same rights to Varasan merchants throughout the markets of Arvenon. Both Varas and Arvenon are today enacting laws to implement this agreement throughout the two kingdoms."

The wide-eyed surprise of the merchant gave way to an animated buzz as he discussed the implications with his fellow merchants. He soon looked up with a satisfied smile, bowing to Lord Haldenset.

"My Lord, I trust that you will convey to the Varasan merchants our regret at any...ah...inconvenience they might have experienced in the recent past. We look forward to welcoming them into the market at Arnost, and we will eagerly anticipate the same welcome in return when next we visit Varacellan."

Lord Haldenset responded with a brief nod.

"You have Queen Essanda to thank for this agreement," the king told the merchants as he dismissed them. "Her Majesty was responsible for the initiative that made it possible."

The merchants bowed deeply to their queen, who acknowledged them with a warm smile. Then they departed.

King Steffan conversed briefly with Lord Haldenset before the ambassador left the audience chamber. The two of them had seen a great deal of each other in recent weeks, and Steffan had developed a healthy respect for the nobleman.

As Steffan and Essanda left the chamber, she asked him, "Why did you give me the credit for this agreement, Steffan? You and Delmar carried out all of the negotiations."

"It would never have happened without you!" he replied. "I was ready to bar the Varasan merchants from the market in Arnost."

Steffan was not exaggerating—Essanda was entirely responsible for this outcome.

His thoughts went back to the day when she had sought Steffan out after hearing about the issue with the merchants.

"Maybe there's a way to resolve this problem," she had said. "Have you thought about discussing it with the Varasan ambassador?"

"Why would the ambassador be interested? Or King Delmar for that matter. I'd just be wasting my time."

"Would you have any objection if I spoke to the ambassador?"

Gazing down at her, he had seen hopefulness sparkling in her lovely eyes. She was young, and the world was full of promise. He felt sure any initiative would be a waste of time, but how could he refuse her? There was surely no real harm in it.

"Of course I don't object. Contact Lord Haldenset if you like. I will be happy to support you."

He knew she would be disappointed if nothing came of it, but disappointments were part of life. He would be there to comfort her.

Before many days had passed Steffan received a formal invitation to a royal lunch at the palace, hosted by the queen in honor of the Varasan ambassador. He had become aware that Essanda was doing a lot of preparation for the event. When he asked her what she was up to, though, she had simply beamed him a mysterious smile and sweetly requested that he wait and see. Steffan was intrigued rather than apprehensive, and more than a little curious to find out how she might be planning to handle the situation.

When the day finally arrived, Lord Haldenset had been admitted to the palace. Approaching the queen with a broad smile, he had bowed deeply to her. "I am greatly honored by your invitation, Your Majesty," he said.

Steffan could see that the ambassador was equally curious about the invitation. The Varasan was also quite obviously flattered to have been singled out.

During the meal the queen had drawn Lord Haldenset out, encouraging him to talk of his family and reflect on his childhood memories. She had also deftly introduced Steffan into the conversation. The two men were soon engaged in an animated and friendly interaction. No matters of any great significance were discussed.

After the meal the queen nodded to the attendants, and a special plate was brought out and placed with some ceremony before the ambassador. His eyes had immediately gone wide in surprise.

He closely examined the food on the plate before leaning forward to sniff it. "Your Majesty!" he said, barely able to contain his excitement as he turned to the queen, "this appears to be cheese from Rillen Dale."

She confirmed his guess with a smile and a nod.

"I am overwhelmed!" He turned to Steffan. "This is a rare variety of Varasan cheese," he explained, "a local delicacy in the east of Varas where I grew up. It's my favorite treat! I haven't had an opportunity to taste it for...for longer than I care to remember."

"Please!" said Steffan, pointing to the food and inviting the ambassador to enjoy it at once.

All conversation abruptly ceased as Lord Haldenset turned his full attention to the cheese. No words were necessary to report his assessment of the delicacy as he sampled it. The enraptured look on his face said it all.

Several minutes passed before he leaned back in his chair with an audible sigh of contentment.

Essanda had said very little during the meal, but she now addressed the ambassador directly. "My Lord, I know that all of us celebrate the strong bonds that exist between our two kingdoms. Those bonds were greatly strengthened as we stood together against a common foe and shared a great victory.

"The cooperation between our armies has never been stronger, and our foreign policies are closely aligned. Is it time, perhaps, to consider strengthening ties in other areas as well?"

She pointed to the cheese with a warm smile. "This cheese is truly delicious—I have tasted it myself, and I am now able to understand why you appreciate it so much. I don't doubt that it could become popular here in Arvenon, if only it wasn't so dreadfully difficult to purchase."

Steffan listened to her in amazement. He had no idea how Essanda had learned of Lord Haldenset's fondness for this particular delicacy, nor how she had managed to procure it.

"I have been wondering if a trade agreement between Varas and Arvenon might benefit us all," she continued. "I know your merchants wish to see our markets opened up to them. Going one step further and opening up the markets of both kingdoms would undoubtedly satisfy all of our merchants, and it could also lead to greater prosperity for everyone."

Lord Haldenset shook his head in wonder. He looked at Steffan with a smile and a bow. "I trust you will pardon my boldness in saying it, Your Majesty, but I can see that a shrewd mind lies behind the gentle manner of your estimable queen. I am well aware of the current dispute between our merchants, and I confess that she has won me over entirely to her point of view. Do you share the same mind on the subject?"

"I do," Steffan told him with a smile. "The perspective presented by Her Majesty enjoys my wholehearted support."

The ambassador rose to his feet and turned to Essanda, bowing deeply. "I am very grateful for your hospitality, Your Majesty, and more touched than I can say by your thoughtfulness toward me personally.

"I can make no promises on behalf of King Delmar, of course. But I can and will promise to contact His Majesty promptly with a proposal to explore the possibility of a trade agreement between Varas and Arvenon."

. . .

THE AMBASSADOR HAD BEEN as good as his word. Before long, Delmar had made contact with Steffan, and the two sovereigns were eventually able to broker an agreement. It had taken a number of weeks to settle on the details, but all parties agreed that it represented a further positive step forward in friendly relations between the two allies.

Since then Steffan and Delmar had jointly initiated negotiations with King Istel with the goal of establishing a tripartite trade agreement that included Castel as well.

Essanda's careful research and skillful diplomacy had set this entire process in motion. Steffan knew that she sought no acclaim for her efforts, but he had readily taken every opportunity since then to freely and widely acknowledge her role. She was already held in high regard within the three kingdoms. Her efforts toward the trade agreement had only enhanced that standing.

Delmar had wryly asked Steffan more than once if Essanda had any cousins. Steffan knew that he was only half joking.

11

———

As they left the audience with Lord Haldenset and the merchants, Steffan turned to Essanda and shook his head. "One of your rare shortcomings is that you're entirely too modest! You need to start recognizing how valuable you are to this kingdom!"

She took his arm affectionately as they walked together through the labyrinthine corridors of the castle. "One of your rare shortcomings is that you're altogether too serious," she said, favoring him with one of her dazzling smiles.

"I haven't had much time for amusements," he told her earnestly. "I've been wanting to go hunting with Torbury and Bottren and a few of the others, but all of us have been far too busy."

"Hmm," she said thoughtfully. "So you've been unable to chase down your quarry in the woods." She paused, releasing his arm. "I don't think you'll do any better in the castle."

So saying, she sprang away from him. "Catch me if you can!" she called back over her shoulder with a teasing laugh.

Steffan's competitive streak needed an outlet, and a challenge from his young wife was more than he could ignore. She flew before him on nimble feet, her hair streaming behind her as she ran. He immediately took off after her in hot pursuit. The shapeliness of her lithe form was not lost on him, and he grinned with delight as he urged his legs to greater efforts.

He was fast, but she was wily. Seeing him drawing close, she quickly abandoned the corridor, pulling open the door to a store-room and disappearing inside. The door slammed shut in his face as he arrived. Steffan swung it open and raced inside, brim full of eager determination.

He found himself in the darkness of a large room with barrels stacked everywhere. Two other openings led into adjoining rooms. He selected one of the rooms at random and sprang inside. She was nowhere to be seen.

"There's no use hiding," he called. "I'll find you!"

A merry laugh sounded behind him as the door to the corridor slammed shut once again. Spinning around, he groped his way back through the storeroom and out into the corridor. He arrived in time to see her shapely form disappearing around a corner. When he reached the corner she was sprinting away, well ahead of him. She threw a glance back over her shoulder, laughing when she saw how far behind he was.

He took up the chase in earnest, gaining steadily with every moment that passed. A startled servant stared open mouthed as his king flew past, the comical look on the man's face drawing a strangled laugh from Steffan.

Essanda had barely reached her apartments and flung open the door when Steffan finally caught up with her. Hurtling into her bedchamber, she threw herself squealing onto the bed. She lay there, sprawled across the covers, disheveled and panting. Little peals of laughter punctuated her breaths.

Steffan came to a sudden halt and bent low with his hands on his knees, grinning stupidly as he sucked in great gulps of air.

Eventually they had both recovered enough to breathe more normally. She went quiet and stared up at him, a shy smile on her face.

For Steffan, the exhilaration of the chase gave way to a tide of passion that rose up within him, threatening to sweep him away. He gazed down at her, breathless once more and with his heart pounding. Everything in him wanted to reach out and scoop her into his arms, to shower her lovely face with kisses. And unless he was entirely deluding himself, she wanted it too. He leaned forward, bending over her slowly until their faces were almost touching.

Then abruptly he drew back, pushing down his eagerness and forcing himself to stand upright again. He knew beyond doubt that if once he started, he would never be able to stop.

It was maddening. But he had promised her on their wedding night that he would give her time to mature. "I won't ask you to take on the full responsibilities of a wife yet. That must wait until you are older," he had said. "They told me you were nineteen, and I give you my word I will wait until you are."

More and more often of late he'd found himself staring at her with helpless admiration. Her innocent way of embracing the world, her cheerful optimism, the little smiles she bestowed only on him, the carefree way she tossed the hair from her face—everything about her was hopelessly endearing.

Increasingly he'd been forced to consciously restrain himself when she was near. Sometimes his hand brushed against her when they passed each other, setting his whole arm tingling. He would have given anything to be able to run his fingers through her hair and hold her tightly in his arms. But he couldn't trust himself.

He found himself agonizing over the promise he had made. It had seemed only right when she was a child. But now? His wife had become an extremely attractive and eminently desirable young woman. But he still couldn't touch her. Not yet.

Meanwhile, the strain of waiting was taking its toll. She haunted his nightly dreams and invaded his every daydream. Outwardly he carried on as normal. He wondered if she had any inkling of his secret struggles.

Seeking a distraction from his inner turmoil, he gazed around her bedchamber. It only made matters worse. A small bunch of wildflowers stood in an earthen jar on a table right beside her bed. He had gathered them on the spur of the moment and handed them to her only two days previously. He could still picture the flush of pleasure that had rewarded his gesture.

Being alone with her in the intimacy of her bedchamber was more than he could bear.

"It was a wonderful race," he told her, trying to cover his awkwardness with a weak smile. "Even if you beat me!"

Then he turned and hurried from the room, trying not to think about the look of surprise in her eyes.

STEFFAN WENT to his bed that night determined for once not to think about Essanda. There was certainly plenty else to occupy his mind. The trade agreement with Varas had been concluded successfully, but many other matters of state remained to be resolved. Steffan tossed sleeplessly in his bed, his mind in a whirl as he attempted to bring order to the chaos of his competing priorities. The common people—and even some of the nobles—expected a king to have unlimited capacity to do whatever needed to be done. The reality was very different, and Steffan was keenly aware of his limitations. He had surrounded himself with wise and capable advisors. But it simply wasn't possible to delegate everything.

Something was niggling away at the back of his mind as he tossed and turned. He eventually identified it and dragged it out into the open. Troubling rumors had begun to emerge from Erestor, and even occasional reports of unrest and disturbance.

He suspected that his own needs and demands had contributed to the problem. At his insistence, Lord Burtelen, the most capable of the Erestorian noblemen, had been located almost permanently in Arnost, the Arvenian capital. He had come to lean so much on the nobleman's wisdom and judgment. Burtelen was not merely wise. He was a rare example of that most valuable of commodities—a nobleman actually capable of getting things done.

Lord Burtelen wasn't his only option for investigating the situation in Erestor, of course. There was always Lord Torbury. He lay there for some time trying to think of plausible reasons why he couldn't afford to send Torbury. He knew that he needed to do it, though. Finally, with a sigh of resignation, he gave in. The following morning he would instruct Lord Torbury to make an extended visit to Erestor.

He could ill afford to lose the services of Torbury. But someone needed to get to the bottom of what was happening in Erestor. Someone he could trust.

Lord Torbury was the newest of his nobles. Once known simply as Will Prentis, he had distinguished himself as commander of the armies of Arvenon and Castel. As an expression of his gratitude King Steffan had elevated him to the Arvenian peerage, christening him Lord Torbury in honor of his decisive victory over the Rogandans at the crucial Battle of Torbury Scarp. The new Lord Torbury had been granted the lands in Erestor formerly held by the Earl of Pisander, the man exposed as a traitor during the siege of Arnost.

More than four years had passed since the appointment, and in all that time Steffan had only once found it possible to release Lord Torbury to spend time at his new holdings. The nobleman was long overdue for another visit.

Steffan's attempt at sleep was fruitless, and he eventually gave up trying. Having propped himself up in bed with pillows, he was sitting there brooding when his door opened. A dark figure, visible only in outline in the firelight, slipped inside and approached his bed.

How had the intruder made it past his guards? Fully alert, he reached for his knife and prepared to defend himself.

A soft voice broke the silence. "It's me, Steffan."

"Essanda! You startled me!"

His thoughts went back to the last time she had entered his bedchamber. It had been at Castel Citadel on their wedding night, and it was the first time he had actually seen her face to face. He was expecting a young woman aged nineteen; he soon discovered that he had been deceived. Little more than a child, she had arrived exposed and vulnerable. She told him that she had celebrated her fourteenth birthday the previous day.

In that moment he had glimpsed the extent of her pluck and determination. It must have taken enormous courage to surrender her childhood and allow herself—for the sake of her kingdom—to be wedded to a foreigner who was a complete stranger.

At the time the situation had left him with a challenge of his own. Should he seek to have the marriage annulled?

One of his most compelling reasons for seeking a wife had been to provide his kingdom with an heir. If he abandoned the marriage the day after the wedding, he would be no closer to achieving that goal.

But if he continued with the marriage, any possibility of producing an heir would be long delayed, because he would not even consider consummating their marriage until she was much older. No other course could satisfy his honor and respect her dignity.

He had quickly decided to allow the marriage to stand. The decision had come with its own set of difficulties and frustrations. But he had stayed the course.

Now she had appeared in his bedchamber once more. But why?

"What are you doing here?" he asked softly.

"Well I am your wife," she retorted, not hiding the amusement in her voice.

"But we decided to wait. Until you were nineteen."

"You decided," she corrected him. "Don't you think I should be allowed a say in such an important decision?"

Her reply startled him. Frustrating as the waiting had been, his head had told him she needed time to mature, and his heart said it would be unfair to rush her simply to satisfy his own desires. It had never occurred to him that she might have strong opinions of her own about the timing. And he had never dared imagine that she might also be chafing at the delay.

With no response forthcoming from him, she continued. "I'm certainly old enough now. Many young women are already mothers by the time they reach the age of eighteen and a half.

"It's been well over four years since the day we married. During those years we've walked together through life. I've observed you closely and been guided by you, and I've watched as you faced difficulties and challenges. Never once have you sacrificed your integrity in favor of taking the easy way. And never once have you treated me with anything less than consideration and respect. I've learned to honor and esteem you more with each passing year."

She drew closer. "And I've grown to love you, too."

Her perfume filled his nostrils, and his heart began to race. She leaned in for a kiss—their first kiss, delicate and lingering. He wanted it never to end.

She drew back slowly and gazed at him with a tender smile. "You're a patient man, Steffan of Arvenon," she said. Then she lowered her voice to a whisper. "But I say we've waited long enough."

***

THE CROWDS PARTED RESPECTFULLY and people stood craning their necks as the royal carriage came to a stop right in the middle of the main marketplace at Arnost.

The young queen stepped out of the carriage and approached some of the merchants, who bowed deeply. She had chosen a location where the stall of a Varasan merchant stood beside that of a local merchant. The queen engaged both men in polite conversation before bidding them farewell with a smile and climbing back into the royal carriage.

The crowds closed in behind the carriage as it pulled away. Soon the noise and hubbub of the market had resumed at full strength, and people bumped and jostled each other good-naturedly as they bustled among the stalls, admiring the wares.

"Don't she look happy!" a young mother remarked to an older woman beside her. The queen, known for her serenity, had appeared to be carrying a special glow about her.

The older woman nodded, a sly smile on her lips. "No wonder, either. She's been visiting the king's bedchamber by all accounts." She reinforced this news with a big wink.

"How do you know that?" demanded the young mother's husband.

"Everybody knows! You can't keep such matters secret. It's all over the palace!"

The husband rolled his eyes. "Who'd be king?" he asked pityingly, directing his question to no one in particular.

"She'll be in her confinement soon," the older woman asserted with a knowing nod.

"Why? What'd she do wrong?" asked a grubby urchin, the son of the young mother and her husband. The boy had temporarily suspended his entertainment—poking his little sister in the ribs—while waiting for the answer to his question.

"She didn't do nothing wrong, you silly," chuckled the woman. "She's in the family way, that's all."

"What does that mean?" demanded the boy, giving his sister another poke.

"She's going to have a baby," his father told him.

"A baby?" the boy exclaimed, screwing up his face. "Why would anyone want a baby?"

This time he didn't wait for an answer. His whole attention had shifted to his little sister, who was scurrying hastily away after kicking him in the shins.

"Why indeed?" asked the father dryly. He raised his eyes heavenward and shook his head as he watched the retreating backs of his two children, both squawking at the top of their voices.

He turned to his wife. "Why *would* anyone want a baby?" he asked.

She came over and put her arm around his waist. "I only want them because they remind me so much of you," she told him with a wink.

12

Four years after the Battle of Torbury Scarp

King Agon of Rogand stormed about his private chambers, shouting at the top of his voice and lashing out violently at any fragile object within his reach. He didn't stop until nothing remained to be broken.

Agon's wild eyes chanced upon the untroubled figure of his slave standing motionless beside the entrance to the balcony. Ennawi seemed rooted to the floor like a statue carved from white marble. The slave's face was dispassionate as always. Nothing stirred in his eyes. If he perceived Agon's behavior as unusual—if he even registered that a human tornado had just been unleashed upon the room —he gave no sign of it. The king stared at him for a long moment before shaking his head in disgust and turning away.

Thrusting from his mind the frustrations that had led to his sudden eruption, Agon stepped calmly into the audience chamber that adjoined his apartments. The servants who cowered there aimed terrified glances in his direction before hastily lowering their eyes. He ignored them. "Bring in the foreign maggots," he said evenly, addressing himself to no one in particular. Two underlings immediately scurried to the door and disappeared outside.

A small throne dominated the room. Agon ascended the steps to its cushioned seat and made himself comfortable. The king was well aware that he could lay claim only to average height, although every detail of his surroundings served to divert attention away from such trivialities.

To Agon such things were indeed trivial. He cared not a whit about his physical stature—he cared only about power.

Two of his servants shuffled forward, offering drinks and delicacies. He waved them away with an impatient flick of the wrist.

The throne had been positioned between two large windows. Strategically placed mirrors directed light from each window onto a cluster of small ornate chairs that faced the throne. The effect was to dazzle anyone fortunate enough to secure an audience with the king. He could read every expression on the faces of his supplicants; they were barely able to see him at all.

The underlings soon returned, escorting three foreign noblemen.

"Sit," Agon commanded the visitors, jabbing a bejeweled finger toward the chairs before his throne.

The foreigners sat.

They squinted uncomfortably up at him, unable to meet his stare. The nobles were as different in appearance and temperament as three men could be, but they had in common the insatiable craving that comes with overwhelming ambition. And of late they shared another important trait—an unhesitating willingness to serve the interests of King Agon of Rogand.

Agon had spent sufficient time with each of them to ensure they were thoroughly under the spell of the Stone of Authority. The first two had been stubborn. It took two tiresome weeks to ensure their full compliance. The third had proven satisfyingly malleable from the beginning—Agon suspected the man would cheerfully run naked through the streets of Rog if he believed it would benefit his new master. Having the opportunity to cut short the necessary period of contact to just one week in his case had been a welcome relief.

All of them were now within his grasp, of that he was certain. If it were not the case, their usefulness—and with it their pitiful lives—would have come to an end. From the beginning their submission had never been in doubt, of course. No one could long resist the Stone of Authority.

Agon frowned down at the men. "Are your plans finalized?"

All of them looked flustered for a moment. Then the compliant nobleman stirred into life. "Our plans are well advanced, Your Serene Majesty, and lack nothing apart from your seal of approval. We carry a continual burden of anxiety while we await your coveted affirmation."

This particular fool might be the most pliable of the three, but his fawning was becoming unbearable. Agon couldn't wait to get the man out of his sight.

Nevertheless, he needed to act the part. "I am gratified to hear that your plans are well advanced," Agon told them, forcing himself to ignore the coarseness of their manners, "and I am eager to hear the details."

The men all began talking at once, interrupting each other constantly in their eagerness to impress him. Through the chaos he somehow managed to glean enough information to satisfy him. The men had not been idle, and their plans actually did offer considerable promise.

"You have done well," he told them, to their evident relief. "I release you to carry out your plans. I will not be meeting with you again. You will, however, find that I have arranged access for you to every resource you could need. My agents will supply you with a more than generous supply of finances and intelligence."

He paused to make sure they were paying full attention. "I trust I have made it very clear what I expect in return," he told them coldly. "Do not dare to disappoint me."

The noblemen bowed very low, and he dismissed them. They

scurried from the audience room, trembling in their haste to be gone from his presence.

Agon pushed through the adjoining door and reentered his chambers. No visible evidence remained of his earlier outburst—order had been fully restored during his interview.

Ennawi appeared not to have moved. Agon made his way past the slave, emerging into the sunshine and open air of his balcony. He observed the three men as they rode away, escorted by an imposing detachment of the royal guard.

The king glanced back over his shoulder at Ennawi. "Life has an irritating way of frustrating and disappointing me," he snarled. "I wield absolute power, and yet I am forced to rely upon creatures such as these foreigners."

He stepped back inside the room. "Am I not a god?" he demanded. "My devoted subjects insist that it is so—they scream it aloud whenever I appear before them in my glory."

Agon examined his slave closely. "Do you believe it to be true, Ennawi?"

The human statue didn't move.

Agon nodded sagely. "Your wisdom is greatly underrated," he told the slave. "I find I cannot argue with your response, nor can I dispute the logic that lies behind it." A peal of mocking laughter issued from his throat.

As his laughter died away, the king's expression became a scowl. "Deity or not, I am surrounded by mortal fools." He shook his head in disgust.

"Consider these foreigners," he added, waving a hand toward the road they had taken. "They are little better than worms." He spat over the balcony. "It physically pains me to be in the same room as such slithering vermin. I am compelled to waste precious hours in their company—feigning interest when I am almost swooning from the tedium. But I cannot delegate this particular task to anyone else," he added more calmly. "There is no one I could trust."

He turned to Ennawi, lowering his voice. "It's the fault of my stone. This mindless little rock doesn't take immediate effect—it requires TIME!" he said with a scowl. "What I need is the Stone of Knowing. That would allow me to see exactly when the Stone of Authority has taken full effect. It would no longer be necessary to waste even a minute with imbeciles like the men who've just ridden away."

He opened his hand, and the Stone of Authority flashed in the sunlight. He studied it for a moment. "How have I become so dependent on a tiny lump of earth?" he asked, staring quizzically at Ennawi. "Surely a god has no need of trinkets."

He smiled ironically. "The truth is that I am entirely reliant on this particular trinket—I might as well be addicted to it. So it seems I am not a god after all, whatever my people tell me."

His hand closed over the stone once more, and he fell silent.

After many months with the stone, he still couldn't claim to fully understand the way it worked.

The scroll had outlined the limits of the stone. Two limitations were especially galling: the stone could be used to target only one person at a time; and no subject could be forced to behave in a way that was inconsistent with their character or deeply held convictions.

The pronouncements of the scroll hadn't deterred Agon from testing the second limitation. He had wasted two entire weeks trying to induce one of his minor nobles to kill himself. The man had gone away confused, but very much alive.

Agon was aware that the stone did not entirely wipe away the will of a person. The effect seemed more akin to training the will to see things the way the holder of the stone saw them. The subject still had the ability to make their own choices. They simply found themselves determined to strive for the same outcome as the stone wielder.

The stone had no impact on the effectiveness of those it influenced—its subjects did not become any more or less capable than they already were. A blunt instrument cut no more finely than it did before, and a sharp instrument lost none of its subtlety and precision.

After a few moments the king turned to Ennawi again. "Of course none of these little maneuvers with the foreigners would have been necessary if only Drettroth had delivered on his promise," he told him bitterly. "He was my childhood companion, and I expected better of him. No one ever equaled him in ruthlessness and effectiveness." He shook his head regretfully. "Those qualities are the only things I truly admire in another human," he added.

His brows furrowed. "None of it matters now. Drettroth is gone. He failed."

The slave showed no sign that he registered Agon's words at all.

Ennawi had been with Agon for so long that it was difficult to remember life without him, yet after all this time he remained an enigma. The slave had been little more than a foreign child when he was first presented to Agon as a food and wine taster. Agon was not told and had never asked how or where his servants had acquired him. He knew only that his new slave was unusually placid.

The other notable thing about Ennawi was that his tongue and both of his hands had been removed by his previous owner. Agon had never inquired as to the reason.

Without hands the slave could not feed himself, and Agon had soon demanded an able-bodied food taster. But he kept Ennawi around, mostly because as king he appreciated the rare freedom to speak freely in front of a safe audience. Agon had long recognized that he could best solidify his thoughts by verbalizing them. But in the murky cesspool of intrigue that was the Rogandan court, he could trust no one with his private thoughts and royal secrets.

No one except Ennawi.

Ennawi was unusually safe. Being unable to speak or write, the slave could not communicate at all—he was in a class of his own. Even if Ennawi had a mind to act on something he heard, he had no way of doing so. The king knew he had nothing to fear from this particular slave.

It had been suggested to Agon that Ennawi was deaf. He didn't know if it was true, but it seemed likely. Apart from rare and fleeting flashes of what might have been conscious awareness, the slave showed no sign whatsoever of understanding a single word that Agon said.

There was, of course, another possible explanation for his non-responsiveness. He was after all a foreigner. Perhaps his hearing was intact, but he had never learned to understand Rogandan.

The king approached him closely and peered into his eyes. "What goes on in that head of yours?" he asked, tapping Ennawi's forehead determinedly.

The slave did not as much as blink.

Agon shrugged. "I'll know once I get my hands on the Stone of Knowing," he said.

The slave's face appeared to twitch momentarily. Then he was still again, his face blank as always.

Agon frowned in bemusement. Had he glimpsed a spark of awareness in those eyes? He stared intently into Ennawi's face, but could see no evidence of cognition.

He shook his head slowly. He must have been mistaken.

THE ARVENIAN FORMERLY KNOWN AS the Earl of Pisander was delighted to be gone from the presence of the unpredictable Rogandan monarch. It gave him no little satisfaction that he had managed to depart from Rog with his head still attached to his shoulders. He glanced across at his fellow conspirators. They appeared to be equally relieved.

Pleased as he was to be gone, he was far from content as the leagues rolled away under the hooves of their horses. King Agon's detachment of guards did not afford their three charges a single moment to relax on their journey across Rogand. The harried former noblemen certainly found no opportunity to speak privately.

The situation did not change until they had almost reached the border with Arvenon. At that point Agon's guards unceremoniously abandoned the three men and pointed their horses toward home.

Left finally to their own devices, the men turned aside from the main road and picked their way slowly through a heavily wooded area. They continued until they were certain they had crossed the border.

By unspoken mutual agreement, they rode until Rogand was well behind them. Then they dismounted and lit a fire. For a long time they sat quietly, none of them saying a word.

The former Arvenian lord finally broke the silence. "We will need to stay in close contact," he said, "although I see no value in remaining together now. It would probably be dangerous to do so. We know where and when to next meet."

There was no response, so he continued. "All of us know how to find Agon's agents, and our saddlebags are stuffed full with enough coin to last us for a considerable time. I, for one, have associates I urgently need to make contact with."

"It's easy for you, Pisander," said the Varasan. "You're in your own country now."

"Don't call it 'my country'," snapped the Arvenian. "My country threw me onto the scrap heap. I was scheduled for execution, and I'd have been dead long ago if I hadn't bribed my way out of a dungeon." He spat into the fire. "This won't be my country again until some radical changes take place."

"You're not the only one who was cast aside," the Varasan replied. "When I was Lord Tarestel I did everything I could to spare my country the ravages of war. My king rewarded me with exile."

Pisander gazed narrowly at Tarestel. He felt nothing but contempt for the Varasan and his relentless self pity. How had he come to be allied with such a whiner?

Both men turned to the Castelan, who sat staring into the fire, brooding. Perhaps feeling their eyes upon him, the former Lord Eisgold looked up. He stared pointedly at Tarestel. "What did you expect?" he asked derisively. "You set yourself up as ruler in place of your king. You're lucky he did nothing worse than exile you."

A bitter tone came to Eisgold's voice. "My only crime was to ignore the orders of an upstart commoner—a foreign upstart at that."

Pisander had more sympathy for Eisgold, if only because he had reasons of his own to passionately hate the commoner who had brought about the Castelan's downfall. He had little respect for Eisgold's intelligence, though—the man seemed to think himself a lot smarter than he actually was.

All of them fell silent again.

Pisander eventually broke the silence. "What are the two of you planning to do next?" he asked.

The others stared back at him. "Surely we've established that already," said Tarestel with a puzzled frown. "Our role is to further King Agon's purposes."

Eisgold appeared equally baffled by the question.

The former Earl of Pisander simply nodded, and all three of them resumed staring into the fire.

So it was true. Agon had somehow turned them into marionettes. He would pull the strings, and all three of them would dance to his tune.

Pisander tried to make sense of what had happened in Rog. He knew that the others had spent two full weeks in the company of Agon. He had found the man insufferable, and done everything he could to shorten the exposure. He had bowed and scraped, fawned shamelessly, and made a pretense of slavish devotion. The Rogandan king had apparently bought his little act, because he satisfied himself with just one week of constant contact.

Was that the reason Pisander seemed to have retained a greater measure of independent thought? He, too, found himself fully supportive of Agon's goals, even though he couldn't make sense of his own reasons for thinking that way. But he also had significant twists of his own that he intended to pursue. The other two didn't seem to have retained any desire whatsoever for independent thought and action.

How could two weeks in the company of Agon cause a man to be so thoroughly bent to his will?

His mind wandered back, as it often did, to the fateful council meeting where he had been exposed as a traitor. His eyes narrowed as he called to mind the young commoner who attended the meeting at Will Prentis's invitation. He ground his teeth involuntarily at the memory of the hated army commander. He shook his head, forcing himself to focus.

The boy seemed to have something in his pouch. At the time, it had prompted him to think about Lord Drettroth's deceptively innocent inquiry after a stolen heirloom—a tiny stone—and his promise of a rich reward if it was returned to him.

How had the youth managed to expose him? Pisander could only wonder if he had access to an object of power, perhaps in the form of a small stone. An object that gave him knowledge of other people's business. Ordinarily he would have scoffed at any such notion. But he had no better explanation for the manner in which he had been undone.

If it was true, how could an unkempt youth have gained possession of such a prize? And why hadn't Prentis simply taken it from him, by force if necessary? Surely Prentis must have known that the youth had it—why else invite him to the council meeting?

He frowned in puzzlement. There were mysteries to unravel here.

None of this explained what had happened with Agon though. Was it possible that the Rogandan king had access to a powerful object of his own? Had he discovered a means of reshaping the wills of those exposed to this power, with the result that they became determined to willingly further his purposes?

He stared into the fire. He would do Agon's bidding—somehow he could not even conceive of doing anything less. But he would also further some plans of his own. He would direct some of his new resources into hunting down the youth who had appeared at the fateful council meeting. And he would initiate some discreet investigations into Agon's remarkable persuasiveness.

There was something incredibly satisfying about the notion of using Agon's own coin for such purposes.

13

A few days after the Battle of Torbury Scarp

With the Rogandan army decisively defeated at Torbury Scarp, the invasion of Arvenon and the occupation of Varas were destined soon to become memories of the past. The allied armies pitched their tents not far from the battlefield, and wild celebrations were underway even before all the burials were over.

Rellan, still reeling from the death of his twin, Kuper, could muster no enthusiasm for celebrating. He instead focused his energy on arranging the burial of his brother. A few of his friends, in particular Will, Rufe, Ander, and Nestor, gathered around him to offer support.

Even Lord Burtelen found time to attend the committal ceremony to pay his respects. After it was over the nobleman sought Rellan out.

"The loss of your brother is very grievous, Rellan," he had said quietly. "It is hard to overstate the significance of your influence at Torbury Scarp. Without the intervention of you and Kuper the army of Erestor would have played no part in the battle. And Will Prentis has described the impact of your three hundred men on packhorses. The timing of your arrival was little short of miraculous. All of us owe both of you an immense debt of gratitude."

Words had failed Rellan in response, but he bowed low to acknowledge the nobleman's tribute.

Having laid Kuper to rest, Rellan rode at once for Erestor. Resolutely pushing the battle and its aftermath from his mind, he set his entire focus on reaching Anneka. His response was instinctive, just as a wounded animal drags itself past other accessible hiding places in an attempt to reach the comfort and security of its own hole.

Only a few days had elapsed since the battle when he reached the forest clearing on the borders of Erestor. He had been riding hard, his mind numb.

Seeing him arrive, a crowd of men, women, and children quickly gathered, eagerly calling out questions.

"Has a battle been fought?"

"Where's the army from Erestor?"

"Did the king defeat the Rogandans?"

Rellan waited for the din to die down. "We won a great victory, with the help of our allies from Castel and Varas," he told them, struggling to maintain his composure. "The war is over."

At his words an excited clamor arose, everyone talking at once.

Desolate and afflicted in spirit, Rellan had nothing further to say.

"Are you injured?" a voice asked suddenly. The hubbub quickly died away.

He shook his head slowly.

"Where's Kuper?" someone asked.

Everything went quiet.

Rellan's chin sank to his chest. He couldn't find a way to answer— the power of speech had deserted him.

The crowd stood silent, staring up at him.

Anneka appeared, stepping in front of his horse protectively. When the people didn't desist with their stares, she called out in exasperation, "Please! Leave him be for a while."

She didn't wait for the crowd to disperse. Taking the reins of his horse, she led him swiftly out of the clearing to a quiet place among the trees. Then she came to his side and stood gazing up at him.

The compassion in her eyes undid him completely. Tears began rolling freely down his cheeks. He slid from the saddle and clung to her desperately.

After what seemed an age, she gently detached herself from his embrace. She guided him back to the clearing, to a small hut set apart from most of the other dwellings. Then she called for Scar. "Make sure that no one disturbs him."

Scar had simply nodded.

Rellan entered the hut and lay down on a straw mattress. He was so exhausted that he went to sleep almost immediately.

As he slept, he dreamed.

In his dream he rode beside Kuper. Since infancy they had been inseparable—as close as twins could possibly be. On this afternoon they were relaxing in one another's company, joking and laughing together. There was no hint of battles or fighting—they were simply enjoying the opportunity to exercise their horses in the sunshine.

"When am I going to become an uncle?" Kuper had asked him.

"Not until I marry and have children, I suppose," Rellan had replied with a laugh.

"Well you'd better get started on it," Kuper had told him. Then he paused and added softly, "When it happens, make sure you tell your children about me."

Rellan had blinked in puzzlement at his brother's remark. Then, in the fraction of a moment it took for his eyes to flick open again, his twin had vanished. Bewildered, he halted his horse and peered around him in every direction. Kuper and his mount were nowhere to be seen.

He woke with a start to find himself lying alone in the hut. Everything was shrouded in darkness—it was clearly still the middle of the night. It took him a long time before he was able once more to fall asleep.

The sun was riding high in the sky when he finally awoke. Even so, he didn't emerge from the hut for another hour. He didn't know how to face people or what to say to them.

The first person he spotted outside was Scar. After acknowledging Rellan with a nod, the bowman ignored him.

It was immediately obvious that the people had taken Anneka's request very seriously. Rellan was met with curious stares, but no one spoke to him. Only the children stared and pointed, persisting until their parents came to shoo them away.

That afternoon Anneka took him aside, and they wandered together beside the small stream near the clearing.

"Tell me what happened," she said.

Rellan wasn't normally one to hoard his feelings, and he knew that hiding himself away was not an option. He needed to get it out.

He drew in a deep breath and released a long sigh.

"It took an age to get everyone through the quagmire below Steffan's Citadel," he told her. "We could easily have missed the battle. As it was, we barely arrived in time. Our mounted men reached the battlefield first. Kuper and I weren't far behind them. We were leading a few hundred men on packhorses."

"And you arrived while the battle was still being fought?"

Rellan began pacing back and forth restlessly. "We arrived at a critical moment. Kuper led us straight in. The Rogandan commander had broken through Will's lines with his bodyguard, and we arrived in time—barely—to push them back.

"I spotted their commander and went for him. It was stupid—I had no one to support me. It would have been the end of me very quickly if it hadn't been for my brother. He saw that I was in trouble and raced in to help me. It was Kuper who killed their commander.

"But then his bodyguard rallied, and Kuper was brought down himself." He raised his arms in a gesture of despair. "It was all over in a matter of moments. There was nothing I could do."

She stood silently for a couple of minutes, pondering his words. "Did you blame yourself?" she finally asked.

"Yes, I did. For a while. Will found me moping the next day and told me to snap out of it. He said that people die in battles, and that Kuper had made his own choices.

"It was obvious that the death of their commander had a big impact on the morale of the Rogandans. It helped change the outcome of the battle. And the credit for that belonged entirely to Kuper. Will said that by taking the blame I was diverting attention from his achievement. I was making it about me."

He winced as he remembered the interaction. "Will didn't pull any punches. He wasn't easy on me. But I knew he was right."

Rellan ceased his pacing. He sat down abruptly on a log and released a heavy sigh that came out more as a groan.

"I don't blame myself anymore, but that doesn't take away the emptiness. All my life Kuper's been beside me—he's been as much a part of me as my two arms. Nothing feels right anymore."

Apart from her occasional questions, Anneka had said nothing. Now she quietly came and positioned herself nearer to him. He found her presence reassuring, even though she remained silent.

After some time she spoke. "When I left our home—with Scar and all the others—I'd just lost my husband and my infant son. I thought life could never be the same again. I found a way to keep my head down and plod through each day, doing whatever had to be done to get all of us through. It went on that way for years."

She swung around to face him. Then she patiently waited until he turned his head and looked her in the eye. "Then you arrived. You're the only reason my situation changed." She spoke calmly, but he sensed the intensity behind her words.

She turned away for a moment and stared off into the distance. "You won't find it easy to adjust. It will take time. Perhaps a long time," she said calmly.

Then she looked at him again, gazing intently into his face once more. "But don't stumble around alone in the dark like I did. I'm willing to help you through it, Rellan. If you'll let me."

.   .   .

Not long after he returned Rellan was asked to repair a roof. As he climbed the ladder he realized that it was the same roof that Kuper had repaired on their first visit to the community. Feeling suddenly lightheaded, he quickly decided to climb down before he fell down. Anneka found him sitting on the ground with his head in his hands.

"Painful memories?" she asked quietly.

He felt his face redden with embarrassment. "Just ignore me! I'll be fine. I need to focus on getting the roof finished."

"No, you're wrong."

The change in her tone of voice startled him, and he looked up at her at once. Her normally unruffled face was pale and strained. He sensed that his current struggles had triggered distressing memories of her own experiences.

"I tried to keep busy, too," she said. "I didn't give myself permission to grieve for the ones I'd lost. So I never actually let them go." Her eyes filled with tears. "I didn't understand the damage it was doing to me."

Only once had he witnessed such a display of emotion in Anneka. Last time it had taken a catastrophic landslide to wring tears from her.

She turned her full attention to him, her eyes still brimming. "Don't you dare drag yourself through life!" she said fiercely. "Give yourself the chance to properly mourn the loss of Kuper. Remember him, think about him, talk about him, miss him—all of those things are important. Even if you can only do it with strong emotion."

He gazed wide-eyed at her for a few moments. Then he slowly nodded.

She wiped her eyes and smiled self-consciously. Then she left him.

Her words made a big impression on him. But her vulnerability had the greatest impact. He thought about the interaction many times in the following days.

And he promised himself he would stop pushing his grief away.

. . .

RELLAN HAD BEEN ATTRACTED to Anneka from the moment they met. Nevertheless the barriers that separated them had seemed insurmountable. Rellan could not imagine wooing a noblewoman, even one who had cast aside her life of privilege. And he came to see that Anneka was so adept at suppressing her emotions she couldn't find a way past her own defenses.

All of these obstructions had been swept away in the aftermath of the disaster at the lake. Their suppressed longings found sudden release and love flamed into life—effortlessly, and almost without conscious intent.

After his return from Torbury Scarp, though, everything had changed. She offered unstinting support as she had promised, but she did so as a caring friend and nothing more. Rellan understood why she was keeping her distance—she was trying to be respectful of his loss. She was giving him room to grieve. But he longed for the closeness they'd enjoyed previously.

The separation felt like a major step backward to him. It meant they needed to start all over again, and in spite of his boldness and bluster, he felt unexpectedly shy.

14

———————

After a couple of weeks of growing awkwardness in his interactions with Anneka, Rellan decided to put aside his hesitation and attempt a romantic gesture. He hoped it might trigger a return to more carefree days.

Making his way to the wildflower meadow he'd found months earlier, he was delighted to find a few flowers in bloom. He picked a small bunch of blossoms, then he rode to the clearing and waited for a moment when Anneka was alone. Approaching her with a tentative smile, he pulled the flowers from behind his back and offered them to her.

She frowned uncertainly. "Are you trying to tell me I've been grumpy lately?"

"Whatever do you mean?" he asked.

"Last time you gave me flowers you told me it was because I was grumpy."

He grinned at the memory. "At the time I seem to remember also saying that you'd been working very hard and deserved a little beauty to lighten your day."

She tilted her head and cocked an eyebrow, which made him chuckle.

Putting mirth aside, he gazed at her seriously. "There's no sting to the message," he said. "I simply wanted to thank you for your support since I lost Kuper. You offered to help me through it, and you've been doing that. I truly appreciate it. It would have been very different without you."

He was entirely sincere, and he felt confident she was aware of that. She accepted the flowers graciously, but her answering smile didn't reach her eyes.

He walked away discouraged. She had apparently received his gesture as an expression of appreciation, not as a romantic initiative.

Anneka's mood over the following days only served to confirm his suspicions. If anything, he'd succeeded in increasing the distance between them.

The incident further shook his confidence. He wished he could have asked Kuper what he was doing wrong. His twin had a knack of stating the obvious, which invariably meant pointing out things that were obvious to everyone except Rellan.

He was none the wiser as the days went by. He slept poorly, and his old insecurities resurfaced. From the moment he first discovered that Anneka had been a noblewoman, he'd felt she was above him. For a time he'd allowed himself to forget the class divide, but the reality of it now came crashing in on him again. How could he have imagined that the chasm between them would simply disappear?

Weeks had now passed since Rellan's return. A day came when he found himself working with Scar repairing the roof of another dwelling, a task that had taken all morning and much of the afternoon. It hadn't gone at all smoothly, and Rellan's annoyance had grown steadily with each setback.

Late in the day Anneka came to check on progress. She arrived at the moment his frustration reached boiling point.

Leaning forward to secure a beam, he lost his footing. He crashed through the structure, wood splintering around him as a large section of the roof collapsed. Thankfully he was able to break his fall by clutching at a crossbeam as he fell, and he landed on a soft pile of hay. Remarkably, he was not injured.

Nevertheless he surveyed the destruction in total exasperation. "What a complete waste of time! I've squandered an entire day. This certainly isn't what I was hoping for."

Anneka fixed him in a stare. "What *are* you hoping for, Rellan?" she asked, clearly irritated. "Do you even know?" Then she spun on her heel and marched off.

Rellan turned to Scar, who was standing nearby. "What was that all about?" he asked, a frown of bafflement covering his brow.

"Her question deserves to be answered," Scar returned, a frosty look on his face.

Rellan looked at him in surprise. "Why is everyone so testy?" he asked.

"I don't exactly know what your intentions are with Anneka," Scar replied bluntly, "but whatever they are, I hope you're well aware that the two of you won't be the only people affected."

"What on earth are you talking about?" Rellan was completely mystified.

"This community has been led by Anneka for a long time," Scar replied. "What's going to happen if she marries you? Are you expecting to become the leader? All of us deserve to know."

Scar turned his back and departed without waiting for a response, leaving Rellan to gape after him.

A number of things instantly became clear. First, it was obvious that Scar had assumed they would marry. He almost certainly wasn't alone in that. Second, Rellan's relationship with Anneka had huge implications for the community, and he had failed spectacularly to grasp that.

More importantly for him, though, what was Anneka thinking? Did she have the same expectations as everyone else? Had she been waiting—perhaps daily—for him to conquer his self doubt and make his intentions clear? If so, his failure to act must have become increasingly painful for her, as well as confusing and unsettling for others. As he finally grasped what had clearly long been obvious to everyone else, his own mortification became unbearable.

Desperately needing time alone to think, he saddled his horse and rode away. He resolved not to return without a complete set of answers—for himself, for Anneka, and for the community.

Having been forced at last to do some honest reflecting, he saw that there was no excuse for his dithering. The loss of Kuper had been very unsettling, but it had never been a reason to leave his relationship with Anneka unresolved.

He had no doubt about his own desires—he wanted to be with her as much as ever. But he realized that deep down he'd never fully believed he could measure up to her. He was a commoner. He suspected that sooner or later she would see him for what he was, and when she did she was sure to reject him.

Everything had seemed so straightforward after the landslide. Now he needed to start again on his own, and his courage had abandoned him.

Why such timidity? He had charged into battle and attacked the Rogandan commander with less hesitancy. Why should the fear of Anneka's rejection be so crippling? He couldn't even pretend to be without hope. She'd told him plainly that his arrival had changed her life.

The situation had to change. His current position was beyond embarrassing, and the longer he left it the worse it would become.

Kuper's appeal finally sealed it. He remembered his brother's words in his dream—*You'd better get started...Make sure you tell your children about me.* He could ignore his own self-interest, but he'd never been able to deny his brother anything.

The time had come, and having put it off for so long, he was now unwilling to wait another minute. He mounted his horse and urged it toward the clearing.

To his relief he found Anneka alone. Best of all, she didn't appear to be distracted by anything pressing.

He took a deep breath to steady himself before approaching her boldly. "Would you take a ride with me please?" he asked.

Anneka's eyes narrowed, but she agreed. She retrieved her horse and accompanied him out of the clearing.

He led her among the trees for several minutes without speaking.

Finally he reined in his horse beside a pleasant meadow and slid off its back. Anneka dismounted as well.

As he turned to her, Rellan's heart began to pound. Her face was an impassive mask.

He shook his head. "I can't go on like this any longer. There are things I need to tell you, Anneka." He took another deep breath, trying to steady his nerves. "My whole world has been shaken since I met you. I never expected to give my heart to a noblewoman."

That earned him a disgusted look. "I told you before," she shot back, "I stopped being Lady Neave a long time ago! That isn't who I am."

"I know you said it, but it still hasn't been easy for me to fully accept it. But noblewoman or not, I can't let things continue the way they've been." He swallowed. "I'm sure you can't stand it any longer either."

The look on her face plainly confirmed it.

He bent down and plucked a wildflower. "You're the most amazing woman I have ever met. I know there's no possibility I could ever deserve you, but I can't bear the thought of going through life without you." He swallowed again. "Would you do me the great honor of becoming my wife?"

As he asked he stretched out his hand and offered her the flower, a delicate and beautiful bloom with large white petals.

She stood looking at him for a long lingering moment. Then she reached out slowly and took the flower from his hand.

"Yes, Rellan, I will marry you," she said. "I would be honored to be your wife."

His joy and his relief knew no bounds. He felt like leaping around the meadow like a young deer. Instead, he stood there staring at her with a stupid grin on his face.

She was magnificent. Reaching out almost instinctively, he swept her into his arms. She gazed up into his eyes, and his heart beat even faster. His eyes dropped to her lips, full and inviting. He bent his head toward her, and a thrill ran throughout his entire body as their lips met for the first time. His eyes closed, and he abandoned himself to the wonder of loving and being loved.

When they finally drew back from each other, he stood there silently, drinking her in, amazed at the tenderness he saw in her eyes. He'd scarcely allowed himself to dream of such a moment.

"I didn't know what to expect when I brought you here," he told her honestly. "I thought you were as likely to punch me as accept me."

She raised an eyebrow. "You're lucky I didn't punch you. I knew you needed to make up your own mind, but waiting for you to do it has certainly tested my patience!"

He took her hands, and gazed happily into her eyes until she began to blush.

Not wanting to embarrass her, he said contritely, "I'm sorry that I'm so annoying at times."

"At times?" she echoed, raising an eyebrow again.

He smiled at the irony in her voice. "I'll try to work on it, I promise."

She rolled her eyes. "And I'll try to restrain my expectations," she said.

He sighed contentedly. "I can honestly say that I've loved you from the moment I laid eyes on you." A cheeky grin came to his face. "Well, perhaps more accurately I've loved you from the moment you stole our horses and tried to trick us into working for you."

"And it would be accurate for me to say," she shot back, "that I've been intensely irritated by you from the first time you tried to flirt with me, which was the instant you met me."

"And yet you love me anyway," he said with a happy smile, reaching for her once more.

"I do," she said, resting her head on his shoulder. "Even though you're so masterful at exasperating me."

A flippant rejoinder came to his mind, but he decided it wasn't the time.

They stood there in silence for a while. Then she pulled away a little so she could gaze into his eyes. "From the beginning I tried desperately not to fall for you. I've never met anyone who drives me so crazy!" Her face softened. "Your brother listed your qualities, though, and he was right. You're kind and generous. And you're also loyal and courageous." She shrugged helplessly. "I gave up fighting it a long time ago."

"Are you sure this is me you're talking about?" he asked with a grin.

She gave him a mock frown before adding seriously, "I'm sorry I snapped at you earlier."

"It's a good thing you did," he replied. "It helped wake me up. That, along with some comments Scar made about whether I would be expecting to lead the community if we marry."

She shot him a glance. Then she drew back a pace, withdrawing her hands from his grasp. "That's an important issue. I'm not sure how some of them are going to feel about it."

"They needn't worry. You're the leader, and that doesn't need to change just because we get married."

She frowned at him. "So you're telling me you'd be willing to be led by your wife? It's hard to imagine how that would work."

"Are you worried that I'll feel less like a man if I'm not the leader?"

She hesitated for a moment, then she nodded.

He shook his head. "You've been my leader the whole time I've been in the community. I don't see why that needs to change, and I don't see why it has to become a problem once we're married. I'm not going to feel inferior if I'm not the leader."

Her skepticism showed clearly on her face.

"Perhaps we have different views about leadership," he said. "I see leadership as an ability—one of many abilities. Kuper was a better leader than me, and I was a better bowman. But neither of us felt superior or inferior because of that. We were twins, and we felt just as valuable as each other."

She offered no immediate response.

"Abilities are useful when deciding who to appoint to do a particular job," he continued. "Take Will, for example. King Steffan and

King Istel appointed him to lead the combined army of Arvenon and Castel because he was the best leader they had. It was the right decision—there's no way we would have won the Battle of Torbury Scarp with anyone else in command. But none of Will's soldiers felt inferior because he was the commander and they weren't. In fact they felt stronger and more capable themselves with an effective leader in command."

"That all makes sense," she replied, "but it isn't how the nobles see it. Believe me—I know from personal experience! To the nobility, a person's value comes from their bloodline. Not from anything else, and certainly not from their abilities. They see leadership the same way. You have no right to exercise authority unless you're born into the nobility."

Rellan nodded his agreement. "I'm sure that's why some of the nobles actively resisted Will's leadership."

"Exactly," she said. "They're nobles and he isn't, so in their eyes that makes him inferior, however capable he is. They wouldn't have been at all happy about coming under the authority of anyone they see as inferior."

She began to look uncomfortable. "You're saying that ability is what qualifies you to lead. If you're right, then I shouldn't be leading the community. The only reason I became the leader was because I was a noblewoman."

He shook his head in denial. "That may have been true in the beginning. But not now. You said yourself that you're not a noblewoman anymore. And yet the others still want you to lead them. It's because they know you're the best leader the community has. I've heard them say so.

"You're the right person to lead. And it isn't going to bother me. I've never seen myself as inferior because you lead the community and I don't, and becoming your husband isn't going to change that."

She looked at him thoughtfully. "I understand what you're saying," she said. "My former husband was always a leader—among the lords and on our estate as well as in our marriage. But he never treated me as inferior, and I never felt inferior. I always felt respected and honored by him."

She raised both eyebrows. "You're an unusual man, Rellan, and you certainly have some unusual ideas. But I believe that you mean what you say." She smiled. "I'm willing to see if we can make it work."

"That sounds good to me," he replied. "I should warn you, though —I'll be leading when it's just us."

So saying, he pulled her firmly into his arms once more. She lifted her face toward him, and he eagerly accepted the invitation, giving full expression to his yearning as he pressed his lips to hers.

The kiss seemed impossibly brief, but he comforted himself with the anticipation that more would follow it. He sighed with wonder as he gazed into her eyes. Why had he ever hesitated?

She smiled up at him, and he smiled back.

"Enough of all this talk about leadership and inferiority," he said. "Let's go tell everyone the news!"

15

Four years after the Battle of Torbury Scarp

In the four years since she married Rellan, the demands on Anneka's time had continued to increase. The community she led, now referred to as Newhaven by its inhabitants, was firmly established and thriving. But growth had brought its share of challenges as children were added, livestock numbers swelled, and cultivated strips expanded ever outward.

Anneka had been enjoying a rare opportunity to relax for a few minutes when Scar burst in. He appeared deeply troubled; it was obvious that he hadn't come with good news.

"Hender and Gunnar have been attacked," he told her. "Near our old dwellings in the clearing. Hender escaped, but Gunnar was killed."

Anneka's eyes went wide with shock. This was not the first time that her people had been attacked and killed—she had witnessed the savagery with her own eyes—but it was just a memory now. The community had long since escaped from those in Erestor who wanted them dead.

Since the day they retreated to the wilderness, no one had died as a result of violent attack. Not even in the days of the Rogandan invasion. She had thought such troubles were behind them.

Her heart sank as she pictured Gunnar. He was a good man, and he would be greatly missed. His wife had long since passed on, but his three children and his steadily expanding group of grandchildren would be shattered when they learned of his loss.

She turned her attention back to Scar. He looked weary, and his face was grim. She could hardly remember seeing him so concerned —certainly not since the Rogandan incursions that had forced them out of their dwellings in the clearing, their first refuge after they fled.

They were secure now in an even more remote location, one with better soil for farming as well as good hunting. But they had never entirely abandoned their former domain, and the awareness that her people were being attacked in their own forest was alarming.

"Do we know anything about the attackers?" she asked.

Scar shook his head. "Nothing at all. But Hender says it was a large party. They were long gone by the time we arrived."

Anneka frowned, completely mystified. She was not aware of enemies in the region, and bandits had been few and scattered. At least until now.

"Was Rellan with you?"

"Yes."

"Where is he now?"

"He stayed behind to do some scouting."

"On his own?"

"Hender is with him, and Petar as well." Scar gave her a knowing look. "Don't worry," he said. "He'll be careful."

She furrowed her brows, annoyed that her private anxieties should be so obvious.

"With your permission," Scar proposed, "I'll take a larger party, and we'll do some more serious scouting. I want to know whether it's a random attack by bandits, or if something else is going on."

Her brows furrowed. "What else do you think might be going on?"

Scar's face clouded. "I'm not sure. But our presence here hasn't been a secret since you and Rellan destroyed the Rogandan army camped outside Steffan's Citadel. Word has undoubtedly spread in Erestor that we're still alive and hiding away somewhere nearby. There might be people who haven't forgotten about us."

"Pisander was thrown into prison. He must surely have been executed long ago. Who else would care?"

"I don't know."

Scar looked very uncomfortable. And she'd learned to trust his instincts.

She nodded decisively. "You're right—we're much too ignorant about what's going on in the world around us. Take as many people as you need, and do a thorough investigation.

"You're right to be concerned, too. We were safe while our existence wasn't known. Now that it's been exposed, we can't be certain about the risks we might face.

"It's time we became more cautious. From now on, no one comes here by the direct route. No exceptions. I don't care about the wasted time. Every one of us needs to take extra precautions to ensure we're not followed."

Scar nodded. "I'll pass on your instructions immediately." He set off without delay.

Alone once more, Anneka allowed Scar's concerns to occupy her attention for a time. He had raised questions that needed to be answered. Uncomfortable questions.

Before long, though, she found her thoughts pulled irresistibly in a different direction—back to Rellan. She sighed, as much frustrated by her own fretfulness as by any reckless streak she could see in Rellan.

Was he reckless, or was she just too afraid of losing him?

Her memory took her back more than four years, to the eve of the decisive battle with the Rogandans at Torbury Scarp. She had watched with dark foreboding as Rellan rode east with Kuper and the host of Erestor. When Lord Burtelen's army had disappeared from all sight and knowledge, her fear told her she would never see Rellan again.

Her heart had dared to hope for a different outcome, and she had never entirely yielded to despair.

Rellan had been the irritant that prodded her back into life. At first she had blocked and resisted him.

Then together they had precipitated the landslide. Yosef and Jon had been lost, and she had almost lost her own life as well. She survived only because Rellan had saved her.

The surging waters had swept away the Rogandans laying siege to Steffan's Citadel—the entire army had simply vanished. Were it not for the endless piles of bodies downstream, there would have been no evidence that the army ever existed. Hundreds of workers had been deployed in the cleanup, and it had taken days to bury the bodies. The landscape had been left radically altered.

But the terrain wasn't the only thing that had changed. Her own carefully constructed emotional defenses had been swept away in the upheaval. Years of pent up feelings were released, threatening to utterly undo her.

To her lasting astonishment, in the days that immediately followed the landslide Rellan had been a rock, a still point in the maelstrom of her inner turmoil. He had been fully present—not his usual brash self, but a caring and considerate Rellan. She had never glimpsed this person. Had his existence been entirely hidden from her since she first met him? Or had she been unable to see it? Perhaps she would never know for certain.

When he had ridden away to war a part of her had died. She was all too familiar with separation, and this latest rending felt no less bitter than the first. Outwardly she carried on with life as before, but all the while her insides had been roiling.

Then, finally, came the day when Rellan returned. He had clung to her, as a drowning man might clutch at a log. There had been no words, only the emptiness in his eyes. He had no need to tell her what had happened.

She had known what to do—she saw at once that it was her turn now. He needed her to provide a place of refuge. Saying very little, she had willingly laid aside for a time the mantle of a leader and clothed herself instead with the compassion of a healer and the empathy of a woman.

Anneka and Rellan had in turn been compelled to part from the ones they loved the most. Each of them had helped the other in their journey through the shadow of the grief and the pain and into the light of day.

She sighed. The challenges of the past might be behind them, but Scar's report had shaken her. What lay ahead?

She got up, the restlessness of her thoughts demanding physical expression. Wandering about the room, her gaze fell on the remains of a bouquet resting on a shelf. Its blooms, once bright and colorful, had long since dried out and faded, but she smiled as she allowed her thoughts to drift back to the day she had been wed.

Fully grasping Rellan's sensitivities about her origins, Anneka had shunned fancy gowns and flashy ornaments. Instead she chose a simple but elegant frock of white embroidered linen. The young women had gathered around and pinned up her long dark hair before adorning it with wildflowers to honor Rellan's first gift early in their relationship.

She recalled the secret gratification of seeing his eyes go wide with wonder as she swept into view. She relived the delight of standing radiant before him as they exchanged their vows.

The reactions of the community had been mixed. They wanted her to be happy, but change is unsettling. Scar in particular had taken a long time to reconcile himself to her new status. But Rellan had spoken truly—he was more than content for her to lead, and he soon directed all of his considerable energy toward bettering the lives of her people.

The community wanted Anneka as their leader, but Rellan was well liked. He was capable, he was kind, and he made people laugh. More than once he had called upon his impish sense of humor to reduce the heat in a tense confrontation.

Rellan loved to poke fun at Anneka, especially in public. Occasionally she found it extremely irritating, but for the most part she took it in good spirit. Whenever it became annoying, she tried to remind herself that by far the most frequent target of his humor was himself.

The merry sound of little voices dragged her back to the present. Moving to the doorway, she gazed out on their twins, playing happily together in the sunshine.

Her life had undergone a total transformation, and she was more than content with the changes.

RELLAN STOOD IN THE OPEN, silent and angry as he surveyed the smoking ruins of the buildings that had once fringed the clearing. Hender and Petar picked among the debris. Neither of them had offered comment, but Rellan could guess how they must be feeling. This place had once been their home. Their home had been violated.

It held memories for him, too, memories that were no less significant. He had met Anneka here.

Rellan had no idea who had caused the destruction, or why. But in destroying the original refuge of Anneka and her people, the unknown marauders had achieved something that not even the Rogandans had managed to do.

He glanced around him, suddenly uneasy. They were too exposed here. He called to Hender and Petar, and they slipped away through the trees to retrieve their horses. They mounted and set off, wary and alert for any sign of trouble.

In the last couple of days they had scouted far and wide and seen no one. But the surrounding forest offered plenty of cover for anyone wanting to remain hidden.

Rellan was grateful to have Hender and Petar with him. Hender was the community's best archer, and Petar was not far behind him. Both men were also outstanding hunters and trackers. He couldn't wish for more capable companions. Nevertheless the surrounding forest felt surprisingly menacing. It was a disconcerting feeling—this had always been their domain.

He wondered what Anneka was thinking about the developments. He had no doubt that Scar had updated her by now. She would be worried about him. He peered out through the trees, a grim smile on his face. Perhaps she had good reason to worry.

After a time they came to a place he knew well. Wildflowers grew beside a tinkling stream that bubbled across a small meadow. He had picked flowers from this meadow and given them to Anneka. And he had come here again after he returned, alone and diminished from the loss of his brother at Torbury Scarp.

He closed his eyes for a moment and allowed the memories to drift through his awareness. Then he turned away from the meadow and the flowers and rode on.

***

"RELLAN!"

The soft call reached him through the trees. If Hender was keeping his voice low it must have been for a reason. Rellan moved quickly to his side.

The bowman pointed away to the east. A group of horsemen could be seen riding toward them, not far away. They were traveling in single file along the forest path and didn't appear to be in a hurry.

"It's a large group," said Rellan, "and they're well armed. We'll observe them, that's all. Let Petar know."

Hender nodded and set off to inform Petar. Rellan tied his horse well back from the path. Then, finding a tree that offered an unimpeded view, he climbed it, carrying his bow and arrows with him. In spite of his close proximity to the trail, he was confident that the leafy foliage would hide him from sight.

He located a forked branch that pointed away from the path, allowing him to remain hidden behind the trunk of the tree. He set his feet cautiously on the branch to ensure that it would readily support his weight and enable him to stand with his legs slightly apart. His perch was perfect—sufficiently stable that he could use his bow effectively if the need arose.

Then he settled himself to wait.

Soon men began passing below him, unaware of his presence. He was not able to get any clear sense of who they were or what their purpose was.

As he continued to peer down at them he started, almost losing his footing in his surprise.

"Will!" he called excitedly. "Rufe! It's me! Rellan!"

The column of men halted abruptly, and every head swung in his direction. The riders appeared more curious than alarmed—they were clearly not on alert.

He scrambled down out of the tree and strode forward onto the path.

"Rellan!" cried Will. He dismounted and embraced the bowman warmly. Then he stood back, surveying him with a grin. "You look much too contented with your lot in life. We'll have to find something that offers you more of a challenge."

"No, thanks!" Rellan replied with energy. "I have a wife and children. They offer more than enough challenge for me!"

Rufe dismounted and pushed his way forward too. "Rellan!" he said, his face beaming his delight. "It's good to see you! I hardly dared hope we'd find a friendly face in this wilderness."

"It's good to see you both," Rellan returned. "What brings you all the way to Erestor?"

Will deflected the question. "We were almost ready to camp for the night. Would you like to join us?"

"Gladly," said Rellan. He turned aside and whistled, releasing a sound that rose slowly in both pitch and volume. Hender and Petar soon appeared from among the trees, and Rellan introduced them to his old friends.

Then Rellan took Will and Rufe aside, beckoning to Hender and Petar to join them.

"You'll need to set guards tonight," Rellan told Will. "I'm sorry to say that this stretch of forest is no longer as safe as it once was."

Will frowned. "What's happening in Erestor? We've heard rumors—rumors of trouble."

"We have no more answers than you," Rellan told him frankly.

"Our community used to live near here, but we've since moved to a more remote location. Some of us still visit from time to time, though."

He pointed to Hender. "A few days ago Hender was here with another of our men. They were attacked by bowmen, and his companion was killed. Since then the three of us have been scouting in the area. We've seen no sign of the attackers, but we've discovered that our old dwellings have been burned to the ground."

He shook his head in puzzlement. "The killing makes no sense. And the destruction seems pointless. We have no idea who is responsible."

Will's brow furrowed. "The king has become aware of trouble in this region. There have been persistent reports of unrest—rumors, mostly. Nothing that's easy to identify. But something strange is going on, and I have no doubt there's purpose behind it. We just don't know what it is yet."

"He must be concerned if he's sent the two of you," said Rellan.

"There are other reasons as well, but he does want us to find out what's behind it," Will replied.

One of the men approached, waiting respectfully for Will to notice him.

"Yes, Jonas?" he asked.

"Would you like us to make camp here, My Lord?" the man asked.

Will turned to Rellan. "Is this a suitable location?" he asked, ignoring Rellan's raised eyebrows.

"Here's as good as anywhere," Rellan confirmed.

Will turned back to Jonas. "Yes, we'll camp here."

Jonas bowed, then withdrew.

"Please accept my apologies, My Lord, for not addressing you appropriately earlier," Rellan exclaimed, a merry twinkle in his eye.

Will looked pained. "King Steffan insisted on elevating me to the peerage. I'm Lord Torbury now. It's another reason I'm heading for Erestor. I'm overdue for a visit to my new estates. They were previously held by Lord Dunnridge, who later became the Earl of

Pisander. His lands were declared forfeit when his treachery was exposed."

He lowered his voice. "Rufe still calls me Will when we're alone. I expect you to do the same."

"Whatever you command, My Lord," Rellan replied with a wink.

Will rolled his eyes.

Rufe had been observing the interaction with barely concealed amusement. Now he turned to Will, his face becoming serious. "We haven't even needed to enter Erestor to find evidence of problems. It's time the men became much more alert. We're not in Arnost now. I'll make sure guards are posted." He got up and moved away, calling for Jonas.

Fires were lit, and the men gathered around them to eat a simple meal. Then they settled down to sleep. Guards were assigned, four at a time, with each group due for relief every four hours.

Will and Rufe had shared some food with Rellan around a crackling blaze in a small clearing. As the air grew colder, Rellan banked the fire, then laid out his blanket. Will stretched out beside him. It brought back memories of nights by a campfire before Torbury Scarp with Will and his companions. They were good memories.

As he lay down, Rellan finally allowed himself to relax. Surrounded by a large group of alert soldiers, his former uneasiness dissipated like an early mist before the morning sun.

RELLAN WAS STARTLED out of deep sleep by the sound of an arrow whizzing past his head. It buried itself into the ground between him and Will. He leaped to his feet, sounding the alarm. The quiet scene immediately descended into chaos as men got up and armed themselves.

"To me, men!" Rufe shouted, and a group quickly gathered around him. He issued rapid instructions before sending them out scouting in pairs.

Within minutes cries could be heard further west along the path.

Rufe and two others leaped onto their horses and spurred them toward the commotion.

Rellan grabbed his bow and arrows and made to join them, but Will placed a hand quietly on his arm and shook his head. Then he swiftly drew Rellan back into the shadows among the trees, well away from the fire.

Rellan looked at him curiously. "What is it, Will?" he asked, keeping his voice low.

Will peered back at him in the gloom. "Was that arrow aimed at you, or was it aimed at me?" he asked calmly.

Rellan frowned, struggling to absorb the implications of Will's question. Then a movement on the other side of the fire caught his attention. He squinted into the dark. Black clad figures were moving among the trees on the other side of the clearing. He could not see faces—their heads appeared to be shrouded with dark hoods.

None of the men with him or with Will were clad in such garb. Then a glint caught his eye—firelight reflected off a naked sword.

Rellan reacted instinctively. He strung and released an arrow almost without conscious thought. A grunt was followed by the thud of a body collapsing to the ground. A couple of figures ran toward him. He put an arrow into the arm of one of them, then Will stepped forward with a drawn sword to engage the other one.

The attacker abruptly changed his mind and turned tail. Rellan sent an arrow chasing after him. A yelp of pain suggested it had found its mark somewhere.

All went quiet. After a couple of minutes Will cautiously made his way around the clearing, sword at the ready. Rellan retrieved his own blade and followed closely.

They found no sign of the attackers. The two wounded men were gone, and it appeared that others had removed the body of Rellan's first victim.

"It will be dawn in a couple of hours," said Will, glancing first at the embers of the fire and then up at the sky. "There's little point attempting anything before then."

Rufe returned a moment later. "They got away," he said. "But not before killing the two scouts I sent west along the path." His tone conveyed outrage. "They didn't have it all their own way, though. A couple of them will do well to survive their wounds."

"Rellan killed another of the attackers and wounded two others," Will replied.

He sheathed his sword, but remained among the trees away from the clearing.

"Who were they, and what was their purpose?" Will asked. "This was no casual raid by local bandits. It was well planned and carefully executed, and we're fortunate indeed if we only sustained two losses." He paused, staring away into the darkness. Then he returned his attention to the clearing, gazing over at the embers of the fire. "I thought the king was overly cautious sending this many men with me. Now I'm beginning to wish I'd brought more."

A dull gray light heralded the imminent arrival of the dawn. As soon as the sun rose, Rufe sent men scouting in every direction, after first instructing them to be doubly cautious. They departed in groups of four.

Once the light had grown sufficiently in intensity, Will and Rellan carefully examined the clearing.

"There's a lot of blood lying around," said Will. "Thanks to you."

Rellan shrugged. "What did they expect?"

"Not you, I'm sure. Very few archers can reliably hit invisible targets in the dark."

Rellan smiled mirthlessly. "It looks like they dragged a body in that direction." He pointed west through the trees.

"So several of them are wounded, and they're carrying a body with them. It won't make it easy for them to move quickly."

"What will you do?" Rellan asked.

"Once the scouts return we'll track them. I want to know who's behind this." He gazed at Rellan. "What about you?"

"I'm going back to the community with Hender and Petar. We need to warn them. I don't understand the purpose behind this attack, but it might have been targeting us. Especially given what happened earlier."

Will nodded. "I understand. We'll be sorry to lose you. We won't only miss your skills, either—it's been good to see you again."

"I feel the same way. It's been too many years since I last saw you both. I hope we'll meet again soon, and in more relaxed circumstances next time."

Rellan called to his two companions, and they mounted and rode away.

"It's a good thing it wasn't just the three of us last night," said Petar.

"I had the same thought," said Hender. "There might be no one riding back to warn the community."

Rellan grunted. "If it had just been the three of us, we wouldn't have been sitting openly around a fire."

"And I would have grumbled about that, even if not out loud," Hender admitted. "It's a reminder of why we need you, Rellan. You're the only one of us with experience that counts."

Rellan didn't acknowledge the remark. His mind was on Anneka and on their children.

He clicked his tongue, and the horse moved forward. They would follow a roundabout route, and they would make doubly sure they were not followed. But they were going home.

16

Jonas glanced up at the sun, now riding high in the sky. It was time he reported back to Will.

Having fought under Will at Torbury Scarp, Jonas still thought of the commander as just Will, even though he was now a member of the nobility. Noblemen needed to be addressed appropriately, and Jonas felt certain he would get caught out sooner or later.

He chuckled to himself. He wasn't complaining. The only reason that addressing the commander had become an issue was that Will—or Lord Torbury or whoever he was—had been giving him more responsibility of late. A lot more responsibility.

That suited him just fine. He was ambitious and willing to do whatever it took to improve his lot in life. Having grown up in grinding poverty, he had no interest in ending his days that way. Direct access to Will must surely bring new opportunities. If it helped him get what he wanted, so much the better.

He soon joined Will's main group. They had been moving swiftly —they weren't far behind the scouts.

Will nodded a welcome as Jonas swung his horse alongside.

"They're still ahead of us, My Lord. By the time we got going this morning they had three or four hours head start. But we're gaining on them."

"Where are they heading?" asked Will.

"I'm not sure," Jonas answered frankly. "I'm not familiar with this region."

"Don't lose their trail," Will told him. "I need answers."

Jonas dipped his head, then pulled his horse clear and raced away. He rode hard until the column was out of sight.

After another hour had passed, he noticed a sudden change—the riders he was pursuing had altered their course, moving into open ground. The result was that the tracks ahead of him had become much easier to follow. He pressed forward eagerly. They couldn't be too far ahead.

He soon discovered the reason for the change. He wasted no time in returning to the main group.

"They've changed direction, My Lord," he said. "They must have realized we were getting close. They've joined the main road, which means their tracks are no longer recognizable. There's been so much traffic on the road that all the signs are confused."

Will frowned in annoyance. "Can we catch them before they reach Steffan's Citadel?" he asked.

Jonas shook his head. "I caught a glimpse of the citadel in the distance. They've probably passed through already." He hung his head. "I'm sorry, My Lord."

"It isn't your fault, Jonas—we were forced to wait for daylight to begin our chase. They've been far too canny from the beginning."

Steffan's Citadel loomed larger as the road climbed to meet it. Soon the fortress towered above Jonas, tall and immensely strong, straddling the only accessible pass through the mountains into Erestor. Its battlements looked down across the plains of Erestor to the west and the forests of Arvenon to the east. He knew that no enemy had captured it in the one hundred and fifty years since it was built by Steffan the First, the predecessor and namesake of the current king. Whoever commanded the citadel controlled access between Erestor and the rest of Arvenon.

Once they had passed through the gates, Will brought them all to a halt.

"I'm going to pay a brief courtesy call on the commander of the citadel," he said. "We need to question his guards at the gate."

He disappeared inside, returning in a few minutes. Jonas followed him to the gates, accompanied by Rufe.

"Did a large party of men pass through here?" Will asked. "It would have been no more than two hours ago."

"No, My Lord," one of the guards replied. "Several small groups of men passed through, but they didn't appear to be connected."

"Was there anything unusual about them?"

The guard paused, frowning. "One group was carrying a body. For burial, they said. A man who had died away from home. They were taking him back to his aged mother, so she could see him off."

"Were any of them wounded?"

"Not obviously," he replied.

One of the other guards spoke up. "One of the groups had a few men who looked like they were ready to fall from the saddle. The person who appeared to be leading the group said they were eager to get to Maranelle as soon as possible, so they'd been riding all night. He said they were very tired."

"Did any of their accents seem different?"

"No, My Lord, although most of them didn't speak. Those who did sounded like locals."

Rufe walked to the middle of the road and bent down, examining it closely. After a few moments he got to his feet, holding up a finger smeared with red. "Blood," he said. He turned to the guards. "These men were a lot more than just tired. They attacked us last night, and some of them were wounded during the fight."

The guards shrugged helplessly. Jonas understood their reaction —the kingdom was supposedly at peace. They would have seen no reason to be especially wary.

"Which direction did they go in?" Will asked.

"They just followed the road to Maranelle," they replied.

Will signaled to Jonas and the other scouts to rejoin the main group. All of them mounted up and passed quickly into Erestor. They rode swiftly, following the road for several hours. They saw no sign of the men they were pursuing.

The sun was sinking low in the sky when they paused to rest the horses. Will called over Rufe and Jonas. "They appear to have eluded us," he said.

Rufe nodded. "They must have found a place where they could leave the road without leaving a trail."

"What do you think, Jonas?" Will asked.

"I think Rufe is right, My Lord. We should have seen some sign of them by now." He shook his head, bemused by what had happened.

Will frowned. "There's no point in continuing to push the horses," he said. "We'll ride on until we find a suitable location to camp. There'll be no sitting around open campfires this time, though. From now on we're on full alert—we will ride and camp as we did during the war."

As soon as he arrived in Maranelle, Will sought out Lord Burtelen. The nobleman usually spent far more time in Arnost than in his native Erestor, but Will had become aware that he was currently in the Erestorian capital to settle some personal business. Will valued Lord Burtelen's effectiveness and reliability as highly as the king did. The nobleman was also well connected in Erestor, and Will hoped he might be able to offer insights into the disturbances.

"It's good to see you, Will. Or rather, Lord Torbury," Lord Burtelen said with a smile. "What brings you to Erestor? Are you paying another visit to your holdings at last?"

"That's certainly one of the main reasons why I'm here, My Lord," Will replied. "But the king is also concerned about rumors of unrest in Erestor, and he wants me to get to the bottom of it."

Lord Burtelen appeared unmoved. "I've heard similar rumors," he replied. "I'm sure we all have. But I don't believe there's any real reason for alarm. I've seen no evidence of unrest."

"Our party was attacked on our way here, and two of my men were killed," Will told him.

The nobleman was clearly shocked. "Were you able to establish who did it?"

"No. They attacked us at night. We pursued them as soon as there was enough light for tracking, but they joined the main road and passed through the citadel before we could catch them. They disappeared somewhere on this side of the pass."

Lord Burtelen's brows furrowed. "It seems incredible. I haven't heard of anything like this. Not since the Rogandan invasion. Could it have been bandits?"

Will shook his head. "Both the attack and their escape were too well planned and executed to have been carried out by bandits. There was purpose behind it, although I am at a loss to understand what it was." He frowned.

"I brought twenty men with me," he continued, "and I only did so at the insistence of the king. I will say, though, that traveling with a large group of men-at-arms no longer seems excessive to me. I would strongly urge you to go nowhere without a strong escort, My Lord."

The nobleman's brows furrowed again in puzzlement. "I don't understand it at all. But I appreciate your advice. And I will take it seriously."

Before they parted, Lord Burtelen had sent word to his holdings with orders for a squad of armed retainers to set out immediately for Maranelle. Will was able to extract a promise from him that he would not leave the capital until they arrived.

WILL ALSO ARRANGED to meet with the king's uncle, the Duke of Erestor.

The king's uncle had acted as regent while the king was absent in Castel seeking out a bride, and he had operated decisively and effectively on the king's behalf, successfully defending the capital during the Rogandan invasion. When the king returned to Arnost after the Battle of Torbury Scarp, the duke had asked the sovereign for permission to return home. Eighteen months passed before King Steffan relented and released his uncle.

The king greatly valued the duke's wisdom and support, and he had only granted permission reluctantly. But he also saw that the regency had wearied his uncle. The duke was no longer a young man, and he had neither the desire nor the energy to continue bearing heavy burdens of state.

All of this was known to Will. In fact he had personally interceded with the king on the duke's behalf. The duke was grateful for his support, and he only left Arnost after extracting a promise from Will to visit his castle when he was next in Maranelle.

Now that Will had arrived in Maranelle, he was looking forward to seeing the former regent. They had worked together closely in Arnost during the dangerous period following the Rogandan invasion, and Will had developed great respect for the duke.

Maranelle Citadel was the duke's ancestral home. It had been built on a rocky promontory above the city, and Will was grateful that his horse was doing the climbing as they traveled up the road to the castle.

When he reached the gates, Will paused to give his horse a rest. He looked down on the city below and beyond to the bay. Fishing boats were drawn up onto the beaches, at this distance little more than dark smudges on the white sand. Others floated in the bay, their sails visible as bright dots on the turquoise water.

He paused for a few moments longer to appreciate the peaceful scene, then he turned and guided his mount through the gates of the castle. One of the duke's retainers took the reins of his horse, and another led him to a terrace that overlooked the bay. He had been admiring the view for several minutes before the duke appeared.

"Lord Torbury! What a pleasure!"

Will bowed low. "My Lord Duke, the pleasure is mine!" Will had never seen the duke so relaxed and content. He waved a hand over the scene before them. "I can see why you were so eager to return to Maranelle."

His host smiled. "It is beautiful, is it not? And it's good to fill my old lungs with fresh sea air," he said. "Will you be in Maranelle for long?"

"Probably not. I need to visit my holdings, but I'll pass through Maranelle again before returning to Arnost."

"You should attend the Council of Lords while you're here. You have a seat on it, of course. In fact the size of your holdings makes you a senior member. The next meeting will be held in a few days."

"I presume you will lead it, My Lord." Will said.

The duke sighed. "I should, although I avoid it if I can these days. The truth is I find myself less and less patient with the petty power plays that occupy far too much of the time at these council meetings. Burtelen is a good man, and there are others, but many of them behave more like unruly children than noblemen. They could use a bit of your common sense."

Will had other things on his mind at that moment, and councils held very little interest for him. He decided to voice his concerns.

"There appear to be signs of unrest in Erestor, My Lord."

The duke glanced at him for a moment, then he redirected his gaze out across the boats on the bay. He didn't speak.

The silence soon weighed on Will, and he began to feel restless. Was the duke aware of the world beyond his walls? He glanced around him. His recent fight in the forest was surely worlds apart from this peaceful environment.

"I have one lasting regret," said the duke. "I had the opportunity to execute Pisander, and I didn't do it."

Will looked at him in surprise. He could not imagine what had prompted the duke's remark. "Surely Pisander is no threat. He was under sentence of death when he fled. He wouldn't be foolish enough to come anywhere near Erestor. Would he?"

The duke redirected his gaze to Will. "Pisander is a subtle and dangerous man," he replied. "Don't make the mistake of underestimating him."

Will shook his head, puzzled. "I don't understand, My Lord. Are you mentioning him because you believe he might be somehow connected with the unrest?"

"I can't tell you for certain who's behind it, Will. But I do keep my ears open. I'm not entirely ignorant of what's going on around me. And if you'll take my advice, you won't ignore any possible threat, however unlikely it might seem."

WILL LEFT the castle with a great deal to think about. The duke had always been a shrewd observer. Could he be right? Was the trouble somehow connected with a traitor who had mysteriously decided to reappear, years after cheating death by bribing his way out of a dungeon?

And even if it were true, how was that information of any use to him? What could he possibly do about it?

17

———————

Jonas had camped overnight with Will and his men almost within the boundaries of Will's holdings. By the time the sun had risen, they were in the saddle and on the move.

Before long they caught sight of an ancient pine tree standing alone at the top of a distant slope. "We're on my land now," Will announced.

They crested a hill, and he reined in his horse. Rufe and Jonas halted on either side of him.

A fertile valley lay before them, with a river winding through it. Will pointed toward a clump of trees far off in the distance. "The manor house is just beyond those trees," he said.

"It's good land," Rufe replied admiringly. "It must yield a worthwhile return."

Will nodded. "It'd been allowed to run down when I took it over. Most of the income for the first three years was consumed paying for repairs and refitting. There should finally be a good return this year."

He clicked his tongue, and they set off again, riding slowly down the slope into the valley.

"I appointed a reliable steward," Will continued, "a man named Timms. He isn't young anymore, but he still has plenty of energy, and he knows what he's about. I'm looking forward to meeting with him again—I haven't heard from him for a while."

Jonas raised his eyebrows in surprise. He couldn't believe that Will had been leaving subordinates to run his estates with so little personal supervision. If landowners expected issues to be dealt with quickly and effectively as they arose, they needed to keep in close contact with their retainers. Jonas had grown up on the land, and he had seen firsthand the consequences of leaving such things to chance. Even if Will was communicating regularly with Timms, Arnost was a long way from Erestor, and the delay between sending a message and receiving a reply must surely create the potential for a lot of problems.

If Will couldn't figure this out for himself he'd be in trouble. Perhaps he wasn't even aware of such basic necessities. He may have never gained personal experience of farming, much less running an estate.

Even if he did understand what was needed, though, it mightn't have helped. King Steffan placed continual demands upon his commander—Jonas had seen it for himself. Will simply didn't have the opportunity to visit his holdings in Erestor as often as he needed to.

Jonas was aware that other noblemen also spent much of their time in Arnost, but he also knew that most of them returned to their estates several times each year. Two visits annually had to be an absolute minimum. Will needed to put pressure on the king to release him more frequently—a lot more frequently. Even if the king was resistant.

Will probably wouldn't raise it with King Steffan unless someone prodded him. Rufe was the man. It wasn't in Jonas's interests to get involved.

As they drew nearer to the manor house Jonas started to become increasingly puzzled. It was gradually dawning on him that something wasn't right here. Where were the farm laborers? Rich land like this should be buzzing with activity. And where were the livestock? Sheep and cattle ought to be grazing everywhere.

Will had clearly noticed it too. He pulled ahead of the others in his haste.

They swung around the trees, and the manor house came into sight at last. Will pulled his horse to a sudden halt.

Jonas expected to see large barns near the main house, and dozens of sturdy little cottages spread out nearby to house the retainers and their families.

There was no sign of barns or cottages. Fire had swept through the area. Smoke still rose lazily from the charred remains of buildings. Apart from the manor house, nothing remained standing except blackened stumps and the remnants of stone chimneys.

Jonas and the others followed close behind Will as he spurred his horse toward the manor house. A few chickens scattered, squawking loudly. Nothing else disturbed the unnatural silence.

The manor house showed no obvious sign of damage until they rode up to the main door. Jonas saw then that the front doors had been torn off. He followed Will inside, trying to peer through the dust disturbed by their passage. He imagined that fine furniture and elegant settings had once graced the parlors and the sitting rooms. If so, all of it was gone. The rooms were largely empty.

An old woman emerged tentatively from within the house and peered fearfully toward them. When she saw Will, she bowed low and began to quietly weep.

"I remember you," said Will gently. "You're Timms's wife, aren't you?"

She nodded dully. "Yes, My Lord." Beckoning him to follow, she disappeared inside.

Will followed her into the building, Rufe and Jonas trailing behind. She soon came to a halt in a dimly lit room. An old man lay on a pallet on the floor.

Will knelt down beside the man. "Timms," he said softly. "What has been done to you? What has happened here?"

Recognizing his visitor, the man tried to get up.

"Stay where you are!" Will insisted firmly.

Timms collapsed back down, panting. "I am sorry, My Lord," he said feebly. "I was not able to prevent them."

"Are you injured?" Will asked.

The man nodded. "They beat me severely, but I think they wanted me to survive. Even if only barely." He grimaced—perhaps intending a smile—then he coughed weakly.

"Who did this?" Will asked.

The man shook his head slowly. "I don't know, My Lord. But I think they were working for...for him." He lowered his voice as he said "him".

If Will had any idea who Timms was referring to, he gave no indication.

"They told me to give you a message," the steward went on. He winced a little, clearly not eager to pass it on.

"Speak freely," Will told him. "I won't hold you responsible for whatever they said."

Timms nodded. "They said to tell you that you have no right to be here. They called you a common usurper and an upstart. They promised they will tear down anything you try to build, and kill anyone who tries to help you." He paused. "That was the message." The effort of speaking had clearly exhausted him.

"Thank you, Timms," said Will. "You need to rest now."

Will got up and left the room, Timms's wife trailing behind him. When they emerged from the house, he turned back to her, looking down into her pleading eyes.

"Can you help him, My Lord?"

Will nodded. "One of my men has some skill with healing. He will remain with you, and I will instruct him to help you in any way he can."

Tears of gratitude came to her eyes. She didn't immediately speak.

He lowered his voice. "The people and the livestock are all gone. Do you know where they went?"

She pointed vaguely toward the north. "The men drove everyone away after they burned the barns and the houses. They took the animals with them. Some of them stayed behind though, to beat my husband," she said.

She was wringing her hands, although she seemed unaware of it. A surge of anger washed over Jonas. What was the purpose of this suffering?

"When did this happen?" Will asked gently.

"The day before yesterday, My Lord," she replied.

"Thank you," said Will.

She bowed and hurried back inside.

Will called for one of his men and sent him in after her. Then he turned to Rufe and Jonas.

"Who did this?" Rufe asked, a baffled look on his face.

"I can't be certain," Will replied, "but I suspect that Pisander was behind it."

"Pisander? How could he have done this?" Rufe was clearly struggling to take such a notion seriously.

"It sounds unlikely, I know. But some recent hints have made me suspect it might be true."

"Are we going after them?" Jonas asked.

"That's certainly what they're expecting us to do," Will replied.

This remark took Jonas by surprise, although it shouldn't have. It was exactly the kind of thing Will was given to say. His ability to outguess his enemies was what made him such an effective commander—and such a dangerous opponent.

Will gazed at Jonas and Rufe expressionlessly. "We wouldn't want to disappoint them, would we?" he asked.

AFTER WILL HAD INSTRUCTED his healer to remain behind to care for Timms and his wife, he and the rest of his party left the manor house without delay.

Since then they had been riding hard for several hours.

Jonas rode near Will. "No need for a tracker," he called. "I've never seen a more obvious trail. There's no way they could hide these tracks."

It was hardly surprising. A large group of people driving all their livestock left a trail that a child could recognize.

"They have no interest in hiding their tracks," said Will.

There it was again. The commander might have managed to make sense of all this, but Jonas certainly hadn't.

The afternoon was well advanced when they finally caught sight of a large body of people, accompanied by cattle, sheep, and goats. They appeared to be milling around aimlessly.

Will called to Jonas. "Scout out the immediate area. I don't expect to find any armed men nearby, but we need to check anyway."

Jonas called to a couple of men, and the three of them rode away in different directions.

Will's instinct proved to be correct. None of them could detect any sign of enemies in the vicinity.

As soon as he gave his assessment of the situation to Will, the commander approached the people.

It was obvious that they were greatly distressed.

"Have you been harmed?" Will asked them.

One of the older retainers stepped forward, bowing. "Most of us are well, My Lord," he replied. "But some of our men have been killed, and all of us are grieving."

"How many men attacked you?"

"There must have been thirty of them at least," the man replied. "They came upon us suddenly, and we had no time to arm ourselves. A number of our men resisted—they were killed without mercy." Tears came to his eyes, and he shook his head. "I don't understand it. I have never heard of anything like this happening before."

"I am as surprised as you are," said Will. "If there had been any history of such happenings in Erestor I would have made sure you were well protected. I am sorry for your losses, and for the way that all of you have been treated. Rest here tonight. You can return to the manor house tomorrow. I will leave behind two of my men to assist you. You will need to set up temporary shelters when you arrive. But while that is being done, the older folk and any women with small children should shelter in the house."

"You won't be coming back with us, My Lord?" The old man was clearly dismayed.

"Not yet. We must ride on. We won't stop until we deal with the men who did this."

The man bowed and turned away.

"Two men won't be able to do much to help them," Rufe observed.

"No, they won't," Will agreed. "But we can't spare any more."

Rufe selected two of the men and gave them instructions.

Jonas was puzzled. These people would never settle while they weren't properly protected. As long as they remained fearful, they wouldn't give themselves wholeheartedly to rebuilding.

What was the point in chasing their attackers? They would most likely escape as they had done previously, in which case it would prove to be a futile waste of time. He shook his head helplessly. The decision didn't belong to him.

Will selected two other men and sent them off to find the trail of the attackers.

"Move out!" Will's ringing call spurred the remaining men into action, and they swung in behind him.

"Rufe! I need you to take half the men. Follow us, but stay completely out of sight. We'll make sure our path is obvious. Jonas, you're with me."

Will's purpose in splitting the group wasn't obvious to Jonas, but he didn't voice his questions. Rufe didn't query the order, either. He selected a group of men and halted them. They were soon out of sight.

The men they were chasing had made no initial attempt to hide their tracks, and Will and his group at first were able to follow swiftly. After a couple of hours the tracks veered off toward a hilly region dotted with rocky outcrops. Will drew the men to a halt.

Jonas surveyed the terrain with narrowed eyes. Then he turned to Will. "If I were looking for a good location for an ambush, My Lord, I wouldn't look any further," he said, pointing ahead.

Will nodded. He waved toward the hills ahead. "If you were setting the ambush, where would you lie in wait?" he asked.

Jonas puckered his brows. "I'd look for a place where the path narrows, and passes between two rocky outcrops. And I'd make sure the trail is easy to follow."

Will gave him a lopsided grin. "It sounds like a perfect plan. I only have one question. Will they think we're stupid enough to fall for it?"

"They'll undoubtedly be hoping we're that stupid."

"What would you do in my position?" Will asked.

"I'd try to do something unexpected," Jonas replied.

"Precisely," said Will with a nod. He turned to another of his men and spoke quietly to him. The man quickly rode away, heading back toward Rufe and his group.

Will turned to Jonas. "I need you to ride ahead. When you find the ideal location for an ambush, come back and let me know. Make sure you stay out of range of their arrows."

Jonas nodded. "What then?" he asked.

"It will be time for us to do something they're not expecting."

"What did you have in mind?"

Will simply smiled back at him.

Jonas shrugged. Then he kicked his heels into his horse's flanks and rode forward.

18

"Keep the noise down!" Gareth growled, glaring at the men spread out around him. The persistent murmur of voices, punctuated by bursts of laughter, slowly died away.

These idiots would betray their position if he didn't keep a close check on them. He frowned. A big bag of money was waiting at the end of this job, and nothing would distract him from that. The others shouldn't need reminding—they were mercenaries, too.

He shook his head. Maybe it was time he considered a different line of work. No one lived forever, and mercenaries typically had shorter life spans than most. It was a high risk occupation, even if it did have the potential to deliver big rewards.

The problem was that a mercenary too often found himself doing dangerous jobs for very dangerous people. The man who had organized this expedition was a perfect example. Gareth had the feeling he would do anything—anything at all—if he thought it might advantage him. He wasn't the kind of person you wanted as an enemy.

Gareth's employer called himself Dunnridge, although it almost certainly wasn't his real name. He had known Will Prentis would be traveling to Erestor, and he had hired Gareth because of his reputation for stealth and reliability.

Gareth had concocted the plan to kill Prentis in the forest. He hadn't been dismayed when the attack failed. It had always been possible that the commander would bring a large group of soldiers with him. So he had devised a backup plan. His new plan was designed to reduce Prentis's force, and thereby to tilt the odds in his own favor.

After burying the dead mercenary and sending away those who were wounded, he had led the remainder of his men to Prentis's holdings. As soon as they arrived he had personally supervised the destruction.

Sparing most of the retainers was no act of mercy—he cared nothing for them. He spared them only because Prentis would be forced to offer them protection. That would compel him to divide his force. Once that was done, all that remained was to lure him to his death.

All these schemes might have seemed unnecessarily complicated to some of Gareth's men. But if you were in charge you got to call the shots. And his employer had accurately predicted that it wouldn't be a straightforward task to kill Prentis. Everyone said that the commander lived a charmed life. Gareth intended to put an end to that reputation.

Gareth wondered why Dunnridge wanted Will Prentis dead. He'd presented it as a simple case of revenge, but Gareth wasn't convinced. It didn't smell right. A deeper game was being played here. He was sure of it.

He was smart enough not to inquire too closely, though. Dunnridge had promised a payout that was more than generous, and that was all that mattered in the end.

Gareth gazed off into the distance, allowing his mind to wander. It was definitely time to consider a change. Sometimes he found himself thinking about buying an inn. Something seedy, filled with rough customers with a liking for ale, and plenty of it. And customers who were willing to pay well for other amusements. There would still be risks, but that was true of every profession. And compared to the risks faced by a mercenary, these would be very manageable.

"I see a rider!" The muffled call came from one of the lookouts he had positioned above the other men hidden among the rocks.

Gareth peered out cautiously. The rider halted his horse well before he reached their position and looked ahead warily. The path wound its way upward with rocky outcrops on either side of it. The rocks offered protection throughout the length of the path, so Gareth had positioned his mercenaries near the base of the outcrops. He wanted to keep Prentis's men out in the open, away from the shelter of the rocks where the mercenaries were concealed.

"Stay out of sight," Gareth hissed. "And don't fire at him! We don't want to alert them."

The rider peered ahead for a few moments, then calmly turned his horse around and rode away.

"It doesn't look like he spotted us," said the lookout.

Gareth's lip curled up in a lopsided smirk. "Remember why we're here," he growled. He kept his voice low, but made it loud enough that all of them could hear. "There's only one man we care about—getting the full payment depends on taking him down. The others don't matter."

As the minutes dragged by he could sense the tension slowly building. Something needed to happen, and soon.

"They're coming!"

"Is Prentis among them?"

"Yes. He's riding near the front of the group."

"Are you certain?" Gareth asked. Nothing could be left to chance.

"Yes. I've seen him plenty of times."

"So he's taken the bait. How many did he bring?"

"There's only about ten of them."

Gareth grunted in satisfaction. "So the fool left half of his men with the rabble as I expected. You know what to do."

Their targets disappeared for a moment as a distant boulder hid them from view. Once they emerged from the other side they would almost be within bowshot range. Gareth's men nocked arrows and bent their bows.

No one appeared. Gareth narrowed his eyes, searching for any sign of their quarry. Where were they? His gut began to twist as the moments passed. He peered about uneasily.

He pointed to two of his men. "You and you! Get down there, and find out what's going on." His finger stabbed toward the area where the men had disappeared, then swung wide to either side to indicate that they should approach from the flanks rather than directly. The men nodded, quickly slipping away among the rocks. They were soon lost to sight.

More minutes passed with nothing but silence. The knot in Gareth's gut began to tighten.

A sudden scream of agony behind him shattered the stillness. Gareth spun around to see archers on the rocks above, shooting down at his men. His eyes went wide as a shaft whizzed past his head.

He began scrambling up the rocks to reach the archers. "Follow me!" he shouted. The men around him responded immediately, emerging from their cover and clambering upward.

An arrow whistled past him from behind and bounced off a rock. He stole a glance back over his shoulder. Bowmen had appeared below, releasing a constant stream of arrows toward him and his men. They were caught in crossfire. Shocked speechless, his mind spun as he tried to dream up a way to regain the initiative. Another shriek beside him shattered his concentration. He glanced to one side in time to see two more men go down with arrows in their backs. It was difficult to think straight.

Abandoning any attempt at reason, he threw back his head and bellowed his fury, other voices joining him to swell the sound. He thrust everything from his mind except the need to visit ruin on his enemies. The archers above him were almost in reach. He leaped over the last rock that stood in his way and drew his sword. With a howl of rage he charged at the bowmen.

They drew their own swords and sprang toward him. He thrust

his sword forward, penetrating his opponent's guard. The man went down, and he straightened, ready to find another.

Then an arrow took him in the square of the back, and he pitched forward onto the rocks. Pain overwhelmed his senses. His mind barely had time to register the futility of life before all awareness was snatched away.

* * *

"You did well, Rufe," said Will.

Rufe shrugged. "It took longer than I expected for us to find a way around that outcrop. Then we had to climb to a position above them. But your plan was good, and it played out as you expected."

"You guessed what they would do, My Lord?" asked Jonas.

Will nodded. "It wasn't difficult."

Jonas raised an eyebrow, glancing in the direction of Rufe, who wasn't looking any wiser than he felt.

"What were they trying to achieve?" asked Will. "That's always been the key question." He gazed off into the distance. "The attack in the forest was carefully planned. It appeared to be targeting either me or Rellan. When I saw what had been done to my estate, it became obvious to me that I was the target of both attacks. The attack in the forest failed. Apparently they had another plan ready just in case."

Jonas nodded. That made sense.

"After they came here and destroyed the buildings and forced the people to leave," Will continued, "I had no choice but to pursue them. Once we caught up with the people and the livestock I had some decisions to make. There weren't too many options."

"And none of them particularly good ones," Jonas agreed.

Will nodded. "The first option was to take the people back and stay with them to provide protection. It wasn't a solution, because I can't stay here forever. Before long I would have needed to return to Arnost. If I took all of you with me, it would have left the people without protection, and these men could come back and finish the job."

"And they probably knew you would figure that out," said Rufe.

Will nodded again. "I could prevent that by leaving most of you here. That would have left me largely unguarded, though. They could have attacked me again on my way back to Arnost, and with much better odds than last time."

It all sounded so obvious.

"The other option was to leave the people and go after the attackers. I've never been one to put things off, especially things that need to be dealt with immediately. They undoubtedly concluded I'd choose that option, because it offered me the only chance of finishing this once and for all."

"With your reputation, they would never have doubted it was going to end in a fight," said Jonas.

"So they pressed on until they found a suitable place for an ambush," added Rufe.

"Right," Will agreed. "But they wanted to find a way to tilt the odds in their favor. So they needed to give me some compelling reasons to divide my force before I set off after them. A prudent leader would leave a few men behind to protect the manor house, and a few more to protect the people. Chasing after them with a reduced force would have been hazardous, but I'm known as a man who's willing to take risks."

"But you took almost everyone," said Jonas. "And you divided our force to let them think you'd taken the high risk option and left a lot of your men behind."

Will nodded. "It was still a risk," he said. "But I am a risk taker."

"And you knowingly walked right into their ambush," said Rufe. "Or pretended to."

Will shrugged. "It seems to have worked out," he said.

Jonas stared at the commander. His reputation was well deserved.

"Whoever's behind this will eventually find out that they failed," said Rufe. "Will they try again?"

Will looked thoughtful. "The more important question," he said, "is why they wanted to kill me at all. They went to a lot of effort and a lot of expense. What was the reason behind it?"

"Some nobleman who doesn't like a commoner joining the nobility?" asked Rufe.

It was what Jonas was thinking, but he was glad that Rufe had been the one to say it. It sounded a bit blunt. "That was the reason given in the message passed on by Timms," he offered.

Will didn't look convinced.

"You said earlier you thought it might be Pisander," Rufe said.

Will nodded. "Timms clearly thought so," he said.

"Is that what he meant when he said these men were working for *him*?" Jonas asked.

Will nodded again. "I believe so. He was only guessing of course. But if Pisander was the one behind it, the question is why."

"You were responsible for his arrest," said Rufe. "Now you've taken over his lands. Someone like Pisander would want revenge."

Will didn't appear to be so easily satisfied. "It would seem to be reason enough. But is it the real reason, or just what I'm supposed to think?"

Jonas frowned. Rufe had already offered a perfectly good explanation. Why look further?

Will was clever, but no one could be right all the time. Jonas couldn't help wondering if he was trying to be too clever on this occasion. Why search for another motive?

Will looked troubled. "Where is he getting the money to pay for all these men?"

"Perhaps he had money hidden away," said Jonas.

Will gave no response.

He glanced back in the direction of the manor house. "I'll need to send men to my estate," he said. "They can provide protection and help with the rebuilding. It will have to be a lot of men. Otherwise the same thing might happen again."

"That's going to mean a few more years without a return from your estate," said Jonas.

"It can't be helped," Will replied. "Rufe, send ten men back to the manor house to help the people. Tell them I'll send others from Maranelle."

Rufe nodded and set off to select the men.

"Do you think we'll be attacked again?" asked Jonas.

"I don't think we're in immediate danger," Will replied.

Rufe returned as his ten men were riding away. "What next?" he asked.

"We'll return to Arnost," said Will. "But first we'll head for Maranelle. I have some pressing business to attend to."

<hr>

THE FORMER EARL OF PISANDER had adopted his original name of Dunnridge, although he no longer used the honorific of "Lord". Being reduced to the status of a commoner might have been a bitter slap in the face, but he welcomed it. It helped ensure that his anger continued to burn hot. He never wanted to allow it to merely smolder.

He eventually learned of the demise of Gareth and the other men he had sent after Will Prentis. One of his informants overheard Prentis's soldiers boasting about it in an inn.

He wasn't at all disappointed to hear that none of his mercenaries had survived. There would be no need to pay them. He had, of course, advanced them an initial sum, but the bulk of the money was due only after the job had been completed successfully.

The mercenaries had never been aware of his true agenda, so they couldn't know that they had already largely achieved their purpose. The fact that they had generously done it almost for nothing only made it more satisfying.

They had failed in one important respect, though. Will Prentis was still alive. It was intensely annoying to discover that.

Dunnridge's own downfall had been at the hands of Prentis, an upstart commoner who had since received the title of Lord Torbury. And this Torbury had the effrontery to accept from the king the ancestral holdings of the Dunnridge family. The only thing he deserved was a painful death.

It made little difference, though. Prentis could celebrate his survival as much as he liked. The fool of a commander might think himself so very clever, but he had no idea what was coming. No idea at all.

19

Will had only been in Maranelle for a few hours before he once again stood with the duke on his terrace overlooking the bay.

"Did you find everything in order at your holdings?" the duke asked him.

"Far from it, My Lord," he replied. "A group of mercenaries destroyed almost everything, and carried away my retainers. I've just spent the morning hiring men to help with the rebuilding and to protect my retainers."

The duke frowned. "So it is worse than I feared." He glanced at Will sympathetically. "I am sorry that this misfortune has fallen on you," he said. "Although I suspect that you will be able to bear it better than most."

He gazed out over the bay and sighed. "I have received reports that Lord Burtelen was attacked on his way to Arnost. Fortunately he was accompanied by a sizable escort." He glanced back at Will. "Was that your doing?"

Will nodded. "Yes, My Lord. I made him aware of the attack in the forest on my way to Erestor and advised him not to travel without an escort."

"Then you saved his life. He is returning to Maranelle, and I expect him to arrive in the next couple of days." His eyes narrowed. "It has not escaped me that the attacks have been directed at the most capable of our leaders."

"Are you taking measures for your own protection, My Lord?" asked Will. "You are the most capable of us all. But you are much more than that—you are also an important figurehead."

"I cannot accept your generous assessment of my capabilities, Will. But please don't be concerned on my behalf. I can look after myself."

Will frowned. He sincerely hoped that the duke was treating the situation seriously enough. The kingdom could ill afford to lose him.

"The council meets tomorrow, and I want you to be there," said the duke. "I have my suspicions about some of the minor nobles."

"Do you suspect them of involvement?"

"Not directly. But some of them are opportunists, and a situation like this provides an unusual opportunity for their loyalty to be tested."

"How do you propose to do that?" Will asked.

"There might be a way," the duke replied. "I'm giving it some thought. In the meantime I need your opinion about the other members of the council."

He went on to share his suspicions in some detail.

It was difficult for Will to know how to respond. Some of the duke's suspicions seemed to him a bit unusual. But Will was also aware that he knew little about the local nobility beyond their reputations. The cost of having spent nearly all of his time in Arnost was that he had been almost entirely insulated from the politics of Erestor.

Nevertheless he heard the duke out, and promised to help in any way he could.

As he left, he made a final plea to the duke. "Please don't go anywhere unless you're well protected, My Lord."

"Thank you for your concern, Will," the duke replied. "I'm sure that nothing unpleasant will happen to me."

There was nothing further Will could say. But he left feeling uneasy, unable to shake off a sense of foreboding.

WHEN WILL ARRIVED in the council room the next day he was welcomed by one of the local noblemen and directed to an empty seat at a huge wooden table. A number of other nobles had already arrived. Some of them eyed him curiously. A few faces wore open hostility.

Will was not particularly concerned by their responses. Since being invested as Lord Torbury, he had been on the receiving end of the full range of possible reactions from the existing nobility in Arnost, and he had learned to take it lightly. His elevation to the peerage had been guaranteed to upset the most conservative of the nobility, especially those who had no personal connection with him. Most of the nobles in Arnost had eventually come around. There were some who would never accept it, though, and he knew there was little he could do about that. He had long since decided he wouldn't let it bother him.

The meeting showed no signs of starting, and the steady murmur of background conversation gradually became more pronounced. Noticing his bemusement, one of the nobles who had displayed a neutral face eventually leaned toward Will. "We're waiting for the duke," he whispered. "He's often late."

Will nodded his thanks. If the duke was merely late, Will didn't mind at all.

Then a servant burst into the room, an expression of alarm on his face. He hurried to one of the noblemen and bent low to speak to him.

The buzz of conversation ceased abruptly.

The nobleman rose to his feet unsteadily. "I have just received terrible news!" he said. "The duke has been murdered!"

This announcement resulted in instant uproar. Men sprang to their feet, and many began talking at once. Will sat dazed. He had tried to warn the duke. But to no avail.

Then one of the noblemen turned to Will. "HE is responsible!" he shouted, pointing an accusing finger at the army commander. Will did not recognize the man, but the venom in his look was not new to him. He had endured worse since his elevation first to command of the army and later to the nobility.

His thoughts flew to his conversation with the duke the previous day. The former regent had clearly anticipated something like this, although Will hadn't taken it seriously enough at the time.

His accuser hadn't finished. "The duke himself warned me about this man. He told me that he feared for his own life. He was aware that this would-be nobleman wanted him out of the way—that he would never rest until he had seen it done."

The assertion was ridiculous—surely no one on the council would believe it. But as Will looked around the room he saw uncertainty on many faces. These men did not know him. By contrast, what possible reason could they have to doubt the word of one of their own?

A second nobleman leaped to his feet. "I can confirm Lord Orkan's account," he said. "I was also present when the duke said these things. He warned us not to trust this pretender."

This second accusation was met with silence. All eyes turned to Will.

Another nobleman rose slowly, raising his hands in an appeal for order. "No lord can be condemned without a trial. Even on the evidence of two witnesses."

"This man is no lord, Rutledge," spat Lord Orkan. "He is not entitled to our privileges."

Lord Rutledge's brows bristled. "He was appointed by the king himself," he protested.

"The king will quickly rescind his decision when he is made aware of the truth."

"There must be a trial," Lord Rutledge insisted.

"We will try him, Rutledge, and we will do it promptly. Then he will hang."

The situation was becoming dangerous. Will began to rapidly consider his options.

A third nobleman, Lord Ryde, rose slowly to his feet. The man was known to Will. In their brief interactions he had treated the new Lord Torbury with exaggerated respect. But there was something slippery about him.

All eyes turned to Lord Ryde, and he waited until he had their full attention. "This is not a time for hasty actions," he said calmly. "Lord Rutledge is right, of course. We must follow an orderly process." Will saw a number of heads nodding in agreement.

"However," he continued, "I must warn you that I, too, have been party to similar declarations from the late duke. This Lord Torbury is a dangerous man, and he must be placed into custody immediately. Indeed it is only right to secure him for his own protection. When our countrymen become aware of what he has done, some of them may well be tempted to respond out of anger."

He tilted his head back and contemplated Will haughtily. Then he sniffed. "A man like this is also unpredictable. He is not one of us. He was not raised to an awareness of the weighty responsibilities that come with privilege. We cannot know what other schemes he has been hatching. Restraining him is also a necessary measure for the protection of others."

Will scanned the room with narrowed eyes, his hands clenching and unclenching restlessly. No good options remained to him now.

It was conceivable that he could break free of the council room using force—he was almost certainly the most capable fighter present, and no guards were in evidence. But any such action would be perceived as an admission of guilt. And some of the noblemen around him might be injured if it came to fighting. That would not be a good outcome.

How could he allow these men to deprive him of liberty, though? With the duke assassinated and Lord Burtelen still on his way back to Maranelle, he had nowhere to turn for support.

His enemies had cleverly seized upon the opportunity presented by the duke's demise to maneuver him into a corner.

But were they merely opportunistic? It occurred to him that they might have arranged for the duke's assassination themselves.

Desperate as his own situation had become, his mind rapidly assessed the broader implications. Why was he a target? Some of the possible explanations were obvious. Conservative elements in the nobility had always struggled to accept a commoner among their ranks. Revenge must also be a consideration as long as Pisander remained alive. None of these reasons satisfied him though. In his mind they did not account for the singleminded persistence of the attacks he had endured.

No, something bigger was at stake. But he couldn't immediately grasp what it was, and unless he could quickly find a way out of his current predicament, it wouldn't matter anyway.

Silence filled the room. Will was still sitting at the table. He had not uttered a word, and every person present appeared to be waiting to see what he would do.

Before he could do anything, a commotion was heard outside the council room. Every eye turned toward the door. A collective gasp arose as a new arrival strode through the door. It was the Duke of Erestor. Rufe Sarjant followed closely behind him with ten of Will's men.

Lord Rutledge sat down abruptly. Only Will's accusers remained on their feet, stunned looks on their faces.

The duke studied them silently for a moment. "You have made some bold accusations on my behalf," he said. "Never fear—I heard every word."

His face set hard. "You claim that I feared for my life, that I accused Lord Torbury of evil intent. You are liars. And I will not tolerate your vicious deceptions."

The duke pointed to the three noblemen. "Arrest them!" he ordered.

Rufe barked an order, and his men moved to seize them.

The third accuser—only minutes before so cool and composed—underwent a sudden transformation. His face twisted with fury. "Perhaps you think you have won," he snarled. "You will live to see otherwise!"

"Perhaps we will," the duke replied. "But you certainly will not. I have learned from my past mistakes, and you will suffer the consequences. The three of you will hang at dawn."

The other two conspirators showed no fight at all. Both of them were dragged from the room pleading for mercy.

The duke ignored them.

When the three men had been removed, the duke turned to Will. "My sincere apologies for subjecting you to this farce, My Lord," he said. "I knew we harbored traitors in our midst and could not ignore an ideal opportunity to flush them out."

He stood silently before the remaining noblemen, coolly assessing their reaction. "Many of you are shocked," he said. "A few of you are angry. You have more reason to be angry than you realize. The actions of a few traitors have brought the entire council into disrepute."

Some muttering arose at his words.

"Perhaps you are tempted to think that these men were acting out of spite, grasping an opportunity to bring down a man elevated beyond his station. You might even think that I have over reacted. Make no mistake. What you have witnessed today was treason, and carefully planned treason. Lord Torbury was targeted only because he has repeatedly proven his value to the king. This little drama has been the third attempt on his life since he came to Erestor. His holding has also been almost completely destroyed."

They listened silently, some of them eyeing Will narrowly. He had the feeling they were not entirely convinced.

"I intentionally misled you in allowing you to believe that I had been assassinated. However, it was not entirely fiction. I barely survived a serious attempt on my life today. It should now be obvious to you who was responsible."

The duke had finally managed to convince them. Many of them gaped at him open mouthed.

"And that is not all. I learned yesterday that Lord Burtelen was also attacked as he tried to return to Arnost."

This final piece of news was met with consternation, and he had to pound the table for silence before he could continue.

"Lord Burtelen and I escaped without injury," he told them. "But only because Lord Torbury warned us both not to travel without a large escort. I now offer you the same advice. From now on, go nowhere without the protection of armed men."

His words caused a sensation, and he was eventually forced to shout them down before he could regain their attention. He waited patiently until they fell silent.

"The men I arrested today are merely dupes," he said. "Traitorous dupes deserving of death, but dupes nonetheless. Erestor will not be safe until we have caught and executed the ringleaders."

He dismissed them, and they scurried away like ants seeking the safety of their nests.

When the room had been cleared, the duke sat down with Will and Rufe.

"I am alarmed to hear that you were attacked, My Lord Duke," said Will. "But I am greatly relieved that you escaped harm. And not just for my own sake, although your intervention today was certainly timely."

The duke smiled grimly. "Perhaps you thought me dismissive of your warnings when we met yesterday. I was paying full attention. And I am grateful to you." He shook his head. "We have become relaxed and comfortable in these years of peace and security, and it has made us careless."

"You hinted at a hidden purpose behind these attacks," said Will. "That is also my belief. I have been wondering for some time if the attempts on my life and the attacks on my holdings were intended as a diversion. Someone wants me dead, and if not dead then at least fully occupied and distracted. But distracted from what? I am now impatient to return to Arnost. I am beginning to fear that Erestor was never the target."

"I know nothing with certainty," replied the duke. "But I suspect you might be right. And Lord Ryde's parting comments could be seen as supporting that view."

"We will leave immediately," said Will. "May I request that you take steps to thoroughly secure Steffan's Citadel? And that you instruct the commander there to be ready to close the border between Erestor and the rest of the kingdom at a moment's notice should the need arise?"

"Such requests must surely be based on dark forebodings, Will. I hope you are wrong. Nevertheless I have long since learned to trust your instincts. I will arrange for it to be done. And I will send one hundred Erestorian soldiers with you—men who can fight with both the bow and the sword. I will also instruct them to take with them an abundant supply of arrows. You may have need of both the men and the arrows."

Will bowed a grateful acknowledgment.

The duke had not finished. "You may rest assured that this time the traitors will not escape. Your own men are guarding them now, and I realize you will need them when you depart. I will arrange for them to be relieved by some of my own men—reliable men that I trust. Tonight I will personally interrogate your false accusers. They will hang at dawn as I have promised."

Confident that Erestor was in firm hands, Will left Maranelle a few hours later.

The duke was as good as his word. Will was accompanied not only by his own men, but by a detachment of one hundred soldiers. Their leaders had been personally selected by the duke, and they in turn had been instructed to choose their best men.

Every rider carried a longbow as well as a sword. Each horse bore a plentiful supply of arrows—bundles of arrows had been secured to the saddlebag on one side of the horse, and an easily accessible quiver with a dozen arrows rested against the saddlebag on the other side. Six spare horses with halters also accompanied the riders. Each of them bore specially designed saddlebags that bristled with many bundles of arrows.

The duke was clearly expecting trouble.

Another strong contingent of the duke's men were also accompanying Will as far as Steffan's Citadel. The men destined for the citadel would be posted there for the foreseeable future. They carried specific instructions to close the border between Erestor and the rest of the kingdom.

The gates would be opened for one hour only twice a day—once in the morning and once in the afternoon. Armed men were to be turned away. If any body of soldiers approached, the gates would be closed immediately and would remain closed until the duke ordered otherwise.

Exceptions would apply only to Lord Burtelen and Will.

Will and his men did not pause when they reached the citadel. They rode for Arnost without delay.

Will heard the gates clang shut behind them as they emerged from the pass. There was something portentous about the sound.

Sealing shut the gates of the citadel provided a tangible reminder of the Rogandan invasion. Once more Erestor stood isolated from the rest of the kingdom.

VOLUME 2—THE STORM BREAKS

20

"**D**adda! Come see!"

Thomas, hard at work in the garden, glanced up with a smile. His daughter had apparently found an egg. A steady supply of eggs was just one of the benefits that flowed from the hens pecking around the cabins hidden in the forest. Chickens had been Elena's idea, and once established they had reliably delivered both eggs and fertilizer for the garden.

Elena appeared and knelt down to admire the two-year-old's discovery. "It's beautiful, Tammi," she said, kissing her on the cheek.

Thomas joined them, and hoisted Tamara into his arms, careful not to dislodge the prize in her little hands. After examining it for a moment, he set her down again. "Go and show Papa," he suggested. She ran inside the cabin, calling for her grandfather.

Thomas's hands were covered with dirt from digging. With a cheeky grin he grabbed Elena by the waist and drew her close. She squealed and pulled away, glaring at him through narrowed eyes. She nevertheless blew him a kiss as he returned to work in the garden.

Thomas had worked without interruption for a couple more hours when he heard Elena call his name. She sounded tense.

Curious, he stood up and brushed off his hands. He caught a glimpse of a man on horseback talking to his wife.

"Well, ain't you a perty little thing," the stranger was saying.

Thomas struggled with the tie on the pouch at his belt and reached in for the stone. Then he headed toward the horseman.

Seeing him coming, the man spun his horse around and rode swiftly away through the trees.

Elena's face was pale. "We never see strangers," she said anxiously. "And I'm glad we don't. Something about this one made me shudder."

"Get Tamara and your father!" Thomas replied, his heart pounding. "We need to leave. Immediately! We can grab a few supplies, but there's no time for anything else. Only take what you can carry on horseback."

She stared back at him, stunned into silence.

He lowered his voice. "I was holding the stone," he said. "I saw why he's here."

He ran off toward the stream. "I'll find Haldek! Hurry!" he called back over his shoulder.

He returned with Haldek to a scene of confusion. Tamara was crying, Rubin was trying to comfort her, and Elena was hurrying back and forth between the cabin and her horse, putting items into a large sack. She had saddled her horse, but Rubin appeared to have done nothing to prepare to leave.

"What's going on?" he asked Thomas.

"I'm sorry," Thomas replied. "But we need to leave urgently. We won't be coming back."

"Whatever do you mean?" asked Rubin. Haldek simply looked confused.

"A group of men have been searching for us," Thomas replied. "They just found us. We need to leave now. If we don't, all of us will die."

"But how can you be sure?" Rubin protested. "This is our home. We can't just leave!"

"You must listen to him, Father." Elena's voice was firm. Thomas had rarely seen her so determined. "For now you will just have to trust him," she said.

Thomas gave her a grim smile of appreciation. "We need to be gone within the next few minutes," he said.

"I am not leaving here," said Haldek.

"You must!" said Thomas.

"How many men?" he asked.

"One. But he will soon return with others."

"Maybe not," Haldek replied stubbornly.

Thomas paused for a moment, his mind racing. "Very well," he said. "Let me suggest a compromise. You stay here, Haldek. The rest of us will ride toward Tallesford. We won't attempt to hide our tracks. After the road crosses the river the trail runs across stony ground for many leagues, and hoof prints will not be visible. We will not cross the ford. The river is shallow for a short distance, and we will instead head downstream in the direction of Arnost. We will find a suitable place where we can leave the river, and we will wait for you there."

"For how long?" Haldek asked.

"The men will be here very soon," Thomas predicted confidently. "But if you haven't reached us by morning, we will return to the cabins," he promised.

"It is good," said Haldek, nodding with satisfaction.

"You must stay out of sight," Thomas insisted. "Don't let them see you!"

Thomas could tell that Rubin was still not convinced. But he agreed to the arrangement, and having done so he actively helped Thomas and Elena prepare to leave.

It took much longer than Thomas expected, and he was extremely fretful by the time they eventually mounted up. Tamara sat in front of him, and he had never been more grateful that all four adults had horses of their own.

"Be careful, Haldek!" he called as they rode out.

Haldek frowned back at him. "I am a soldier!" he declared, pounding his chest.

· · ·

HALDEK CAUGHT up with them as the sun was setting, his face red with anger.

"They burn our cabins. Destroy our garden. Even kill our chickens!" he said. "I want to fight them. But they are five, and Haldek only one."

"Were they Rogandans?" asked Rubin.

"No," replied Haldek. "They are speaking your language."

"Did they follow our trail?" Thomas asked.

"Yes. I ride behind them. Their leader say you all go to Tallesford. Just like you want him to think. They cross ford, and they go." Haldek flicked his fingers in the direction of Tallesford. "Then I ride here, along this river."

Rubin shook his head in bafflement. "What possible reason could they have for doing this?"

Thomas shrugged. "Perhaps we are known to be friends of Will. And also of the queen," he said. "I don't doubt that all of them have enemies."

His father-in-law shook his head again. "We have no choice but to leave now," he said. "There's nothing left for us to go back to."

Thomas suspected that neither Rubin nor Haldek would be at all satisfied with what he had told them so far. They must surely be wondering how he could have known so much based on so little evidence.

He moved his horse closer to Elena's. "Do you think the time has come to tell them about the stone?" he asked, keeping his voice low.

"I've been asking myself the same question," she said. "The stone is what's putting them in danger, so maybe it's fair that they know."

They rode in silence for a while. "Perhaps there's another way," she said finally. "Could you tell them what you're able to do, but not explain how exactly you're able to do it?"

"You mean tell them I can see into people's thoughts, but not tell them it's a stone that lets me do it?"

"Yes, I suppose so."

"Maybe. I can try."

Thomas was not sure how quickly the men pursuing them would

discover their mistake. So he suggested they ride on into the evening and stop only when night was well advanced.

They were all weary when they finally made camp. Little Tamara had spent some of the journey sleeping fitfully in Thomas's arms. Back on solid ground again she was soon soundly asleep.

Their location was well hidden, so they decided to risk a small fire. They had brought food, and they sat down together around the fire and shared it.

Thomas glanced at Elena, and she smiled encouragingly at him. He swallowed nervously, then he broke the silence. "I imagine you're wondering how I knew that our visitor would come back. And why these men were searching for us in the first place."

His comment was met with silence, but it was obvious to him that he had hit the mark.

He glanced at Elena. "I've been hiding a secret," he said. "I haven't told you because it's a dangerous secret, and I thought you would be much safer if you didn't know." They looked puzzled, but there was no immediate response. "Hiding it from you hasn't been helping to keep you safe anymore, though."

"I'm wondering if I really want to know," said Rubin. "But I think you should tell us."

Thomas nodded. "It's very likely that the men chasing us know little more than you," he said. "They almost certainly haven't been told the real reason why they were sent to find us."

He took a deep breath. "I have the ability to see what other people are thinking," he said.

Haldek looked doubtful. Rubin simply frowned.

"I won't try to prove it to you," Thomas said. "I long ago decided never to use this ability to pry into the thoughts of anyone close to me. So you are safe from me.

"The visitor who arrived today was different—I examined his thoughts because I needed to know if he was a threat. He turned out to be far more dangerous than I could have imagined. He knows nothing of my gift, but he was looking for me. He was also looking for you, Haldek, although he doesn't know why. He knows all of us have been seen together."

He paused to assess their reaction. Both of them were frowning now.

"They are mercenaries. Their instructions were to kill us all and to bring our bodies back to the man who hired them. Our visitor knew that, but not a lot else."

"Who hired them?" asked Rubin.

"He doesn't know. He was hired by the leader of these men. I doubt that even the leader knows who the real employer is."

"Where did your gift come from?" asked Rubin. He still appeared to be skeptical.

Thomas sighed. "That knowledge is very dangerous. For all of us. Would you be willing to trust me with it?"

Rubin looked at Elena. "Are you aware of this?"

She nodded, blushing as she did. "I'm sorry, Father. I never wanted to have secrets from you."

"I trust you, Elena," he said without hesitation. He turned to Thomas and gazed thoughtfully at him. Then his face softened. "I trust you, too, Thomas. We need speak no more about it."

Thomas glanced across at Haldek, raising his eyebrows questioningly.

Haldek spread his hands. "I know nothing," he said. "So it is easy."

"Where will we go now?" Rubin asked.

"I think we should go to Arnost," Thomas replied. "Briefly, anyway. It isn't a good place to remain hidden for any length of time. But I would like to consult with Will. And my parents would want to meet Tamara."

Elena nodded eagerly. "And I want her to meet them too."

Rubin pondered for a moment, then he also nodded. "And after that?" he asked.

"I don't know," Thomas replied. "I traveled with a soldier—his name is Rellan—who lives in a small community somewhere near Erestor. They are in a remote location, hidden from the world. The people went there fleeing from trouble. They keep to themselves, and I think we would be safe there. Will might know how to find them."

Conversation soon dried up, and they lay down and tried to sleep.

Thomas had a restless night. He'd spent plenty of time on the run, but it felt like long ago. He'd been foolish enough to believe it was all behind him.

They rose before dawn, setting out as soon as they had broken their fast.

They continued their journey toward Arnost without incident for three more days, avoiding roads and any signs of habitation. Twice they came within the vicinity of a village. Each time they gave it a wide berth.

Late on the morning of the fourth day their progress came to a sudden halt.

A fox bolted across the path of Thomas's horse, spooking it. The horse reared up, whinnying shrilly. Tamara had been perched in front of her father, and she was flung from the saddle before he could prevent it. Thomas launched himself toward her, managing to catch and cradle her as they both hit the ground. He landed hard on his back, knocking the wind from him. His head connected heavily with a rock, and his vision filled with stars.

Elena swung down out of the saddle and raced to Thomas and Tamara.

Thanks to Thomas's efforts, their daughter appeared to be unhurt. The toddler stared wide-eyed at her mother for a moment. Then she opened her mouth, filled her lungs, and began to scream. Elena picked her up and tried to examine her injured husband while comforting her.

"Take her somewhere else!" said Rubin, rushing out his words when Tamara paused for breath. "We can tend to him," he said, waving her away.

Reluctantly she followed his advice.

The moment her daughter had calmed down, Elena returned

anxiously to Thomas. His eyes were open, but he looked dazed. He hadn't moved.

Rubin took her aside. "Haldek says he's seen similar injuries on the battlefield," he said grimly.

Elena struggled to remain calm. "What is he expecting will happen?" she asked.

"It's possible that Thomas might lose consciousness," her father replied.

"And after that?"

"It's difficult to be certain," said Rubin.

She had the definite impression he knew more than he was willing to say.

"We have to get help," said Elena desperately.

"Where from?" her father asked. "Who could we ask that will be safe? We've been trying to keep away from people."

"I know. But we can't just leave him like this," she said, tears welling up in her eyes. She continued to agonize uselessly, unable to think of anything worthwhile to do and unable to accept the situation as it was.

Her father moved back and forth restlessly for a few minutes. Then he seemed to reach a decision. "I'm going to find help," he said.

"Where?" she asked.

"I don't know," he replied frankly. "There must be other people nearby. Surely one of them can do something for us."

She looked at him uncertainly for a moment. Then she nodded. They had to try.

Once Rubin had gone, Elena returned to Thomas's side. "How are you feeling?" she asked him softly.

He didn't answer immediately. He appeared distracted. Finally he said, "My head hurts."

Her agitation slowly began to grow. Tamara, apparently sensing her distress, became fretful and demanding. Haldek took it upon himself to distract her, and his antics soon had her giggling uncontrollably. Elena shooed them away to give Thomas some peace and quiet.

The wait felt interminable, but in reality no more than thirty minutes had passed before Rubin reappeared, accompanied by another rider.

Elena saw that the new arrival was a woman, small in stature and clad in bright garments. Large gold earrings flashed brightly beside her dark curls. She was attractive—she might almost have been beautiful were it not for the hardness on her face.

Her mouth curled into a smile. To Elena the gesture appeared forced.

"We don't often see travelers in these parts," she said. "Rubin here tells me that one of your number is injured." She peered down at Thomas lying on the ground. "What happened?"

"His horse threw him when he was riding with our daughter," Elena replied, her voice trembling. "He managed to protect her, but he hit his head."

The woman turned to Elena, scrutinizing her for a long moment. Then she put on a cheerful voice. "I live in a small community," she said, "and one or two among us have some skill with healing. You must bring him to us."

"We can't move him," said Rubin.

"No, he will need to be carried." She paused to think. "I will get help. Wait here until I return."

She wheeled her horse around and rode off.

"I do not like this woman," said Haldek.

"She looks rough. But she seemed sincere," said Rubin hopefully.

Elena didn't reply. Something about the woman made her uneasy, and she didn't feel enthusiastic about her offer of help. But what choice did they have?

Her insides churned unrelentingly. It wasn't just her anxiety about Thomas. Her own responses to the stranger left her feeling extremely uncomfortable. Throughout her childhood she had managed to remain generous in her assessment of other people, even when they were unkind to her. She knew from bitter experience that people were capable of great evil, but she had learned to extend her generosity of spirit even to those who did her harm. Neither had her nature changed when she and her father began to emerge from their self-imposed isolation after meeting Thomas.

Now, desperately in need, she had received an offer of help. Yet she was filled with suspicion and mistrust. What was happening to her?

She was aware that her outlook had shifted when she became a wife and mother. Was she being reshaped by these new responsibilities? Or did the changes signal a more sinister process? Was she gradually becoming hard-hearted, just like so many others in the world around her?

Long after the rider had disappeared, Elena remained rooted to the spot, staring after her.

21

After leaving the injured man and his companions, the woman rode swiftly toward her home. She didn't slow her pace until she reached the outer ring of the camp where she lived.

Twenty five colored wagons stood before her in a field, drawn together into a rough circle. A familiar sense of belonging washed through her as she slid from her horse and stepped among the wagons. This was where her heart lived, among the Clan, among her people.

Her serenity was short-lived though, as it always was. A wave of bitterness surged over her as she glanced around, sweeping away any traces of contentment.

After standing motionless for a moment to settle herself, she strode over to the largest and most brightly painted of the wagons. The Clan's leader sat outside it, brooding over a blazing fire.

He glanced up, a surly look on his face when he saw who it was. "And what have you been doing?" he asked brusquely, spitting into the flames.

"I have been meeting new friends," she said.

"How many of them? Are they wealthy? Are they well armed?"

"There are three men, a woman, and a small child. They are not well armed. They appear to be poor, although they have four good horses. One of the men is injured."

He spat again. "Then we will pay them a visit. I'm sure they'll be delighted to make us a gift of anything of value they might have. At the very least we can find a new home for their horses."

She shook her head firmly, setting her dark curls swaying. "I have invited them to join us. I told them we have healers among us."

His face became red with fury in an instant. "How dare you invite them here? I gave you no such permission!"

Her jaw set stubbornly. "The leadership is not yours by right, Viggor—even if you were elected. So don't expect me to bow and scrape to you."

He pushed himself to his feet and towered over her menacingly. "One day you'll push me too far, Ronya."

She raised her chin defiantly. He might talk tough, but he would never dare to touch her. "I will need a litter. And two men—to carry back the one who is injured."

He made no response. The contempt on his face rendered any response unnecessary. He sat down again, ignoring her.

An angry retort rose to her lips. Somehow she managed to swallow it, inhaling slowly to steady herself.

Viggor's reaction was hardly surprising. She had extended an offer of hospitality to these strangers, a magnanimous gesture that was no more appropriate than it was sincere. It was foolish and empty for her to play at being leader of the Clan.

Without support from Viggor, she would have to find two litter bearers herself. They would need to be men willing to weather the displeasure of their leader. Perhaps Andri might be agreeable.

Could there be another way, though? She turned back to Viggor. "I get a feeling about these people," she murmured. "A lucky feeling." Then she added, "The woman—she is very beautiful."

He studied her with an unreadable expression. Abruptly he stood again and bowed expressively. "How could anyone dismiss a lucky feeling of yours, my lady? You may choose the litter bearers yourself. The Clan will be honored to host your new friends."

Viggor was a fool. And a predictable fool. "The woman is also married with a child. You will keep your wandering hands to yourself."

He snorted. "Or what?"

"Or I will make it my business to see that you regret it."

A scornful look flashed across his face. Then he threw back his head and burst into laughter. "The Clan's fierce little kitten has claws," he said. "I trust that your new friends will not get themselves scratched."

<hr>

THE WAITING HAD BEGUN to feel unbearable. Much as she mistrusted the woman and her offer, Elena now found herself longing for the promised help to arrive.

Her heart pounded in her chest as she peered down at her husband's pale face. How badly hurt was he? Was it possible that he wouldn't recover? She pushed the thought from her mind, refusing even to consider such a possibility. She placed a hand on her heart and sent a fervent prayer into the heavens. Surely there must be something that could be done for him.

As she stared anxiously at him, Thomas's lips moved weakly, and he shifted his gaze to her. He groaned.

She bent low to caress his brow. "Thomas!" she whispered tenderly.

"Where am I?" he asked, his voice weak. "I can't see properly. Everything's blurry. What happened?"

"You hit your head when you fell. But you saved Tamara from harm."

He peered back at her. He seemed to be struggling to grasp what she was saying.

"Help is on the way," she added.

Something must have penetrated through the haze, because a

frown slowly came over his face. "The stone," he said, slurring his words. "Can you get it?"

His question startled her. He was right, of course. He couldn't be expected to protect it while he was incapacitated. And they couldn't allow the woman and her people to get their hands on it.

She fumbled at the drawstring of his pouch, eventually freeing it. Then she took out the stone.

"Take it," he breathed.

"I will keep it safe for you," she promised.

"No," he said slowly, wincing as he tried to shake his head. He went quiet for a moment. Then he murmured, "I want you to have it."

Her eyes grew wide with alarm. "No! I can't!" Keeping the stone safe for Thomas was one thing; receiving it as a gift was another matter entirely. She had no desire to bear the burden of its revelations.

The effort of speaking had come at a cost. His eyes rolled up, and his head lolled to one side.

Thoroughly alarmed, she put her ear to his mouth. To her profound relief he was breathing steadily.

After a few moments he stirred again, opening his eyes. She was still bending over him. "You must take it," he said with an effort. His eyes fluttered closed once more. "I give it to you," he breathed.

Her life changed forever in a single moment.

A flood of sensations swept over her, leaving her gasping in shock. Thomas's inner world lay exposed, his thoughts and memories naked to her gaze. Her entire body froze. Even as it did so, her mind was racing—probing, absorbing, analyzing. She did it instinctively and without conscious thought, unable at first to prevent herself.

Then Elena's self awareness forced its way past the overwhelming deluge of impressions, and her will reasserted itself. Registering too late what she had been doing, she shook herself free of her paralysis and spun away from Thomas.

She could immediately have prevented herself from staring at Thomas had she understood exactly what he was intending. But she had been caught entirely off guard, and her response had been involuntarily. Did that absolve her for not turning away more quickly though?

In her heart she felt that she had violated him, and a flush of shame flooded her face.

She knew that Thomas had managed to avoid doing this to her— she had seen it in his memories. Her own sense of betrayal distressed her beyond words.

Having first been weighed down by anxiety, she now found herself confronted by an ugly set of unfamiliar emotions—her suspicion of the woman, and now shame at her own behavior. The tranquility that had always defined her lay shattered. Her whole world had tilted, in just a few hours.

Once Elena had witnessed a small boat drifting unattended down a river. She felt as if her inner self had broken loose from its moorings.

She glanced at the stone, nestling in her palm. It appeared so innocent and attractive, so small and insignificant. But its potency appalled her. Thomas had made her aware of the stone's capabilities, but nothing could have prepared her for the reality. She hadn't gone close to guessing at the extent of its power, or imagining the impact it would have on her.

She closed her hand over it, extinguishing its gleam, and thrust it into a hidden pocket in her clothing.

It would remain there, untouched. Because she was never going to use it again, no matter what happened.

RONYA RETURNED to find that the little group had not moved. They seemed relieved to see her, but at the same time she couldn't help noticing the wariness in their response. They had reason to be wary —more than they could know.

"My name is Ronya," she said brightly.

"I'm Elena," the young woman replied. "Thank you for your willingness to help us." Her tone was humble, and she was clearly worried about her husband. But Ronya nevertheless saw that she was very much in two minds about the offered assistance.

Elena pointed out each of the others in turn. "You've met my father, Rubin. This is our friend, Haldek. My daughter here is Tamara. And you've already seen my husband, Thomas."

Was it her imagination, or had Elena emphasized the word husband? Ronya ignored it, smiling an acknowledgment.

She introduced the two men who had ridden in with her. "This is Andri, and this is Olver."

Andri and Olver nodded to the others without speaking, their eyes lingering on the young woman.

Elena's beauty was impossible to ignore, and Ronya felt the sharp pangs of envy. She herself was not unattractive—she had seen the way men looked at her. But alongside this young woman? Could the moon outshine the sun?

The men dismounted and placed the now unconscious Thomas onto a litter they had brought with them. Elena supervised the process anxiously, her child perched on her hip.

Ronya studied her attentively, all the while pretending disinterest. When they had first met, Elena seemed anxious and on edge. Now she was restless as well, unable to remain still for more than a moment. Ronya noticed her sucking in sharp breaths and pushing them out slowly between clenched teeth. She gave every appearance of being deeply troubled. Ronya took careful note, wondering how she might make use of this information.

Andri and Olver set off for the camp, carrying the litter between them. Ronya took their horses in tow and rode behind them at a slow walk. The other strangers mounted and followed her.

The terrain became rough at times. At one point the men stumbled, almost tipping the patient off the litter. He stirred, mumbling incoherently, although his eyes didn't open.

"Be careful!" she snapped at the bearers. Then she frowned, unsettled by her own reaction. She had claimed she had a lucky feeling about these people, and she had told the truth. Why then was she so brittle? Perhaps it was her frustration over Viggor's leadership.

Or could it be the provocation of the young woman's beauty? Ronya chewed at her lip, annoyed at being so easily discomposed.

The bearers soon needed a break. Rubin and Haldek offered to share the burden, and the journey resumed. With the two pairs of men alternating, they were able to continue without interruption.

After a night in the open, they reached the camp late the following day.

Viggor came forward to greet them.

"Welcome, weary travelers!" he said. "Please, set your injured friend down over here. Our healers will examine him very soon. I am Viggor, and I lead these people. I will invite our good Ronya to introduce you all."

Viggor's false congeniality irritated Ronya more than ever, but she nevertheless obliged, naming each person in turn. As she had expected, Viggor's full attention was captured by Elena. Ronya's eyes narrowed as he flashed the young woman his oily smile and overflowed with his insincere benevolence.

"I do have one request," said Viggor regretfully. "We are unable to welcome visitors to our camp if they are carrying weapons. I am sure you will understand. I trust you will allow my men to examine you and your possessions. Any weapons will, of course, be returned to you when you leave us."

He nodded to Elena congenially. "Please do not be concerned. I would never permit any of my men to approach you," he said, beaming her a smile. "I am certain that Ronya can oblige."

None of the travelers looked at all happy, but they were smart enough to recognize that they had no choice but to submit. The men were searched first, very thoroughly. Few weapons were found, but every item of any possible value was promptly removed, "Purely for safe keeping," as Viggor explained apologetically.

Even the unconscious Thomas was meticulously searched. The pouch at his belt attracted special attention, but it proved to be empty.

If the travelers had been carrying items of value on their journey, they had clearly hidden them before Ronya returned. Such a possibility would certainly occur to Viggor. If they had secreted items of value, he would find an effective way to motivate them to reveal the location. She didn't doubt that he would quickly obtain their enthusiastic cooperation.

She thought it unlikely they had anything to hide. Apart from their steeds, they appeared to possess nothing of value.

The horses were a notable exception. They were fine animals, and all of them were in excellent condition. At least one of the travelers understood how to care for horses. She wondered how they had acquired them. Perhaps they were stolen. Something told her that was unlikely.

By the time the men had been searched, the true nature of Viggor's hospitality must have been obvious to them all.

Only Elena remained.

Ronya approached her. The young woman's face was expressionless, but she appeared to be struggling to keep it that way. A careful search at first revealed nothing at all of interest. Then Ronya felt a lump within her clothing. It was so small she had almost missed it. Could it be a precious gem? She immediately focused her entire attention on uncovering it.

The object had been secreted in a hidden pocket, and Elena's obvious alarm at its discovery only intensified Ronya's interest. As she removed it, Elena lunged forward and snatched it away from her. As she did so, her eyes went very wide. She glanced first at Ronya, then at Viggor, then down at her hand as Ronya grabbed her wrist, determined to wrest it from her grasp.

The young woman clearly had little experience of physical violence. It took only moments before she cried out in pain and released the object. It fell to the ground and disappeared in the dirt, buried by their scuffling feet.

Ronya got down on her hands and knees and poked around until she felt something small and hard. Standing up again, she dusted if off and held it up with great anticipation. She frowned in disappointment. It was only a small stone. Its coloring gave it an attractive appearance, but it was otherwise unremarkable. It was almost certainly worth nothing.

Was all the fuss about this small stone? A glance at Elena confirmed that it was. The young woman stood before her with a pitiful expression of dismay twisting her lovely face.

"What is it?" Ronya asked, unable to account for the misery caused by the loss of such an insignificant object.

"It's a family heirloom," Elena replied, grimacing as she rubbed her wrist.

Ronya stared at it, frowning. It wasn't hard to believe that the stone had no worth at all apart from sentimental value.

"It doesn't belong to you!" Elena exclaimed indignantly, glaring at Ronya.

Ronya looked up. "It does now," she said, staring coldly back at her.

Until that moment, Ronya had been considering returning it to her. Now she was determined to keep it, if only to spite her rival.

The young woman's face twisted with anger, or maybe fear. The emotion, whatever it was, looked entirely out of place on her.

The clanswoman glanced at her contemptuously. Clearly Elena had lived an untroubled life—she had never needed to face the hardships that Ronya had endured. Every benefit that came with great beauty was hers to enjoy, and she could probably make a reasonable claim to virtue as well, questionable though its benefits might be. But she was weak. And from now on she would have to do without her little heirloom.

22

Elena stood behind a small wagon, pacing back and forth restlessly as she gazed up into the night sky. It had become clear to her that the responsibility for finding a way out of their current predicament rested on her shoulders, and hers alone. And she knew she would never find a solution if she wasn't able to take control of her own emotions and reactions.

All was silent in the camp. At that moment the world around her was at peace. Her own sense of inner peace had deserted her. She had been in turmoil even before they arrived at the camp of the Clan.

It was time for that to change. She had faced trouble before, and she had never allowed it to define her. Her troubles might have multiplied from the moment Thomas was thrown from his horse, but the same choices were still available to her.

The wagon beside her had become a temporary home for the little group. It was adequate, if a bit crowded, and it was at least providing shelter for Thomas. The previous occupant—an elderly man well past his prime—had vacated it to make way for them, moving in with the family of his daughter instead. The elderly man and his daughter were not at all satisfied with the arrangement, but Viggor had not offered them a choice.

True to Ronya's promise, healers from the camp had tended to Thomas soon after their arrival. Elena quickly warmed to them. The healers were a married couple with no children of their own, and they seemed genuinely caring. They had not been alarmed by Thomas's condition, and they had every expectation that he would fully recover in a few days if he continued to enjoy quiet and rest.

Thomas had regained consciousness soon after they reached the camp. He had spent much of the day sleeping, but he was lucid when he was awake. Thankfully he had accepted without question the need to rest. He reported that his head was pounding much of the time, and the discomfort was undoubtedly contributing to his meek acceptance of being confined to bed.

Elena had not told him about the stone. She knew he would have wanted to do something to retrieve it. Any such attempt would likely prove dangerous, and it would certainly do nothing to promote his recovery.

Rubin had quietly taken responsibility for his granddaughter. Throughout their first full day in the camp Tamara played happily with the other children, watched over by Rubin. Elena was grateful for his help—she had far too many things on her mind.

They had little contact with members of the Clan. Ronya had sauntered by a couple of times. After what had happened with the stone, Elena found it difficult even to be civil with her. She knew, though, that her attitude and approach to Ronya was the first thing that needed to change.

Even if she was struggling to feel sympathy toward the clanswoman, Elena did at least understand her. In the moments before the stone had been forced from her grasp, Elena had been able to rapidly scrutinize the thoughts of both Ronya and Viggor. Although further investigation was now impossible, she had come away with an abundance of insights to draw upon. She was under no illusions about Viggor's true intentions and motivation, and she fully comprehended the reasons why Ronya was behaving as she did.

After her mistake with Thomas, she had vowed never to use the stone again. She was now seriously considering the unhappy possibility that the stone might offer the only way she could extricate them from this situation.

ELENA RETURNED with Tamara from a walk across the fields to find Thomas out of bed and sitting up eating some food.

Tammi ran to him, a happy cry on her lips. "Dadda!"

Elena watched on with a smile as the little girl reached up and kissed him on the cheek. Then she ran off to find the other children.

"How are you feeling?" Elena asked.

"Much improved," he said brightly. "I expect I'll be able to ride again soon. We should be able to leave before long—maybe even tomorrow."

Elena had said nothing to Thomas about the reality of their situation there, and clearly her father and Haldek hadn't either. She had especially avoided any hint about the loss of the stone, out of fear of threatening his recovery.

She'd never been good at hiding her emotions, though.

"What's wrong?" he asked, a frown of concern appearing on his face.

Her stomach twisted as she stared at him. What should she say? Was it fair to hide the truth from him? She sighed in resignation, simply unable to do it.

It all came out in a rush. "They searched us when we arrived here. They took everything of value, especially the horses. We're little more than prisoners." She paused, trying to steady herself. "And Ronya found the stone. She's taken it."

Tears had begun to well up in her eyes as she was speaking, and now she began to sob quietly. Thomas had entrusted the stone to her care, and she hadn't been able to keep it safe even for two days.

Thomas came and held her close. "I will get it back," he said fiercely.

She pulled away from him. "No, no! You mustn't!" she cried. She had seen into their minds, and she knew what they were like. Especially Viggor. Thomas must never find out what Viggor had in mind for her.

"Please," she said, "you have to let me do it."

"But how?" he asked, holding his head and slowly shaking it.

"See!" she said. "You'll hurt yourself."

She took a deep breath to calm herself. "I was able to look into the minds of both Ronya and Viggor," she told him. "I believe there's something I might be able to do."

"What?" he asked, frowning doubtfully. He didn't look well. These problems were more than he could reasonably be expected to cope with at that moment.

"I need you to trust me, Thomas. Can you do that?" she asked plaintively.

He had never been able to resist her when she pleaded with him.

He sighed deeply, then nodded slowly in resignation and lay back down on his bed. The fact that he had given in so easily said a great deal about how far he still needed to go before he could say he'd recovered.

She had told him there was something she might be able to do. As soon as she rose the next morning she would attempt it.

Viggor had ridden out of the camp at dawn with two youths, and Elena had overheard someone saying that he wasn't expected back before nightfall. Elena had been waiting for much of the morning for the right opportunity to talk with Ronya. When she noticed the clanswoman striding alone through the field not far from their wagon, she felt sure that her moment had finally arrived.

Elena hurried toward the brightly clad woman.

"Ronya, may I please speak with you?" She was trying hard not to tremble.

The clanswoman paused, looking Elena up and down with casual disinterest. Finally she shrugged. "If you have something worth saying," she said, "then say it." Her tone suggested she had no expectation whatever of hearing anything of value.

"You hate Viggor," Elena began tentatively, trying not to notice the suspicious glare that came immediately to the eye of the other woman. "You hate him because by rights he should not be Clan leader. The succession should have passed to you."

"Who told you this?" Ronya demanded angrily.

"No one told me. I had no need to be told," Elena replied, somehow succeeding in her efforts to keep her voice calm.

The clanswoman snorted. "So you are claiming you have the Sight?" she said, curling her lip sarcastically.

"Viggor got you out of the way. For long enough for him to be appointed instead. And now that an appointment has been made, nothing can be done about it."

Ronya scowled. She clearly was not impressed. Elena could have learned this information from anyone in the little community with a loose tongue. More would be needed.

"And you are interested in Andri," she continued. "You believe he is interested in you, too, and you're upset and disappointed by his failure to take any initiative." She paused. "Would you like me to continue?"

At first Ronya had been shocked at the mention of Andri's name, but her surprise rapidly transformed into fury. Before Elena could blink, Ronya had a knife at her throat. "Who have you been speaking to?" she hissed. "Have you dared to spread these lies?"

"I have spoken to no one," said Elena, trying desperately to remain calm. "I have no desire to embarrass you. I only wanted to get your attention." She strained her eyes downward toward the knife without daring to move her head even slightly. "I appear to have succeeded," she said uncomfortably.

The clanswoman held her position for a moment longer, then she lowered the knife and stepped back a pace. "Very well, you have my attention," she said. "Why do you want it?" Her voice was steady, but it held a tone of menace.

"I can help you, Ronya," Elena said. "If you will let me."

"You? Help me? How?" Ronya spat dismissively onto the ground.

"Before I tell you, I have two conditions." The words tumbled out, in spite of Elena's attempts to settle herself.

Ronya's eyes narrowed. "I could just slit your throat right now."

Elena shook her head. Why did Ronya have to be so stubborn? "You would be the loser," she retorted.

"What are your conditions?" the clanswoman asked.

Elena found that she had regained her courage. "First, when I have helped you, you will freely allow us to leave with our horses and all of our possessions."

"And the second condition?"

"You return my heirloom to me, right now." Her voice held steady, and her gaze didn't waver. It was her turn to be stubborn.

A calculating glint came into Ronya's eye. "You seem very interested in this heirloom," she said suspiciously. "Could it be that your second sight is granted by this little stone?"

"You should be able to answer that question yourself," returned Elena boldly. "You're the one who has it." She placed her hands on her hips. "Has it made you any the wiser since you stole it from me?"

The clanswoman frowned. After a moment's hesitation, she reached down and lifted a finely wrought chain from beneath her clothing. A clasp hung from the chain. She had mounted the stone on it and fastened the chain around her neck. The clasp had been fashioned from a thin sheet of gold with four tiny arms to hold the stone in position.

The clasp spun lazily on the chain, the glitter of the stone alternating with golden flashes from the clasp.

Elena held out her hand for it, a frown of determination on her face.

Ronya hastily tucked it away again. "I'm not going to give it to you," she said mockingly. "You've done some clever guessing, but you've done nothing to benefit me. Why should I do anything at all for you?"

"Look, Ronya," said Elena, frustration rising in her voice. "Your healers have cared for my husband, and we're grateful for that. But that doesn't excuse what you've done. You came to us when we were vulnerable and in need, and you lured us here with offers of help. All you ever intended was to rob us! You and your people have taken everything we had. Everything! And don't imagine I'm ignorant about Viggor's intentions toward me!" An involuntary shudder shook Elena's body. She closed her eyes for a moment, trying to push the memory of Viggor's thoughts from her mind.

She opened her eyes again and frowned at Ronya. "I've already proven to you that I have second sight. And I'm willing to use that ability to help you, even though most people would call me crazy for even considering it. But you seem determined not to give me a single reason why I should."

Elena set her jaw. "You might have been defrauded of your birthright, but no one forced you to spend your energy preying on the helpless and unwary. I thought I glimpsed something more than that in you. But if you want my help, you're going to have to show me I wasn't just imagining it."

Ronya was silent.

Elena threw her hands into the air. "What have you got to lose?" she asked. "My heirloom is of no use to you. And any dealer in gems would tell you that your gold clasp is worth more than the stone you've mounted onto it."

Ronya lifted out the stone once more and stared at her for a long moment. Then she shrugged. Removing the chain from her neck, she handed it to Elena.

"Take it," she said. "I'm giving you what you wanted—now it's your turn. I'll be watching you. And I'll be very eager to see what you do for me in return. It better be good." Her face went hard. "Don't imagine I'm giving it to you permanently, though. You'll return it to me when the sun sets tonight. Or..."

Elena looked Ronya in the eye as her hand closed over the stone. "Or you will take Tammi away from me until I give it back," she said with a sigh, placing the chain around her neck and hiding the stone beneath her own clothing. "I know what you're thinking, Ronya. It isn't necessary for you to tell me."

Ronya's startled eyes stared back at her. The clanswoman was impressed, and it showed on her face.

Elena no longer needed visual clues to guess at her reactions, though. With the stone in her possession, she knew exactly what was going on in the other woman's mind.

She turned on her heel and headed back to the wagon.

Thomas was waiting for her. "I stayed out of sight," he said, "but I overheard that entire conversation." His eyes shone with admiration as he drew her close. "You were incredible, Elena!"

She smiled gratefully at him. After the blows she had sustained over the last few days, his support came as a welcome relief. He held her tightly, and she allowed her anxiety and weariness to fall away as she relaxed into the familiar security of his love.

And his encouragement was timely too, because she knew that a challenging day lay ahead of her.

ELENA WAS EXHAUSTED by the time she finally returned to the wagon that night. Only Thomas had waited up for her—the others were already asleep. He embraced her, his eyes full of concern, then he encouraged her to lie down and sleep. Thankfully he seemed to understand that she had no energy left to talk about what she had been doing.

She had spent the afternoon moving from wagon to wagon, studying people as she spoke to them, men as well as women. By the time she had finished the entire camp was buzzing.

Her actions had been motivated by a single purpose. The stone's brief insights into both Viggor and Ronya had exposed an injustice, and also revealed a possible way of making it right. And she had told Ronya the truth—she had seen that there was more to the clanswoman than her actions had so far suggested. That insight had prompted Elena to do what she could to right the wrong, in spite of the way that Ronya had behaved toward her and her family.

Before returning the stone to Ronya, her final visit had been to

Andri. He glanced up when she arrived at his wagon, then nodded her to a seat beside his small fire.

"Why haven't you told her how you feel?" Elena asked him gently.

His brows drew together, but he had nothing to say.

It was immediately clear to him that his intimate feelings were no secret to her, but he wasn't offended by her directness. She knew, because she had the stone.

Elena decided to steer in a different direction. "Her situation offends your sense of justice," she said.

He shrugged. "What can anyone do?"

"There is something that could be done," she said. "Let me make you aware of it."

She began to speak quietly, her words weaving a tapestry that portrayed what was and what still might be. A faraway look came to his eyes as he listened, and he leaned back, the tension in his body slowly easing.

When finally she halted, weary and depleted, he removed his cap and got to his feet, his face glowing with a new light. He bowed respectfully to her, then stood silently as she hurried away to meet Ronya.

It quickly became apparent that Ronya was well aware of what had been happening around her. Her eyes were wide with awe when Elena approached her. The clanswoman would not have refused if Elena had insisted on keeping the stone, but they had made an agreement, and that was enough for Elena.

The stone had done everything she asked of it. But it had also done much more than she expected. As she spent time with each of the Clan members, its revelations had aroused her compassion as never before. She was beginning to see that it held almost limitless potential to bring about changes for good in people's lives.

She handed it over to Ronya with mixed feelings. A large part of her was relieved to be rid of it. At the same time, she had gradually become attuned to it, learning to hold her ground against the deluge of impressions, to sift through the emotions and memories to find what she needed. Never could she have imagined the depth and complexity of the mind of another person—the accumulated years of experiences, good and ill, and the far-reaching consequences of the ways each person had chosen to respond to those experiences.

It was completely overwhelming. How could she possibly manage to disengage from it all?

Elena crawled into her bed utterly spent. Never before had she talked to so many people in a single day. Given her reserved nature, it was surely one of the most difficult things she had ever done.

She wondered if she would sleep at all that night. Nevertheless sleep took her almost from the moment she climbed beneath the blankets.

23

The sun was shining brightly when Elena finally awoke the next morning. Thomas was already out of bed, and he greeted her with a happy smile and a warm and lingering embrace.

"I feel almost normal," he said. He looked it, too.

There was to be no chance to celebrate his recovery, though. At that moment Ronya appeared. "I need to speak with you, Elena," she said. She sounded tense.

Elena smiled at Thomas, then she stepped out of the wagon and followed Ronya a short distance into the field beside it.

"I've just learned something," said Ronya. "Something that might be of great importance to you." Her face was grim. "I've found out that one of the clansmen encountered some men a few weeks ago. They were searching for a small group of people, and they offered a reward for information about them. The group supposedly included a young married couple and two older men, one of the men Rogan-dan." She glanced significantly toward the wagon.

"Viggor has recently heard about this—that's why he left the camp yesterday. He didn't find the men, but he thinks he knows where they might be, and he's planning to send his sons to meet with them. He returned to the camp this morning to make sure none of you leave. He wants the reward!"

Elena's mouth hung open in dismay.

"I don't doubt that he also hopes to find a way to get the reward and keep you as well," she added darkly. "In the meantime, though, you need to come with me. You stirred up a hornet's nest yesterday. The people have been gathering, and trouble is brewing."

Elena called to Thomas, asking him to bring Rubin and Haldek. Then she followed Ronya, doing her best to push the alarming news to the back of her mind.

The entire Clan had gathered in the space between the wagons. As Elena appeared with Ronya, a murmur went up. Thomas came and stood beside her, followed by Rubin with Tamara and Haldek.

"Ronya is a fool," Viggor snarled. He stabbed an accusing finger at the new arrivals. "She brought these people here! They've done nothing but abuse our generosity. But I've learned the truth. They are fugitives, fleeing justice!" He turned to two of his men. "Seize them!"

The murmuring became loud calls of anger as the men stepped forward.

"She has the Sight!" called a voice.

"Do you dare to bring bad luck on us all?" cried another.

Viggor watched on with fury as his men backed away. "Are you cowards?" he shouted.

At that moment Andri stepped forward. "You are not the rightful leader of the Clan, Viggor," he said calmly.

Viggor scowled at him. "I was appointed by the gathering in the ancient way," he said.

"After you arranged for Ronya to be drugged so she couldn't participate," said Andri.

"That is a lie," spat Viggor. "And even if you could prove it, which you cannot, the decision of the gathering is binding."

"Yes, it is binding," Andri replied. "But our laws allow for the leader to be challenged."

"A ritual challenge, with knives?" Viggor laughed contemptuously. "Let Ronya challenge me if she dares."

"Our laws also provide for the challenger to be represented by a champion," said Andri.

Viggor's eyes narrowed. "Who told you this?"

Andri did not respond.

"Let the Law Keeper speak," someone said.

All eyes turned to an old woman, her face wizened with age. She rose slowly to her feet. "That condition has always been a part of our law," she called in a thin voice. "Perhaps it is not well known, but it has never been a secret." She sat down abruptly, shaking her head.

Viggor's eyes sought out Elena.

Others saw it too. "She knew," a voice called from among the gathered Clan. "She has the Sight."

Looking back at Viggor, Elena saw raw hatred in his face. In spite of his lustful intentions, he would have killed her then and there if he dared—that much was obvious to her, even without the stone. But the people of the Clan would never permit it. Not when they believed she had the Sight.

She had established her standing in just one afternoon, and with very little effort. She made no attempt to manipulate anyone. Nor had she tried to influence them to act in any particular way. She had done nothing more than show concern.

Sitting down with individual family members, she had probed their thoughts and memories as they conversed. As she had done with Andri, she quickly gained their respect by mentioning innocent secrets known to them alone, then proceeded to reveal things they were not aware of.

She had set out to reveal mysteries hidden deep within them that she believed they would benefit from knowing. She had done it in her own gentle way, choosing only to disclose insights that would encourage and restore them.

She hadn't lingered—she had soon moved on. Within a few hours she had bonded deeply with many of the adult members of the Clan. Word of mouth had done the rest. Glancing around at them now, she had no need of the stone to see that these people would never allow harm to come to her. Viggor was not without his supporters, but they were a small minority, and most of them also held her in awe.

If only Viggor knew, it was his own mind that had provided her with the crucial information about their laws. He was well aware of the right of a challenger to appoint a champion, and he had done everything he could to keep it quiet.

He had also persistently used his influence as leader to weaken Ronya—to isolate her and keep her wrong footed. He arranged for some of his supporters to whisper to Andri that Ronya secretly despised him. Others went to Ronya pretending that Andri had confided in them. They claimed that he had no interest in her.

Viggor intended to ensure that even if the relevant provisions of their law came to light, none of the Clan would ever consider championing Ronya.

His scheming could not be hidden from the stone, though. And it took little more than a few well placed words from Elena to quickly undo much of the damage done by the whispering.

"Ronya is the rightful leader of the Clan," said Andri loudly. "I challenge Viggor on her behalf."

He did not wait for a response. He slowly stripped to the waist, exposing his muscular physique. One or two of the older women whistled their appreciation. He ignored it.

Andri was powerfully built. He had the frame of a fighter, and his jaw was set with determination. After pounding his massive chest, he reached down for a pair of knives, carefully balancing one in each hand. Then he began to feint forward and back, stabbing and slashing in precise motions. His face was calm, but Elena could see that fierce anger bubbled not far beneath the surface. Andri had a point to prove.

Viggor went pale. He was a big man, but he had established himself by cunning rather than by physical prowess.

He also had the right to appoint a champion. But Elena already knew that the Clan boasted no fighter to compare with Andri. And she guessed that none of them—including Viggor's supporters— would risk their chances against Andri. Not for Viggor's sake.

There could only be one possible outcome from the looming fight. And in spite of Viggor's dishonor and deceit, Elena had no desire to see him or anyone else die that day.

She stepped forward. "There is no need for blood to be spilled," she called, trying to keep her voice steady. "Your law provides another way."

No one said a word.

"Viggor can yield to the claim. He can separate himself to establish a new camp. He must go far away—a journey of at least five days. But he need not go alone. He has supporters who can help him."

She turned slowly, facing each of his supporters in turn. Some of their faces colored quickly. Others glared back at her with angry expressions. But she continued until every one of them had been clearly identified.

Elena's action had been carefully considered. Viggor might accept her compromise while quietly instructing a few of his followers to remain with the larger group to undermine and spy on Ronya. Elena had preempted any such ploy by openly identifying every one of them. No one would doubt the accuracy of her insights. She knew where their loyalty lay. She had the Sight.

Her words hung in the air. Andri stood silent, waiting for a response from the leader.

After a long pause, Viggor turned and spat on the ground. "I will go," he said. "For years I have selflessly served the interests of this camp, and this is how I am to be repaid? Your disloyalty shames you. You are not worthy of my leadership."

Then he pointed at Elena. "You have torn our Clan apart. But your turn will come. You are being hunted, and every hour brings the hunters closer. I will make sure they know where to find you."

Her heart skipped a beat. She was careful not to show it.

He glared at her poisonously. Then he spat again, turned on his heel, and left. His supporters followed close behind him. All of them quickly began to prepare their wagons for departure.

Those who remained gathered around Ronya immediately to

anoint her as their leader. They drew Elena into their midst, and it was some time before she managed to steal away.

Noisy celebrations had begun, and as Elena left the revelers, she saw that gaps had appeared in the circle of wagons. Viggor and his supporters had already departed.

Spotting Rubin, she ran to him. "We need to leave!" she said urgently.

He nodded. "We've saddled our horses. We're ready to go right now," he assured her.

"There is one thing I need to do first," she said. He nodded as she ran back to find Ronya.

Andri stood at her side, her hand clasped firmly in his own. Their faces were glowing.

"Ronya, I must speak with you."

Ronya smiled at Andri, then left him and followed Elena away from the celebrations.

"We must leave," said Elena. "Viggor did not speak truly—we are not fleeing from justice. But the men pursuing us do not wish us well."

"You have used your gift to benefit us all, and I honor you for it," said Ronya, bowing her head. "It has also earned you a new set of enemies. We will help you in any way we can."

"If the men who are hunting us arrive here," said Elena, "perhaps you could send them in a different direction from the one we will take."

"Gladly," said Ronya with a smile.

The new Clan leader gazed upon Elena with respect in her eyes. "I thought you were weak," she said, "and I held you in contempt. I was jealous of your beauty, too. But you have shaken me."

She shook her head in wonder. "I was raised to lead the Clan, but the opportunity was stolen from me. You have given me a chance to fulfill my birthright. And thanks to you, the man I love is now standing beside me as well." She stole a glance across at Andri. He caught her glance and grinned back at her.

"All my life I have witnessed violence, scheming, and unscrupulous behavior from everyone around me. I believed there was no other way to accomplish anything worthwhile. Yet you have done all this without resorting to violence or deception. And when I treated you unjustly, you refused to sacrifice your honor in an attempt to get even." She shook her head once more. "I promise you that I will learn from what you have done."

She dipped her head respectfully. Then she smiled. "If there is anything I can do for you, Elena—anything at all—you need only ask."

"Thank you, Ronya. What you have said means a great deal to me. I truly need nothing from you though—apart from my heirloom, that is."

The smile vanished from Ronya's face in an instant. "I haven't told you!" she said. "So much has happened, and this matter was pushed entirely from my mind."

Dismay twisted the new leader's face, and she passed a hand across her eyes. Then she shook her head. "Viggor is a greedy man. You already know that he planned to take you for himself when he thought the time was right. He also witnessed me snatching away your heirloom when you first arrived, and he has been lusting after it ever since. It wasn't because he cared about it for its own sake—he didn't even know what it was. He simply couldn't bear for me to have something that he didn't have. When we met this morning he took it by force. I no longer have it!"

Elena felt the blood drain from her face.

"I am so sorry, Elena," said Ronya miserably. "Andri and I will gather some men and pursue him right now. We will do whatever it takes to get it back."

Elena shook her head firmly. "No. You have separated peacefully from Viggor, and you must not turn to violence now. We will pursue him."

Ronya opened her mouth to argue, but Elena cut her off. "Perhaps there is a way you can help us. Would you be willing to send us away with a few supplies? We must leave quickly, though."

Ronya agreed without hesitation. Then she hurried away, calling for Andri's help.

Thomas joined Elena. "We are ready to go," he said.

She took his hands and peered wretchedly up into his eyes. "Viggor has taken the stone," she whispered.

Thomas was thunderstruck. He shook his head in anger. Then he groaned, placing both hands over his face.

"Look at you, Thomas! You're not even fully recovered yet," she exclaimed. "I know what you'll want to do. But it's still my problem. I'm the one who lost the stone, and it's my responsibility to get it back."

"But how?" he asked.

"I'm not sure. But I'll find a way somehow."

He gazed into her eyes, then he shrugged helplessly. "You've already achieved more than I would have ever believed possible," he acknowledged.

Thomas turned to Rubin. "Viggor has taken something that belongs to us. We must retrieve it from him before we continue our journey."

Rubin raised his eyebrows, but he didn't argue.

While they were waiting for Ronya, Rubin brought out a simple sling he had fashioned during their time with the Clan. It was designed to hold Tamara while she was on horseback. His intention was to avoid any repetition of the incident that had led to Thomas's head injury.

Rubin now put on the sling, and Thomas handed Tamara up to him. She was soon perched snugly and securely in front of her grandfather, while he retained full use of both hands. Seeing how well it worked, all of them were enthusiastic in their praise of his innovation.

At that moment Ronya returned and pressed two bulging sacks into Thomas's hands. They thanked her warmly, and Elena embraced her.

As soon as they were all mounted they said their goodbyes and set off after Viggor.

. . .

THE WAGONS HAD LEFT A PLAINLY visible trail, and they followed it swiftly. They caught up with Viggor after little more than an hour had passed.

When he became aware of them he stopped his wagon. The other wagons quickly came to a halt as well. "So you have come to throw yourself upon my mercy," he said mockingly.

"You have something of mine," said Elena, her voice trembling. "An heirloom that you took from Ronya. I want it back."

So much had changed for her since Thomas's accident. She had turned Ronya from an enemy into a grateful friend. One at a time she had won the respect of most of the members of the Clan. And she had orchestrated a bloodless change of leadership. She had also made a bitter enemy.

All of it, the good as well as the bad, had come at considerable cost. The pressure within her had built up relentlessly until she was almost at breaking point. The tension from this latest crisis was finally more than she could bear. Her body began to tremble. She tried to master it, but failed miserably. Soon she was shaking uncontrollably.

The woman sitting beside Viggor on his wagon turned to him in alarm. "She is going into trance," she said. "Who knows what might happen? Give her what she wants! Now. Quickly, before she does something that ruins us all!"

Viggor stared at Elena with wide eyes. Then he pulled the chain with its golden clasp from a hidden pocket and threw it to the ground.

"Take it, then!" he said. "You've done enough to us already. Leave us in peace!"

He called to his horse, snapping the reins sharply. His wagon began to move away, the others soon following.

Thomas climbed down from his horse. He retrieved the chain, looking curiously at the stone held within it. Then he brought it to Elena and placed it into her shaking hand.

Viggor's face appeared from around the side of his wagon as it rumbled away. Her tension subsided at the sight of him leaving, and she finally managed to control her shaking.

The ease with which she had retrieved the stone astounded her, and the means by which it had happened was no less remarkable.

Back at the camp she had reached a crucial turning point. She had thrust aside the suspicion, fear, and shame that had assailed her since Thomas became incapacitated, choosing instead to return to what she knew best—a gentle manner that sought to encourage rather than to disapprove.

She remembered something she had heard many years earlier from Brother Vangellis, the monk who later become Thomas's mentor. He had told her, "God's grace is all you need—his power is strongest when you are weak."

It hadn't made sense to her at the time, but it did now. She hadn't outsmarted Viggor with her cleverness, nor had she come after him with overwhelming force—that simply wasn't her way. Strange as it might be, her weakness had been the means of resolving this latest crisis. Somehow that seemed fitting.

Slipping from her saddle, she handed the stone to Thomas. "It's yours!" she whispered spiritedly. "I'm giving it to you!"

He tore his gaze hastily away from her, looking instead toward Viggor's wagon. She followed his glance and caught a final glimpse of the deposed leader as his head disappeared behind the wagon.

She understood why Thomas had avoided looking at her once he regained possession of the stone. Gently taking his face in her hand, she turned it back toward her. His eyes went wide as the stone showed him the reason for her action. A fleeting look of disappointment crossed his face, but it was quickly replaced by awe and amazement as he perceived everything she had achieved while he was laid low.

He closed his eyes and looked away again.

She gazed earnestly up at him. "I know you never wanted to see into my mind. But I needed you to understand."

"I do understand," he said, "and I don't blame you. It wasn't your fault that you saw into my mind when I gave you the stone."

He slipped the stone into his pouch along with the chain and the clasp.

"Let's not do it again," he said.

She nodded her agreement, leaning forward and kissing him gently on the lips.

"We need to go!" he said. "I caught a glimpse of Viggor after you gave me back the stone. He's very angry, and he'll make us pay if he can find a way to do it."

She looked at him in surprise. "I saw him, too—as I was handing it over," she said. "All I could see was his pain. His parents never praised him—not ever—and he's been trying his whole life to prove he's worthwhile. Now he sees himself as more of a failure than ever."

They stared at each other in confusion for a lingering moment.

Then they remounted. Thomas retrieved Tamara and the sling from Rubin, and the little party set off.

THEY RODE until well after dark, aided by the light of a moon that was almost at its full. When they eventually made camp, they didn't risk lighting a fire.

Tamara soon fell asleep. The others sat quietly with not much to say.

"These men that chase us," said Haldek finally. "They want your little heirloom?"

Thomas groaned inside. So many eyes were now upon the stone. Keeping it unknown and out of sight was becoming almost impossible. He looked at Haldek then across at Rubin.

"Haldek and I have been talking," Rubin confirmed.

Thomas sighed. "The man who found us doesn't know exactly why they're chasing us," he said. "I can't speak for the others riding with him. But I won't try to pretend that the heirloom has nothing to do with it."

Rubin turned to Elena. "I don't understand what happened back at that camp," he said, "and I'm not sure I want to know. But I have a bad feeling that you're now mixed up in it as well."

Elena glanced at Thomas. "The heirloom belongs to Thomas," she replied. "He gave it to me so I could keep it safe while he was injured. As you know, Ronya stole it from me, but we got it back in the end. More could be said, but those are the important parts."

Neither Rubin nor Haldek looked satisfied, but Rubin did make a final promise. "Haldek and I will keep this to ourselves. And we will do anything we can to protect you both."

Both Thomas and Elena quietly expressed their gratitude for the support and the discretion shown by the older men. Then Rubin and Haldek lay down with their blankets and were soon asleep.

Elena and Thomas settled beside each other.

"You said that the stone belongs to me," whispered Thomas. "That's not completely true anymore."

"What do you mean?" she whispered back, alarm in her voice. "It's yours! I don't want it!"

"You let me into your mind," he replied, "so I saw what you did when you were with those people. None of that would even have occurred to me. I just don't think the same way you do. And even now that I've seen what you did, I still don't think I could do it."

He paused, trying to find a way to properly express his thoughts. "When I have the stone I can see what people are thinking and planning, and I see their motives. I see what they're feeling, too, but it never occurs to me to dig down to understand why they feel that way. That doesn't particularly appeal to me."

"There's a lot I don't see either," she said. "I've learned to overlook the mean and unpleasant side of people and to find reasons to excuse them. Like my final glimpse of Viggor when he was leaving. Even with the stone in my hand I think I completely missed a lot of what was going on in people's minds."

"And that turned out to be a good thing. You probably wouldn't have wanted to help Ronya if you'd only seen her ugly side. But you looked past that, and now their whole Clan has changed as a result.

The truth is, Elena, that you're a much more generous person than I am."

Seeing that she was about to protest, he hastily added, "I'm glad you think I have some good qualities, too. Especially now that you've seen into my mind!"

He paused again. "What I'm trying to say is that even though the stone gives both of us complete access to another person's mind, we see different things. There's far too much there for one person to grasp anyway, and we can only sift through a tiny part of it. So we find our way to whatever makes most sense to us."

Her head nodded in the dark. "You're probably right."

"So...I see part of the picture, and you see a different part of the picture. Together we see a lot more."

"What are you suggesting?" she asked.

"That it's time we shared it," he said. "We can pass it back and forth between us as the need arises."

She appeared too nonplussed to respond.

"As far as I'm concerned it's settled," he concluded. "If you still need convincing in the morning, we can talk about it then."

He leaned forward and kissed her delicately on the lips. "You are the most gracious and generous person I have ever met," he said, "and I still can't believe that I was the one fortunate enough to marry you."

All conversation ceased as she leaned in to kiss him back.

24

The little group of travelers paused in sight of Arnost, standing just off the main road as they discussed their plans.

Thomas had donned his usual broad rimmed hat to hide his face, but an unfamiliar cloak covered his frame. Ronya had sent them away with ample provisions, thoughtfully including cloaks for each of them along with the food. The fabric of Thomas's new garment was more colorful than anything he had worn previously, and he decided that it suited his purposes perfectly for that very reason.

Not wishing to stand out more than was necessary, Elena had clad herself in her usual black hooded cloak rather than the much more attractive one sent for her by Ronya. She had long since abandoned her old hunchback disguise—a hunchback crone with a young child was sure to attract attention.

Although they had seen no sign of their pursuers, Thomas felt sure that the approaches to Arnost would be watched. They therefore decided to split up before they joined the main road.

Rubin and Haldek had no plans to enter the city at all, and Thomas intended to separate himself from Elena and Tamara before they reached the gates. As they stood together discussing it near the main road, they noticed a wagon filled with produce approaching. Elena hurried to the road and spoke to the man and woman driving the wagon. After confirming that the farmer and his wife were heading for the market in Arnost, she asked if she could ride with her daughter in the back. They readily agreed, and she clambered aboard with Tamara in her arms.

With Elena's horse in tow, Rubin set off with Haldek for the place where they had agreed to meet after Thomas and Elena eventually left the city.

Thomas directed his horse out onto the main road and followed along behind the wagon, careful to keep his distance. He had arranged to rejoin Elena and Tamara inside the city walls, far enough from the gates to avoid attracting the attention of anyone keeping watch for them.

The stone hung from the chain around his neck beneath his clothing, his close fitting tunic holding it firmly in position. Many times already he had silently breathed his thanks to Ronya for her innovation. The stone's insights were available to him for as long as the clasp held it against his skin.

The flow of revelations became a relentless onslaught whenever other people were constantly in view. Thankfully, though, it was easy for him to take a break. He only needed to briefly lift his tunic away from his skin and rotate the clasp, bringing the thin layer of gold instead of the stone into contact with his skin. With a little practice he was able to do it relatively unobtrusively.

DUSK HAD FALLEN by the time he eventually reached the city walls, still trailing behind the wagon.

Thomas led his horse through the gates of Arnost, keeping his head down and avoiding eye contact with anyone. The stone was not idle though, and what he saw disturbed him greatly.

The walls had fallen away behind him when he heard Elena's voice calling to him softly. She appeared from the shadows as he was slipping from the horse's back. Lifting Tamara from her arms, he held his daughter close. She snuggled into him, too tired for chatter.

All traces of light had faded from the sky by the time they arrived at the little cottage beside the stables. Thomas quietly opened the wooden gates, and they hurried inside. He took Elena aside to the stables and handed Tammi back to her. Then he groped his way in the dark to the cottage and tapped lightly on the door.

After a long delay, Axel Stablehand opened the door a crack and peered out suspiciously. His eyes went wide when he realized who it was. He didn't invite Thomas inside. "Wait there," he whispered. Then he closed the door.

Moments later Thomas heard a muffled cry. The door swung open again, and Thomas saw that the candles inside the cottage had been extinguished. The only light came from the flicker of the fire. Then his mother appeared and flung herself into his arms.

"Thomas!" she whispered excitedly. "Is Elena with you?"

"Yes," he whispered back, immediately leading her toward the stables.

His father quickly closed the cottage door and hurried after them. Arriving first, Axel steered them to one of the smaller stable buildings. A dark figure soon joined them. "I'm here," said Elena quietly.

Axel ushered them all inside and closed the door firmly. Then he lit a candle.

Thomas's mother could barely contain her excitement when she found herself face to face not just with Elena, but with a granddaughter. "This is Tamara," whispered Elena with a smile.

Tears of joy flowed freely down Marya's face as she embraced Elena and gazed down at the child sleeping peacefully in her arms.

"You came!" she said. She turned to her husband. "I told you we needed to wait."

The stable master raised his hands helplessly. "I've been telling her she needs to leave. I wanted to send her south to her brother's farm again—where she stayed during the Rogandan invasion. But she wouldn't go. She insisted that the two of you would come, and she refused to leave before she'd seen you."

"And I clearly did the right thing," said Marya with evident satisfaction.

"Why do you need to send Mother away?" Thomas asked his father. "Are either of you in any danger?"

"We haven't personally been threatened," the stable master replied. "But Arnost has become a dangerous place. Even more so than during the invasion." He shook his head. "I never thought I'd live to see such a day."

"Where is the king?"

"The king and the queen both left to confer with the kings of Castel and Varas. They set out a couple of weeks ago, and nothing has been heard of them since."

"What about Will?"

"He's gone to Erestor. He left before they did. He took Rufe Sarjant with him."

"Who did the king leave in charge?"

"Lord Bottren. Supposedly he is still in authority in Arnost. Everything is done in his name. But I can't find anyone who has seen him —not for more than a week. The man who is actually in control now calls himself Lord Lygell. I have no idea where he comes from, but the men who answer to him are no good."

Marya looked at Thomas and Elena with worry on her face. "Everything has changed so quickly. I wouldn't have believed it was possible. And men have been snooping around here. Asking after you, Thomas, and your Rogandan friend. We knew you were off living in a forest somewhere, but we had no idea exactly where, of course, so we couldn't tell them anything."

"Have you been harmed in any way?" Thomas asked her in alarm.

"Nothing's happened so far," his father replied. "But I've been worried about when that might change. I'll feel much better when your mother is safely away from here."

"Enough of our troubles!" said Marya. "Tell us about you! And your beautiful little daughter!"

"I've been longing to share it all with you," said Elena eagerly.

"I've so much wanted you to meet Tammi! But how will we make it work? It sounds like it isn't safe here anymore. Not for any of us."

Thomas nodded. "We clearly won't be able to relax and talk freely until we're somewhere else. Perhaps we could all leave the city for a while."

"Leaving the city quietly won't be easy," said his father. "Our absence would certainly be noticed. You need to be aware that your mother and I are being watched. It's been obvious to me for some time. Did anyone see you when you came here?"

Thomas shook his head. "I don't think so. We were very careful. We split up before entering the city, and we only came here after dark."

"What prompted you to take precautions?" asked his father. "Were you aware of our situation?"

"No," Thomas replied. "A group of men have been hunting us. We were living in a very isolated location, but they somehow found us anyway. They destroyed our home."

"You could come with me!" said his mother excitedly. "To your uncle's farm. We'd all be safe there!"

"Before I go anywhere else," said Thomas, "I need to pay a visit to the castle."

Marya's face showed her apprehension. "Why would you want to do that, Thomas? It's too dangerous. You know that people are looking for you."

"I owe it to my friends—to Will and the others—to find out what's going on here."

Seeing that Thomas's mother was opening her mouth to say more, Elena drew her aside and began eagerly sharing the details of Tamara's birth. Marya was immediately captivated, and the two of them moved off to one side and settled themselves on bales of hay.

"You'll be taking a big risk if you go into the castle, Thomas," his father warned. "You won't find too many friendly faces—almost everyone you knew before has gone."

"There aren't many horses in the stables," said Thomas. "Where are all the soldiers?"

"As you know, most of the army was made up of farmers or tradesmen during the invasion," his father replied. "They simply returned to their homes after Torbury Scarp. The king still has a lot of permanent soldiers of course, and a good few of them went with the king and queen to protect them. Another large contingent just left for Erestor. We've heard rumors of a rebellion there, supposedly led by none other than your friend Will Prentis—Lord Torbury."

"That's ridiculous!" Thomas exclaimed. "Will would never rebel against the king."

"Of course he wouldn't," said Axel. "No one who knows him at all would ever believe it. What reason does Erestor have to rebel anyway? The old duke is still in charge there, and he's the king's uncle. He was the regent during the Rogandan invasion while the king was away from Arvenon, and always fiercely loyal. But that isn't all. Another force was sent to the borders of Castel. Supposedly the Castelans have threatened to invade Arvenon."

Thomas stared at him in disbelief.

Axel shook his head in disgust. "All of it is complete nonsense. Why would Castel attack us? They're our allies! They fought at our side against the Rogandans. And our own queen came from there." He raised his hands helplessly. "None of it makes any sense."

Thomas frowned. Something very odd was going on. And he couldn't ignore a pressing burden of responsibility to learn more. Tempting as it might be to simply slip away from Arnost with his family in search of an even more isolated place to hide, he knew he couldn't do it. He had the stone, and that gave him a better chance than anyone of getting to the bottom of whatever was happening.

Such considerations could wait until the morning, though. For that moment, he was glad to be with his parents again. Having a child had given him greater appreciation for his own parents—even his father—and he had been looking forward to them meeting his daughter. Tammi was fast asleep, but they still wanted to see her and to hear every little detail about her. Tammi already had a loving and involved grandparent in Rubin, but sharing the experience with his own parents, and witnessing their enthusiasm, proved to be just as rewarding as Thomas had hoped.

They could have talked all night, but eventually his mother brought blankets for the new arrivals, and they slept among the hay.

Thomas and Elena stole away from the stables before dawn had begun to lighten the sky. Tamara was still asleep, cradled in Elena's arms.

Marya came with them. She brought with her a large sack into which she had placed a few essential belongings. She was not intending to return to the cottage—Axel had finally convinced her to join her brother on his farm away to the south.

Thomas knew that his mother entertained hopes that he and his little family would accompany her. He had no intention of joining her, though. There was no doubt in his mind that sooner or later he would be pursued, and he would never knowingly place either her or her brother's family at risk.

At the very least it should be possible for them to enjoy some time together before they parted. The first priority was to depart from the city without being observed.

The little party arrived at the city gates as the first hint of daylight appeared in the sky. A number of wagons were lined up within the city walls, waiting to leave Arnost as soon as the gates opened. Once again Elena found a friendly farmer willing to allow her and Tamara to hitch a ride. She also carried his mother's sack of belongings into the wagon with her.

Thomas watched carefully as the wagon rolled through the gates, making sure to keep the stone in contact with his skin. No one that he could see showed any interest in the wagon or its passengers. Marya soon followed them on foot, and once again he saw no sign that she was under observation.

Axel was intending to slip out of the city just before the gates were closed that evening. He would return the next morning as soon as the gates opened. If they were fortunate his absence would not be noticed. All of them planned to spend the night in a secluded location not far from the city—they would brave the cold and sleep under the stars. Marya at least would be able to spend an entire day with Tammi before they parted.

Having seen his family safely through the gates, Thomas turned away from the wall and began to retrace his steps. He would not be leaving the city until he had paid a visit to the castle.

The sun had risen by the time he arrived at a little used side entrance to the castle. He knew that countless people would be stirring within its walls—from the kitchens, where cooks and their helpers stoked the kitchen ovens, to the reception hall, where servants scurried about piling logs onto the great fireplaces. Thomas planned to move purposefully—just another underling eager to perform his tasks without attracting attention.

Pulling his hat down low over his face, he pushed through the side entrance into the castle. Finding himself in a familiar passage, he hurried along it, turning in different directions as the mood took him. All the while he allowed his eyes to roam freely, absorbing information greedily whenever his gaze happened upon another person.

It took no more than a few minutes for Thomas to establish that most of the people scurrying about the castle were anxious and unhappy. The only exceptions were the mercenaries. He encountered far too many of them, and they were sauntering about as though they owned the place.

Before an hour had passed it was clear to Thomas that the kingdom was in serious trouble. Lord Bottren was leader in name only—he and his most trusted retainers had taken up residence in the dungeon with the rats. Lord Lygell was now firmly in charge. The stone soon laid bare abundant evidence of both the ruthlessness and the effectiveness of the new leader. But it also revealed that he was little more than a pawn. Thomas had not been able to uncover any details about Lygell's agenda, but he knew that the man was acting on behalf of another.

Thomas now faced a difficult decision. Should he remain in the castle until he caught a glimpse of Lygell? Or should he leave now, before trouble found him?

While he was pondering his next move, a harsh voice snapped him out of his reverie.

"You! Who gave you permission to be here? Come here. NOW!"

Thomas's head jerked involuntarily toward the speaker. He was alarmed to see that the man was pointing directly at him.

His eyes saw a mercenary. The stone showed him a man with a reputation for brutality—a reputation that the hired soldier carefully cultivated. The man enjoyed throwing his weight around. And his full attention was now focused on the intruder.

Thomas didn't pause to consider his options—he turned and fled.

"Stop or die!"

Thomas sprinted away, pursued by increasingly strident threats.

A growing commotion behind him told Thomas that others were also joining the chase. The hunt was on.

He had been in the castle many times during his childhood but had never explored it fully. The majority of its labyrinthine ways were unfamiliar to him. He dashed into the first side passage that presented itself, throwing himself forward heedlessly with no idea where he was heading. He twisted and turned through passages, at one point emerging in a corridor behind his pursuers, having somehow managed to come full circle. Someone noticed him, and the chase resumed.

A door appeared before him. Thrusting it open, he cast himself forward into a medium sized meeting room. At the same moment, a lavishly dressed nobleman in early middle age entered the room through another door off to the side. Thomas caught a quick glimpse of sharp eyes peering out at him from a narrow chiseled face. The man calmly regarded the fugitive, an expression of casual malice on his face. His robe was even more arresting than his countenance. Thomas's eyes were drawn irresistibly to the dazzle of shimmering silk that flowed in a rich red cascade around the lord.

No more than a glance had been necessary to assure Thomas that he had stumbled upon Lord Lygell himself. In the brief seconds that his eyes lighted upon the nobleman he learned all he needed to know and more.

Several of Lygell's retainers trailed in behind him, even as Thomas's pursuers burst into the room. Thomas's eyes darted around wildly as he sought a way of escape. Two other doors faced him. He selected one at random and flung himself through it before anyone could utter a word.

Fear lent him tremendous speed. Lygell's face haunted him. The nobleman had the eyes of a killer—death would overtake Thomas swiftly if he was caught. Such an outcome had to be prevented at all costs. And not just for his own sake. The stone must never be allowed to fall into the hands of such a man. Or, even worse, into the hands of the traitor who had employed him.

Thomas unexpectedly found himself in a familiar passage. He raced along it before pushing through a narrow entrance and dashing toward the winding stone stairway that lay beyond it.

Bounding up the stairs two at a time, he emerged breathlessly into a small tower room. He glanced around him. Once again he stood in the private retreat where he had whiled away many happy hours with Will and Rufe. There was no opportunity to savor it though.

He shut and bolted the door. Someone had almost certainly seen him enter the passage that led to the stairs, and pursuers were undoubtedly close behind him. But he didn't care. Kneeling down, he pushed aside the large rug that covered the floor to expose a round piece of wood with a metal handle set into it. He tugged at the handle, lifting the wooden cover to reveal a small opening in the floor. A flight of stone steps was dimly visible below it. He lit a candle before carefully positioning the rug over the wooden cover. He knew from experience that as soon as he closed the cover, the rug would slide back into place to completely hide the opening.

Climbing down the steps, he carefully lowered the wooden cover into place, sealing the hole above him. The cover settled with a satisfying thud as it dropped into position. Holding the candle in front of him, he made his way carefully down the stone steps into a small chamber that lay below the main stairway.

It had been Rufe who revealed the chamber to him. On occasion the three friends had climbed down into it, and they had sometimes joked about hiding in it to baffle unwelcome intruders.

Only Thomas, though, had ever ventured out of the chamber's small window onto the flying buttress that lay below it. Such forays were beyond foolhardy, and having dared it once he saw no need to prove a point by doing it again. The buttress stretched upward over his head, but a larger horizontal buttress lay below it. On the far side of this lower buttress another small window beckoned to him.

He could see no way of climbing safely down onto the lower buttress. If he could somehow find a way to do it, though, clambering across it and climbing into the far window should be relatively straightforward. He had once searched out the room to which the other window belonged, and he knew that another stairway led down from it into a lightly trafficked section of the castle.

A bird could fly from one window to the other in little more than a heartbeat. Thomas was no bird, but at that moment other options were not available. And he could ill afford to delay. He needed to make good his escape before the entire castle had been roused against him.

Taking a deep breath, he climbed out of the window onto the buttress, willing himself not to look down.

<h1 style="text-align:center">25</h1>

Perched high above the ground, Thomas took a deep breath and tried to calm his jangled nerves.

The horizontal buttress below him was no wider than the one on which he stood, so there was no way to step down onto it. He knew he would not even be able to see the lower buttress if he looked straight down. Without a rope there was no simple means of descending safely.

No alternative presented itself that seemed better than dangling his legs over the side of the higher buttress and planting his feet on the lower one. The challenge would be to get the rest of his body down without toppling over the edge.

Thomas had once witnessed a cat successfully complete the journey from one window to the other. Somehow the cat had made it onto the lower buttress, but try as he might he could not recall how.

Muffled voices called in the tower room above him. The mercenaries must have broken down the door. He couldn't delay any longer. Placing both arms across the upper buttress, he lowered himself over the edge. At this point, near to the tower, the lower buttress was not far below him, and he was able to get his feet onto it.

He tried to find a handhold that would allow him to lower himself in safety. He could see nothing vaguely suitable anywhere within reach.

Thomas was not left searching for long. He abruptly discovered he was not alone. Disturbed by his clumsy maneuvering, a pigeon leaped into the air, wildly flapping its wings right in his face. Startled out of his wits, he lost his grip. As he fell, he reached desperately for the lower buttress, somehow managing to get both hands onto it. He clung precariously to it, far above the ground, panting with fear.

The buttress was almost as tall as he was, and a childhood memory came to him of scaling stone walls in the stable. He stood head and shoulders above the stable walls now, but they had seemed tall at the time. Partly from memory and partly by instinct, he bent his knees and planted both feet lightly onto the stonework below him. Then he carefully hooked his right leg up until his heel caught the top of the buttress beside his hands. With three points of purchase, he strained upward until he had positioned his body atop the buttress. He sat transfixed, wide-eyed and quivering with shock. Forcing himself not to think, he crawled across the buttress until he arrived at the far window. Then he clambered through it and cast himself down trembling onto the floor.

After a few minutes he picked himself up and plodded unsteadily down the stairs. He had no idea what he would do if he met another person, but somehow he made it outside the castle without even catching sight of anyone.

Finding a place where he could remain hidden, Thomas considered his options. He had now become frantic to leave the city. Horses were available in plenty in the stables, but he knew that the stables were being watched.

Before he could reach any conclusion, hoofbeats sounded. Slipping deeper into the shadows, he looked on in silence as a dispatch rider appeared. The rider brought his horse to a halt not far from Thomas and swung himself down from the saddle, immediately disappearing into the castle.

Thomas didn't pause to consider the risks. He strode boldly to the horse, whispering soothingly to it as he approached. Then he climbed into the saddle and rode swiftly away from the castle, heading in the direction of the city gates.

As the walls of Arnost appeared before him it occurred to Thomas that the alarm might have been raised and the gates closed against him. To his relief, though, the gates stood wide open, and the guards were no more vigilant than usual. He rode through, keeping his head down and trying not to hurry.

Once clear of the city, he headed toward the agreed meeting place in search of Elena and his mother.

Thomas parted with the horse soon after leaving the city, pointing it in the direction of the city gates and slapping it on the rump. It was not impossible that the animal might somehow manage to find its way back to where its rider had left it. If it did, no trace would remain of Thomas's escape.

He hurried to the agreed meeting location, half walking half running. As soon as he arrived Tamara stretched out her little arms to him. He lifted her up and held her tight, finally able to master his agitation after the tension of the stone's revelations at the castle and his narrow escape. Turning to Elena and his mother, he managed with an effort to speak to them calmly. He was, however, unable to prevent himself from pacing restlessly back and forth while he waited for his father to arrive.

All the while his mind was churning over everything that had taken place in the city. So much about the experience was disturbing, but Thomas at least had the satisfaction of knowing he had left Lord Lygell and his lackeys with a puzzle. He was confident that he had not been recognized—the stone hadn't shown him anything that suggested otherwise—so it was likely that Lygell's men would be reduced to guessing who he was and why he was wandering around the castle.

From their perspective it must seem that he had somehow contrived to vanish completely. Even if they found the hidden trapdoor in the tower room—which seemed unlikely—it would leave them none the wiser about where he had gone. They would almost certainly believe he was still hiding in the castle somewhere. As far as he was concerned, they could search for him there as long as they chose.

It was quickly obvious to Thomas that his mother had become anxious by the time he arrived. Elena, by contrast, had never doubted that he would find a way to safely extricate himself from the city. He guessed that she was trusting in the stone to help him find a way through. If so she was setting too much store by it. Thanks to the stone he was aware of what other people were thinking. Such insights were extremely useful, but they offered no guarantee of keeping him out of trouble.

It was now Thomas's turn to become restive. His father should already have arrived. If the stable master had been detained for some reason, Thomas would have no alternative but to return to the city. That prospect filled him with apprehension.

The sun had set by the time Axel finally appeared. Nevertheless, Thomas would not hear of any of them resting until they had relocated to a safe location much further from the city. They finally found a place where Thomas was willing to light a fire and sit down around it to talk.

"What's wrong with you, Thomas?" his father asked, traces of his old irritability creeping into his voice.

"I met Lord Lygell," said Thomas, unable to suppress a shudder. "Now I know what he's planning. I have to find the king and warn him."

His father stared at him curiously in the firelight. "What is he planning?" he asked.

"It's safer if you don't know," Thomas replied. "It's easier to behave normally if you have nothing to hide." He spoke in a tone that did not invite disagreement.

Axel frowned. "I need to know what I'm going back to," he insisted.

"You can't go back!" Thomas said in alarm. "You need to join

Mother. You'll both be safe at my uncle's place. Stay there until all of this is over."

"I can't just abandon the stables!"

"Other people will care for the horses," Thomas told him. "They have no choice—they need them."

He peered at his father anxiously. "Did you bring any coin with you?"

His father snorted. "I have no lack of money—I brought all of it. My savings are no longer safe at our house." He shook his head in disgust.

Thomas brightened immediately. "Wonderful! Then there's no reason at all for you to go back. You can leave at once."

The stable master frowned. He opened his mouth to speak, but then he closed it again.

"Is the situation really as bad as that?" asked Thomas's mother.

"It's worse," Thomas told her. "Much worse. Until the king returns to restore order, Arnost isn't safe. Not for any of us."

Thomas didn't say it, but the king would never get an opportunity to restore order in his kingdom if Lygell and his employer had their way. He had enough sense to keep that knowledge to himself. His mother looked alarmed enough already.

Axel was choosing not to argue, which surprised Thomas—it was something to be grateful for. Nevertheless it was obvious to him that his father had by no means made up his mind to leave Arnost.

Only Elena appeared to be entirely peaceful, no trace of any shadow darkening her lovely features. Reflecting on all that had been demanded of her in the brief period of time since they left their refuge, Thomas could only marvel at her calm demeanor. She was a remarkable person. And for some mysterious reason she had chosen to bind herself to him. He shook his head once more at the wonder of it, a surge of joy momentarily easing the crushing burden of the challenges that confronted him.

The night was well advanced before any of them even attempted to sleep. Only little Tammi had slept uninterrupted through the hours of darkness, and apart from her no one could muster much enthusiasm for the new day.

Tamara greeted the dawn with seemingly boundless energy. When Thomas groaned aloud at her noisy exuberance, his father responded by taking her little hand and leading her to a nearby meadow. After a few minutes Thomas followed them to ensure that she wasn't wearing out her grandpa. He discovered his father patiently pointing out the wildflowers and the worker bees attracted to the pollen in their blooms.

Elena later retrieved Tammi to offer her some food. After she had eaten she loudly called for "Gampa". Grandpa was by no means displeased, and the two of them happily spent a busy hour in one another's company.

Thomas had the feeling that if Elena and Tammi had been going with his mother to her brother's farm, his father would agree to accompany them without hesitation. He needed to find the king, though, and he was unwilling to part from his wife and daughter, even if he might be leading them into danger. It was clear to him that the stone's capabilities could be used much more effectively if he shared it with his wife.

Once Elena had settled Tammi for an afternoon nap, Thomas's father surprised them all with a sudden pronouncement. "I can afford to leave the stables for a while. It's not essential for me to be there—not with the king away. I have a couple of capable assistants who come in each day. They're more than able to provide basic care for the horses."

Thomas stared at him wide-eyed.

"I will leave Arnost and go with your mother, Thomas," said the stable master. "On one condition."

"What's your condition?" asked Thomas. His father's face was an unreadable mask, and Thomas was left guessing whether he should be pleased or suspicious.

"It's obvious that you'll need to settle again soon—if only for the sake of your daughter. When you do, I would like you to allow us to visit you." He paused, before adding roughly, "I know your mother would like that."

Elena was overjoyed at the suggestion, and wasted no time in letting him know.

"I agree to your condition with pleasure," Thomas assured him. He was working hard to conceal his utter astonishment at any such initiative from his father. "You will be welcome to stay with us, of course—for as long as you like."

His mother said nothing, although she brushed tears from her eyes. His father contented himself with a grunt by way of acknowledgment. But he looked pleased. Thomas had the feeling that the credit for his sudden change of heart belonged entirely to Tammi.

His father hadn't quite finished. A look of concern came to his face. "I don't pretend to understand how you've become caught up in the affairs of the king again, Thomas," he said, studying his son thoughtfully, "but be careful. The king is a good man, and we owe him our loyalty. But you have a wife and daughter to consider now."

Unsure of how to respond, Thomas said nothing.

"My father and Haldek will be wondering what has become of us," said Elena, deftly changing the subject.

"You're right," Thomas replied. He turned to his parents. "Come with us," he suggested. "They will be pleased to see you."

RUBIN AND HALDEK were indeed pleased to see Axel and Marya again, and greatly relieved at the safe return of Thomas and Elena and little Tamara. They enjoyed an evening and most of a day together before Thomas informed them of his intention to leave. Keenly aware of his responsibility to find and warn the king, he was becoming more restless with each passing hour.

Axel and Marya were also ready to depart at once. They had managed to secure a ride with a farmer who was heading south in the general direction of Marya's brother's farm. The farmer couldn't take them all the way, but they were confident they would find another ride when they were closer to their destination.

Although Thomas's parents had invited Rubin and Haldek to

accompany them, the two men had no hesitation in deciding to remain with Thomas and Elena. Rubin knew how much they appreciated his help with Tammi, and Haldek felt as protective as ever toward Elena and her little daughter.

All of them promised to meet up again as soon as they could.

Tammi cried when her grandpa and grandma said their goodbyes and left the little company. Axel had been holding her, and she parted from him unwillingly and with many tears. Marya wept openly, and even Axel appeared to be trying a bit too hard to look normal. Thomas could only marvel at the difference a grandchild had made, especially to the attitude of his father.

As his parents were about to climb into the farmer's wagon, Axel approached Thomas. He nodded toward Elena and Tamara. "Look after them, son," he said, before adding, "And you be careful too." Then he pulled Thomas into a quick embrace, slapped him once on the back, and released him. Thomas was too astonished to do more than nod.

As the wagon rolled away Elena came to Thomas and nestled her head into his shoulder. They waved his parents off together.

"Well that was unexpected," he murmured, glancing down at Elena. She simply smiled at him.

Once his parents had left, they all mounted their horses and set off together on their search for the king. Their journey would take them north, but they initially headed southwest, since Thomas wanted to skirt around Arnost to stay well clear of any mercenaries in the area who might be searching for him.

Their efforts to avoid the main road slowed them down at first, but once they were well clear of the city they swung north. Crossing the main road, they headed into the rolling hills and fertile valleys to the north.

Travelers were not unusual in these parts. Their horses set them apart from the common folk, but to a casual observer they might have appeared to be a small group of merchants or wealthy farmers going about their business.

A considerable period of time had now elapsed since their last sighting of the men who destroyed their home in the forest. If those men were still continuing their pursuit, there was no indication of it. Thomas dared to hope that they had made good their escape.

He was mounted on a fresh horse with a blue sky above him. His little family was at his side, and he had the surprise of his father's farewell to savor. Thomas finally allowed himself to relax.

26

———

In the wide world the sun was shining brightly. Inside the cabin the time of day might as well have been twilight. Alfic squinted about him. The scattered rays of sunlight that filtered through the single narrow window of the room succeeded in picking out the specks of dust in the air, but did little to penetrate the gloom.

Alfic peered testily into the darkness across the room. The man who was hiring him had positioned himself behind an elaborate chair in the corner. He was visible only in outline. It was obvious that he had planned it that way.

The man's eyes glittered with an unwavering intensity. "Do you understand what's required of you?" he asked.

"I know what you want," Alfic growled. "Trying to achieve it with forty men is absurd."

The dim figure shrugged. "Hire one hundred, then. The payment will be the same either way. You can share it with as many men as you want."

Alfic scowled, although the other man probably couldn't see it.

"You're not going to need an army." The voice was beginning to sound impatient. "There's no reason to panic—this entire exercise has been meticulously planned."

"No one's panicking," grumbled Alfic, furrowing his brows even more deeply.

"Good. Then carry out your role exactly as you've been instructed, and everything will go smoothly. If you try to get creative you'll fail and end up with nothing."

He paused as if waiting for a response.

Alfic offered none. The patronizing attitude of the other man was beginning to irritate him. Having never been told the name of his employer, Alfic silently dubbed him Count Nothing. He had the feeling that it would give the plotter considerable satisfaction if he could somehow find a way of paying nothing.

The voice continued as if sensing his thoughts, "You'll be well paid—when the job is done."

A bag sailed through the air in his direction. "Here's the first installment."

Startled, Alfic reached out instinctively. Catching the bag cleanly in the dark proved impossible, though, and it crashed to the floor. Filled to overflowing with coins, the bag burst open as it landed, spilling its contents freely.

Alfic bent down, cursing loudly. The coins had scattered far and wide, and retrieving them in the dark was a slow and frustrating task. He was reduced to scrabbling around on his hands and knees.

Eventually he stood to his feet and straightened, clutching the bag possessively. He knew he hadn't managed to retrieve every coin.

Count Nothing observed him silently. His face was hidden, but Alfic didn't doubt that he was gloating. Furious and humiliated, Alfic left the room without a word, pushing his way out of the cabin into the bright sunlight.

He had no idea of the identity of his employer, but a bitter hatred of the man welled up within him. There was nothing he could do about it, though—the bulging bag of coins held him in thrall. In that moment he hated his own greed as well.

He made his way to his horse, muttering angrily to himself. After stuffing the coins into a saddlebag, he climbed into the saddle.

As he rode away he reflected on the interaction. Reluctant as he was to admit it, his shadowy employer was right. Even two hundred men wouldn't be enough if the rest of the plan wasn't carried out properly.

If he trusted in the plan, though, it also meant that he wouldn't even need forty men. His lip curled upward in a sneer. He would hire thirty, and he would pocket the coins intended for the other ten.

Now it was his turn to gloat. That didn't mean Alfic had forgiven Count Nothing for humbling him. He never forgot an insult, and he would never pardon any person foolish enough to deliver one.

IN THE CABIN two other men emerged from the shadows. "Will he get the job done?" one of them asked gruffly.

"He might not be happy about the terms," the first man replied, "but he'll do it. And based on his reputation, he'll do it well."

The third man said nothing. Spotting something on the floor, he bent down and picked it up. Silver glinted in the dim light as he held it up to inspect it. He slipped it quietly into a fold in his cloak before returning his attention once more to the floor.

The first man turned away, shaking his head.

"WE'RE ALMOST THERE, YOUR MAJESTY!"

The coach driver's news came like a much longed for tonic, and Queen Essanda drank it in gratefully. Leaning forward, she peered out of the carriage window, bracing herself against the constant jolting and lurching.

The coach was following a track that could barely be called a road, and it seemed to catch every possible rut. Not far ahead, though, located in the heart of a lush valley, stood a large manor house, surrounded on three sides by barns and other dwellings.

The site had been chosen primarily for its location. It lay within

Arvenon, but it was much closer to the Castelan and Varasan borders than to Arnost.

A river flowed lazily on the far side of the buildings. The scene was breathtakingly beautiful. If her situation had been different she might even have thought of it as idyllic.

Columns of soldiers formed an escort that stretched out before and behind her. A few of those riding ahead had almost reached the house.

The maid traveling with her in the carriage poked her head briefly out of the window. "Not exactly royal apartments," she muttered under her breath.

The queen laughed. "This isn't Arnost, Ava. Count Lonnigen has been very generous in offering his mansion for the gathering."

"Did you say 'mansion', Your Majesty?" The maid raised her eyes heavenward. "I actually heard someone claiming this place is called Paradise Valley," she added with a disdainful grunt.

Her reaction drew another laugh from Essanda.

Ava was the perfect companion—sensitive, levelheaded, and even-tempered. She did, however, have a way of taking instant offense when anything less than absolute perfection was offered up to her mistress. Her expectations were impossibly unrealistic, but Essanda found her concern endearing.

With the destination now in sight, Essanda allowed herself to indulge in the anticipation of lying down at last—on a motionless feather bed. Everything possible had been done to ease the journey for the heavily pregnant queen, but the bumping and shaking had steadily worn her down. It was no one's fault except her own, of course—she was attending this gathering at her insistence.

More than once she had asked herself why she was so determined to travel all this way to meet with the three kings. She knew it was partly because she had become so invested in Arvenon and every-thing that affected it. Arvenon had been nothing more than a neigh-boring kingdom for the first years of her life. From the moment she was crowned queen, though, it held a claim on her loyalty. And Arvenon had become far more than that to Essanda—in yielding up her heart to its king she had also transferred her allegiance to his kingdom. Arvenon's future was her future now. And the future of her unborn child as well.

It occurred to her there were probably other motivations as well. She wanted to see her father one more time before she gave birth. And perhaps it had a lot to do with her stubborn determination not to be parted from Steffan, especially at this point in her pregnancy.

She gave up trying to understand herself and sank back into her seat.

No more than a few minutes passed before the coach finally rolled to a stop. Count Lonnigen was on hand to greet Queen Essanda, and he himself helped her down from the carriage.

"Welcome to Paradise Valley, Your Majesty," he said with a bow. "You honor us with your presence at my humble home. A suite has been prepared for you—it is available right now if you would like to rest after your journey. I can arrange for refreshments to be sent up to you."

"Thank you, My Lord, you are most gracious. The prospect of resting is very welcome indeed."

A small but impressive staircase faced her as she entered the count's mansion. Her host had thoughtfully assigned her a suite at ground level, though, and he directed her to it. She found King Steffan resting inside it.

He leaped to his feet with great delight when he saw her, embracing her tenderly. "It's such a relief to see you, Essanda! I was very concerned for you once I saw the condition of the road."

"You told me exactly what the journey would be like, and you're generous not to remind me of it," she replied with a weary smile. "I'll admit that I did have second thoughts, especially once we left Arnost behind and the roads started to deteriorate. But it was a bit late by then."

She took Steffan's arm and eased herself onto a bed with a sigh. "None of it matters now, because I've arrived, and with no harm done. I'm not even going to think about the journey home—that can wait until it happens."

Resting her hands atop her ample belly, she closed her eyes and exhaled noisily. It wasn't very elegant, but her current condition didn't exactly lend itself to elegance.

Count Lonnigen had freely offered his own retainers to serve the monarchs during their stay at his estate. Nevertheless the task was beyond the capabilities of his own people, so he had soon sought additional resources from elsewhere. One of his nephews had joined the monastery led by Brother Elias, and the count had established a connection with the abbot. Hoping to enlist the aid of the monks, he sent a message to Brother Elias with a request for assistance.

The abbot had readily agreed. In his reply he noted that he understood the challenges that came with the exercise of authority, and he saw it as a privilege and an honor to serve those who bore the heaviest leadership burden of all. He also felt confident that a change of environment would prove worthwhile for his monks.

Brother Elias had duly arrived with twenty white-clad monks. He set them to work without delay.

Brother Ander and his fellow monks would have gladly released Brother Elias from physical work. The old abbot was not content simply to organize his brothers, though—he insisted on working alongside them. Any attempt to limit him would have been a waste of time.

The truth was that in spite of his age and apparent frailty, Brother Elias was entirely capable. His energy had not been noticeably diminished by the passage of the years, and his desire to serve had never been stronger.

And he somehow managed to do whatever was needed without complaining. His cheerfulness set the tone for all of the brothers.

Once the kings and their retinues arrived, the monks became increasingly busy. Count Lonnigen's mansion was able to accommodate the three monarchs in comfort, but it had never been designed to host entertainment on such a scale. However a large barn stood adjacent to the main house, and the count had arranged for it to be cleaned out and decorated and equipped with tables and elegant chairs. Daylight flooded into the barn through a pair of large doors at one end, and the overall atmosphere was pleasant and cheerful.

A makeshift but well supplied kitchen had been established at the far end of the barn, with clusters of candles for lighting and access through a side door. The monks were soon working alongside the local cooks.

Brother Ander was approached by his mentor one afternoon.

"I'm sure you must recognize some of these kings and their noblemen," said Brother Elias. "Does it bring back uncomfortable memories for you?"

Brother Ander shook his head. "No, I've left that life behind. It's been more than four years since I joined the monastery, and my days as a soldier seem..."

"Abhorrent?" the old monk asked.

He puckered his eyebrows in response. "I'm not even sure what that word means," he replied. "What I wanted to say was that becoming a healer has changed everything for me. I have no desire to be a soldier anymore. I can't even imagine what it would be like to go back to it."

Brother Elias smiled. "I have no doubt you were very effective when you were a soldier. But you've certainly been developing into an extremely capable healer."

***

KING STEFFAN SAT with Queen Essanda in the barn, enjoying the opportunity to relax before the other kings joined them. His wife had slept well after her long journey and appeared somewhat refreshed.

Count Ranauld stood at their side, and Steffan waved him to a seat.

Steffan glanced around the barn, impressed at how much Count

Lonnigen had achieved in a short period of time. The count had confessed to him that a few weeks earlier it had been just another dusty outbuilding. The nobleman had nothing to be ashamed of. Now it was a pleasant and well appointed living area. Comfortable seating surrounded tables covered with clean white cloths and adorned with flowers. Large benches at the far end of the barn held a variety of food and drinks.

After admiring the setting, he found his eyes drawn to the monks, and one of them in particular. "That monk over there," he said, leaning toward Ranauld and nodding in the direction of the white-robed figure in question. "There's something familiar about him."

The man towered above most of the other monks, and something about the way he moved set him apart from his brothers.

"He used to be a soldier, Your Majesty," Ranauld replied, speaking quietly. "He commanded a large group of men at Torbury Scarp, and he fought well. His name is Ander."

Steffan shook his head. "What's he doing here dressed like that?"

Ranauld shrugged. "I'm not sure," he replied. "But I know that Lord Torbury agreed to release him from the army."

Essanda had been listening to their interaction. "It wouldn't be the first time a soldier decided to renounce fighting and became a monk," she said thoughtfully.

Their conversation was interrupted by the arrival of King Delmar, accompanied by several nobles who had traveled with him from Varas.

Steffan rose from his chair, dipping his head. "Your Majesty," he said, greeting his fellow sovereign warmly.

Count Ranauld had also stood, and he brightened as he saw Lord Karevis enter the barn behind his king.

Steffan singled out the Varasan army commander for a special greeting. "My Lord Karevis."

Karevis smiled before bowing low in response. "Your Majesty."

Essanda shared his respect for the Varasan nobleman, and she was clearly pleased to see him too. "We are honored to have you with us, My Lord," she said with a warm smile.

"The honor is mine, Your Majesty," he replied respectfully.

Karevis headed for Ranauld, and the two of them were soon engaged in animated conversation.

Last to arrive was King Istel, followed by several Castelan nobles. The old king had a disheveled look about him, and his hair was in disarray.

"My apologies for being late," he said, addressing no one in particular. "These days I like to take a brief nap after my midday meal." He raised his hands helplessly. "Unfortunately I don't always wake exactly when I intend to." He shuffled over to Essanda and kissed her on the head. "You look radiant, my dear," he said fondly.

"I confess that I don't feel especially radiant," she replied. "But thank you all the same, Father." She smiled up at him affectionately.

Steffan was impatient to begin, so the moment King Istel had seated himself, the Arvenian king turned to his father-in-law.

"You called this meeting, Your Majesty," he said, "and I for one have been very curious to understand the reason. Please tell us what has been concerning you."

Istel's face took on a grave look. "I don't doubt that all of us have appreciated the peace and stability enjoyed by our kingdoms after our victory at Torbury Scarp. None of us wish to see that tranquility threatened. However I have become aware that such a threat exists, and the information I have to share will be of grave concern to us all." He paused to scan their faces.

Steffan's brows furrowed. Castel might be a small kingdom, but in recent years it had boasted a formidable network of foreign agents.

He had witnessed their effectiveness himself. His mind flew back to his first visit to Castel. Istel had warned him about a traitor among the Arvenian nobility, right at the time of the Rogandan invasion. Steffan had been dismissive at first, but the information proved accurate. Will Prentis had later unmasked the Earl of Pisander as the renegade.

The Arvenian capital of Arnost would have fallen if the traitor had not been identified at a crucial moment. Will had credited

Thomas, the stable master's son, with exposing Pisander, although it wasn't at all clear to Steffan how he had managed it.

The traitor had later bribed his way out of prison and escaped. Steffan still harbored frustration that his uncle, acting as regent at the time, had not decisively dealt with Pisander while he had the chance. His uncle, the Duke of Erestor, had otherwise shown himself to be very effective as regent, and Steffan didn't want to dwell on one blemish. Pushing the matter from his mind, he returned his attention to his father-in-law.

"I have learned that certain men—none that I can identify, unfortunately—have been hiring mercenaries with a view to creating unrest. The initial target is apparently Erestor."

Steffan frowned. This information could explain the reports he had been receiving from Erestor. Sending Will to investigate was now looking like an astute decision—he could hardly imagine anyone better suited to ferret out whatever might be going on.

"Varas was also mentioned," Istel continued. "And I don't doubt for a moment that my own kingdom is also a target."

Delmar had offered no comment, but it was obvious to Steffan that the Varasan king was deep in thought.

"There were no details on offer," Istel continued, "but since all three kingdoms appear to be affected, it seemed important to pass on the information and coordinate our responses."

Steffan nodded his thanks. "I certainly appreciate your initiative."

"There's more," Istel said grimly. "This most recent information didn't reach me until after I set out for this meeting. My agents believe that the purpose goes far beyond unrest. It seems that the ultimate goal is assassination." He poked a finger first in the direction of Steffan, then at Delmar. "Removal of the monarchs. I don't doubt that I am also on the list."

No one spoke.

"One last piece of information," said King Istel. "I am told that the plotters have access to almost limitless financial resources."

"Agon," said Steffan bitterly. "Who else has vast financial resources, and who else would be eager to see us all brought down?"

Delmar locked eyes with him for a moment. Then he nodded slowly.

"Strangest of all," Istel added, "my agent almost had the feeling that the original information about the mercenaries had been leaked intentionally."

Steffan frowned skeptically. "Why would they want to do that?"

"Perhaps they were looking for a way to bring all three kings together," said Lord Karevis. "They might reasonably expect Your Majesties to meet in a central location. Of necessity, any central location is going to be remote, and therefore less secure than the capitals." Karevis became increasingly restless as he spoke.

"But each of us brought at least two hundred soldiers," Steffan protested, "and they're stationed in the fields around us. It would require a small army to deal with a force that size, and I've had no reports of armies on the move."

The kings went quiet. The noblemen found nothing to say either.

King Delmar eventually broke the silence. He turned to Lord Karevis. "Am I right in thinking that the perimeter guard duty is currently assigned to our men?"

"Yes, Your Majesty," the Varasan commander replied.

"Double the guards," Delmar ordered, "and make sure that all of them are on high alert."

Lord Karevis nodded and left the barn immediately, slipping out through the side entrance.

Delmar turned back to his fellow sovereigns. "Hunting down and dealing with these plotters is clearly a pressing priority," he said. "In the meantime we find ourselves here together, whether by our own design or that of another. That offers us an opportunity to combine our resources. We need to make the most of that opportunity."

27

Alfic and his band of mercenaries had been watching the barn all day from the cover of a thick stand of trees some distance away.

They had watched the kings emerge from the mansion and enter the adjacent barn to be served their evening meal. A number of nobles had accompanied them, but few soldiers joined them inside the barn. The only other people in the vicinity were a group of monks who had apparently been brought in to serve the meal.

Careful observation throughout the daylight hours had shown that each king had no more than a dozen members of their royal guard stationed at the mansion where they were staying. However Alfic knew that the surrounding fields hosted busy encampments, each of which housed a substantial contingent of soldiers.

Three army camps had been established—one for each kingdom. The encampments were sited so that they were completely independent of each other, and they had been situated far enough away from the mansion to ensure that a hostile force coming from any direction could be challenged well before it came anywhere near the kings.

Between them the kings had brought several hundred soldiers—more than enough to heavily guard all approaches to the mansion.

Alfic had not been deterred. His men had avoided roads and trails and slipped through the trees in ones and twos under cover of darkness. The guards had not presented any difficulties. They had been well positioned, but they'd been far too relaxed. They clearly weren't expecting trouble.

The role of observing had quickly become tiresome. None of Alfic's thirty hired men showed any aptitude for waiting patiently. He had repeatedly been forced to warn them to keep quiet and stay out of sight—every one of them was now ready to erupt at the slightest provocation. They needed action, and the sooner it started the better.

As for him, he was focused entirely on the payout waiting for him at the end of this job. It was unlikely he'd ever need to work again once this exercise was behind him. The anticipation of the reward made him willing to put up with a lot.

Others had been tasked with dealing with the encamped soldiers. He didn't know the details—his employer insisted that Alfic already had plenty to focus on—but the other pieces had better be in place. He and his men would do what they had come here to do, but none of them would be alive for long if the rest of the plan fell apart. He pushed such considerations from his mind. His employer was right—he had more than enough of his own business to worry about.

As soon as the light began to fade he gathered his men. All of them were armed with bows, and each of them was a capable marksman. Their first task would be to deal with the soldiers outside the barn. They'd have no further need for the bows after that. Inside the barn it would be a matter of swordplay.

"You two. Stick close to me once we're inside." He jabbed a finger at his key Castelan and Varasan contacts. He needed them to identify King Istel of Castel and King Delmar of Varas. He had no need of assistance in identifying King Steffan—he had seen the Arvenian king often enough himself.

He pointed to four others. "Once we've dealt with the soldiers, torch the mansion. And make it quick! We need as much confusion as we can get. Then join us in the barn."

He pointed to two of the men. "There's a side entrance near the back of the barn. Find a way to block it, then join the rest of us."

He pointed to another two men. "Once all of us are inside, you two will close the main doors at the front and guard them. No one gets in or out. No exceptions."

He turned a stern face on his men. "Kill everyone you find in there—women as well as men."

He eyed them critically. "Do all of you get it?"

They grunted in response.

"Good. When we've dealt with them all, we'll burn the barn as well. Then we get out of here. Fast. The only thing left to do after that will be to collect our reward."

IN THE HALF light of dusk, an old horse plodded across the fields, pulling a wagon behind it. A gray haired crone trudged along in front of the horse, guiding it forward. She headed toward the encampment housing the Arvenian soldiers that had accompanied King Steffan to the gathering.

A sentry challenged her as she approached.

"A luv'ly evening to you, good sir," she gushed. "It's only old Gretchen, here with a tiny treat from the king. Something wet to grease the insides of his loyal soldiers on a cold night." She waved at the barrels in the back of the wagon.

The sentry brightened, and called to some of his comrades. "Let's have some help over here! Unload those barrels!"

"Now, now!" scolded the crone. "Don't you be greedy! Just four of them barrels, and no more. There are other soldiers camped out as well, you know."

"Only the Castelans and Varasans. None of them would be thirsty," insisted the sentry.

"Don't you be playing your silly tricks on old Gretchen!" she cried, wagging a finger at him. "I know what's what. You keep your grubby little mitts off them other barrels!"

"All right, old woman. No need for a fuss." The sentry turned to his fellows. "Just take four of 'em," he instructed.

Ale was already being drawn from the barrels, and someone handed the sentry a large mug, delivering it with a hearty slap on the back.

Tilting back his head, the sentry took a swig. He screwed up his face. "I've tasted better!" he exclaimed.

"It's a fresh barrel," said Gretchen soothingly. "The first sip always tastes a bit off." She winked at him. "The next mouthful will slide down better."

The sentry took another swallow. He grimaced slightly, but kept drinking.

"I'll be on me way, then," said old Gretchen. "Others might be thirsty too!"

She tugged at the horse. It pulled obediently at the load, and the wagon lurched into motion, its wheels squeaking in protest.

She smiled toothlessly to herself as she left the encampment behind. "Enjoy your evening, boys," she mumbled. "It'll be your last."

Before long she reached the Castelan encampment. The soldiers there were no less thirsty, and she departed after leaving them four barrels of their own.

Everything was going perfectly.

The final encampment belonged to the Varasans. As soon as she had delivered the final four barrels, her job would be done.

Once again she was challenged. "Who are you, and what are you doing here?" the sentry demanded.

"I've brought a nice little surprise for you all, courtesy of the king," she replied.

"What surprise?"

"Some tasty ale. Just the thing to warm your insides."

"Which king?" asked the sentry.

"Eh?" asked the crone, bewildered.

"Courtesy of which king?" the sentry repeated, rudely this time.

"Your king, of course. King Istel, bless him."

"Istel isn't our king." The sentry looked her up and down suspiciously.

"I meant King Steffan, of course," Gretchen replied. She berated herself for her sloppiness, and the attention it was drawing to her.

"Go find Lord Karevis!" the sentry called to another soldier. The soldier disappeared immediately.

Gretchen's heart began to race. She felt like turning and running, but she knew she wouldn't get very far. Besides, the situation might still be retrievable. She tried to calm her ruffled nerves.

A nobleman appeared, presumably Lord Karevis.

"What's your business here?" he asked her. He wasn't rude, but she had the impression that not much got past him. All at once she found herself feeling very uneasy indeed.

"I'm just delivering some ale to you and to your men, Your Worshipfulness," she said.

"Who arranged this?"

"King Delmar," she said with a deep bow, finally getting the name right.

"She told me King Istel sent it, My Lord!" the sentry said indignantly. "Then she said it was King Steffan!"

Lord Karevis looked at her searchingly for a long moment. "Detain her," he told the sentry. "Don't allow her to go anywhere. I will return soon."

He called for his aides and his horse, and left immediately.

Lord Karevis dismounted beside the barn and followed a servant through the side entrance.

An industrious group of monks were serving food, and the tables were laden. The kings were relaxing together in comfortable chairs, surrounded by members of the nobility who had accompanied them.

Karevis approached King Delmar discreetly. "Could I please steal you away briefly, Your Majesty?"

Delmar rose without hesitation and followed his friend. Karevis retraced his steps through the side entrance and paused once they were outside the barn.

"Did you arrange for ale to be sent to the men?" Karevis asked him.

"No," the king replied with a smile. "But I wish I had. It's an excellent idea."

Karevis shook his head. "Something very suspicious is going on," he said. "An old woman has appeared at our encampment with barrels of ale—supposedly sent by you. I've had her detained."

The king's smile faded.

"Do you have any idea who might be behind this?" Karevis asked. "It could be innocent, but something tells me otherwise."

King Delmar frowned. "Let's find out. I want to be present when you interview this woman."

He called for a horse, and the two men quickly mounted and rode away, followed closely by members of the king's guard.

NOT LONG AFTER Lord Karevis left with King Delmar, Alfic's men at last sprang into action.

Two men ran to the side entrance of the barn to block it.

Four others sprinted to the mansion bearing flaming torches. All of them carried rocks, and they smashed the windows of the mansion, thrusting forward their torches until the heavy drapes were alight. Then they threw the torches inside.

One of the men also carried a small cask of oil. Unstopping it, he splashed oil liberally inside the entrance way of the mansion. Then he smashed it and threw the pieces inside, followed by his torch. A roaring blaze now commanded the entrance to the building.

The four men positioned themselves around other doorways. Fugitives were soon flying from the building in mindless terror. Alfic's men ignored the servants, allowing them to flee in confusion into the gathering darkness. They struck down every other person who escaped the building. Nobles and soldiers alike met the same fate.

Smoke now billowed throughout the mansion and flames licked at the roof.

As the trickle of fugitives came to an end, the men ran to the barn to join the others.

ALFIC SPOTTED King Steffan as soon as he entered the barn. The king was positioned across the other side of the open space, laughing with a small group of noblemen. Alfic pointed to the Arvenian king, and six of his men ran across the barn toward him.

Alfic turned to his Castelan confederate. The man pointed out King Istel, who was sitting very close to the barn entrance. With a wave of his hand, Alfic directed several men to the Castelan king. They reached him in a few strides, putting him to the sword even before he understood what was happening. The men around the king drew their weapons and frantically began to defend themselves.

When Alfic turned to his Varasan accomplice, the man was frowning.

"Delmar isn't here," he said.

"Are you sure?" Alfic asked.

"I'm certain!"

Alfic spotted Queen Essanda sitting apart from her husband, with members of the Arvenian royal guard around her. Alfic pointed to them, and the Varasan set off with several others.

Small knots of fighting men had spread out around the barn, and Alfic now directed his remaining men to throw their weight behind those attacking King Steffan and Queen Essanda.

Two of his men had closed the doors of the barn and now stood guard just inside them. The four who had torched the mansion arrived and were quickly admitted to the barn after supplying an agreed signal.

A group of monks had apparently been serving food, and they had huddled together at one end of the barn. Alfic sent the new arrivals to kill them.

In the chaos it was difficult to determine with certainty what was happening. The location of King Delmar of Varas was a mystery. But the Castelan king was dead, and Alfic was confident that nothing could save the Arvenian royals.

DURING HER CHILDHOOD, Gretchen had seen her beloved father defrauded and mistreated by a noble family. Her father was a gentle man, and the action taken against him had left him in desperate circumstances. He had quickly declined as a result, to the point where he was unable to work.

With the breadwinner transformed into a burden, the entire family had been plunged into grinding poverty. From that time Gretchen had nursed a bitter hatred of every member of the upper classes, along with all those who willingly served them.

Now she stood beside her horse and wagon with growing anxiety. She had organized the horrific deaths of many unsuspecting men that night, but her grisly handiwork was not the reason for her distress.

While she was bolder than most, she was by no means fearless. Now she had been caught, and she greatly feared the consequences.

She soon began to weep. "What is to become of me? And all I've done is bring ale to some thirsty soldiers." Her tears were only partially faked.

A few other soldiers happened to be within earshot. "What's this about ale?" one of them asked.

"Lord Karevis said not to touch it," the sentry replied, lifting his chin officiously.

"He said no such thing!" Gretchen retorted. "He made no mention of my ale." She began to weep again.

"What are you doing to this poor woman?" another of the soldiers demanded.

The sentry scowled at him. "I'm detaining her. By order of Lord Karevis!"

"And what about the ale?" The soldier pointed to the wagon.

Other soldiers had arrived, and a small crowd now awaited his answer with keen interest.

"She claims it's a gift from the king. Lord Karevis wasn't convinced. And I'd suggest you move along if you don't want to get in trouble with him."

"Who gave you the right to speak on his behalf?" the first soldier asked. "If the king sent us ale, what business is it of yours?" Growls of assent rose in a rough chorus.

The men didn't wait for an answer. Eager hands reached for the barrels, and they were quickly pulled from the wagon.

"You'll answer to Lord Karevis for this!" yelled the sentry.

Some of the men held back uncertainly, but others broached the barrels and began passing around mugs of ale. New arrivals soon appeared, and before long they were pushing and shoving to get their share. The scene quickly descended into chaos. When the sentry tried to intervene he was shoved to the ground.

Gretchen took her opportunity and slipped away. She was forced to leave the horse and wagon behind, but she didn't care. She would be paid handsomely for her efforts.

She chuckled to herself as she waddled away. She would be out of sight before the fool of a sentry noticed she was missing. And by then he would have plenty else to think about.

King Delmar and Lord Karevis arrived at the encampment to a scene of unimaginable horror. Many of the men were thrashing around in agony on the ground, and more succumbed even as they watched. The remaining soldiers looked on in helpless dismay.

Karevis had no doubt that the men were in their death throes. He quickly located the sentry. "What happened here?" he demanded.

"I tried to prevent them from touching the barrels, My Lord," he replied miserably. "But they wouldn't listen. They pushed me to the ground."

"Where is the woman?"

The sentry hung his head. "When I got up she was gone."

Karevis turned to the king. "The ale was clearly poisoned," he said, grimacing as he surveyed the devastation.

He drew the king aside. "This was a carefully planned attack, Your Majesty," he said. "I fear we would find a similar scene if we visited the Arvenian and Castelan encampments."

He furrowed his brows. "We need to get you to safety. And I need to warn the other kings!"

Delmar opened his mouth to protest, but Karevis shook his head determinedly. "Can you imagine what's going to happen to Varas if we lose you? Preserving your life has just become our most pressing priority!"

He called to the sentry. "Find six men who didn't drink any of the ale and get them mounted. Then bring them to me. And hurry, man!"

The captain of the king's guards and a detachment of his men had followed Karevis and the king from the barn. Karevis turned to the captain. "Round up anyone else who hasn't touched the ale, and tell them I'm placing them under your command. Get King Delmar away from here, as quickly as possible. Escort him somewhere safe, somewhere defensible. As soon as you're confident you have the situation under control, send someone to find me. I'll be with the other kings in the barn."

The captain nodded and immediately sent several of his men to gather survivors.

The sentry arrived with six mounted men.

"You!" Karevis pointed to one of them. "Go to the Arvenian encampment. Tell any soldiers who are still alive to ride to the barn immediately and protect their king and queen!" He pointed to another soldier. "Do the same at the Castelan encampment. Get moving!"

The two soldiers rode off in great haste.

Karevis faced the five remaining soldiers. "The rest of you follow me," he said. He galloped away without a backward glance.

28

—————

Lord Karevis drove his horse forward as fast as he dared. Nevertheless, his unease increased as he began to imagine what might be happening in the barn. He tried not to think about the possible consequences should any of the kingdoms be stripped of their leaders.

Someone was behind this, but the mystery of who it was would have to wait. He could afford no distractions.

A glow in the night sky heightened his alarm. Drawing closer he saw that the mansion was ablaze. He urged his horse to a last burst of speed.

Bodies lay scattered around the flaming building, and he forced himself to ignore the feeble cries and moans that reached his ears. He sent his horse sprinting instead for the barn.

As the huge structure came into sight, sounds of fighting reached him. Karevis drew his sword and leaped from the saddle. He spared no attention for the men who had followed him. They shouldn't need to be told what to do.

The main barn doors were shut, and he burst through them, crashing into two men on the inside who had been standing in front of them. The first was knocked to the ground; the second immediately attacked him. Dancing away from a slashing sword, Karevis took his opponent in the side with a precise thrust of his own weapon. Without waiting for the outcome, he skewered the other man before he could regain his feet.

His five soldiers ran into the barn, and clustered behind him. He paused then, glancing rapidly around him.

King Steffan of Arvenon stood at bay across the barn with Count Ranauld, fighting off four opponents. They were barely holding their own. Karevis could see no sign of the Castelan king, Istel. He spun around to face his men. "Help him!" he commanded, pointing to Steffan. They immediately raced over to join the fight.

Then he noticed Queen Essanda huddled in a corner of the barn, defended by just one soldier. Even as he watched, the defender went down. Karevis didn't pause for thought—he immediately sprinted toward her.

One of the men stepped toward the queen, raising his sword high. But his blow never fell. A sword point emerged briefly from his back before disappearing again. He stood rigid for a moment, then slowly crumpled to the ground.

Underestimating the heavily pregnant young queen had cost the attacker his life.

Four remained, and the queen faced them alone, a determined expression on her pale face. Before any of them could move, Karevis smashed into them from behind. He ran one of them through with his sword as he burst past them.

He came to a halt beside the youthful queen, panting from the exertion. They raised their swords and confronted their enemies together.

HAVING SERVED THE FOOD, the white robed monks were clearing tables when the attack in the barn began. Seeing they were trapped, they scurried to Brother Elias and thronged around him fearfully.

Unperturbed, the old monk was surveying the scene as if trying to assess where he might best be of use.

Brother Ander stood silently beside his mentor. Such a situation could not have been fashioned more precisely to challenge the transformation that had taken place within him. What kind of a man could remain detached while witnessing cold blooded murder? And he was a seasoned warrior—how could he stand by and do nothing? He looked on with growing alarm as King Istel was struck down and King Steffan beset. His hands began to twitch involuntarily.

Everything within him demanded a response. He knew what to do, and it was obvious that his skills were sorely needed. But he had chosen a different path. He had vowed to follow the way of peace.

His mind wrestled mightily with his instincts. God was not dependent on him to save these people. The destiny of every person was in his hands. And if the Almighty chose not to send others to help, he must have his reasons.

But was there a reason why he found himself there at such a time? Was he the one that God had sent?

It couldn't be. He knew from experience that violence only gave rise to more violence, and he had turned his back once and for all on resolving conflict by the sword. He shook his head in a vain attempt to dispel his inner turmoil.

"Get rid of those monks," a harsh voice called. "Leave no witnesses!"

His alarm turned to anger as four men with drawn swords stepped toward his brothers. His eyes narrowed. What kind of men would slaughter defenseless monks?

He turned to Brother Elias. How could his mentor remain so calm?

The old abbot caught his eye. "You must allow God to direct your ways," he said quietly.

What did Brother Elias mean? Ander looked from him to the advancing killers and back again. The four men had almost reached them.

Brother Ander himself was not afraid to die. But how could he stand idly by and allow these butchers to snuff out the lives of his brothers?

The attackers must have realized that Brother Elias was the leader of the monks, because two of them headed straight for him. Brother Ander saw the death of the abbot in their eyes.

He could not permit it—he *would* not permit it. The twitching in his hands became uncontrollable.

The killers raised their swords to strike the abbot down. They had no way of knowing it, but they had just pronounced their own death sentences.

Brother Ander's inner debate ceased abruptly as his anger hit boiling point. Completely overcome with indignation, he stretched down for a wooden bench. The two men reached Brother Elias just as he hefted it into the air. He brought it smashing down on their heads.

The attackers collapsed to the floor and lay unmoving. Their companions came to a sudden halt, staring at him open mouthed.

The big monk waded into the attack, wielding the bench as a club. His opponents ducked and weaved frantically as he swept his makeshift weapon back and forth like a scythe. They were not nimble enough to completely avoid his blows.

No one could long survive such bludgeoning. A heavy blow to the side of the head sent one of them crashing to the floor. The full force of the former warrior's fury was now turned on the remaining attacker. The man made the mistake of turning to flee. The entire weight of the wooden bench slammed into the back of his skull, breaking his neck. He slumped lifeless to the floor.

The monks were now safe, at least for the moment. Brother Ander was just getting started.

Quickly scanning the chaos in the barn, he chose another target. Then, roaring a challenge, he sprinted toward the men who had dared to bring death and destruction into the peaceful barn.

Lord Karevis accepted that he could not himself survive, but he was determined to keep Queen Essanda alive for as long as he could. Unwilling to allow her to remain at his side facing their attackers, he tried to push her behind him.

She refused to budge. And in spite of her condition, she was by no means proving to be an easy kill.

At first their enemies targeted her, two of them coming at her at once. With their attention diverted, Karevis saw an opportunity. Deflecting a blow from the remaining attacker, he leaned forward and punched him in the face. As the man staggered back, Karevis attacked the other two from the side. He thrust his sword into the nearest man, shoving him against the other as he collapsed.

The queen did not waste her chance. While the other attacker was unbalanced, she stabbed forward with her blade and took him in the neck.

One opponent remained. Having recovered from the blow to the head, he renewed his attack on Karevis, a nasty look on his face. Off balance himself, Karevis did well to survive the first frantic moments of this new onslaught.

And even before he had settled into a rhythm, he saw from the corners of his eye two new attackers heading in their direction.

Brother Ander threw the heavy wooden bench at two more attackers. Snatching up a discarded sword, he stabbed down at them while they lay stunned on the ground. Then he ran on, grabbing hold of a large earthenware jug in his other hand as he ran past a table.

He became aware of Queen Essanda's plight just as two additional men joined the assault on her and her defender. Recognizing the Varasan nobleman at her side, Brother Ander raced to his support.

Having vented his initial rage, he found that his head had cleared. Rather than roaring a new challenge, he chose subtlety. Running up behind the men, he smashed the heavy jug over the head of one, then plunged his sword into the back of the other. The third attacker glanced behind him in alarm, and paid for his distraction as Lord Karevis ran him through.

"Get her out of here, My Lord!" Brother Ander cried, pointing to the now unguarded doors. "I'll cover you."

They hurried outside, the nobleman taking the queen's elbow and helping her forward. The queen's maid, Ava, who had been cowering behind them in the barn, scurried out after her mistress. The big monk followed them watchfully.

With no immediate need to defend herself, Queen Essanda began to look increasingly distressed. Brother Ander marveled at her pluck in facing what must have seemed like certain death. With limited support, she had somehow outlasted her attackers. It occurred to him that the unborn baby might well have been put at risk by the almost superhuman efforts she had been called upon to make. He sent up a fervent prayer for the safety of them both.

Arriving outside, they met a dozen soldiers in Arvenian livery belatedly approaching on horseback. Their faces wore haunted looks, and the men appeared dazed and disoriented.

They came to their senses when the monk bellowed at them to protect their queen.

Brother Ander pointed to Lord Karevis. "This man is the commander of the Varasan army. I fought beside him at Torbury Scarp. Do whatever he tells you to do!" he ordered. "I'll need some of you to come with me."

He jabbed a finger at four of them, and they dismounted. Drawing their swords, they followed him back into the barn.

FROM THE MOMENT the attack began, King Steffan's only thought was for the safety of his wife. Determined to protect her, he set out at once to move to her side. He quickly found his path blocked completely by attackers. Their relentless onslaught offered him no chance to go anywhere, and little opportunity to think of anything beyond his own survival.

Of the nobles who surrounded him, only Count Ranauld had fought in a battle. Most noblemen routinely carried a sword, though, if only for symbolic reasons, and all of them were trained from an early age to use it. As a result, every one of his companions mounted a vigorous defense.

Nevertheless they were outnumbered and outmatched. Their host, Count Lonnigen, was the first to fall. Before long just Steffan and Ranauld remained. Between them the others had accounted for only two of their attackers.

The king and Ranauld now fought side by side, with the barn wall at their backs.

Steffan barely found time even to glance elsewhere. But he was aware that his father-in-law was dead. He saw Lord Karevis arrive, and realized that his pregnant wife was alive only thanks to the help of the Varasan nobleman. Unable himself to reach Essanda, he saw that he had no choice but to rely on others to protect her.

Other Varasan soldiers had arrived with Lord Karevis, and five of them now ran to his aid. For a time the odds tilted in Steffan's favor, but more enemies came against them, and the attackers gradually regained the initiative.

Steffan caught a glimpse of Brother Ander when he joined the fight, and saw to his relief that his wife had been rescued and ushered to safety.

There was no opportunity to enjoy the moment, though. One by one his new defenders were overwhelmed. Once again he fought side by side with Ranauld against superior numbers.

Another attacker joined the fight—one who appeared to be the leader of his enemies. He wondered who the man was, and what had motivated him. But his thoughts were forced back to the basic necessities of block, thrust, twist, turn.

He felt so weary. Where were his soldiers? Why couldn't Will Prentis have been here, and Rufe Sarjant?

Brother Ander reentered the barn followed by four Arvenian soldiers. Perhaps help was arriving at last. Some of the new arrivals must surely have gathered around Essanda to protect her. He felt as if a huge weight had been lifted from his shoulders.

ALFIC GROUND his teeth in frustration. After a very promising start, the attack had become completely bogged down. If only he had a few more men. A flush of anger washed over him. He would have brought forty if his employer's barbs hadn't stung him into hiring thirty.

The only victory—and it was increasingly feeling like a minor one—had been killing Istel. Delmar had somehow contrived to vanish before the fighting started, and Steffan was proving unexpectedly difficult to kill. Every time the resistance of the Arvenian king appeared to be ending, more soldiers arrived to defend him.

You always needed to expect the unexpected. But there had been far too many unforeseen developments. Where had the Varasan nobleman come from? He had killed the men guarding the door, sent his soldiers to rescue Steffan, and still somehow managed to save the Arvenian queen.

The most ruinous surprise had been the monk's intervention. Monks weren't supposed to be fighters. How could he have anticipated that one of them would turn out to be such an efficient killer? The big monk must have killed more of Alfic's men than any other person.

When the monk disappeared outside with the queen, Alfic saw his opportunity. He would finish off Steffan, then get out of there fast. He waded into the attack.

"The monk! He's back!"

The warning held a tone of panic. If Alfic wasn't careful, his few remaining men would turn and run. He pressed forward with renewed urgency.

He lunged at the Arvenian king with his sword. The king twisted aside, blocking the blow with his own blade. Instead of drawing back, in one smooth motion Alfic pulled a knife from his belt and thrust forward with his other hand.

King Steffan had no time to avoid the blow and no armor to protect him. The knife took him in the side, and he went down with a cry of pain.

Alfic heard a roar behind him, and spun instinctively to the side, barely avoiding the monk's sweeping sword. The moment he regained his balance, he sprinted for the doors of the barn, dodging fallen tables and leaping over chairs and wooden benches.

More soldiers were running into the barn. He crashed through them, knocking two of them to the ground, and ran off into the night. He didn't pause until he was well hidden among the trees. No one appeared to be pursuing him.

He finally came to a halt, doubling over with his hands on his knees and gasping in air.

The monk had nearly ruined everything. As it was Alfic could claim only one confirmed kill and one probable kill. The third king had avoided his trap, and the Arvenian queen had apparently escaped entirely.

He should still receive half of his reward. And there wouldn't be too many of his hired men left to share it with. He doubted that more than two or three of them had escaped. A smile of satisfaction crossed his face.

He would find his horse and ride to the agreed meeting point. Then he would wait for other survivors.

But not for long.

29

Queen Essanda stood outside the barn with her maid, Ava. A small group of soldiers surrounded them. Most of them were glancing around nervously, as if expecting to be attacked at any moment.

Only Lord Karevis projected calm. He stood beside the queen, shooting frequent glances at her face and her bulging stomach. He was clearly concerned for her.

"Don't worry about me," she said, forcing the words between clenched teeth. "The king needs our help!" She took a deep breath, willing herself to ignore the painful tightenings of her abdomen.

"Ander—Brother Ander—will do whatever is necessary," he replied. "We need to get you somewhere safe, and somewhere comfortable." He paused. "Then I must see to my own king," he added apologetically.

"Of course, you should go! Do what you need to do," she told him.

"I'm not going anywhere until you're safe," he insisted.

She was too exhausted and too distressed to argue with him. Her father's life had ended that night, and she had been permitted no opportunity to mourn his passing. Grieving would have to wait.

Outside in the open, the roar of the flames filled her ears, and even at a safe distance the heat from the fire beat upon her. Glowing embers billowed up into the night sky with the smoke from the burning mansion. It was a terrible and imposing sight. She tried not to notice the bodies strewn around the building.

The angry red glow of the fire filled her vision, but her heart was with her husband. Essanda could think of nothing else. As she was helped from the barn she had caught a glimpse of him. He looked weary and vulnerable, but he had risked a glance in her direction. She knew it would comfort him to know she was safe.

She knew a queen should be thinking of her subjects at such a time, but she was fearful and burdened and had nothing to give.

A man ran from the barn and disappeared into the trees. Two more men followed him. Then Brother Ander emerged with Count Ranauld, carrying King Steffan.

Her pain and weariness forgotten, she ran to him, crying out his name.

"He's unconscious," Brother Ander told her. "But he's alive. He took a knife in the side."

A group of monks emerged from the barn, the oldest of them hurrying over to join them. He knelt with Brother Ander beside the king, examining him.

"He's badly wounded. He's lost a lot of blood, and he needs immediate attention," the monk said gravely.

Brother Ander responded at once. "Tell me how I can best help, Brother Elias!"

"You can begin by praying," Brother Elias said simply.

Brother Ander bowed his head. But he appeared shamed rather than prayerful.

Brother Elias saw his response. "I don't want you to limit yourself to praying," he said. "God uses our hands as well as our prayers. And you were made to be a healer—I have never seen anyone learn so quickly or apply that learning so effectively."

Brother Ander remained silent, but he joined his mentor at the side of the king. The two of them worked swiftly to expose the wound. An anguished sob shook Essanda's frame when she saw the damage, and she tore her eyes away, blinking back her tears.

Unable to watch, she fixed her gaze on the two healers. There was something incongruous about them. One was old and wizened and slight of frame. The other had the build of a burly warrior in the prime of life. Yet both were clad simply in the robes of monks, and both had eyes only for their patient. Both of them were clearly competent, although the big monk deferred to the older man.

Brother Elias was surprisingly deft, the nimbleness of his fingers belying his age. He did not seem dismayed by the task before him, and her trembling gradually subsided as she allowed his calm demeanor to wash over her anxieties. She closed her eyes and slowly released a long shuddering sigh.

A Varasan soldier galloped up, leaping from the saddle the moment he spotted Lord Karevis. He bowed, then leaned in and spoke to the Varasan commander in low tones.

Karevis nodded, and turned to Essanda. "Our men have located a farmhouse not far from here. They have set up defenses around it, and King Delmar is using it as a temporary base. He is not aware of what has happened here, but he requested me to invite his fellow monarchs to join him. Everyone here will be welcome."

Of the Castelan lords who had accompanied King Istel, just one —a pompous nobleman called Lord Eravitt—appeared to have survived the attack. "Will you join us?" Karevis asked him.

A look of disdain came across the noble's face. "I have just located four Castelan soldiers who survived," he said. "We leave immediately for Castel." He frowned darkly as he glanced around him. "This is not a time for playing at alliances. No outsiders need expect a warm welcome in our kingdom. I will be instructing our soldiers to seal off Deadman's Pass immediately."

Essanda glared back at him. "What are you saying, My Lord?" she demanded.

The nobleman winced. "As a native of our land, you will of course always be welcome, Your Majesty." He bowed stiffly. "I must go. Your brother is now the king, and the Council of Lords will need to appoint a regent."

Her heart went out to her brother. Prince Rupert—King Rupert, she corrected herself—was all that remained of her family now. The youth was barely seventeen. She had seen him just once since leaving Castel, and then only briefly. "Please convey my love and best wishes to my brother. Our prayers will be with him in these difficult times."

She took a breath to steady herself. "What of my father?" she asked.

The nobleman bowed. "With your permission, we will take his body with us," he said. "I regret that we will not be able to transport him with the dignity that is his due. But he will be buried in state in his capital."

She nodded, unable to find words to speak.

Eravitt bowed again, then hurried away, calling to his men. She turned her back as they brought out the body of her beloved father and tied it to a horse. She could not bear the thought of it, and could not allow such a sight to become her final memory of him. The Castelans rode quickly away into the night.

Tears of grief rolled down Essanda's face as they left. Better men than Eravitt had died tonight, her own father chief among them, but there was nothing she could do to help Castel at that moment.

She returned her attention to the pressing matter of her husband.

Lord Karevis was kneeling beside Brother Elias. "Can King Steffan be moved?" he asked.

The abbot shook his head unequivocally. "Not by horse," he replied.

"My carriage!" cried Essanda. "Is it still intact?"

"Yes, Your Majesty," a soldier replied. "I saw it earlier. It was moved away from the house, and the flames have not reached it."

Brother Elias pondered for a moment, then he nodded. "He would certainly be better off in proper shelter. We must move him slowly and carefully, though."

"Fetch the carriage, and quickly!" Count Ranauld ordered.

As a number of his men scurried away to do his bidding, another monk drew near. Beyond him, a group of monks huddled together. Their eyes wore a haunted look. Some of them were staring openly at Brother Ander.

The new arrival first addressed the big monk. "Thank you," he said simply. When Brother Ander did not respond, he turned instead to Brother Elias. "How can we help?" he asked.

"I must go with the king," the old monk replied. "I am leaving you in charge of your brothers, Brother Gerome. Please tend to any wounded who might benefit from your help. I will send for you all later."

Brother Gerome nodded and returned to the other monks, speaking quietly to them. They quickly dispersed.

After what felt like an eternity, a group of men returned with the carriage. King Steffan was gently lifted into it, both Brother Elias and Brother Ander climbing in beside him.

Ava appeared at the side of the queen, pale but determined. "You, too, Your Majesty," she insisted.

Lord Karevis nodded his agreement and offered Essanda his hand. Then he helped Ava up as well. "Pay close attention to her," he murmured.

After closing the carriage door, Karevis briefly conferred with Count Ranauld. Then the Varasan commander climbed up beside the driver.

Count Ranauld stepped forward and called to the men around him. "I need five volunteers! The rest of you can follow the carriage to King Delmar's new base."

No one moved at first, but five men eventually stepped forward. Count Ranauld nodded his thanks to them. "We must find mounts and ride to each of the encampments," he said. "Others may have survived. We will gather the survivors and bring them here. Be alert —we don't know if any enemies are still in the area."

"We will send a guide and instruct him to wait for you here," Karevis told him. "We will also return the carriage for the other wounded."

Count Ranauld nodded, and led his men away.

Karevis called to the Varasan soldier, "Lead on!"

The carriage rumbled slowly forward, and the rest of the men followed it, some on horseback, others on foot.

Essanda winced at every jolt. Could the ride have been this bumpy when she traveled from Arnost? Ava found her a cushion and insisted she take it.

Brother Elias turned away from his patient to address the queen. "When we arrive, you must leave the king with us for a time," he said gently, indicating himself and Brother Ander. "You need to care for yourself too." He glanced briefly down at her belly before directing a significant look toward her maid.

Ava nodded an acknowledgment.

Essanda gazed back at him for a moment, then gave a single nod. She knew she wouldn't find it easy to leave Steffan's side, but she recognized the wisdom in the monk's words. It was impossible to know how much the baby had been affected by the upheaval. She sent a fervent prayer into the heavens for her unborn child.

Brother Ander had nothing to say, so Essanda leaned over and placed her hand on his arm. "I owe you my life," she said. "For that you have my heartfelt thanks!"

He bowed his head, but offered no other response.

Sudden insight came to her as she gazed across at him. "Perhaps you have paid a price of your own in fighting to save me and others. Was it possible to help us only by laying aside your principles?" she asked. "If so, I am truly sorry that our situation demanded that of you."

His head sank lower still. It was obvious to her that she had hit the mark.

"I have survived," she said, "in spite of the best efforts of the murderers who attacked us tonight. I am praying that my baby is unharmed too. Perhaps we are still here because that is what God intended."

Brother Ander's head came up slowly, and his eyes met hers. Then he stole a glance at Brother Elias.

The old monk gazed back at him quietly. "I have firmly taught you to renounce violence," he said. "But I cannot presume to understand God's purposes. It is difficult to imagine that your presence in the barn tonight was an accident. God brought you to us by a winding path, and that same path led you to the barn. You were in the right place at the right time—of that I have no doubt. Be at peace, my young friend."

Essanda's delicate fingers still rested on Brother Ander's arm, and the old monk covered them with his own worn hand. A gentle smile softened his wrinkled visage. "The queen has spoken wisely," he said.

She smiled back at him, even though she felt more perplexed than wise.

She stared at the prone figure of Steffan. Who had done this, and why? She could make no sense of the blood crazed savagery that lay behind them.

Tearing her eyes away from her husband, she stared out of the carriage window into the night sky. Thin wisps of cloud draped themselves across the face of the moon, and a dazzling array of stars winked down at her.

Brother Elias followed her gaze for a moment. Then he turned to her. Glancing across at him she saw the deep contours of his face twisted with sorrow. "It is strange, is it not?" he asked. "How is it that such beauty can coexist with the madness we have witnessed?"

He might have been reading her mind.

He peered back out into the starlit night, and slowly his face became calm again. "It is as beautiful as it is unwavering," he said. "Everything above us in the heavens continues its stately procession. Day follows night, night follows day, and seasons give way to seasons, just as they always have. The whole of nature dances and sways in time to a divinely ordered rhythm."

He shook his head sadly. "Humankind alone resists it."

She gazed absently out of the window, a single tear welling up in her eye and rolling down her cheek.

.   .   .

THEY HAD JOURNEYED for no more than thirty minutes when the carriage at last rolled to a stop.

Men with torches appeared, and Lord Karevis issued a rapid set of instructions. A litter was found, and King Steffan was carried into the farmhouse, the two monks remaining at his side.

Essanda heeded Brother Elias's words, and stayed away from the room where her husband had been placed.

Instead she dismissed Ava with a tight smile and wandered aimlessly outside in the dark, passing among the soldiers settling in around the farmhouse. Most of the men who weren't on duty had positioned themselves before one of a number of roaring fires. They stared into the flames, silent and brooding. They could almost have been struck dumb.

With her uncertainties about the future weighing heavily on her, the oppressive atmosphere only served to heighten her fears and doubts.

Physical exertion had also taken a heavy toll on her body. Her abdomen was becoming increasingly uncomfortable, and her head had started to throb. When she also found herself shivering uncontrollably with the cold, she hurried indoors.

Ava had been waiting anxiously for her return, and the maid ushered her to a rough bed that she had prepared.

COUNT RANAULD eventually reached the farmhouse. The queen had been resting when she was told of his arrival, and she felt strong enough to get up and seek him out.

She discovered that he had brought twenty men with him. Three of them were Castelan, and he was in the act of excusing them to follow Lord Eravitt when she joined him. She greeted her former countrymen solemnly and wished them well on their journey. They managed to thank her politely, but they seemed barely able to focus. It was obvious they were traumatized by the things they had witnessed. The men rode away the minute they were released.

Essanda mustered up a smile for Ranauld. "It's pleasing to see that you found more men, My Lord," she said. "Are others following behind you?"

He bowed formally. "As far as we can tell, Your Majesty," he said, "there are no other survivors."

Her face fell. "You visited all three encampments?" she asked in dismay. "And you found no one else?"

He shook his head without speaking. The tension on his face hinted at the horrors he had seen.

"Lord Karevis has told me that the men were deliberately poisoned," she said. "I must go to our encampment tomorrow to pay my respects to the fallen."

He responded with immediate alarm. "You must not, Your Majesty!" he insisted. "Not in your condition—it would be much too distressing!" He hesitated, then added, "Their...their end was not a pleasant one."

She contained her emotions with an effort. "How are they to be laid to rest?" she asked.

He shrugged unhappily. "I do not know," he said. "There are so many of them and so few of us. Defending our monarchs must be the priority for the moment. But I have sent to Arnost for reinforcements."

"If only Will had been here," she murmured.

Ranauld nodded slowly. "The same thought has come to me more than once. I can't help thinking that the outcome would have been different if Lord Torbury and Rufe had been here." He passed a hand across his eyes. "I'm not at all sure how I survived."

"I saw you in there. You're alive because of your skill and your determination," Essanda told him. "And the king is still living only thanks to you."

"Each of us did what we could, Your Majesty," said Ranauld. "I would not be here without His Majesty's skill and determination."

She found nothing further to say.

Ranauld eventually broke the silence. "Where is Brother Ander?" he asked.

She took a deep breath to steady her voice. "He is inside. Caring for the king."

Ranauld nodded. "If it hadn't been for him," he said, "none of us would still be alive."

***

NONE of the men guarding the approaches to the mansion had been affected by the poison, since they were not in their encampment when the ale was handed out. By agreement between the kings, the perimeter guard duty was shared on rotation among the three contingents. The Varasans had been taking their turn at the time, and King Delmar had ordered the guard to be doubled not long before the ale was delivered.

As a result, King Delmar's contingent had been least affected by the attack. Even so, three Varasan noblemen had died in the barn, as well as a high proportion of the soldiers present in the Varasan encampment.

King Delmar was eager to return to his capital of Varacellan as soon as possible. It seemed likely that the assault in the barn was part of a larger strategy, and Delmar was eager to assess the state of his kingdom and put in place a range of security measures.

He also intended to seal tight his border with Arvenon. The Rogandan invasion a few years previously had taught him the consequences of half measures.

He was keenly aware, though, that most of the surviving soldiers belonged to him, and that the small number of Castelans had already returned to Castel. If he departed now, he would leave the remaining Arvenians vulnerable. Doubly so since King Steffan could not be safely moved, and the queen could not ride a horse in view of her pregnancy.

Out of consideration for his friend and ally, Delmar decided to delay his departure until reinforcements arrived from Arnost.

Varasan reinforcements finally appeared after four days, led by Lord Nilsean, one of Lord Karevis's senior commanders. With no sign of the Arvenians, even though Arnost was relatively close at hand, Count Ranauld reluctantly concluded that his messenger had met with an accident. Although he could ill afford to do so, he now sent two more men, with instructions for them to return promptly with medical help as well as soldiers.

The following day King Delmar called a meeting with Queen Essanda and Count Ranauld. He also invited Lord Karevis.

"I must be direct with you," he said to the queen. "I have delayed my departure as much for your sake as for my own. But I cannot afford to delay any longer."

Queen Essanda nodded, her face unreadable.

"All of us came to this location for the sake of our security. Now that my reinforcements have reached us I no longer feel quite so vulnerable as I did previously. I am confident we now have more than enough men to ensure our safety during our return to Varas. Lord Karevis agrees with me." He nodded to his commander, who bowed in response.

"I am therefore willing to leave fifty of my soldiers here under Lord Nilsean. I will instruct Lord Nilsean to report to Count Ranauld. I will leave them with instructions to return to Varas as soon as your own reinforcements have arrived."

"We are exceedingly grateful, Your Majesty," said the queen.

"Please, there is no need to thank me! I have not forgotten that King Steffan lent me more than one thousand of his own soldiers to help me take back Varas from the Rogandans. This tiny gesture in no way erases that debt."

Queen Essanda nevertheless thanked them sincerely, expressing her profound appreciation for their help and friendship at a time of great need. She assured them too that she would never forget her own personal debt to Lord Karevis for his life-saving intervention during the attack in the barn.

.   .   .

KING DELMAR and Lord Karevis rode away in no doubt of Queen Essanda's staunch support should they ever find themselves in need of it.

"What do you make of the Arvenian situation, Karevis?" the king asked his friend. "It seems surprising that reinforcements have not arrived."

"I admit to being greatly concerned about it, Your Majesty. And not just for the sake of King Steffan and Queen Essanda, who are friends as well as allies. We share our most accessible border with Arvenon. If Arvenon stumbles, we are certain to be affected."

Delmar offered no response, and they fell silent for a time.

"What do you expect us to find when we reach our own kingdom?" asked the king.

"The reinforcements reported no hint of trouble at the time they left, Your Majesty. But I'm not sure if that means a great deal. Even if there is no obvious trouble, we would be wise to keep our forces on high alert."

The king drew his horse closer to Karevis. "And what of our foreign agents?"

Karevis lowered his voice. "We've worked very hard to strengthen and broaden our agent network. I think it's time we put them to work."

30

———

Alfic stood once again in the darkened cabin with the man he thought of as Count Nothing.

"Have you completed the job?" he was asked.

"I kept my part of the agreement," he replied. "To the degree it was possible."

"What does that mean?" asked the Count.

"Istel is dead. Steffan is as good as dead—I knifed him myself."

"What about Steffan's woman?"

"She's still alive."

"What? You had clear instructions to kill everyone. That included her!"

"She had unexpected help."

"What help?"

"From a monk."

"A monk? A large group of mercenaries couldn't handle a monk?!"

"This was no ordinary monk. And I've already told you—we dealt with the king."

"She's pregnant with his heir, you fool. You didn't even get half of the job done. And what about Delmar? You made no mention of him."

"He wasn't there."

"What do you mean he wasn't there?"

"He was there for most of the day, but he disappeared just before we moved in."

"So even by your own account, you only dealt with one king. You were supposed to deal with three kings, a queen, and an unborn heir."

"I told you, Steffan is as good as dead."

"One king means one fifth of the pay. And you won't get that until we confirm your story."

"You call me a fool, but you're the fool if you think you can cheat me and my men," growled Alfic.

"You surely can't expect to be paid for work you didn't do," was the retort. "I would never have hired you if I'd realized you were so incompetent."

Alfic's eyes narrowed. All his life he had taken the risks, while men like this sat back and criticized from their couches. Fury began to slowly build inside him.

"Anyway, you'll still be very well off," the voice continued, "even with a fifth of the payment. It doesn't look like you have too many men left to claim a share."

A bag of coins flew through the air. Alfic was ready this time and caught it cleanly.

"That's a down payment. You'll get the rest when Castel announces the death of Istel. And there'll be more if Steffan does die."

Alfic left with the money. But he was furious.

The contract had always been to kill everyone present. But payment was only ever about the three kings. There had never been any suggestion that the amount depended on the queen and her unborn child.

Count Nothing had claimed that Alfic was better off because fewer men would share the money. But Alfic had never expected to share the payment with all of them. No one in this line of business would imagine for a moment that an entire group of mercenaries would survive such an operation.

Some of Count Nothing's money would be used against him. Alfic would begin making discreet inquiries about him. And he would have him constantly watched, starting immediately.

No one cheated Alfic and got away with it.

KING AGON GLARED down at his agent. "Get up and tell me what's been going on!" he commanded irritably.

The man abandoned his bow and scrambled to his feet, standing awkwardly at attention. He was Agon's best agent—more accurately the best of those who hadn't yet lost their heads—and the deep lines under his eyes suggested he hadn't managed to sleep for some time. He had probably been riding all night. Most likely he hadn't eaten in a while either.

That awareness did nothing to diminish Agon's impatience. His subjects existed solely to do his bidding.

"Have my pet foreigners delivered on their promise?" he demanded.

"They have been successful at least in part, Your Majesty. The kings of Arvenon, Castel, and Varas were successfully drawn into meeting in a remote location," the agent told him. "One of our agents planted the idea in King Istel's mind, and he took the bait. The kings were attacked after most of their soldiers were disposed of."

"Well? What was the outcome?" Agon's heart began to hammer with annoyance. Why couldn't the idiot get to the point?

"At least one of the kings is dead, Your Majesty. Another is believed to be close to death. The foreign noblemen were vague about specifics of how he managed to survive."

Agon felt the blood rising to his head. "I give you every agent you ask for!" he howled. "And you're relying on foreign dupes for information?"

"No, no, Your Majesty!" said his agent, cringing. "The foreigners made bold claims about what they had achieved. But every fact that is known for certain about the kings comes from our own sources!"

Agon's eyes bulged as he tried to master his fury. "I gave them unlimited resources," he shouted. "And this is the best they can do?"

After all the bold plans and confident expectations of the foreign noblemen, the fools had somehow managed to bungle it.

"What is being done about the survivors?" the king demanded, seething in anger.

"The foreigners are very confident they will be able to finish the job, Your Majesty."

Agon felt like his eyes were about to pop out of their sockets, and his head had begun to throb painfully. He realized he needed to act quickly, before he did something he would later regret—he knew he could never replace this particular agent.

"Get back out there!" he shouted. "Deal with this situation!"

Agon noted with satisfaction the panicked look in his eyes. All of his servants needed frequent reminders that the king could not be trifled with.

The agent fled from the room without risking a backward glance.

Agon's head was pounding now, and he headed immediately for his rooms. He needed to get there before his vision began to blur.

As soon as he reached his suite he stretched out on a couch. As always, Ennawi stood close at hand.

"I am surrounded by fools," Agon moaned. "I have the power to make my servants want what I want. But what use is it if they are incompetent idiots?"

He covered his face with his hands, trying to shut out the light.

"I expected by now I would be entering Arvenon as its new over-lord. But my highly paid assassins have failed to kill the king. Or his wife. And the woman is pregnant with his heir!"

He closed his eyes and groaned.

"And they're still no closer to bringing me the boy with the other stone—the Stone of Knowing. They're chasing him all over Arvenon, and they haven't caught him."

He groaned again. The pain was becoming unbearable.

It was infuriating. He could not afford to leave his servants unsupervised. But there was nothing for it now—he had no choice but to lie down in the quiet and the dark and try to sleep.

Queen Essanda entered the small room that had been hastily erected for her convenience on the side of the farmhouse. Count Ranauld and Brother Elias had already arrived in response to her invitation. She eased herself into the rough wooden chair—the best the farmhouse had to offer—and squirmed awkwardly, trying without success to make herself comfortable. This was not at all a good time to be so far advanced in a pregnancy.

"Thank you both for joining me," she said. "Our situation has been weighing on my mind, and I would value your counsel."

Ranauld's face showed no obvious emotion, but the stiffness of his posture betrayed a hint of the underlying tension that she knew he must be feeling. Brother Elias appeared unmoved, no more affected by their current circumstances than the mountains distantly visible to the north.

She first directed her attention to Ranauld. "What is your assessment, My Lord?"

Ranauld bowed his head briefly. When he lifted it his face was grim. "We are confronted by unknown enemies, Your Majesty, and the king has been gravely wounded. We find ourselves in a barely defensible location with only twenty five of our own men and the fifty Varasans that King Delmar left behind with Lord Nilsean. We have sent two separate requests for reinforcements to Lord Bottren in Arnost, and have received no response."

He waved his hand around the room. "And this is the best we can offer you, Your Majesty. In your condition. In short, I am deeply concerned!"

"What do you suggest?" she asked calmly.

"It appears that Varas is the only place where the king's safety can be assured. I would recommend that we set out for the border at once. If it is safe to move His Majesty, of course."

She shook her head firmly. "I understand your concerns, My Lord, but I have no doubt that the king would not countenance such an action. The assassins who attacked us apparently intended to destabilize all three kingdoms in a single blow by removing their monarchs. It was a bold strategy, and it appears to have been carefully planned. But the attackers were few in number. We have no information to suggest that an army has invaded Arvenon, or that Arnost has been attacked."

Ranauld frowned, but he offered no response.

"Our attackers didn't manage to kill us," she continued. "But if we flee the kingdom in a panic, that must surely be almost as good from their perspective." She shook her head once more. "If the king needs to be moved, it will be to Arnost."

"But we've heard nothing from Bottren," Ranauld replied.

"The attackers may have been lying in wait for any messengers," said the queen. "They may not find it quite so easy to deal with seventy five soldiers."

Ranauld bowed his head, but he was clearly troubled.

The abbot had been watching the exchange impassively. "What are your thoughts, Brother Elias?" the queen asked.

He dipped his head. "I would not presume to offer anything other than medical advice, Your Majesty."

When she nodded, he immediately continued.

"As you are aware, the king has been gravely ill. A couple of days after the attack his wound became red and swollen and he became feverish. We applied poultices to the wound, and we fed him broth laced with feverwort. Thankfully his fever shows signs of abating, and his wound no longer looks quite as angry. Nevertheless he cannot be moved without risk."

He sighed and shook his head. "And yet he is at great risk here, too—perhaps at greater risk. We only expected to serve food when we came here. Our supplies of herbs are severely limited, and we carried no medical texts with us. The resources available to the king in Arnost—or in Varacellan—would be vastly superior."

Noticing the queen opening her mouth to protest, he added, "Varacellan is much further away, of course. A journey to Arnost would be much less taxing for His Majesty." He glanced at Ranauld. "Assuming that such a journey could be completed safely."

The queen sat silently, trying to ignore her own discomfort.

Brother Elias looked at her thoughtfully. "If you do decide to move the king to Arnost, Your Majesty, I think it would be wisest if my monks do not accompany you. We would only get in the way. However I will not leave either His Majesty or yourself untended. Two of our number at least will accompany you."

Her face lit up in a grateful smile. She knew that her husband was alive only thanks to the efforts of Brother Elias and Brother Ander.

THE FOLLOWING morning they broke camp. The queen sincerely thanked the farmer and his wife for their hospitality, presenting them with a generous payment to cover their costs. The couple bowed deeply in response. They had been attentive and respectful hosts, but Essanda didn't doubt that they would be relieved to finally have their farm to themselves again.

Soldiers had been busy preparing the royal carriage. As soon as they had driven it to the front of the farmhouse, several monks brought out the king, still weak and unconscious, and laid him carefully within it. With the help of her maid, Ava, the queen clambered up after him. Ava followed her into the carriage.

Brother Elias came to speak with the queen. "Brother Ander has agreed to accompany you, Your Majesty. He is the best healer we have."

"We are very grateful," Essanda replied.

"He particularly asked me to convey to Your Majesty that he is not willing to fight again. Under any circumstances." The abbot paused before adding, "This is his own decision. I have not tried to influence him."

"His skills as a healer will be more than adequate," she assured the old monk.

"Brother Gerome has also agreed to travel with you," said Brother Elias. "I believe that Brother Ander will welcome his support, both spiritually and medically. But he has also assisted in the delivery of babies whenever need has arisen." He glanced down at her swollen abdomen.

"Thank you, Brother Elias," she replied gratefully.

"Brother Ander is a capable rider," he concluded. "But Brother Gerome is not. Would you be willing for him to ride with you in the carriage? That will also allow him to attend to the king while you travel."

"Brother Gerome will be most welcome," she assured him.

The monk climbed into the carriage and positioned himself beside the king.

Count Ranauld placed his twenty five soldiers ahead of the carriage, while Lord Nilsean and his men brought up the rear. At Ranauld's command, the column moved forward, heading in the direction of Arnost.

Looking back, the queen saw Brother Elias standing in the road behind them. His head was bowed in prayer. He wasn't looking in their direction.

She redirected her eyes back into the carriage, acknowledging to herself that they were going to need all the help they could get.

THOMAS and his little group of travelers had not long crossed the main road west to Erestor. They were heading north.

"See that hill," said Haldek, pointing to a high point not far to the east. "I am going up it to look around."

Thomas nodded. "We'll wait for you over there." He pointed to a thick stand of pines not far north of their current position.

Checking to see if they were being followed was a sensible precaution, and Thomas realized he should have thought of it himself. He'd never been more grateful to have a former soldier traveling with them, even one who'd fought with the Rogandans.

The others followed him to the shelter of the pines. They dismounted while they were waiting.

Haldek was away longer than Thomas expected. When Thomas eventually spotted him, he was heading toward them and riding swiftly.

The moment he arrived, Haldek gabbled out something urgently in Rogandan. Thomas frowned, struggling to make sense of it. Elena had made considerably better progress in learning Rogandan, and she turned to her husband at once with a frown of concern.

"Haldek says that a large group of armed men—maybe as many as two hundred—is heading this way. They're coming from the direction of Arnost. If they leave the road where we did and follow us, they'll reach us in less than half an hour."

Haldek spoke rapidly again.

"Another group of armed men is approaching from the other direction—from Erestor. They're half the size of the first group. They're not using the main road. And they'll be here even sooner."

"What should we do?" Thomas asked Haldek anxiously.

"Not run," he replied. "No time. We hide here."

They led their horses in further among the trees. Then Thomas signaled to Haldek, and they ran back to the outskirts of the wooded area.

After ensuring that he was out of sight and the stone was in contact with his skin, Thomas settled down to wait.

He didn't have long to wait.

Only a few minutes had passed before a rider appeared from the west, most likely a scout from the smaller group. He didn't approach their position—instead he headed for the same hill that Haldek had used.

As he passed, Thomas got a good look at him. He grabbed Haldek's arm in great excitement, and ran back to the others.

"Mount up!" he told them. "That was one of Will's men!"

They reappeared in the open at the same moment the scout left the hill. The man was clearly in great haste and probably wouldn't have noticed them. But Thomas urged his horse forward, calling out at the top of his voice.

"Wait! Can you take us to Will Prentis? It is very urgent!"

Surprise showed on the face of the man. Slowing his horse, he glanced rapidly toward their little party before nodding once.

"Follow me if you can. I can't wait for you though. Armed men are heading toward us, and I think they spotted me."

Without further comment he spurred his horse back the way he had come. It sprang away with Thomas and the others racing after it.

The scout was a competent rider, and the horse he rode was swift. He had soon opened up a substantial lead on them. Thomas could have kept pace, but Elena was riding with Tamara perched in front of her in the sling, and he wasn't willing to leave them.

At one point the scout disappeared entirely. Haldek had seen the group from the hilltop, and he didn't pause even for a moment. They followed Haldek over a small rise and suddenly found themselves in the middle of a group of riders. Will and Rufe were among them.

"Well met, Thomas," said Will with a tight smile, nodding briefly to the others as well. "We don't have time for pleasantries. Are you up for some hard riding?"

They all nodded. Thomas came alongside Elena and retrieved both Tamara and the sling. The moment his daughter sat securely in front of him, the entire group raced to the west, away from Arnost.

They rode until they came to a river. Splashing across it, they swung around, dismounting and taking cover among some trees that lined the bank. The men lifted arrows from their quivers and thrust them point first into the ground before them. Then they unslung their bows from their backs and tested the strings.

"I need all of you to stay out of sight," Will instructed Thomas.

They responded immediately, hiding themselves among the trees. Elena took Tammi again, speaking to her quietly.

Before long a number of riders came into view. They rode toward the river, slowing as soon as they saw the line of bowmen waiting for them on the opposite bank.

"Why are you pursuing us?" called Will. "Who are you, and what do you want?"

One of the riders came forward. "We mean you no harm," he said. "We're searching for a youth and a young woman with a small child. Two older men are traveling with them. They're wanted for questioning. Have you seen them?"

"We've just ridden in from the west," Will replied. "We haven't seen anyone heading that way who matched that description."

"Why aren't you riding on the main road?" the other man asked. He managed not to sound imperious, but he couldn't keep a hard edge from his tone.

"There's been unrest where we came from," Will replied evenly. "We're simply being cautious."

The other man considered them carefully. "Where are you headed?" he asked.

"Arnost," Will replied.

His interrogator seemed satisfied. "If you see them, report it when you arrive in Arnost," he said.

Will nodded. "You can count on it," he lied.

The other man called out a command, and the whole group turned about and headed back to the main road. When they reached it, a couple of riders split off from the main group and headed back toward Arnost. The others continued riding west in the direction of Erestor.

"There'll be more riders heading our way before long," Will predicted confidently. "Most likely a lot more."

He turned to Thomas. "What brings you all out here?"

"Can we talk in private?" Thomas asked, moving his head to indicate Will and Rufe.

Will nodded, and the three of them moved out of earshot of the main group. "I'm sure I don't need to tell you to keep it brief," said Will.

Thomas came immediately to the point. "Lord Bottren is nominally in charge in Arnost, but he and any other loyal leaders are in the dungeons. The person who's really in charge is a man known as

Lord Lygell." Thomas shuddered. "He's an evil and devious man. He has many plans, and none of them are good."

Then it occurred to Thomas to add, "The men you just spoke to are working for him."

"In that case we can definitely expect to see a large number of riders heading in our direction," said Will grimly. "I'm fairly confident that some of those men recognized me."

"How do you know all this, Thomas?" asked Rufe in amazement.

Will gave him a warning frown, and Rufe subsided, clearly still baffled.

Thomas ignored the question. "It's much worse than that," he continued. "The king and the queen have gone to a remote location that's near both Varas and Castel to meet with King Istel and King Delmar. The idea of the meeting was planted by the people who are paying Lygell. A group of assassins is planning to go there to kill them all."

"The king would have taken soldiers for his protection," Will said. "Plenty of them, I expect. The other kings would have done the same."

"There was some kind of a plan to poison the soldiers," Thomas replied.

Rufe was listening with his jaw agape.

Thomas quickly added, "None of the others know all this. They know we're trying to find the king to warn him, but I haven't told them any details."

Will simply nodded. He didn't seem especially surprised. The look on his face suggested that a lot of things had finally become clear to him.

"How long do we have?" asked Will.

"I don't know," Thomas replied.

"When did the king and queen leave for the meeting?"

"More than two weeks ago. Nothing's been heard from them since."

"In that case the attack has already happened," said Will. "It's possible that Arvenon, Castel, and Varas are all without leaders right now."

Thomas saw his own shock mirrored on the face of Rufe.

Will simply looked grim. "Do you know the location?"

"I think it was somewhere called Paradise Valley," said Thomas.

Will nodded. "Count Lonnigen's holdings. I know roughly where it is." He turned to Rufe. "Mount up the men. We need to get there, and get there quickly. It might be too late, but it's possible that someone has survived."

Rufe hurried away, calling to the men.

Will gazed off into the distance for a moment. Then he shifted his attention back to Thomas. "If we arrive in time to save anyone, Thomas, the kingdom will have you to thank."

31

Will kept his men in the river for as long as he possibly could, then they splashed out onto firm ground and headed north. The little diversion wouldn't delay a determined tracker for long, but it should give them a head start.

Since that time they had barely paused. Will could not afford to slow the pace, but he occasionally managed to spare a thought for Elena. Whenever she caught him glancing at her, she simply smiled, and he gradually permitted himself to believe that she was coping with the pace. He acknowledged to himself that she was more resilient than he'd given her credit for.

Will had scouts ranging ahead, although they were hard pressed to stay far in advance of the main body. Rufe had a couple of men following behind. They were doing whatever they could to confuse the trail as well as keeping an eye on their pursuers.

As far as Rufe's scouts had been able to estimate, at least three hundred men were now in pursuit of them. It was now almost certain that someone had recognized Will. Lygell had wasted no time in sending a strong force to intercept him. The pursuers were a few hours behind, but that was nowhere near enough of a gap to be comfortable.

Will never doubted that Lygell would be sending men to Paradise Valley as well. He could only hope either that the assassins had failed entirely in their mission, or that any survivors had fled from Count Lonnigen's lands before Lygell's men arrived.

As soon as they paused to rest the horses, Will called Rufe, Jonas, and Thomas aside. "We have to suppose that some people have survived the attack. But it wouldn't be wise to assume that we will find them at Paradise Valley. If they're unaware of what's been happening at Arnost, they will try to go there. So we will need to send scouts to watch for anyone heading in that direction."

"What of the men pursuing us?" asked Rufe. "It won't help to have them breathing down our necks when we join forces with any fugitives."

"It's time we arranged a little surprise for them," replied Will. "The duke told me he'd selected a hundred of his best men to accompany us. Erestorians pride themselves on their ability with the bow. It's time we gave them an opportunity to demonstrate their skills."

* * *

Rufe waited with fifteen bowmen behind a hastily erected barricade. Will's scouts had found the perfect location for an ambush. The terrain narrowed to a pass between two low cliff faces that resembled a long and slender neck. The only way to avoid the pass would be to journey far to the east or to the west to divert around the area entirely. Any such diversion would waste the better part of a day.

A few trees had been felled to form a barricade halfway along the pass. Twists and turns in the neck of the pass meant that the barricade would not be visible until the riders were almost upon it. Unfortunately the twists and turns also meant that Rufe's bowmen could not get a clear view along the full length of the pass. For that reason, men under the command of Jonas scrambled up the low cliffs on each side. As well as the fifteen bowmen waiting at the end of the pass, another twenty were now spread out on each side of it as well.

When the pursuers approached, a signal was passed from the

men on the cliff to Rufe and his bowmen. Riders soon filled the pass, milling around aimlessly when they reached the barrier.

Rufe barked a command, and archers appeared at the top of the barrier, pouring a steady stream of arrows down upon the men in the pass. Those at the front tried to push back the way they had come, but downed horses and men hampered their efforts. Almost fifty mercenaries fell in the first few minutes. Then the rain of arrows came to an abrupt end.

The panicked men in the pass discovered that their attackers had abandoned the barrier and simply melted away. They quickly began working to dismantle the barrier, soon discovering that its construction made it easy to clear a pathway wide enough for a horse, and difficult to dismantle it entirely. They chose the easy solution.

As soon as a solid mass of men had filed through the opening, they charged together along the pass, hungry for revenge. Instead of bursting free into open terrain, though, they found another barrier waiting for them at the end of the pass. They immediately turned back, frantic to escape the latest trap. The original barricade halfway through the pass had not been entirely removed though, and there was no quick way for the men to escape. To their horror, they soon found themselves beset from above on each side as well, arrows raining down on them from the cliffs along the entire length of the pass.

Fifty five bowmen poured a continuous stream of arrows into the confused ranks. Another hundred riders fell in the next few frenzied minutes. Soon no rider was left alive in the pass. The only survivors were those able to retreat well out of bowshot range.

Once again Rufe's and Jonas's bowmen melted away. They left behind them a demoralized mob. In the space of a few minutes their pursuers had been reduced from three hundred men to a force half that size. The battle had not cost Will a single soldier.

The men pursuing Will's force now hunted with new caution. Scouts were sent out to probe ahead of the main body of mercenaries. Jonas responded by setting ambushes for the scouts. After several of them failed to return, the scouts too learned to be extremely wary.

Will's men were no longer closely pursued, and Will took the opportunity to hasten his advance. His men traveled into the night as well as all day.

The pursuers were glad to put the pass behind them. They left their dead unburied. The carrion birds had barely gathered when three of Rufe's men appeared in the pass and sent them flapping to safety.

The duke might have provided an abundant supply of arrows, but Will was conscious that the stockpile was by no means unlimited. Rufe accordingly left behind three of his men with instructions to gather spent arrows and rejoin the column whenever it was safe to do so.

Having collected a large pile of reusable shafts, they tied them together in bundles. Then they remounted their horses and rode away.

THE PACE soon began to wear on Tamara. She somehow learned to sleep in the sling while bumping along on horseback, but she never slept for long enough or frequently enough. Whenever she was hungry or thirsty she began to wail. "Dadda! Hungy!"

"What's a kid doing here?" spat one of the soldiers rudely. When it became clear that no one was going to back him openly, he went to great efforts to ensure he never traveled anywhere near her. He wasn't the only one.

Others responded very differently. "Come on, Dadda! Where's the food? The poor little mite's fading away!" Before long Thomas faced a continual stream of good-natured wisecracks if he failed to deliver food or water to the toddler quickly enough.

Whenever they stopped for breaks, men would gather round Tammi and engage her in childish banter. She warmed to the smiles and the attention, and her endearing ways soon made her a great favorite with most of the men. Hardbitten soldiers as they were, before long they had adopted her as their mascot.

Thomas was just as concerned about Elena, and not only because of the punishing pace of travel. It was impractical for her to constantly cover herself entirely, and she reluctantly accepted the necessity of having her face openly exposed to a large group of men. Never in her life had she been so directly confronted with the reactions of so many men. The soldiers gradually became accustomed to her presence, but it was a rare moment when one of them wasn't staring directly at her.

Once again she showed her resilience, but Thomas could see that it was far from easy for her. He hovered nearby as much as he possibly could, and neither Rubin nor Haldek ever left her side for more than a few minutes at a time.

Nevertheless, there was bound to be trouble sooner or later. On the second night when Will finally called a halt so they could sleep, Elena briefly moved away from the others to find a quiet place to relieve herself. As she was returning to the camp, one of the soldiers confronted her.

"How about a little kiss, darlin'?" he demanded.

Thomas stepped out of the darkness. "Leave her alone," he said calmly but firmly.

"Or what, little boy?" the soldier retorted scornfully. Reaching out, he shoved Thomas in the chest. Thomas landed hard on his back. The soldier stood over him, drawing back his foot to kick him in the head.

Before Thomas could respond in any way, the soldier let out a howl of pain and hopped backward on one foot.

Elena stood glaring at him, fully prepared to repeat the treatment by stamping down hard on his other foot.

"So the little vixen has a bite, has she?" the man snarled, reaching out to grab her by the arm.

At that moment the giant form of Rufe appeared from out of the gloom. The big guardsman grabbed the soldier by the collar and lifted him bodily off the ground. The man was left with his feet dangling in mid air.

Rufe pulled the soldier toward him until their faces were almost touching. "Go near her again, or her husband," he snarled, "and I'll separate you from the source of your trouble." He shook the man hard. "Do you take my meaning?"

The soldier hesitated, then he attempted a nod.

"I didn't hear that," said Rufe loudly.

"Yes," the soldier croaked, unable to breathe properly.

Rufe responded by dropping him. The man picked himself up, then turned to glare first at Rufe, then at Thomas, and Elena.

Rufe stepped toward him with menace in his eyes. That was too much for the soldier. He turned tail and fled.

Others had witnessed the confrontation, and Thomas knew that word would spread quickly.

Rufe left nothing to chance, though. From that moment, he made sure that he always rode and camped within easy reach of Thomas and Elena.

THOMAS WAS RIDING BESIDE WILL, answering a range of questions about what he'd learned in Arnost. Their conversation ceased abruptly when a scout appeared, riding in from the northeast. As soon as the scout spotted Will he headed for him, pulling his mount alongside.

"I've just seen a group of soldiers," he reported breathlessly, "fewer than a hundred men, traveling slowly toward Arnost. They have a carriage in the middle of their column. From the markings on it, it's the royal carriage."

Will called for Rufe and Jonas, and they quickly joined him. Then he turned back to the scout.

"Go on," he said.

"There's a larger group, well over two hundred men, coming from the direction of Arnost. The two groups are likely to meet."

"When?" demanded Rufe.

"A few hours at the most," the scout replied. "They're not much further away than we are."

Will nodded. "Lygell will have sent them from Arnost. Can we get there first?"

The scout didn't hesitate. "Yes, if we hurry."

"Is there a vantage point that allows all of these groups to be seen at one time?" Will asked.

The scout shook his head. "No, the terrain isn't well suited to visibility over long distances. I only know about the second group because I've just met with one of our other scouts."

Will nodded in satisfaction. He quickly halted the column. Then he stood up in his stirrups, and called out, "The king and queen are ahead of us. More of our enemies are heading right for them! Ride as if the hounds of hell are chasing you!"

So saying he spurred his horse forward. The troop followed hard behind him.

Elena rode as fast as she could, but she couldn't match the pace of the soldiers. Thomas, Rubin, and Haldek remained with her, and before long all of them were bringing up the rear. When the soldiers galloped over a ridge a short distance ahead of them, Thomas lost sight of them entirely.

At that moment a soldier reappeared over the ridge, riding purposefully toward them with a drawn sword. Quickly bringing the stone into contact with his skin, Thomas recognized the man as Elena's attacker, and saw exactly what he was intending to do. He signaled to the others to halt and swung his horse protectively in front of his wife.

Haldek drew his sword and rode past them to engage the soldier.

The soldier spat. "Ha! So the filthy Rogandan thinks he can fight, does he?" He spurred his horse forward, raising his sword to strike Haldek. Ducking under the swipe, the Rogandan raised his own sword, managing to nick the soldier's arm as it flew past. Cursing with fury, the man swung his horse around wildly and crashed it into Haldek's mount.

Haldek's horse reared up with a scream, thrashing its forelegs in the air. Haldek was thrown from the saddle. Unhurt, he scrambled to his feet and cast about for his sword. As he reached out to grasp it, the soldier swept his horse around and prepared to ride him down. Thomas looked on helplessly, berating himself fiercely for his ineptitude with weapons.

As the soldier rode toward Haldek with his sword raised, he suddenly threw his arms into the air and slumped forward, tumbling from the saddle. Thomas stared down at him in amazement. He lay unmoving on the ground, an arrow protruding from between his shoulder blades.

Jonas rode up, his bow still in his hand. "Rufe sent me back to keep an eye out for you," he said. Glancing down at the dead soldier, he shook his head. "What a senseless idiot!"

Thomas stared at him with relief. "Thank you!" The words felt woefully inadequate.

Jonas nodded curtly. "There's no time to bury him—the buzzards can have him. We've got some hard riding to do!"

Haldek remounted, and all of them raced toward the ridge with the riderless horse trailing behind them.

32

Hazor narrowed his eyes as he gazed across the rolling hills ahead of them. Paradise Valley wasn't far off, and they'd seen no sign of fugitives.

He spat in annoyance. They should have set out days earlier.

Hazor had personally squeezed every last scrap of information from Ranauld's messenger before he died. He knew that the few soldiers who'd survived the poisoning were spooked and distracted, and that the royals who'd evaded the assassins were unprotected as never before. King Steffan was badly wounded—if he was still alive—and his queen was heavily pregnant. They wouldn't be going anywhere in a hurry—riding a horse was not an option in their condition.

A hundred men could have finished it off at that point if they'd moved quickly.

But Hazor had been ordered to wait. Lygell wanted to assemble an overwhelming force, whatever that meant, and he didn't want any of the king's soldiers included in it. He wanted men he could rely on, which meant mercenaries.

So here they were. It was laughable—two hundred and fifty men hardly constituted an overwhelming force. By now the wounded king and his pregnant queen were probably on their way to Varas. It was even possible they were already sheltering behind a Varasan army. Lygell might be a dangerous man to cross, but he wasn't the smartest person Hazor had worked with.

Hazor's thoughts were interrupted by the arrival of one of the scouts.

"I've caught sight of a body of soldiers ahead. There aren't many of them. Barely a quarter of our number. They must have decided Arnost isn't safe—they're heading away from us in the direction of Varas. They have a carriage with them. We've finally found the royals!"

"Stick to the facts," Hazor snarled. "I'll draw the conclusions."

"They had scouts trailing behind them," the rider added.

Hazor frowned. "Did they see you?"

The scout nodded.

"You idiot!" snapped Hazor. "Now they'll run."

He swung around to face his men. "Move!" he shouted. "The chase is on!"

Hazor charged forward with his men close behind. He'd already caught one distant glimpse of his quarry, and he knew the carriage must be slowing them down significantly.

A small stand of trees stood in their path, and Hazor raced around them, his men close behind him. As they passed the trees an arrow whizzed past his face, barely missing him. The whistle of flying arrows soon filled the air. Glancing behind, he saw several of his men tumble from the saddle.

His men were already swinging around to confront the bowmen.

"Keep riding!" he shouted.

The men swung back into line and urged their horses forward. As they raced past the last of the trees, Hazor glanced back once more. Judging by the number of riderless horses, he must have lost thirty men. He cursed in exasperation.

It wasn't entirely bad though. Their attackers had already been left far behind. That meant fewer men to protect the carriage.

A river appeared before them, and Hazor spotted a suitable ford without even slowing. Reaching the ford, his mount splashed across it and scrambled up the opposite bank. His men were soon strung out in a line leading to the ford.

Barely three quarters of his force had crossed the river when a new hail of arrows rained down from a ridge on the opposite bank. Hazor looked on in fury as arrows found their targets. The ford was soon littered with bodies, staining the river red.

Hazor ground his teeth. His enemies were deploying a simple but effective strategy. If he stopped to fight, a small number of attackers would succeed in bogging down his entire force. If he left behind enough men to deal with the bowmen, they would have succeeded in splitting his group.

He wasn't taking the bait. Let his enemies be the ones to diminish their numbers.

"Ride on," he shouted again, and his men galloped away from the ford, leaving their dead and wounded behind them.

The trail left by Hazor's enemies was broad and impossible to miss. He had no need of scouts. Rolling hills lay before him with no obstructions and no obvious locations for further ambushes. Furious after his losses at the ford and impatient for revenge, he charged forward at the head of his men.

Before another hour had passed, Hazor crested a high ridge. The position commanded a view of the entire area, and he quickly brought his horse to a halt. His scouts guided their horses onto the ridge beside him as he peered out across the terrain.

Below him lay a broad plain, stretching out many leagues into the distance. Far ahead a small cluster of horsemen rode swiftly away from him, heading for Varas. He could see no sign of a carriage.

Hazor cursed again. They must have hidden the carriage somewhere along the way. In his eagerness he'd led his men right past it.

"Find that carriage!" he ordered his scouts.

The scouts turned their horses immediately and rode back the way they had come. Hazor and the rest of the troop followed behind them.

———————

ONE OF LORD Nilsean's riders drew his mount alongside the nobleman and pointed back the way they had come. "They've made it to the ridge, My Lord."

The nobleman stared over his shoulder, slowing his horse without completely stopping. A row of tiny figures could be seen silhouetted against the horizon.

"Do you think they'll follow us?" the rider asked.

Lord Nilsean shook his head. "No, they're not interested in us. They'll be looking for the carriage. It's the king and queen they want."

"What do we do now?"

"We keep going. We've done what Will Prentis—Lord Torbury, that is—asked us to do. It's up to him now."

"Will the king survive?"

The nobleman shrugged. "The king is vulnerable in his condition," he said. "The queen too, since she can't ride. But Torbury's with them now, so they're in good hands. He did the impossible at Torbury Scarp, and I'd never place a bet against him."

Lord Nilsean turned away from the ridge and focused his attention on the distant mountains on the horizon ahead. They would come to a broad river before they reached those mountains—the border of Varas.

They were going home.

———————

HAZOR'S SEARCH for the carriage had so far been a miserable failure, and his frustration and rage grew steadily as the sun slowly made its way toward the horizon.

Four of his scouts had now failed to report in. The horses of the missing men eventually led to two of the scouts. The horses were found grazing peacefully, with the bodies of their riders lying nearby.

Both men had been felled with arrows. Hazor gave the other two up as lost.

The phantom bowmen were attacking his riders with impunity. His entire force had been ambushed as they rode beneath a steep hill. Hazor sent men scrabbling up the slope in pursuit of the archers. Not many of them made it to the top alive. Those who did reported that the bowmen had already ridden away.

Night fell without any sign of the carriage. Hazor called a halt, and his men began to set up camp. They were soon building campfires and preparing food.

Before they could relax, arrows came streaking out of the dark, picking off men sitting beside their campfires. Hazor set off after the attackers personally with a large group of his men. They eventually returned weary and empty handed.

Conscious that he couldn't risk losing even more of his mercenaries, Hazor ordered them to put out the fires. They went to sleep cold and hungry.

The tension steadily escalated as the next day progressed. By the time a scout brought him the news he had been waiting for, Hazor was almost ready to erupt.

"I found the carriage," the scout reported.

"Where?" demanded Hazor.

"West of here. It was empty."

Hazor ground his teeth in fury.

"It is the one they were using, though. I searched the surrounding area and found a blood soaked bandage. And there were fresh tracks nearby—wagon wheel tracks."

Hazor forced himself to remain calm. "Which direction were they heading?"

"Southwest."

"So they're not heading for Arnost."

The scout shook his head. "No, they're heading in the direction of Erestor. I followed the tracks until they disappeared across stony ground."

"They'll be forced to travel slowly. We can still catch them."

With his other scouts either missing or out searching, Hazor selected several more men. "Forget the royal carriage," he told them. "You're looking for a body of soldiers protecting a wagon. Get going!"

His scouts rode away.

Hazor faced the rest of his men. "No more distractions. If we're attacked again, we ignore it. Whatever happens we keep riding."

JONAS PEERED over the tip of the rise, watching his enemies ride past below him. They were heading in the wrong direction, and he would make sure that his next ambush pointed them even further away from their intended target.

His nighttime raid had forced the mercenaries to forego their hot meal and bed down in the cold, and he knew that they would be weary and disgruntled. But such successes also came at a cost to him and his men. They couldn't afford to use fires either, and he couldn't remember when they'd last enjoyed an uninterrupted sleep.

Will had given him more authority, which was what he wanted. But the role also came with more responsibility, and no shortage of risk.

Will would surely look after him when everything returned to normal—at least Jonas was counting on him to do so. But who could say when that might happen? And there was always a chance that one or other of them wouldn't survive. War was an uncertain business, and no one was invincible. They'd done well to stay alive as long as they had.

His biggest concern was for his aging parents. He did everything he could to support them, and he didn't like to think about their chances if anything happened to him.

His mind went back, as it so often did, to his big sister. She'd been his best friend from the earliest time he could remember—the two of them had been inseparable. Her future looked bright. Everyone agreed she was the most beautiful young woman they'd ever seen.

She could have taken her pick from among the young men in the village.

Then she became sick.

His parents couldn't afford a healer. They'd barely been able to feed their family even before the baron seized their milking cow for his latest feast. Jonas had watched on helplessly as his beloved sister slowly wasted away.

It was no use dwelling on the past though.

Jonas sighed as he turned away and remounted his horse. Life was unpredictable. And it certainly wasn't fair.

Queen Essanda sighed with relief when Will called a short break. The cart carrying her and Steffan rolled slowly to a stop, and Ava hurried to help her down from it. All around them men quickly dismounted, gratefully accepting the opportunity to stretch. Brother Ander remained in the cart with Steffan, attentive as always at his side.

The occupants of the royal carriage had been transferred to a farmer's cart as soon as Will and his men connected with the royal party and its largely Varasan escort. The empty carriage became nothing more than a decoy, and Lord Nilsean had agreed to take charge of it. His squad of Varasan soldiers changed course and headed in the direction of Varas, intending to hide the carriage somewhere suitable along the way. Count Ranauld and his small squad of Arvenian soldiers parted from their Varasan friends and attached themselves to Will's force.

On the journey to Paradise Valley Essanda had thought of the royal carriage as uncomfortable. Now she remembered its cushioned seats and sheltered interior ruefully. By comparison with the wagon, the carriage was impossibly luxurious.

Noticing Brother Gerome approaching, Queen Essanda managed a weak smile of greeting.

"I am truly sorry that we cannot offer you more appropriate traveling conditions, Your Majesty," he said regretfully.

"It isn't your fault, Brother Gerome," she replied.

He glanced forthrightly at her distended belly. "Would you be willing to discuss your condition with me?" he asked.

Essanda turned to Ava and gave her a significant nod. The maid raised an eyebrow, but she bowed respectfully and left them without comment.

"Do you know when you are due, Your Majesty?"

"At the time I left Arnost my best guess was another six weeks," she replied.

His eyes went wide.

"I know," she said with a sigh. "You don't need to say it." She glanced across at the prone figure of her husband in the wagon. "It was my choice to accompany the king, and I'm not sorry that I did."

Brother Gerome noticed Elena nearby. "May I invite Elena to join us? She has personal experience with the birth process, and her insights might prove helpful."

"By all means," Essanda replied.

Brother Gerome called to Elena, and she quickly joined them.

"Have you noticed anything different or unusual, Your Majesty?" asked the monk.

Essanda hesitated momentarily before deciding to be direct. "I've been experiencing sharp pains at times. I've wondered if they were contractions."

"How often?" asked Brother Gerome.

"Infrequently. Sometimes two or three times in a hour, then nothing for long periods."

The monk nodded. "You are most likely experiencing false labor."

"I had similar pains," Elena confirmed, "especially in the weeks leading up to Tamara's birth."

"Has the baby been moving?" asked Brother Gerome.

"Yes. I felt some kicking just a few minutes ago."

"Any bleeding?"

She shook her head.

Brother Gerome had many more questions, but he seemed satisfied with her answers when he left. Essanda was grateful for their concern, and told them so frankly.

She saw now that her need for reassurance had been more pressing than she'd realized. Since the horrors of the fight in the barn at Paradise Valley and the death of her father, Essanda had endured the constant stress of fleeing under rough conditions with a gravely wounded husband. She now acknowledged her growing concerns about how these experiences might have affected her baby.

Having confronted her own anxieties, Essanda bent her thoughts once more to Steffan. She returned to the wagon and stood beside it gazing helplessly at the prone figure of her husband.

Brother Ander looked up, and their eyes met. The compassion in his eyes still astounded her. She couldn't forget his fury in the barn as he single-handedly wrested control away from the attackers. Difficult as it had been to comprehend his transformation from fierce warrior to gentle healer, she readily acknowledged that Steffan was in capable hands.

"He's improving, Your Majesty," Brother Ander told her, answering the unspoken question in her eyes. "I am hopeful."

"Thank you, Brother Ander," she said, her voice trembling. She brushed away the tears welling in her eyes, and turned aside to compose herself.

Will called the men to horse, and the wagon rumbled forward again. Essanda sucked in a sharp breath as another contraction compressed her abdomen. She gritted her teeth against the pain and tried to think of anything except the desperate state of their circumstances.

WHEN THE RIDERS next stopped for a break Essanda clambered down out of the cart to stretch her aching muscles. Glancing up, she saw Elena coming to her. Tamara arrived as well, pausing for a few moments to stare wide-eyed at the queen's distended belly before running off to play. Essanda paid no attention to her undignified appearance—she was beyond caring about how she looked.

The queen greeted her friend warmly, a wry smile covering her face. "I seem to remember us talking about what it would be like to have babies of our own, back when we were chatting in the castle at Arnost," she said. "The idea seemed so exciting at the time. In practice it hasn't been working out quite the way I imagined." She sighed deeply.

Elena's concerned eyes peered back at her. "Can I do anything to help, Your Majesty?" she asked.

"Yes, you can," Essanda replied without hesitation. "Stay and talk to me for a few minutes. It's been far too long, and I've missed you!"

As the soldiers saw to their horses, the queen and the commoner wandered together arm in arm among the scattered trees of a forgotten valley. For a time the bouncing of the wagon, the condition of the king, and the uncertainties of the future slipped away, as Essanda laid aside her burdens to share her self with a true friend.

When the order came to move out, Elena helped the queen back into the wagon. Essanda squeezed her hand, allowing the moisture in her eyes to express without words the overflow of her heart.

Awareness returned slowly to Steffan, with dim hints of a blue sky above and a shaking and jolting below. The only certainty was unbearable pain.

A face swam into view as a monk bent low over him. The monk attended to him silently. The face seemed somehow familiar, but Steffan slipped into oblivion before understanding why.

When next he awoke he sensed through a haze of pain that Essanda was sitting nearby. She seemed peaceful and well, and the knowledge comforted him for reasons he couldn't recall. When the blackness came for him once more, he surrendered to it calmly.

. . .

THE SKY WAS dark when Steffan woke again. The bouncing had stopped, and he lay peacefully beneath a starlit expanse. His side throbbed incessantly, but he decided he could bear it. His beloved Essanda came to him, her face flickering in the firelight. Tears glistened in her eyes, but she smiled tenderly down at him, whispering words of comfort and hope. He tried to smile back, but his mouth wouldn't cooperate, twisting awkwardly as a wave of pain washed over him.

He reached up a hand, and she took it, squeezing it gently.

Memories came to him then, dull memories of fighting and of fear. More than anything, he remembered his weariness.

He decided to close his eyes, just for a moment, and everything slid away again.

THOMAS RODE alongside Rubin to retrieve his daughter, then he steered his horse closer to the royal wagon so Tammi could catch another sight of the queen's bulging belly. The toddler was fascinated by the idea that a baby was hidden inside the bump, almost ready to come out.

Humble as the farmer's cart was, Thomas couldn't help thinking of it as the royal wagon. In reality, there was nothing regal about it beyond its passengers. Brother Ander sat beside the king, wincing every time the cart bounced across an especially rough patch of ground. The monk had packed straw beneath King Steffan's prone body in an attempt to cushion the king against the jolting, but the effectiveness of the makeshift mattress was questionable.

The only other passenger was the queen. She appeared pale and preoccupied. This rough mode of transport was surely doing nothing useful for her unborn child.

Seeing him riding behind the wagon, Elena guided her horse toward him. Thomas knew that her gentle heart had been deeply stirred by the plight of the king and queen. Whenever the wagon bounced and shook its passengers, she saw more than just the reigning monarchs. She also saw a gravely wounded man and his heavily pregnant wife. More than that, since Elena's first visit to Arnost the queen had been her friend. Their current helplessness tugged at her compassion.

"How are you feeling, Your Majesty?" she asked the queen.

"A little better, thank you Elena," the queen replied. She sighed. "If circumstances were different, I'd very quickly be exchanging places with Ava."

Both women glanced briefly back at the queen's maid, riding serenely behind the wagon.

Ava had taken Thomas by surprise—she was proving to be much tougher than she appeared. The maid had surprised everyone by announcing that she did not require a seat in the farmer's cart. She promptly climbed into the saddle of a spare horse, explaining breezily that she had grown up around the animals.

The other passenger displaced from the royal carriage was Brother Gerome. Since then, he had spent the daylight hours perched uncomfortably on a horse, trying desperately to absorb everything Thomas was teaching him about riding. The former horse master was encouraged by the monk's progress—Brother Gerome was doing much better than he himself realized.

Brother Gerome rode closer to the wagon. "How is the king?" he asked his fellow monk.

"He's slipping in and out of consciousness," Brother Ander replied. He frowned. "This jolting isn't helping his recovery."

"It's time for me to take a turn," Brother Gerome told him. "You need to stretch your legs."

For a moment Brother Ander looked as if he might argue, but then he nodded once and leaped nimbly from the moving wagon. Brother Gerome rode to him and stopped his horse. After climbing awkwardly from its back, he ran alongside the wagon and clambered in. He turned first to the queen, speaking quietly to her, then he moved to the side of the king.

The big monk swung himself into the saddle and immediately

rode away at a trot, clearly relishing the opportunity to be on horse-back again.

Thomas still hadn't fully adjusted to the changes in Brother Ander. He had last seen his old traveling companion when he visited the army camp at Hazelwood Ford after the Battle of Torbury Scarp. The big soldier had announced his intention to become a monk at the time, but it still felt strange seeing him in his white robe. Hearing him referred to as "Brother Ander" was even stranger.

Strangest of all were the stories floating around about Brother Ander at Paradise Valley. It was said that he had destroyed the enemies of the king and queen almost single-handedly, rising up like an avenging angel. Thomas couldn't get his head around it all.

The big monk might be taking a brief break now, but it was apparent that his attention was focused almost entirely on his patient. On one occasion when Thomas had been openly staring at the former soldier, Brother Gerome hastened to assure him that Brother Ander was the best healer he had ever seen. Thomas had no reason to doubt it. He had simply been struck by a memory from the past. In his mind's eye he could still picture Brother Ander as the patient hovering on the brink of death.

Tamara laid her head back and went to sleep. Thomas decided to use the opportunity to speak to Will.

Clicking his tongue, he directed his horse forward to where Will was riding. Will glanced across at him without speaking, and they rode together in silence for a time.

Thomas felt tense and uneasy. Something had been weighing on his mind, and he wasn't sure how to approach it.

"I wanted to ask you something," he began. Then he shrugged. There was no easy way to say it. "I've learned to use the stone sparingly—I try very hard not to abuse it. It still occasionally reveals things by accident though. The last time that happened I was with Jonas."

Will looked at him with a raised eyebrow.

"I don't want to give the wrong impression," Thomas added

hastily. "I'm very grateful to Jonas—he rescued us when one of the men tried to assault Elena."

"I heard about that," growled Will. "The fool got what he deserved."

"Do you completely trust him?" Thomas asked bluntly. "Jonas, I mean. I only had a brief glimpse, but his motives are...complicated. He isn't just fighting because it's the right thing to do—he's hoping to benefit personally."

Will's lip curled up in an ironic grin. "How many of us could truthfully claim that our motives are never mixed?"

"Of course. But..." Thomas shrugged helplessly. He didn't know what else to say.

"I realize that you're trying to help, Thomas, and I do appreciate it. But there's no need for concern in this case. Jonas isn't going to betray us."

Both of them fell silent again.

After several minutes of awkwardness, Thomas asked a question to change the subject. "Where are we heading?"

Will's eyes flicked in his direction. "We're going to try to find Rellan."

Thomas couldn't hide his surprise. "Isn't he living somewhere inaccessible? I thought I heard he was in the wilderness near Erestor."

Will nodded. "Inaccessible sounds very attractive right now."

Thomas stole a glance back at the king. "How long will it take us to get there?"

Will shrugged. "The speed of the wagon is entirely dependent on the terrain. Our arrival time also depends on the people pursuing us. If they manage to track us down, we probably won't get there at all."

33

Hazor spurred his horse to the top of a rise and peered in the direction his scout was pointing. A moderately sized group of men was riding away from him, clustered around a wagon. They were moving slowly.

He rode back down the slope and faced his men. "We'll finally get our revenge!" he shouted. Then he spun his horse around, and charged over the hill. Eager for blood, his mercenaries raced after him.

As they drew closer to the group ahead a hail of arrows flew toward them. Men went down around him, but Hazor ignored it. He wouldn't be denied. Drawing his sword, he shouted his fury.

The riders had spun around to face him now. But they were greatly outnumbered. When Hazor's men crashed into their line, they turned and scattered.

The wagon had been pulled aside into a small wooded area. "To me, men!" Hazor shouted, and led his men into the wood. More arrows flew their way, but Hazor had caught sight of the wagon now. He charged up to it with sword raised.

Then he bellowed in frustrated rage. The wagon was empty, just like the carriage.

Once more his enemies had offered him a decoy, and once more he had fallen for it. He had lost more men, and he was no better off. The handful of enemy dead behind him were cold comfort for Hazor.

How many more decoys would there be?

His only consolation was the knowledge that the king and queen must surely be in a wagon somewhere, and they couldn't be too far away.

HAZOR SCOWLED when he looked up and noticed another of his scouts riding toward him. He turned his head away and spat onto the ground. It hadn't been a good day, and his scouts weren't known for bringing good news.

"What is it?" he snapped.

"I just ran into a scout from another group sent out by Lord Lygell. They were following Will Prentis, but they lost him."

"Prentis! He's around here?" A number of mysteries were suddenly being resolved for Hazor. Will Prentis's reputation was legendary.

"How many men are with this other group?" Hazor asked.

"Fewer than two hundred. They started out with three hundred."

Hazor scowled. He must have lost at least ninety men himself. He had no idea how many were riding with Prentis, but whether it was few or many, he'd been using them very effectively to tilt the odds in his own favor.

"Who's leading our other group?"

The scout shrugged. "Apparently the leader appointed by Lord Lygell has been killed. A man named Jobin is leading them now. He doesn't seem to have much of a clue."

"Take me to this Jobin. Now!"

Hazor was actually smiling as they rode out. He'd just found a way to more than make good his losses. For once his day might actually end well.

. . .

"WILL Prentis and his bowmen make it impossible," said Jobin despondently.

Hazor couldn't argue with that. Arrows had been buzzing around like angry hornets for days. And apart from one small skirmish over a decoy wagon, he'd barely managed to catch a glimpse of his opponents, much less draw them into open battle.

He wasn't about to give up though. Prentis appeared to have sucked the life out of Jobin, but Hazor wasn't so easily intimidated.

Sooner or later Prentis would make a mistake—no one was infallible. And Hazor was more than happy to be the one to end his run. With over three hundred men under his command, it was time to take the fight to Prentis.

His first step would be to divide his force into three. It would allow them to cover more ground, and three groups would be harder to ambush than one. The main goal hadn't changed—find the king and queen and finish them off. If he could do away with Prentis at the same time, so much the better.

HAVING SEARCHED out a quiet location to confer with Rufe and Jonas, Will withdrew with Count Ranauld and his two senior leaders to discuss his plans. Rufe and Jonas had recently arrived in response to his messages requesting them to ride in to meet him as soon as possible.

"It's time for a change of strategy," he told them. "But first I want to acknowledge the excellent work you've both done to keep the mercenaries away from the king and queen. Fortunately for us the real wagon hasn't been exposed yet. We have you to thank for that."

"Your strategy has been working brilliantly," Rufe told him. "My men have been ambushing them from every possible location. The ambushes haven't cost us a single man, either. Our only losses were when they caught up to the small group with the decoy wagon."

"They still haven't found our decoy wagon," said Jonas, "and we haven't lost anyone either. We've been harassing them day and night." He grinned. "They're too frightened to light fires at night now."

Will grunted in satisfaction. "So small mobile groups have been working well."

Rufe nodded. "We're very fortunate that the duke sent those archers along with us. They've made all the difference. We've been able to constantly harry the mercenaries without needing to fight them directly."

"Are you running low on arrows?" asked Will.

"Yes!" Jonas replied. "We've followed your suggestion to retrieve arrows whenever we could, but even so we're running dangerously low."

"We don't have many left either," said Rufe, "but I'm not too concerned. One of the duke's commanders has told me about a large stockpile of arrows. Apparently the duke ordered fresh arrows to be hidden securely on both sides of Steffan's Citadel."

"Does the commander know where they are hidden?" asked Will.

Rufe nodded. "Yes, and I've sent him with a couple of men to retrieve them. They've probably already returned."

Will nodded in satisfaction. "We have a lot to thank the duke for. We wouldn't have made it this far without his foresight. I knew we would have to fight, but the extent of it has been beyond anything I imagined."

Jonas grunted his agreement. "Even with more arrows, we have a big task ahead of us," he said. "We've whittled down their numbers significantly, but they still have a much larger combined force than us."

"And they're finally getting smarter," added Rufe. "I've just learned that they've split into three smaller groups. That will make our task more difficult."

"We've almost reached our destination, so it's time for us to combine our forces," Will told them. "Sooner or later they'll probably merge again as well."

"Are we going through Steffan's Citadel into Erestor?" Rufe asked.

Will shook his head. "It's more important to remain hidden, at least until the king recovers and the queen delivers her baby—I've been confronted with a few too many traitors in the recent past."

"Have you made contact with Rellan?" asked Rufe eagerly.

"Yes, we have," said Will, his delight showing on his face. "They've had people watching for intruders, and it wasn't long before they spotted our scouts. He's agreed to lead us to Newhaven, his community. It should be a secure place for the king to recover in peace and quiet."

"Won't the mercenaries simply follow us in?" Jonas asked.

"Getting there is not at all straightforward," Will assured him. "You need to know exactly where you're going."

"If we don't go to Erestor, our medical resources will be limited," said Jonas. "Is Brother Ander good enough as a healer?"

Will nodded. "He knows what he's doing. He's been treating the king while we've been traveling, and he expects the king to recover as soon as we can stop shaking him around."

"Is the king conscious yet?" asked Rufe.

"He's conscious for at least some of the time now," said Will. "Brother Ander says he isn't out of danger though. It's a key reason why we need to get to somewhere quiet and safe."

He bent down and drew in the dirt. "This is where we are now. And here's where Rellan will be leading us. Tomorrow you need to bring in your men. All of us can go with Rellan together. We'll be much less likely to be followed if we disappear at the same time."

Hazor threw up his hands in frustration. "What's Prentis doing? Our scouts have been watching every approach to Steffan's Citadel, and there's been no sign of him or any of his men."

"The army Lord Lygell sent to Erestor is camped outside the citadel," Jobin replied. "Prentis isn't likely to go anywhere near them —it would be too risky. He's supposedly leading a rebellion against the king."

Hazor smiled ironically. "People are incredibly gullible if they believe Prentis would turn rebel. He's probably the only friend the king has right now."

Jobin shrugged. "People will believe anything. If a lie is outrageous enough, they're even more likely to buy it."

Hazor waved a hand dismissively. "Forget all that. I want to know what Prentis is up to. Spread the word—there'll be a reward for anyone who gets me answers."

ONE OF HAZOR'S scouts appeared. He looked excited. "I've heard there's a reward for information about Prentis. We've captured one of his men!" He pointed to a man who was being pulled from his horse.

Hazor wasn't impressed. "How do you know he's one of Prentis's men? He could be anybody."

The scout looked smug. "He's one of Prentis's commanders. One of the men who fought at Torbury Scarp recognized him and even remembers his name—he's called Jonas."

Hazor narrowed his eyes. "Bring him here. I want to question him."

The man was dragged over.

"Who are you?" asked Hazor.

"I'm a local farmer," the man replied. "I was just going about my business when your men grabbed me. I have no idea why they're interested in me."

Hazor sneered at him. "You're heavily armed for a farmer."

The man shrugged. "These are dangerous times."

"You have two options," Hazor told him. "Help us, or die. Which will it be?"

The man looked pained. "There has to be a third option, surely."

"Prentis isn't going to care if you live or die," said Hazor. "He's Lord Torbury. Who are you? You take the risks, but who gets the rewards? Are you any wealthier since you started fighting for him?"

The man appeared to flush slightly, but he quickly hid it behind a bored expression.

Hazor smiled to himself. He'd clearly found an open wound.

"Be smart, Jonas," he said reasonably.

The man started.

"Yes, I know who you are," Hazor added calmly. "Look, my employers reward all of us handsomely for our efforts. If you're smart you can have your own share in the spoils."

Jonas was pretending boredom again. It wasn't entirely convincing.

"I know you think you're supposed to be loyal to Prentis. But what about the people you care for, the people who've depended on you? Have the wealthy and powerful shown any loyalty to them?"

This time Jonas wasn't able to fully mask his reaction. Hazor would have been willing to bet that Jonas had watched someone suffer cruelly from poverty or injustice. Someone he cared about.

"If you have it in your power to act, and you stand back and wait for a lord or a king to make it right, you're as bad as they are."

He paused to let his words sink in.

"I'm willing to be reasonable," said Hazor. "I won't ask you to slip a knife into anyone. All I want is information. I want to know where Prentis is heading. Before long we'll find out for ourselves anyway, so it isn't as if you'd be compromising anyone."

Jonas's face was expressionless. But he wasn't looking bored.

Hazor was careful not to appear smug. "Here's what will earn you a share of the reward..."

THOMAS AND TAMARA stood with Elena, Rubin and Haldek, watching a crowd of soldiers milling around on the path behind them.

The royal party had been positioned ahead of them. The king lay on a stretcher that was currently resting on the ground, with Brother Ander hovering protectively near him. The queen stood beside them, with Brother Gerome and Ava flanking her on either side. A stretcher lay on the ground ready for her use as well. Ten guards commanded by Count Ranauld stood around the little party.

Thomas watched in admiration as Will walked among the soldiers, turning chaos into order.

While Will was forming up the soldiers into disciplined lines, Rellan approached Thomas, slapping him heartily on the back.

"Look at you, Thomas—you're all grown up! And you're a father!"

"This is Elena, my wife," said Thomas, smiling warmly back at him. "Elena, this is Rellan—you've heard me talk about him."

Her beautiful face lit up. "It's a great honor to meet you, Rellan!"

"The honor is all mine," he replied, offering her a sweeping bow. He surveyed Thomas with raised eyebrows. "I must say I'm in awe of the transformation you've performed on our Thomas," he added with a wink.

"I am sure he must have changed a great deal since you saw him last, but none of the credit belongs to me," she protested with a merry laugh.

Then he turned his attention to Tammi, perched wide-eyed in her father's arms and gazing at him coyly.

"This is Tamara," said Thomas proudly.

Rellan pulled a face and rolled his eyes at Tammi, and the toddler rewarded his antics with giggles of delight.

Will arrived before Thomas could introduce Rellan to his father-in-law and Haldek.

"Are you ready, Rellan?" Will asked.

Rellan nodded. "I'll join you right now." As he departed he called back over his shoulder to Thomas and Elena, "I'll look forward to introducing you to my own lovely wife and children."

Thomas reached out his arm and drew Elena in. As she nestled into his shoulder, he briefly closed his eyes, savoring the moment alone with his own little family. Then they headed over to join Rubin and Haldek.

While they waited for the column to move out, Thomas spotted Jonas among the soldiers, making his way to the rear. He immediately reached down and twisted the clasp on the chain suspended around his neck. As the stone came into contact with his skin, he caught a fleeting glimpse of Jonas before he disappeared out of sight. The little he saw filled Thomas with alarm.

Excusing himself from his family, he hurried toward Will. Finding the commander was easy; getting a quiet moment with him was another matter entirely.

Will eventually glanced in his direction. Noticing Thomas, he paused what he was doing and came over to speak to him.

Will gave him a wry smile. "I know that look, Thomas—something's bothering you." Before Thomas could respond, he added, "You're still worried about Jonas, aren't you? You have no reason to be."

Someone called loudly for Lord Torbury, and the commander hurried away without giving Thomas an opportunity to say a word.

The contact with Jonas had been too brief to allow Thomas to build a complete picture, so perhaps there was more to it than he had seen.

Thomas shook his head helplessly. What more could he do? Will had understood his concern before he even voiced it. Thomas could only hope that Will's insight into Jonas was equally uncanny.

Will ordered Count Ranauld to move out, and the royal party set off with their escorts around them. Both the king and queen were carried on stretchers. Thomas and his little group followed close behind them. Will didn't order Rufe to follow with the soldiers until the royal party was long gone.

The path twisted and turned from the very beginning of the journey, with the result that Thomas rarely caught a glimpse of the soldiers behind them. At one point when the soldiers were out of sight, Rellan led the party down from the main path through some thick bushes. A faint animal trail soon appeared before them, and they hurried along it. At first the animal trail must have run alongside the main path, because Thomas occasionally heard the sounds of soldiers tramping along above them. In time the trail turned away, though, and they descended until they reached the banks of a swiftly flowing river.

Rellan left them at that point and headed back along the animal trail.

A large raft had been pulled up onto the near bank, and Ranauld led the group aboard. The raft was soon floating down the river. As the landing place slipped away behind them, Thomas peered back for any sign of Rellan or the soldiers. He saw nothing, and a bend in the river soon hid the scene entirely from view.

The river carried them for more than an hour, then the raftsmen pulled in to the opposite bank, and they continued the journey on foot. Cultivated fields eventually came into sight, and a large cluster of huts appeared before them, smoke rising lazily from many roofs.

Men and women hurried out to greet them, led by a woman of noble bearing.

"My name is Anneka," she said. "We are honored to welcome the king and the queen to our midst, and we bid all of you welcome to Newhaven. We established this community as a place of peace and security where all could prosper without interference. We trust that your needs will be met and your hurts will be healed here."

"Thank you on behalf of us all, Anneka," Queen Essanda replied. "We are grateful for your willingness to offer us sanctuary at a time of great need."

The king and the queen were brought into a large and well appointed hut, and every effort was made to make them comfortable.

Thomas kept watch for many hours, his uneasiness growing as he waited for Will and Rellan to arrive with the soldiers. The sun slipped below the horizon, and stars began to twinkle in the sky. Still he saw no sign of them.

34

One of Hazor's scouts called the mercenary over and pointed beneath a bush. Hazor bent low, noting with satisfaction the small piece of scarlet cloth lying there. Jonas might have kept them waiting for a few days, but he was keeping his end of the bargain.

"Keep moving!" he shouted.

Hazor's men had been following a path dotted with such markers for a couple of hours. The surrounding trees were closely set, and thick undergrowth covered the ground between them. Only the path was easily accessible. It had been a necessary decision to leave their mounts behind when they entered the deep forest.

Based on what Jonas had said, Hazor expected them to break free of the dense canopy soon. Before long the prize would be in reach.

It wouldn't be easy to kill the king and queen—Prentis would make certain of that. But surprise would give them a huge advantage. No one was expecting them to reach the hidden community.

The men were much too spread out, and Hazor moved to the rear to bunch them closer together. He was still at the back when he heard cries and shouts break out far ahead. The bends and turns of the path made it impossible to get a clear line of sight, so he hurried forward, impatient to discover the cause of the commotion. As he ran, arrows whistled over his head from behind. His men were under attack from the rear.

Shoving aside anyone who stood in his way, Hazor rounded a bend and came to a long section of path that ran along the base of a steep hill. An appalling sight awaited him. Huge rocks bounded recklessly down the slope, crushing men before his eyes. Even worse, the slope was clearly unstable. Rocks and loose soil began to flow down as he watched, covering the path and burying alive anyone unable to flee in time.

The only possible direction in which to flee was down, away from the slope. His men leaped from the path, forcing their way through the undergrowth among the trees below it. Hazor followed them in.

He was soon panting from the effort. As he sucked air into his lungs his nostrils tingled. A steady breeze was blowing along the path from behind him, and it carried with it a strong smell of smoke. He paused for a moment with his nose to the air, and a white-tailed deer bounded past him, springing nimbly away between the trees. A large buck followed close behind it. The behavior of these creatures told him that a forest fire was coming his way, and coming fast.

Panicked cries sounded behind Hazor now, and he resumed his headlong flight downhill. A large boulder struck a tree nearby, bringing it crashing to the ground. The tree narrowly missed him, and he ran faster, with heart pounding and ragged breath. After what seemed an age he pushed through the last of the trees, emerging onto the banks of a river. The river was narrow at this point, and it ran swiftly down to a series of rapids not far below him. The roar of the water was almost deafening.

Other men had arrived before him, and they stood unmoving, staring nervously back toward the forest. Already wisps of smoke were appearing among the trees. Men continued to spill out of the forest onto the riverbank, many of them coughing and hacking from the smoke. Hazor bent double, panting from his exertion.

At that moment arrows began to fly across the river from the opposite bank. Missiles soon filled the air.

He could hear the crackle of flames now, and thick smoke billowed from the trees. With a fire behind and death raining from the sky above, a few men panicked and cast themselves into the river. Hazor watched wide-eyed as they were swept into the rapids.

"Follow me!" he yelled above the din. Some of the men heard him and hurried to his side. He began weaving a path among the trees at the edge of the river, working his way upwind and upriver. The ranks of his companions thinned as arrows found their marks, but the trees offered some protection, and shafts began to fall uselessly to the ground as they moved beyond the range of the bowmen.

In time the smoke ahead cleared as well, and Hazor guessed that the fire was almost behind him.

Sounds of fighting began to reach him, and he belatedly realized that it had been very fortunate that his men had not all bunched together. Some of them at least had been able to avoid the rocks and the fire.

He drew his sword and crashed through the trees.

Men fought desperately all around him. Archers had perched themselves in the trees, and he watched them calmly picking off any of his men who strayed too close.

He cursed the almost total absence of archers among his own ranks. He was not himself an archer, and he had recruited men like himself who were good with the sword. It had proven to be a colossal mistake. Capable archers invariably came from Erestor—he would make sure he recruited heavily from Erestor next time.

As small knots of men fought back and forth among the trees it became increasingly clear to Hazor that his men were not giving a good account of themselves. He cursed Will Prentis—the very name of the man was enough to weaken the hands of the fainthearted. He was beginning to wonder if his men dared to believe they could defeat Prentis.

Hazor was beginning to doubt it himself. He had brought a huge advantage of numbers into this fight, and once more Prentis had found a way to even the odds.

The more he pondered it, the more Hazor began to realize that the chances of his men breaking through to the king and queen were fast diminishing. Seen in that light, it became clear that his responsibility had changed. He now had a rough idea of the location of the community sheltering the king and queen, even if the specifics of the route were far from certain. That information needed to be brought to Arnost. Lord Lygell could assemble a real army, one big enough to brush Prentis aside and finish the job.

He began edging around the battle lines, avoiding the fighting whenever he could and killing anyone who got in his way. Eventually the conflict lay behind him. He crept through the trees, desperate to stay out of sight of any bowmen watching from the branches above.

To his intense annoyance he noticed other men slinking away from the fighting. He had a good reason for leaving; their motivation could be nothing more than cowardice. He cursed them silently before completely ignoring them.

Slipping from tree to tree made for slow progress—the return journey took him more than twice as long as following the path. Nevertheless he finally came within sight of the place where his men had left their horses. He peered about him in surprise. There was no sign of the animals.

Drawing closer he noticed several bodies lying on the ground. It quickly became clear that the men he had left to guard the horses had been killed and the animals scattered.

Hazor cursed silently. His task had just become much more challenging.

The trees thinned out ahead of him, offering little cover. The only sensible option was to settle down and wait for darkness.

The day was almost spent when Hazor noticed a horse wandering nearby. Unwilling to miss such an opportunity, he leaped to his feet and sprinted toward it. He had covered half the distance when he saw that the horse was not alone. A dismounted rider stood behind it. It made little difference to him—he was more than happy to dispose of the horseman. He drew his sword and ran on.

The rider came out from behind the horse, and Hazor caught a glimpse of his face. Before him stood Jonas. The man had treated Hazor's bargain with contempt. Jonas had ruined any hope of finding and killing the king and queen and had brought about the destruction of Hazor's entire army.

Infuriated with the monstrous repercussions of his own blindness, Hazor bellowed a challenge and charged.

A WRY SMILE came to Jonas's face when he realized that the man running at him was Hazor. Quickly unslinging the bow from his shoulder, he nocked an arrow and waited calmly until his enemy was almost upon him. Then he put the arrow into Hazor's chest. The mercenary crashed to the ground.

Jonas gazed thoughtfully down at Hazor's body for a long moment, reliving their interaction. Measuring Jonas by his own standard, the mercenary had managed to convince himself that the lure of riches would be enough to win the loyalty of his captive.

Jonas shook his head scornfully. Then he spun on his heel, mounted his horse, and rode away.

WILL and Rellan stood together surveying the destruction from a high vantage point. A vast pall of smoke still covered the entire area.

"The fighting is over," Will told his friend, "but we'll need to guard the approaches for many days. Any mercenaries who survived are hiding in the forest. They've been trying to creep away, and they've kept my men busy."

"I'll leave you to organize the guard duty if you're willing," Rellan replied. "Our people have been fully occupied ferrying the wounded to Newhaven and setting up shelters for your men."

Will nodded. "We can handle it." He glanced at Rellan. "Newhaven isn't hidden now. How does Anneka feel about that?"

"It's a big adjustment—for her and for everyone. But we couldn't remain cut off from the world forever. And it's not as if Newhaven has suddenly become easy to find. We only found it by accident in the first place. Even if the mercenaries had made it to the end of that path we lured them onto, they'd have discovered it doesn't lead anywhere. It's hard to imagine any strays appearing on our doorstep."

"No," agreed Will. "But my men know how to get there now. We can ask them to keep it quiet, but word will leak out eventually."

Rellan shrugged. "We couldn't turn away the king and queen, and that meant we needed to welcome your soldiers as well. If it all leads to dire consequences, then so be it. There's no point in worrying about the future before it comes."

Will grunted his assent. "In the meantime, we'll make sure that no one else gets in or out of here."

THOMAS AND ELENA stood together at Newhaven, watching Tammi play with some of the other children. Their daughter had settled in almost immediately. Both Rubin and Haldek longed for the solitude of their old home in the forest, but they were doing as well as could be expected.

Thomas was feeling foolish and discouraged. Earlier that day Jonas had arrived at Newhaven, escorting a group of wounded soldiers. Thomas noticed his arrival and quickly used the stone to find out if his earlier concerns had been well founded. He soon discovered that he had completely misread Jonas. It was becoming apparent to him that superficial attitudes, thoughts, and desires weren't always a reliable indicator of how someone would behave when tested.

Thomas was relieved at the outcome, and equally dismayed about getting it so wrong. It was especially embarrassing that Will had assessed Jonas so much more accurately than Thomas, and he had done so without recourse to an all-seeing stone.

When Jonas next came into view, Thomas retrieved the stone from around his neck and handed it to Elena. "Could you please take a look at Jonas?" he whispered.

Elena frowned at him.

"It's important to me!" he insisted.

Somewhat reluctantly, she took the stone and turned her gaze upon Jonas. After a while she returned the stone to Thomas, who quickly slipped it back over his neck.

Jonas noticed them looking his way and came to join them.

Elena greeted him warmly. "Hello, Jonas. It's wonderful to see that you made it through safely!"

Thomas mumbled a welcome as well.

Jonas returned a friendly greeting of his own, but he appeared distracted.

Elena considered him for a moment. "I remind you of your sister, don't I?" she asked.

He gazed back at her in surprise. "How did you know?"

Elena smiled. "A lucky guess?"

Jonas shook his head in puzzlement.

"Tell me about her," Elena suggested gently.

Jonas stared at Elena for a moment. Then his head went down, and he shrugged. "She was the best person I ever knew. We were very close."

"And she became sick?"

He nodded without speaking.

Elena gazed at him compassionately. "You're a good man, Jonas. She would have been very proud of you."

Jonas looked up and met her eyes. Then he released a long shuddering sigh.

"Perhaps you couldn't save her," Elena said, "but you've been doing whatever you can for the helpless ever since, haven't you? I've benefited personally from that." Reaching out for his hand, she squeezed it briefly before releasing it.

Finding a way to master his emotions, Jonas returned a lopsided smile. "You're like her in more than just looks, Elena," he said. "Thank you."

The soldier's attention was captured by the arrival of a new group of men. "I'd better return to my duties," he said apologetically. Then he hurried away.

As he left Thomas raised his hands helplessly. "You're so much better at this than I am!" he told Elena.

She smiled and put her arm around his waist. "Not better, just different. We don't seem to notice the same things when we look at people with the stone."

He sighed. "If I've learned anything at all today, it's that I need to dig a lot deeper than initial impressions."

***

THE NEWHAVEN COMMUNITY boasted a modestly sized hut for the sick, but the number of men wounded in the recent battle far exceeded its capacity. A large hall had been built for community activities in cold weather, and the hall quickly became the main accommodation for the wounded.

Every available healer was needed to treat the men, and Anneka, Brother Ander, and Brother Gerome rarely left the building.

King Steffan was well on the way to recovery, but Brother Ander insisted on complete rest while his patient rebuilt his strength. Accordingly, the monk had relocated the king to the healing hall. Having all of his patients in easy reach allowed him to closely monitor the king's progress while also responding to the more pressing needs of the many wounded.

The queen had no objection whatever, and she soon spent a good proportion of her time there. She didn't limit herself to visiting her husband.

The men were curious about the king's wounds, and word gradually spread about the attack in the barn and his bravery in fighting off so many attackers. His willingness to convalesce among them lifted their spirits.

Once Essanda's exploits became known, men never tired of hearing of the heavily pregnant queen's courage in taking up a sword and vigorously defending herself and her unborn child. In the recovery hall, though, they saw only her gentleness. Many of the wounded were in pain, and the visits of the queen cheered them enormously. They waited patiently for their turn as she made her way slowly among them, resting her hands on her belly as she paused at each bed to speak a quiet word with the patient.

Reports of Brother Ander's intervention also circulated among the men, and the tales quickly grew in the telling. His deeds eventually achieved legendary status without him ever knowing it. Men followed with their eyes as the big monk walked among them, quietly going about his business.

The queen did not limit herself to visiting the wounded. In the evenings she spent time among the able-bodied soldiers and community members, expressing appreciation for their help and listening to their stories and concerns. With Brother Ander's permission, the king often joined her for brief periods.

The royals had been distant figures to those without personal contact with them. As the men basked in the attention of the recuperating king and the pregnant queen, their reverence slowly ripened into an ardent devotion.

The day soon came when the queen did not appear in the recovery hall. The men quickly noticed that the king had become tense and distracted, and the news was whispered abroad excitedly that the time for the queen's confinement had arrived.

KING STEFFAN HAD BEEN ASSURED by Anneka that the queen would be well cared for when the time came to deliver her baby. Newhaven might have been isolated from the rest of the world, but the community was not entirely unprepared for such an event. As chief healer,

Anneka could lay claim to a wealth of experience as a midwife. And the king knew she would also call upon Brother Gerome if the need arose.

As soon as Essanda's labor began, Anneka whisked the queen away to a specially prepared birthing room, ejecting everyone except two of her trusted helpers.

Several hours passed without news of any kind. Steffan waited anxiously in the recovery hall, conscious that all eyes were on him and trying hard to remain calm. Finally a woman bustled in and hurried to his side. Every head turned as the woman bowed, then leaned forward to whisper in his ear.

"It's a boy!" he cried jubilantly, and the room erupted around him.

Steffan threw an eager glance in the direction of Brother Ander.

"Go, Your Majesty," the monk exclaimed with a smile, waving an arm toward the door.

The king left the hall and hastened to his wife's side. Arriving to see her pale and tired, he stared at her in concern.

Anneka noticed his reaction. "Her Majesty has done extremely well," she assured him briskly. "You should be very proud of her!"

Steffan broke into a pleased smile, and he was relieved to see an answering smile appear on Essanda's face. Anneka brought his baby to him, and he held the infant awkwardly, staring down wide-eyed at the wrinkled little face. As he watched, his son opened his mouth, filled his tiny lungs, and let out a mighty squawk. The baby's lower lip trembled pitifully as he wailed.

Anneka retrieved him with a matter-of-fact air and returned him to his mother's breast. "You won't get your milk for a couple of days, Your Majesty," she told her. "But this will comfort him in the meantime."

She turned back to the king. "Her Majesty needs rest," she advised him gently.

He left reluctantly, but the contented smile on Essanda's face eased his mind as he went.

A wave of joy flooded over Steffan as he returned to the recovery hall. His beloved wife had presented him with a son. He had become a father.

Whatever storms the future might bring, they would weather them together.

THE LITTLE PRINCE'S naming ceremony was not marked with the pomp that would have accompanied it in Arnost, but the king and queen were at least spared the insincere flattery that would have been served up by some noblemen and courtiers. They instead found themselves surrounded by simple men and women who truly wished them well.

Brother Gerome conducted the ceremony, managing to provide a dignified sense of occasion while showing no sign of being overawed by the responsibility.

King Steffan and Queen Essanda proclaimed together, "We name our son Aiden!"

The crowd broke into loud cheers for Prince Aiden, and a procession of people filed past the royal family, presenting modest gifts and hearty congratulations. Steffan and Essanda thanked the most humble of the well wishers with the same sincerity they offered to Will, Rufe, and their other friends.

The recovery hall was empty—even the few remaining convalescent soldiers had been brought outside for the occasion—and the whole community made their way to a huge bonfire where freshly cooked venison and other treats awaited them.

BEFORE THE FEASTING was fully over, Thomas and Elena were summoned by King Steffan to a conference. They arrived to find the king and queen already there with the baby prince, along with Will, Rufe, Jonas, Count Ranauld, Anneka, and Rellan.

Thomas and Elena had brought little Tammi with them, and late as the hour was, she was soon playing happily with Anneka and Rellan's two-year-old son, Kuper, and his twin sister, Bella.

"Will tells me that the duke has sealed off Erestor," began the king. "Apart from that, the rest of Arvenon is now controlled by the mercenaries. Thomas, I hear from Will that you can provide more information about who the mercenaries answer to."

Thomas bowed deeply. "Yes, Your Majesty. I made some discoveries while I was in Arnost a number of days ago. Lord Bottren has been imprisoned, and a man known as Lord Lygell is in charge of the capital. He commands the mercenaries, but he is not the real leader. He was placed there by the Earl of Pisander."

The king scowled. "I'll have that traitor's head!" he exclaimed.

"Pisander seems to have access to a lot of resources," said the queen. "Those resources must have come from somewhere."

Thomas nodded. "Your Majesty is right. His money and most of his spies have been provided by King Agon of Rogand. I understand that King Agon wants to take over Arvenon, and Castel and Varas as well."

Steffan slowly shook his head. "Drettroth so nearly succeeded in annexing the three kingdoms. It was too much to expect that Agon would simply walk away from that failure."

A puzzled look came to Essanda's face. "Surely our soldiers won't simply follow the orders of these usurpers!"

King Steffan shrugged. "So far our own men haven't been called upon—mercenaries seem to have done all the fighting."

Thomas nodded. "My father told me that the soldiers have been sent away from Arnost, Your Majesty," he said. "Some were sent to Erestor. A story has been put out that Will...Lord Torbury, I mean," he added awkwardly, "has stirred up a rebellion against the king in Erestor."

Will simply raised his eyebrows. "Pisander won't want us to make contact with those men. If he realizes that we're anywhere nearby, he'll undoubtedly arrange for them to be sent somewhere else."

"The rest of the soldiers have been sent to the border with

Castel," Thomas continued. "They were told that the Castelans are planning to invade Arvenon."

The queen shook her head in anger. "Surely no one believes this nonsense!" She turned to her husband. "Can't you simply reappear and tell people the truth?"

"The king needs to be careful, Your Majesty," said Will. "His life will be at risk the moment his whereabouts become known. Pisander has done his preparation well—he appears to have far too many highly placed traitors in his pocket. And right now he has more fighting men available than we do. He will be eager to finish the job one way or another."

"I'm sure our soldiers are loyal at heart," said the queen.

"Soldiers do what they're told," the king replied grimly. "If Pisander—and ultimately Agon—can find a way to control the leaders, he'll control the army too."

"Either that, or Pisander will disband the army," said Ranauld. "It would be safer for him to rely on men who answer only to money."

Thomas said nothing, but his thoughts were churning. He knew from the scroll that the Stone of Authority was somewhere at large in the world, and he had seen hints at Arnost that Pisander might not simply be acting on his own behalf.

Thomas was beginning to suspect that Agon had indeed found a way to control people. But how could he voice his suspicions without exposing his own secret?

He decided that for the moment he would do nothing. He would discuss it later with Elena.

Will knew about his stone as well of course. If it seemed important enough, Thomas could always choose a suitable moment and pass on his suspicions to Will.

The cooking fires had long since died down to glowing embers, and the feasters had scattered. Steffan and Essanda stood alone together beneath the stars, cradling little Aiden.

"It appears that I no longer have much of a kingdom to pass on to my son and heir," Steffan said gloomily.

Essanda frowned up at him. "We can't let these people win. It isn't just about Aiden's inheritance—we've already seen what they do to anyone who gets in their way. The common people will suffer most."

Steffan nodded. "I don't know how we can turn the tide, but we will find a way."

He glanced down at the prince, then out into the night. "Whatever else happens, I'm not going to sit here hiding for the rest of my life," he vowed. "I will win the kingdom back, or I'll die trying."

EPILOGUE

Agon's best agent stood before him, trembling with fear. The man had delivered a full report, and Agon was not at all satisfied with what he'd heard.

"So this boy you've been tracking has slipped through your fingers—you have no idea where he's gone?"

The agent could only nod mutely.

"And you sent a small army after Will Prentis—hundreds of men —and not one of them has returned?"

The agent winced, but he nodded again.

"I'm plagued by fools and incompetents!" the king shouted. "Is nothing ever done properly unless I do it myself?"

The man didn't dare to look at him.

"Get out of my sight!" Agon bellowed.

The agent scurried away.

The king shook his head in fury.

He'd poured in so much money, and what did he have to show for it? His search for the Stone of Knowing had stalled, and he still couldn't claim full control even over one of the three kingdoms.

Closer to home, he'd made no progress at all on uncovering the priests' secrets around extending life. It was true that one or two unlucky priests had fallen into the hands of his men, but either they knew nothing, or they were tight lipped fools.

He ground his teeth.

Perhaps he would execute all of his agents and start again fresh. The thought almost calmed him.

"Ennawi, there you are!"

The slave barely seemed to have moved since Agon had last seen him.

"I'm planning a little trip—to Arnost, the capital of Arvenon. You can come too. You'd like that, wouldn't you?"

As usual, the slave offered no response.

Agon ignored Ennawi's apparent lack of interest. "I'm going to base myself in Arvenon for a while. It seems I must be there in person if things are to be done properly."

He patted a hidden pocket in his cloak. "I'll take my little prize with me of course."

He'd arranged for a cloak to be specially designed with a pocket to hold the Stone of Authority securely. Now he could simply slip his hand into the pocket whenever he needed to put the stone to use.

Agon felt almost cheerful. He saw no reason to be entirely dissatisfied with his efforts so far. He had recently recruited a new agent—a tracker without peer. His new tracker would find the Stone of Knowing, and the fool who had dared to take possession of the stone would be dragged before Agon.

Much as Agon liked to rail at his agents, his plans hadn't ended in complete failure. Castel had closed its borders, but it was now ruled by a child. Although Varas had withdrawn into its shell, isolation had done nothing to guarantee its security last time.

Neither country mattered, though. Controlling Arvenon had always been the key to controlling the region, and his pet Arvenian nobleman had largely done as he promised. The former Earl of Pisander now controlled the entire country apart from Erestor, and Pisander was ready to welcome Agon into the capital.

Once he was in Arnost, Agon would spend time with key Arvenian noblemen and the leaders of the army—enough time to bring them thoroughly under the control of the Stone of Authority.

Then he would deal with Erestor. Best of all, he would use Arvenon's own armies to do it. Castel would come next, and then Varas.

The Stone of Knowing would have nowhere to hide.

He turned back to Ennawi with a self-satisfied smirk. "I hear it's very pleasant in Arnost at this time of the year," he said.

The End

The saga continues in
The Struggle for Authority
Book Four of Allan N. Packer's
The Stone Cycle

LIST OF CHARACTERS

- *Agon* - king of Rogand
- *Ander* - Arvenian soldier who traveled with Will and later commanded soldiers at the Battle of Torbury Scarp; decided to become a monk after the death of Brother Vangellis
- *Andri* - respected member of the Clan
- *Ava* - handmaid to Queen Essanda
- *Axel Stablehand* - master of the Arvenian royal stables at Arnost, and the father of Thomas
- *Alfic* - mercenary leader
- *Anneka* - former noblewoman who leads a community hidden away in the forest near Erestor
- *Bottren* - high-ranking Arvenian nobleman and close confidante of King Steffan; liaison to Will Prentis at the Battle of Torbury Scarp
- *Burtelen* - high-ranking Arvenian nobleman from Erestor who is a close confidante of King Steffan; played a crucial role in bringing an army from Erestor to the Battle of Torbury Scarp

- *Delmar* - king of Varas, a neighboring kingdom to Arvenon, and ally of King Steffan of Arvenon
- *Drettroth* - high-ranking Rogandan nobleman who commanded the Rogandan army during the invasion of Arvenon; known as Vilkami during his childhood
- *Duke of Erestor* - the uncle of King Steffan of Arvenon, and the regent during the king's absence during the Rogandan invasion; the senior member of the nobility in Erestor
- *Dunnridge* - nobleman who later became the Earl of Pisander (see *Pisander*)
- *Eisgold* - Castelan nobleman formerly commanding the Castelan army; exiled after the Battle of Torbury Scarp for ignoring orders at a crucial moment in the battle
- *Elena* - young woman living in hiding with her father Rubin in the forests of Arvenon
- *Elias* - abbot at the Monastery of St. Rodrig the Martyr where Brother Vangellis was hiding away
- *Ennawi* - slave of King Agon of Rogand
- *Eravitt* - Castelan nobleman
- *Essanda* - queen of Arvenon, formerly a princess of Castel
- *Gareth* - mercenary leader
- *Gerome* - monk at the monastery led by Brother Elias; close friend of Brother Ander
- *Haldek* - former Rogandan soldier who unwittingly helped Will on significant occasions; living in a tiny forest community with Elena, Rubin, and Thomas
- *Hazor* - mercenary leader
- *Hender* - young bowman living in Anneka's forest community
- *Istel* - king of Castel, a neighboring kingdom to Arvenon, and father-in-law and ally of King Steffan of Arvenon
- *Jobin* - mercenary leader
- *Jonas* - senior army leader and close confidante of Will Prentis; fought at the Battle of Torbury Scarp
- *Karevis* - Varasan nobleman and commander of the

Varasan army; played a key role at the Battle of Torbury
Scarp

- *Krasmir* - wealthy and powerful Rogandan baron
- *Kuper* - Arvenian soldier from Erestor who led a cavalry
  force to the battlefield at Torbury Scarp with his twin
  brother Rellan; killed at Torbury Scarp
- *Lonnigen* - Arvenian count with holdings in northern
  Arvenon
- *Lygell* - nobleman directing mercenaries from Arnost
- *Marya* - wife of Axel Stablehand and mother of Thomas
- *Nestor* - Arvenian soldier heading Will Prentis's spy
  network; traveled with Will's small band during the
  Rogandan invasion
- *Nilsean* - Varasan nobleman and senior army commander
  under Lord Karevis
- *Nistinaa* - slave who cares for Ennawi
- *Pisander* - earl and former head of King Steffan's foreign
  spy network who remained in Arnost during the
  Rogandan siege; imprisoned for treason during the siege,
  but bribed his way out of prison before his execution
- *Ranauld* - Arvenian count and a senior leader in the army
  at Torbury Scarp; a close confidante of King Steffan and a
  friend of Will Prentis
- *Rellan* - Arvenian soldier from Erestor who led a cavalry
  force to the battlefield at Torbury Scarp with his twin
  brother Kuper; connected with Anneka's forest
  community
- *Ronya* - member of the Clan
- *Rubin* - father of Elena
- *Rufe Sarjant* - respected and physically imposing Arvenian
  soldier; a close friend of Will Prentis and a key leader in
  the army
- *Scar* - respected leader in Anneka's forest community
- *Steffan the Second* - king of Arvenon
- *Tamara* - daughter of Thomas and Elena

- *Tarestel* - Varasan nobleman who became puppet ruler of Varas after the Rogandan invasion; exiled after the defeat of the Rogandan army at Torbury Scarp
- *Thomas Stablehand* - possessor of the Stone of Knowing; son of Axel and Marya
- *Torbury* - title granted to Will Prentis by King Steffan; Will Prentis was elevated to the Arvenian peerage as Lord Torbury in honor of his efforts in defeating the Rogandans
- *Vangellis* - Arvenian monk who became a key mentor to Thomas; killed at Lord Drettroth's stronghold
- *Vilkami* - noble-born Rogandan who became Lord Drettroth
- *Viggor* - leader of the Clan
- *Will Prentis* - commander of the Arvenian army, greatly respected by his soldiers as well as King Steffan due to his remarkable qualities; fluent in Rogandan and widely traveled

NOTE FROM THE AUTHOR

Thank you for reading *The Stone of Authority*—I hope you enjoyed it. Please consider leaving a review on Amazon for the benefit of other readers. It makes a big difference to me to receive reader feedback as well!

I've appreciated the opportunity to journey with the expanding group of travelers as they've made their way through Arvenon and the surrounding kingdoms. And the journeying is far from over—the saga reaches a new climax in *The Struggle for Authority (The Stone Cycle Book 4)*. The cover and outline appear below.

Before reading *The Struggle for Authority*, I recommend reading *The Seer: A Prequel to The Stone of Knowing* if you haven't already done so. See below for more information.

And if you haven't caught up on the origins of Anneka and her community, I've released a free novelette that provides the backstory. It's a complete story (no cliffhanger ending) that can be read at any point in the series, and it's available in ebook and audiobook format. To get it, simply sign up to my mailing list at www.allanpacker.com. The mailing list will keep you up to date on new releases, it's low traffic so won't clutter up your inbox, and new subscribers will receive the exclusive bonus novelette, *The Rending: A Prequel to The Cost of Knowing*, described below.

But first, *The Struggle for Authority (The Stone Cycle Book 4).*

Arvenon is controlled by a traitor. The kingdom of Castel teeters on the brink. With the unseen hand of King Agon of Rogand pulling the strings, a mantle of oppression is slowly settling over the four kingdoms.

Having recovered from the assassination attempt, King Steffan of Arvenon sets out to wrest back control of his kingdom, vigorously supported by Will, Rufe, Thomas, and familiar allies. Unlikely influences might ultimately tip the balance.

In a desperate attempt to block Agon, Will and Thomas set out for Rogand. What each of them encounters there will shake them to the core. The fate of four kingdoms will hinge upon the Stone of Authority.

How did the stone come to be where Thomas found it? The answer can be found in *The Seer: A Prequel to The Stone of Knowing,* a novelette, 5 chapters (13,500 words) in length. It is a standalone story, and as such can be read independently of other books in *The Stone Cycle* series, although it is recommended pre-reading for *The Struggle for Authority (The Stone Cycle Book 4).* The novelette is described below.

Eyes see no more than a glimpse

Sheylha is a seer—a woman with unique

and extraordinary abilities. Powerful men want to control her, to use her to dominate others.

Kalvor is a warrior of unusual tenacity, a hunter who never gives up. Driven by his past, he has become a dangerous enemy.

When Kalvor is sent to find and capture the seer, each of them will be tested in ways they could never have imagined.

In time the outcome will determine the fate of kingdoms.

The Seer: A Prequel to The Stone of Knowing is available at Amazon's Kindle store.

By signing up to my mailing list at allanpacker.com you'll receive the free prequel to *The Cost of Knowing,* as well as being kept up to date on new releases. The prequel novelette, *The Rending: A Prequel to The Cost of Knowing,* is a complete story four chapters (13,000 words) in length. It provides additional context to Anneka's story from *The Cost of Knowing* without introducing spoilers for other books in *The Stone Cycle* series. The novelette is described below.

Endings may be beginnings in disguise

Anneka is comfortable and confident, a noblewoman of consequence living a life of privilege. Until the day her world is torn apart.

After losing everything she most cares about, she must abandon her home and her way of life in an attempt to secure the future of those who depend on her.

No one, least of all Anneka, could anticipate a deeper significance to her struggle. Yet her journey will one day influence the fate of kingdoms.

RESEARCH NOTES

Spoiler Alert!

The reader is advised to avoid this section before finishing *The Stone of Authority*.

Head Injury

Modern medicine would likely describe the head injury suffered by Thomas as a subdural hematoma. Information about signs and symptoms can be found at:

https://en.wikipedia.org/wiki/Subdural_hematoma

Poisons

Gretchen's poison of choice was strychnine, a poison in use since ancient times. It typically takes effect ten to twenty minutes after being administered. More information can be found at:

https://en.wikipedia.org/wiki/Strychnine_poisoning

ACKNOWLEDGMENTS

I'd first like to thank my wife Merilyn, my reliable and effective alpha reader as well as my best friend. Her insights have improved the story enormously. This story is dedicated to her.

Special thanks to my beta readers, Deborah, Ray, Andrew Menzies, Jen Neal, Alison George, and Cherilyn White. Their feedback makes a difference and encourages me to keep writing.

Mary Novak did her usual outstanding developmental edit. I continue to find her feedback invaluable. Deborah followed up with her typically thorough proofread.

Karri did another superb job on the cover. I appreciate her patient persistence.

I am indebted to Brian Plush for his wonderfully detailed map. The map beautifully illuminates the pathways throughout Arvenon and the surrounding kingdoms.

This year promises a number of exciting new beginnings, including the wedding of one of our sons. And with one daughter, Melanie Cellier, now well established as a writer of young adult fairy tale retellings and fantasy, we are eagerly anticipating the imminent debut release of a young adult fantasy series by our other daughter, Deborah Grace White. Walking the journey with each of them has been a rich privilege.

The past year provided many special moments as well as multiple reminders of the uncertainty and fragility of life. I'm grateful to God for providing each new day as a fresh start, for supplying strength to navigate through the challenges, and for offering hope for the future.

ABOUT THE AUTHOR

Allan Packer writes epic fantasy. The books in *The Stone Cycle* series are his first published fiction.

Allan grew up surrounded by books and became an avid reader during his childhood. In his university years fantasy displaced science fiction as his favorite genre, thanks primarily to J. R. R. Tolkien. He later shared this love with his four children by reading *The Lord of the Rings* to them aloud—a three-month marathon he completed twice during their formative years.

Born in Australia, Allan has lived and worked on three continents, and spent one quarter of his working years abroad. Having worked as an IT professional throughout his career, he was first published as a technical author.

Today he lives with his wife in Adelaide, South Australia, near their children and a small but growing band of grandchildren.

Allan is currently working on the next installment in his series *The Stone Cycle*.